D1024103

Stephanie Bond was seven years deep into a systems engineering career and pursuing an MBA at night when an instructor remarked that she had a flair for writing and suggested she submit to academic journals. But Stephanie, a voracious reader, was only interested in writing fiction—more specifically, romance fiction. Upon completing her master's degree, and with no formal training in writing (her undergraduate degree is in computer programming), she started writing a romance novel in her spare time. Two years later, in 1995, she sold her first book, a romantic comedy, to Harlequin Books. In 1997, with ten sales under her belt to two publishers, Stephanie left her corporate job to write women's romance fiction full-time. She now writes contemporary romantic comedies for Harlequin Books, and comedic mainstream women's fiction for Avon. Stephanie lives in Atlanta, Georgia.

USA TODAY bestselling author **Janelle Denison** is known for her sinfully sexy heroes and provocative stories packed with sexual tension and emotional conflicts. She is the recipient of the prestigious National Reader's Choice Award, has been a RITA® Award finalist and has garnered many other awards and accolades in the romance-writing industry. Janelle enjoys hearing from readers, and you can write to her at janelle@janelledenison.com. For information on upcoming releases, visit her Web site at www.janelledenison.com.

Stephanie Bond
Janelle Denison

Christmas Party

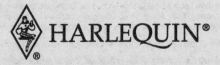

HARLEQUIN®

TORONTO • NEW YORK • LONDON
AMSTERDAM • PARIS • SYDNEY • HAMBURG
STOCKHOLM • ATHENS • TOKYO • MILAN • MADRID
PRAGUE • WARSAW • BUDAPEST • AUCKLAND

HARLEQUIN BOOKS

by Request—CHRISTMAS PARTY

Copyright © 2004 by Harlequin Books S.A.

ISBN 0-373-23029-X

The publisher acknowledges the copyright holders of the individual works as follows:

NAUGHTY OR NICE?
Copyright © 1998 by Stephanie Hauck

CHRISTMAS FANTASY
Copyright © 1999 by Janelle Denison

This edition published by arrangement with Harlequin Books S.A.

® and TM are trademarks of the publisher. Trademarks indicated with ® are registered in the United States Patent and Trademark Office, the Canadian Trade Marks Office and in other countries.

www.eHarlequin.com

Printed in U.S.A.

CONTENTS

NAUGHTY OR NICE?

Stephanie Bond

1

THE STYLIST HELD A HANDFUL of dark hair high above Cindy Warren's head, the scissors poised only inches from her scalp. "Are you sure you want to do this, ma'am?"

Cindy bit her lower lip, wavering. Long hair was easy, uncomplicated. *And a security blanket,* her mind whispered.

Standing behind another salon chair a few feet away, Jerry cleared his throat meaningfully and pushed the fuzzy Santa hat he wore back on his bald head. An institution at the Chandelier House hotel, the elderly black barber gave trims to male guests, but declined to use his artistry on female heads. His implied subtle comment nettled her. Whose hair was it, anyway?

She looked up once again to the length of hair, then to the woman's name tag. "Tell me, Bea, how long have you been working in our salon?"

"Counting today? Hmmmm. Three—no, four days. I graduated from beauty school two weeks ago, ma'am."

Cindy digested the information as Jerry spun his seated customer around to face the action. "Well, I'm due for a change," she murmured, to no one in particular, sitting erect with new resolve. "Long, straight hair is ridiculous at my age. I need to either have it cut, or become a country music singer."

Jerry gave her a pointed stare. "Hum a few bars."

"What's wrong with long, straight hair?" Jerry's customer asked.

Cindy's gaze darted to the man's reflection and her

breath caught in appreciation of his appallingly good looks. "Excuse me?" she squeaked, then warmed with embarrassment.

The visitor, a striking man with pale blue eyes and a prominent nose, sat tall in the chair, his long, trousered legs extending far below the gray cape Jerry had draped over his torso. His dark curly hair lay damp and close to his head, compliments of Jerry, and a mirror trimmed with glittery gold tinsel reflected his crooked smile. "I said, what's wrong with long, straight hair?"

Squashing a zing of sexual awareness, Cindy bristled. "I-it makes me look like a coed."

"Most women would be thrilled," the man offered with a shrug.

"Well, not this woman," Cindy said, growing increasingly annoyed with her unexpected—and unwanted—physical reaction to him.

Jerry leaned over the man's shoulder and said in a conspiratorial voice, "She's trying to impress someone."

"Jerry," Cindy warned, narrowing her eyes.

The customer nodded knowingly at Jerry in the mirror. "Figures. Man?"

"Oh, yeah," Jerry drawled, pulling off the plastic cape to reveal the man's crisp white collarless dress shirt and burgundy leather suspenders.

"Jerry, that's enough!"

"Boyfriend?" the man asked Jerry.

"Nah," the barber said sadly, shaking the cape. "Ms. Cindy doesn't date much—works day and night."

"Really? Day *and* night." The man made a sympathetic sound. "Then who is she trying to impress?"

"Some corporate fellow," Jerry said, whipping out a brush and whisking it over the man's neck and broad shoulders.

"Jerry, I've never impressed anyone in my life!" Suddenly, she realized what she'd said. "I mean, I've never *tried* to impress anyone."

The old barber ignored her. "Headquarters is sending a hatchet man next week to check us out, and to check out Ms. Cindy, too, I reckon."

"Other than the obvious reason—" the man flicked his glance her way for a split second "—why would this fellow be checking out Ms. Cindy?"

"'Cause," Jerry said, nodding toward their topic of discussion, "she runs this whole show."

His customer looked impressed. "Is that so?"

"Yes," Cindy said, looking daggers at Jerry. "That's so."

"Ma'am?" prompted a shaky Bea.

"Don't do it." The man leaned forward, resting his elbows on the padded arms of the chair.

With ballooning irritation, Cindy scoffed and waved off the stranger's opinion. "If men had their way, every woman would have hair down to her knees."

The man steepled his fingers and glanced up at Jerry. "I would have said ankles. How about you, Jer?"

"Amen."

"Ma'am," Bea pleaded, "my arms are about to give out."

Cindy raised her chin. "Cut it. This will be my early Christmas present to myself."

"Punishment for being naughty?" the man asked Jerry.

"Punishment for being nice," Jerry amended.

Fuming, Cindy nodded curtly to the hesitant hairdresser. "Do it."

"Don't do it," the man said, his voice rich with impending doom.

"Whack it off," Cindy said more forcefully. "Layers all over. Make me a new woman."

The handsome man's eyes cut to Jerry. "Is there something wrong with the old woman?"

Jerry pursed his lips. "She's a little impulsive."

Cindy set her jaw. "Let's get this over with."

Bea swallowed audibly. "I'll leave the back shoulder length, ma'am." The woman closed her eyes.

Alarm suddenly gripped Cindy. "Wait!" she cried just as the shears made a slicing sound. Bea opened her eyes and stared.

The man winced, and Jerry grunted painfully when the hairdresser held up more than a foot of severed dark tresses. As the remnants fell back to her shoulders, Cindy tried to squash her own rising panic and painted on a shaky smile, encouraging the new stylist to continue.

Maybe, she thought, keeping her gaze down and dabbing at perspiration along her neck, this woman would stay longer than the seven days their previous hairdressers had averaged. Cindy had urged her staff members to give the salon their patronage, and felt compelled to take the lead. But twenty minutes later, when Bea stood back to absorb the full effect of her latest creation in the mirror, Cindy understood why none of her employees used the unproved stylists.

"Good Lord," Jerry muttered, shaking his head.

The man whistled low. "Too bad."

"You hate it, don't you?" Bea asked Cindy, her face crumbling.

"N-no," Cindy rushed to assure her. She lifted a hand, but couldn't bring herself to touch the choppy, lank layers that hugged her head like a long knit cap. "It'll just take some getting used to, that's all." She inhaled and smiled brightly.

"Think he'll be impressed?" the man asked Jerry, doubt clear in his voice.

"If he can get past the hair," Jerry said, nodding.

"*Do* you two mind?" Cindy snapped, feeling a flush scald her cheeks. She tugged the cape off her shoulders and stood, brushing the sleeves of her blouse. Jerry, she could overlook. But this, this...arrogant guest was tap-dancing on her holiday-frazzled nerves.

The infuriating man stood as well, and in her haste to leave, Cindy slipped on a pile of her own hair and skidded across the marble floor, flailing her arms and legs like a windup toy. He halted her imminent fall with one large hand, his fingers curving around her arm. Cindy jerked upright to stare into his dancing blue eyes, then pulled away from his grasp. "Th-thank you," she murmured, her face burning.

"The haircut must have thrown off your balance," he observed with a half smile.

Feeling like a complete idiot, Cindy retrieved her green uniform jacket and withdrew a generous tip for the distraught Bea, then strode toward the exit. Her skin tingled with humiliation and her scalp felt drafty, but she refused to crumble. She simply had too much on her mind to dwell on the embarrassing episode with the attractive stranger— the upcoming review, going home for Christmas and now her hair.

Cindy squared her shoulders and lifted her chin. No matter. After all, the unsettling man was simply passing through. And Manny would know what to do with her hair.

"OH, MY," Manny said when she walked within earshot of the concierge desk. "Cindy, *tell* me that's a wig."

Cindy smiled weakly at her blond friend. "It's a wig."

"Liar," he said smoothly, then emerged from behind his desk to touch her hair, a pained expression on his handsome face.

Hiring Manny Oliver as concierge over a year ago had been one of Cindy's greatest achievements in her four years managing the Chandelier House. Next to most of the odd-ball staff members she had inherited, Manny was a breath of fresh air: good-looking, polite, helpful and witty. A true friend, *and* he could cook. Cindy sighed. Why were all the good ones gay?

"Don't tell me," he said, stroking her head as if she were a pet. "You've been to see Bea the Butcher."

"You know about her?"

"I arranged a free dinner to console a lady she hacked yesterday."

Cindy felt like crying. "Now you tell me."

"You know I don't bother you with details. What were you *thinking* to cut your beautiful hair?"

"I was trying to drum up confidence in the salon among the staff."

"Now you're a walking billboard, all right."

She grimaced. "So can my hair be saved?"

He smiled. "Sure. There's this great little hat shop down on Knob Hill—"

"Manny!"

"Shh, I get off at one. I'll meet you in your suite," he promised. "If you get there first, plug in your curling iron."

Cindy frowned. "Curling iron?"

Manny pursed his lips and shook his head. "Never mind—I'll bring the tools."

She lowered her voice and scanned the lobby. "So, have you seen anyone who looks like they might be under-cover?"

He leaned forward and whispered, "Not a trench coat in sight." When she smirked, he added, "What makes you think this Stanton fellow is going to come early to spy on us?"

"Because *I* would."

"It would be nice if we knew what he looked like."

"My guess is he's in his fifties, probably white—although I can't be sure—and walking funny because he's got his shorts in a knot.'' She leaned close. ''And he might be in disguise. So be on the lookout for someone we'd least suspect to be on a corporate mission.''

At that moment, Captain Kirk and Mr. Spock look-alikes strolled by in full costume. Manny looked at Cindy. ''Could you be more specific?''

''Okay,'' she relented. ''Spotting a spy will be difficult in this hotel, but keep your eyes peeled. I'll see you at the staff meeting.''

She cruised by the front desk and smiled at the dozen or so smartly suited reservations handlers, not missing their alarmed glances at her hair. Engineering workers were hanging garland and wreaths on the wall behind the reservations desk and at least a hundred over-coiffed females—guests who'd attended a cosmetics convention—waited in lines fashioned by velvet ropes to check out. Cindy slipped in behind Amy, the rooms director, and asked, ''How's it going?''

''Fine,'' the brunette answered, then lifted a hand to her forehead. ''Except for a raging headache.''

Cindy tried to conjure up a bit of sympathy for the woman, but while Amy had proved to be very capable on the job, her tendency toward hypochondria remained legendary around the watercooler. ''Must be the perfume,'' she offered in her most soothing tone, nodding toward the aromatic crowd.

Amy sighed noisily. ''Don't worry—I'll survive. Once we get the makeup ladies out of here, we'll have a full two hours before the bulk of the Trekkies arrive.''

''May the Force be with you,'' Cindy said solemnly.

Amy laughed. ''Wrong flick, Cindy.''

''I have thirty free minutes before the staff meeting. Any problems I can take off your hands?''

Amy gave her a grateful smile, then rummaged under the

desk and came up with a clipboard. "Room 620 wants a better view, 916 wants a TV without the adult movie channel and room 1010 wants a smoking room with a king-sized bed."

"And do we have alternative rooms for them?"

Amy made check marks with her pencil as she moved down the list. "No, no and no."

"And 'no' means a personal visit," Cindy said wryly, taking the clipboard.

Grinning, Amy said, "Take it up with the GM—it's one of her policies."

"Touché."

"By the way." Amy squinted and tilted her head. "What happened to your hair?"

Cindy frowned. "I'll see you at the staff meeting."

Retracing her steps through the lobby, she noticed every detail. The gray marble floors were polished to a high sheen, the sitting areas populated with antique furniture and overstuffed couches were neat. Christmas was a scant two weeks away, and while everyone else in the world shopped and anticipated holiday gatherings, Cindy knew she and her staff had many grueling hours ahead of them during their busiest time of the year.

Top that with headquarters' announcement they were sending a man from a third-party downsizing firm to look over her shoulder for the next couple of weeks... And not just any man—Cindy shivered—but a highly touted, much-feared hatchet man named Stanton. Her intercompany contacts informed her he was ruthless, and the fact that he was coming at all did not bode well for the future of the Chandelier House. No uptight corporate stiff would appreciate the nutty flavor of her eccentric staff.

Avoiding the crowded elevator corridor, she headed toward the sweeping three-story staircase in the front of the lobby. The climb up the dark-gold-carpeted stairs gave her an impressive view of her front operation.

The hotel's signature item, an enormous sparkling chandelier, presided over the lobby. She gave the dazzling piece a fond wink in memory of her grandfather, thinking of his stories of the hotel in its heyday, then turned her attention to the pulsing activity below. Every employee seemed occupied, from the valets to the bellmen to the lobby maids. Greenery, garlands and lights, thanks to engineering, were slowly enveloping the lobby walls and fixtures. Jaunty Christmas Muzak kept everyone moving and lifted Cindy's spirits as well.

A new beginning lay just around the corner. A clean slate. A promising year for the Chandelier House, a better relationship with her mother, maybe even a man in her life.

Cindy smirked. Why settle for one Christmas miracle?

At the top of the stairs, she paused to catch her breath, then caught an elevator to the sixth floor. An owlish-looking middle-aged man answered her knock to room 620. Wearing suit slacks, dress shirt and tie, he held a pad of paper under his arm and, oddly, the room's antique desk lamp in one hand. Cindy raised an eyebrow, then quietly introduced herself and explained that a room with a better view of the city was available, but it was a suite, and therefore, considerably more expensive.

The man frowned behind thick glasses and complained loudly, but Cindy remained calm, her eyes meaningfully glued to the lamp. In the end he huffily claimed the room to be adequate and slammed the door. Cindy shook her head, then jotted a reminder to send him a complimentary prune Danish the following morning. The man was obviously constipated.

The robed couple in room 916 cleared up a misunderstanding—they weren't complaining about having access to the adult channel, they were complaining because they thought the channel should be free. No, Cindy explained, but an evening of pay-per-view was still relatively cheap entertainment in San Francisco.

She was two for three approaching room 1010, thankful the complaints were small compared to what her staff normally dealt with. Wrinkling her nose at the ancient orange carpet bearing a nauseating floral pattern, she pledged to put the case forcefully to headquarters about the need for new hallway floor coverings, then lifted her hand and rapped lightly on the door.

Within seconds, the handsome stranger from the hair salon stood before her, minus his dress shoes. His imposing masculinity washed over Cindy and his smile revealed white teeth and slight crow's-feet at the corners of his ice-blue eyes. Late thirties, she decided. "We meet again," he said pleasantly.

"Um, yes," Cindy murmured, resisting the urge to pull her jacket up over her head. She checked the clipboard. "Er, Mr. Quinn?"

"Eric Quinn," he said, extending his hand.

She returned his firm and friendly shake. "I'm Cindy Warren, Mr. Quinn, I—"

"—run this whole show…I remember."

She flushed. "I'm the general manager, and I came to discuss your request for another room."

He crossed his arms and leaned against the doorjamb, smiling lazily. "Do you personally oversee every guest request, Ms. Warren?"

"No, I—"

"Then I'm flattered."

He was an extremely handsome man, Cindy decided as she struggled to regain control of the situation. And very full of himself. "No need, Mr. Quinn," she replied coolly. "My reservations staff is swamped at the moment, so I'm pitching in. If you're interested, we have a smoking room available, but it doesn't have a king-sized bed.''

Mr. Quinn frowned and stroked his chin with his left hand.

No ring, she noticed, then chastised herself. The absence of a ring didn't mean the man was available. And despite her mother's increasingly urgent pleas for her to find a nice man and settle down, even if he *was* available, Cindy wasn't in the market for a relationship with a guest…who rubbed her the wrong way…at the most professionally chaotic and emotionally vulnerable time of the year.

Mr. Quinn shook his head ruefully. ''No, a smaller bed will never do. I can afford to go without cigarettes more than I can afford to go without sleep. I'm a big man,'' he added unnecessarily.

To her horror, Cindy involuntarily glanced over his figure again, then felt a heat rash scale her neck. She fidgeted with the clipboard, clacking the metal clip faster and faster as her pulse rate climbed.

He shrugged. ''I guess I'll stay put since I need a big, roomy bed.''

Cindy's hand slipped and the metal clip snapped down on her fingers, sending pain exploding through her hand. ''Yeeeeooooow!''

Mr. Quinn grabbed the clipboard and released her pinched fingers in the time it took for Cindy to process the distress signals from her brain.

''You're bleeding,'' he uttered, clasping her fingers.

''It's nothing,'' she gasped, bewildered that such a minor injury could produce so much blood—and agony—and wondering what it was about this man that made her behave like the Fourth Stooge.

''Come in and wash your hands,'' he said, tugging gently at her arm.

"Uh, no." Cindy knew there was a good reason to turn him down, but the rationale escaped her for a few seconds.

"But you need to stop the bleeding."

Suddenly Cindy's brain resumed functioning—oh, yeah, she *lived* here. "I have my own suite," she explained hurriedly.

"Be reasonable, Ms. Warren. You'll ruin your clothes." His mouth curved into a wry smile. "Not to mention this, er, lovely carpet."

She relented with a laugh, gritting her teeth against the pain. "Maybe I will borrow a wet washcloth, if you don't mind."

He stepped back and swept his arm inside the room. "This is your hotel. I'll wait here."

"I'll just be a moment," she murmured. As he held open the door, she slid past him, their bodies so close she could see the threads on the buttons of his starched white shirt. The proximity set what hair she had left on end.

Keeping her eyes averted from Mr. Quinn's personal belongings, she stepped over his barge-sized dress shoes in the doorway of the bathroom, squashing down her instantaneous thought of the anatomical implications. She also ignored the masculine scents of soap and aftershave as she turned on the cold-water faucet and grabbed a washcloth.

Glancing into the mirror was a mistake—her hair looked straight out of the seventies and her makeup needed more than a touch-up. Cindy groaned, then gasped when the water hit her fingers. *What an idiot I am.*

She applied pressure with a white washcloth and looked toward the bedroom. The door he held open cast light into the room from the hallway, sending his long shadow across the carpet. No doubt he was belly-laughing at what must seem like her talent for self-destruction.

Cindy removed the washcloth, relieved the bleeding had slowed.

"You'll find a couple of bandages in my toiletry bag," he called out, and for the first time she noticed a slight Southern accent. "It's on the back of the door. Help yourself."

She hesitated to go through his personal belongings, but then told herself she was being ridiculous over a couple of lousy bandages. Cindy stepped back and closed the bathroom door, immediately smelling the soft leather of Mr. Quinn's black toiletry bag. Her hand stopped in midair at the sight of pale blue silk pajama pants barely visible behind the large hanging bag. A picture of the handsome Mr. Quinn in his lounge wear zoomed to mind and the urge to run overwhelmed her.

With jerky hands, she unzipped the left side of the toiletry bag, but to her dismay, a barrage of small foil packets rained down on her sensible pumps. Condoms. At least a dozen in all varieties—colored, textured, flavored.

Oh, good Lord. Cindy dropped to her knees and snatched up the condoms, then stood and crammed them back into the pocket, knocking down Mr. Quinn's pajama pants in the process. *Dammit.* She yanked up the flimsy pants, remembering too late the cuts on her hand. And silk was nothing if not absorbent. Cindy watched in abject horror as the pale fabric soaked up her blood. She dropped the garment as if it were on fire.

"Are you all right in there?" he called.

Cindy nearly swallowed her tongue. "Y-yes."

"Did you find what you were looking for?"

Her heart thrashing, Cindy tore open the right zippered pocket of the toiletry bag and fished out the bandages amongst shaving cream, shampoo and toothpaste. "Got them!" she called. Quickly she rewashed her fingers and slapped on the bandages despite the tremor of her hands. Finally, she turned and carefully picked up the silk pants to assess the damage.

One clear red imprint of her hand embellished the backside, as if she'd grabbed the man's tush.

Cindy closed her eyes, her mind reeling. Why did things like this happen to her?

"Is everything okay in there?"

She leaned on the sink for support. *Should I tell the man I found his stash of rubbers and fondled his pajamas?* Then Cindy straightened. She could have the pants cleaned, then slip them back inside his room before tonight—Mr. Quinn would never know. Considerably cheered, she wadded the pants into a ball and shoved them down the back of her skirt. Thankfully, her jacket covered the lump.

Cindy took a deep breath and emerged from the bathroom, nearly faltering when she had to sidle past him again to reach the hall. "Thank you," she said, as she retrieved the clipboard.

"No problem."

At the sight of his devilish grin, Cindy remembered the man's sexual preparedness and told herself he was a ladykiller to be avoided. Recalling her original errand, Cindy cleared her throat. "And I'm sorry about the room, Mr. Quinn. Of course you're welcome to smoke in the hotel lounge."

He shrugged. "Perhaps I'll take this opportunity to rid myself of a nasty vice."

Backing away on wobbly legs, Cindy nodded curtly. "Well, good luck." Then she turned and fled, horrifically aware of the man's pants jammed in her pantyhose.

ERIC STEPPED INTO THE HALL and watched her hurry away. He was at a loss to explain why he'd felt so compelled to tease the woman. In scant days Cindy Warren would see him in an entirely different light, and laying a friendly foundation wouldn't hurt, he reasoned. He ignored the fact that such a gesture had never seemed necessary in past assignments. Perhaps the thought of her cutting her lovely hair to impress the hatchet man had made the difference.

From the reports concerning the Chandelier House, he had known the general manager was a woman, but nothing had prepared him for her youth or her beauty. Yet after observing her in the salon for only a short time, he understood why Cindy Warren held the top position in the grande dame hotel. She had fire in her beautiful green eyes and a firm set to her chin. And even with the haircut from hell, she was still pretty damn cute.

Eric stepped back into his room, pushing the stiff leather suspenders over his shoulders to fall loosely past his waist. Crossing to the antique desk where he'd abandoned a stack of paperwork, he reclaimed the surprisingly comfortable chair.

Using a pen with the hotel's name on it, he jotted down notes about the room he'd received as an incognito business traveler. His head pivoted as he surveyed the space.

Although the wood furnishings were far from new, the bed, armoire and desk were charming and smelled pleasantly of lemon furniture polish. The bed linens were a restful combination of taupe checks and plaids, and the worn areas in the carpet had been cleverly concealed by attractive wool rugs. The electrical outlets worked and the spacious bathroom smelled fresh and sunny, although the Sweet Tarts on the pillow struck him as slightly odd.

He scribbled a few more notations, then stopped and dragged his hand over his face, picturing the determined set of Cindy Warren's shoulders. Frustrated by the attraction he felt for her, he reminded himself of the danger of getting too involved with someone who might suffer from his assignment.

Craving a cigarette, he expelled a noisy breath, then reached for the phone and dialed out. After a few seconds, a familiar voice came on the line.

"Lancaster here."

"Bill, this is Stanton. I just wanted to let you know I'm on-site."

"Great. How's the preliminary—is the place as nutty as we've been told?"

Eric fingered the package of Sweet Tarts. "Too early to tell."

"Well, I spoke to our liaison from Harmon today. If you discover in the next few days that the Chandelier House doesn't fit the future profile for a corporate property, we won't even send in the rest of the team."

Eric frowned. "I'm good, but that hardly seems fair."

"Sounds like Harmon wants to get rid of this property."

"If the numbers are that bad, why don't they just dump it?"

"Because the numbers aren't that bad. And some old cow on the board of directors has a soft spot for the place, so they need justification. We're it."

Eric leaned back in his chair. "Look, Bill, I came here to do a job and I'm not turning in a phony report. Plan on sending the team as scheduled. My reputation aside, there are people here to consider."

His associate snorted. "People? I'm sorry, I thought I was talking to Eric Stanton. Are the holidays making you soft?"

Cindy Warren's green-gray eyes flashed through his mind. "No—I guess I'm just tired."

"Have you met the GM?"

"Yeah." *Oh, yeah.*

"Is she on to you yet?"

Eric pinched the bridge of his nose. "Nope, she's not on to me yet." *But she's already under my skin.*

2

CINDY TRIED TO ERASE Eric Quinn's image from her mind as she approached the executive meeting room. If ever there was a time not to be distracted by an attractive guest, it was now, when the fate of her staff depended on her. Worry niggled the back of her mind. Working in the close confines of the hotel, co-workers rapidly became like family, and she felt responsible for their future.

In the two years since Harmon Hospitality had purchased the Chandelier House, she and her staff had received countless memos from the home office mandating changes that would force their beloved hotel to fit into a corporate mold. So far, she had resisted. Her employees had no concept of a corporate direction—at any given time, most of them had no idea which direction was *up*. Yet somehow jobs were done and guests were delighted enough to return time after time.

"Good morning, everyone," she said, flashing a cheerful smile around the room as she walked to the head of the long table. Six directors and a handful of assorted managers chorused greetings and exchanged barbs while vying for a choice doughnut from the boxes being passed around.

The meeting room reeked of the mingling brews gurgling from appliances in the corner: regular coffee, cappuccino, sassafras tea and something scarlet dripping from the juicer. Cindy wrinkled her nose and refilled her cup with black coffee.

"New haircut, Cindy?" Joel Cutter, the food and beverage director, covered a smile by biting into a powdered doughnut.

Amidst the good-natured chuckling, Cindy threw him her most withering look, which didn't faze him. A valued employee and personal friend, Joel oversaw the restaurant, the lounge and catering. Hot coffee sloshed over the edge of her happy-face mug as she set it on the table. She tucked herself into an upholstered chair, ignoring the unsettling lump at her back. "Pass the doughnuts. And thanks for the opening, Joel. We'll begin with the hair salon. Amy?"

All eyes turned to the wincing rooms director, who was shaking white pills from one of the four bottles sitting on the table in front of her. She downed them with a drink of the scarlet liquid. "If it wasn't for Jerry, I'd say turn the place into an ice-cream parlor. I talked the new stylist into staying through tomorrow, but after that, we'll be short-handed again." Amy smiled sheepishly. "Jerry said she hasn't stopped crying since you left, boss." The room erupted into more laughter.

Cindy waved to quiet the melee. "Ha, ha, very funny. Seriously, what seems to be the problem with keeping a qualified stylist?"

Amy leaned forward. "Most hairdressers I've interviewed want to keep their skills sharp in areas other than simple cuts, like perming and coloring. In my opinion, we need to offer a full range of services."

Nodding, Cindy made a few notes on a yellow legal pad. "Fine."

Amy angled her head. "And it would help if Jerry—"

"—would agree to wait on female customers," Cindy finished for her. "I know. But Jerry's good at what he does, and we can't afford to lose him. He's a legend."

"Much like your new hairdo," Joel mumbled into his napkin, prompting more laughter.

Ignoring him, she shifted her gaze to Samantha Riggs, director of sales. "How's business, Sam?"

"Never better," Sam replied, completely at ease in full Klingon war regalia, including the lumpy forehead mask. "If the Trekkies are happy with the way we handle the regional conference, we're bound to get the business of the Droids and the Fantasms." She adjusted her chain-metal sash for emphasis.

Cindy hoped her smile wasn't as shaky as it felt. Although the buying power and loyalty of the role-playing groups was strong, she'd heard the hotel was getting quite a reputation at headquarters as well—as the Final Frontier.

Sam counted off on her black-tipped fingernails as she spoke. "The crystal readers will be here at the end of the week, the vampires are arriving at midnight on Saturday and the adult toy trade show starts next Monday."

Panic seized Cindy. "Adult toys next Monday?"

"Isn't that corporate fellow arriving next Monday?" Joel asked casually, reaching for a honey cruller.

Cindy nodded, trying to mask her alarm. She didn't mind hosting the X-rated trade show, but the timing couldn't have been any worse.

"Let's hope he has a sense of humor," Amy chirped.

"And a sex life," Manny interjected.

"Don't worry," Joel said, "Cindy has cornered the market on celibacy."

"You're a laugh a minute, Joel," Cindy said dryly, ignoring the burst of applause. Joel and his wife were constantly trying to fix her up, but their matchmaking attempts had produced one disaster after another. "Sam, let's keep the trade show as low-profile as possible, okay?"

Sam nodded convincingly. "You want low-profile, Cindy—you got low-profile."

"Said the woman in the Klingon costume," Manny pointed out.

"Hey, whatever makes the customer happy," Sam said smoothly.

Cindy looked to William Belk, director of engineering, a burly fellow who rarely spoke. Smiling broadly, she asked, "William, how goes the search for the perfect lobby Christmas tree?"

He glanced around uneasily, twisting his cap in his big hands. "The nursery is still looking."

Cindy's stomach pitched. "We're running out of days in the month of December," she said with mustered good humor. "I'd like to see the tree up and decorated before our visitors arrive next Monday."

"Uh, yeah."

She smiled tightly and wrote herself a note to follow up with the nursery. After discussing a few administrative details with the comptroller and the human resources manager, she glanced at Joel and lifted one corner of her mouth. "Would you like to close out the meeting, or is my hair too distracting?"

"I'll try to be strong," Joel responded fiercely, then added, "Farrah."

Cindy rolled her eyes heavenward. "Start with banquets."

"Booked to 90 percent through New Year's."

She blinked. "Great. The restaurant?"

He pushed a newspaper article toward her. "The *Chronicle* gave us a mediocre review."

"That beats the flogging they gave us last spring," she said. "Anything else?"

"I doubt I'm the only one wondering about this axman, Stanton."

Cindy glanced around the room, which had suddenly grown so quiet she could hear her hair moaning. After a deep breath, she rested her elbows on the table. "The corporate review was next on the agenda, but I'm glad you brought it up, Joel." She wet her lips. "As most of you know, a third-party firm has been hired to study select properties under the corporate umbrella." She smiled. "And we're one of the lucky ones—the Chandelier House is going to be treated to the works."

Cindy counted on fingers that hadn't seen a manicure in months. "An audit of our accounting procedures, our reservations process, sales, customer service—if we do it, it's going to be scrutinized."

Manny cleared his throat. "Is there a reason we're being studied so closely?"

Cindy clasped her hands in front of her. "The inspection might be related to the fact that I've resisted efforts to change the way the hotel does business."

"And that you have breasts," Amy muttered.

"I have no reason to believe this has anything to do with me being a woman," Cindy said with sincerity, then grinned and pointed her thumb toward the slight curves beneath her jacket. "Besides, your point is debatable."

Laughter eased the tension in the room.

"They want to turn us into a cookie-cutter corporate operation," Joel supplied.

Cindy weighed her words. "It would seem that headquarters would like for us to conform more to a corporate profile, yes." She forced optimism into her voice, then swept her gaze around the room. "A Mr. Stanton is scheduled to arrive next Monday with an examination team. But I wouldn't be surprised if he arrives a few days early to check us out. Let me know if you notice anyone suspicious."

"Should we be worried?" Amy asked, massaging her temples. "I think I'm getting a migraine."

"We should all be *aware*," Cindy corrected gently. "Aware that everything we do will be under a microscope. As soon as Mr. Stanton arrives, I'll call an executive committee meeting and make the proper introductions." She conjured up an encouraging smile. "Now, if there's nothing else—"

"Whoa," Joel said, raising his hand. "Don't forget about the Christmas party tomorrow night."

Cindy nearly groaned. Nothing could have been further from her mind. "How could we forget?" she croaked.

"With cutbacks on the horizon, should we bring a bag lunch?" Sam asked.

Everyone laughed, but Cindy shook her head emphatically.

"Forget the lunch," Joel said, "but feel free to bring a date for Cindy."

Amid the laughter, Cindy narrowed her eyes at Joel. "*You* are treading on thin ice." She smacked her hand on the table. "This meeting is adjourned."

As everyone filed out of the room, Joel fell in step beside her and she poked him in the shoulder. "What makes you so sure I'm not bringing a date? It just so happens that I might."

Joel's look of incredulity made her wish she actually *did* have a date. And the flash of Eric Quinn's face in her mind exasperated her further. "You don't have a date," Joel scoffed. "Name one eligible bachelor in this town you haven't neutered with indifference. Your name is on the bathroom wall—for a hard time, call Cindy Warren."

"You flatter me."

"Cindy, if you bring a date tomorrow night—" He looked toward the ceiling. "I'll cover for you all day Wednesday."

She straightened. Since her home consisted of a small suite near the top of the hotel, excursions outside the walls—especially for an entire day—were rare. This could be her last chance to go Christmas shopping before the hotel descended into seasonal chaos. "You'd cover my office calls?"

"Yep."

Her last chance to buy a few casual clothes before she headed home to Virginia on Christmas Eve. "My pager?"

"Sure thing." Then he grinned. "Of course, if you come stag, I get your parking spot for a month."

And hadn't the lock on her garment bag jammed the last time she'd traveled to L.A. overnight on business? She definitely needed new luggage. "And all I have to do is produce a man?"

"He has to be straight," Amy qualified, walking on the other side.

"Right," Joel agreed sternly. "I expect to see definite heterosexual groping before the night's over."

Cindy put her hand over her heart. "I'm wounded—you two honestly think I can't find a date?"

"Right," they said in unison.

She squinted at Joel. "You're on, buster."

Joel rubbed his hands together and squeezed his eyes shut. "VIP parking—I can hardly wait."

"Well, *I* can't wait to meet this mystery man," Amy said over her shoulder as she followed Joel toward the stairs.

Cindy stopped and stared after her friends, dread surging in her stomach. "Neither can I."

ERIC SPENT the next couple of hours touring various areas of the hotel as unobtrusively as possible, occasionally ducking into alcoves to scribble on index cards. If employees stopped to offer assistance, he either manufactured requests for directions or said he was waiting for someone.

The covert stage of his job had always been his least favorite. Eric didn't have a problem with pointing out deficiencies in an operation, but he much preferred doing it face-to-face with the staff.

He spotted Cindy Warren twice as she practically jogged from one task to another, but he stayed out of her line of vision despite his urge to talk to her again. He typically made his most valuable observations early in the review process and he liked as much done as possible in the first couple of days, since he never knew if or when his cover would be blown. After that, the sucking-up factor set in— an ego trip for some consultants, but merely a hindrance to productivity in his opinion.

After he'd exhausted his many checklists, he made his way to the concierge desk, where a pleasant-looking blond man offered him a professional smile.

"Good afternoon, sir. How can I help you?"

Eric sized him up in seconds—he knew from the man's demeanor he was an asset to Cindy Warren. "I'm looking for a dinner recommendation."

"Any particular type of cuisine, sir?"

"Maybe a good steak."

"Unless you want to see the city, our chef grills a great rib eye."

Eric inclined his head, silently applauding the man's response. "Sounds good—I'll try it. How's the lounge?"

"Great drinks, but not much action on Monday night."

Shaking his head slightly, Eric laughed. "Fine with me."

The concierge extended his hand. "I'm Manny Oliver."

Eric clasped his hand in a firm grip. "Quinn. Eric Quinn."

"Glad you chose the Chandelier House for your trip, Mr. Quinn. Let me know if there's anything I can do to make your stay more enjoyable."

At that moment, Eric caught sight of Cindy across the lobby. He hadn't realized he was staring until Manny's cool voice reached him. "That's our general manager, Cindy Warren."

Eric tried to appear casual. "We met briefly in the salon this morning. I was quite impressed with her, um, professionalism." *And her legs.* Eric watched her move alongside a barrel-chested man, gesturing from floor to ceiling in the curve of the magnificent staircase.

"She's first-rate," the man agreed. "The Chandelier House is lucky to have her."

"She seems young for so much responsibility," Eric said, fishing.

"Early thirties," Manny offered.

"Is she single?" The words came out before Eric could stop them, and he wasn't sure who was more surprised, himself or the concierge.

Manny straightened, his defenses up, and Eric wondered if the man had romantic feelings for his boss. "Ms. Warren is unmarried," he said tightly.

Mentally kicking himself, Eric simply nodded. "Thank you for the meal recommendation, Mr. Oliver." He withdrew a bill from his wallet, but before he could extend it, Manny stopped him with the slightest lift of his hand. "Don't mention it, Mr. Quinn. It's my job to take care of *everyone* in the hotel."

Manny's friendly smile didn't mask the glimmer of warning in his clear blue eyes.

"I'm sure you're good at your job," Eric said lightly.

"The best," Manny assured him as another guest approached his station. "Enjoy that steak, Mr. Quinn."

Unable to resist another peek in her direction, Eric was treated to an inadvertent display of lower thigh as Cindy stretched her arm high to make a point to the man, presumably in preparation for installing more seasonal decorations.

Feeling Manny's stare boring into his back, Eric dragged his gaze away from Cindy Warren. Checking his watch and finding he had plenty of time for a drink before dinner, he moved in the direction of the lounge, trying to shake off the undeniable surge of attraction he felt for the general manager. The nostalgia of the season must be getting to him, he decided. Making him sappy. Or horny. Or both.

The name "Sammy's" stretched over the entrance to the lounge, one of the few areas in the hotel Eric had not yet staked out. He walked down two steps and into the low-lit interior, fully expecting the lounge to resemble the hundreds of other generic hotel bars he'd visited during his fifteen-year stint in the business. Instead, he was pleasantly surprised to find a motif of antique musical instruments. An old upright piano sat abandoned in a far corner. The strains of Burl Ives played over unseen speakers, evoking memories of past Christmases. A bittersweet thought; family gatherings hadn't been the same since his mother's death.

The place was practically deserted, with only a handful of customers dotting the perimeter of the room. A knot of Trekkies indulged in a down-to-earth pitcher of beer.

But to his pleasure, Jerry the barber sat on one of the upholstered stools, still wearing the Santa hat. He chatted with a thick-armed bartender and smoked a sweet-smelling cigar.

"Weeeeell, if it isn't Mr. Quinn." Jerry grinned and nodded to the stool next to him. "Have a seat. Tony'll get you a drink."

Eric slid onto the stool and rested his elbows on the smooth curved edge of the bar. "Bourbon and water," he directed Tony with a nod. "Taking a break, Jer?" He patted his shirt pocket for a cigarette, then remembered he had left them in the room.

The older man nodded and took a long drag of his cigar. "I'm through for the day—got tired of that woman caterwauling."

"Excuse me?"

Jerry used the cigar as a pointer while he talked. "That woman who whacked off Ms. Cindy's hair—she's been bawling all day."

"It wasn't her fault," Eric said with a laugh. "We warned your boss."

"You know Cindy?" Tony glared as he slid Eric's drink toward him.

Another besotted employee, Eric surmised. "Not really," he said lightly.

Tony sized him up silently, flexing his massive chest beneath his skintight dress shirt. The red jingle bell suspenders did little to soften the man's looks. Finally Tony walked down the bar to help another customer.

"Don't mind him," Jerry said with another puff. "He's Ms. Cindy's self-appointed bodyguard."

"He looks dangerous."

Jerry glanced around, then leaned toward him. "Just between me and you, he did a stint at San Quentin."

Eric glanced up from his drink in alarm. "For what?"

"Never asked," the man admitted. "But he's fine as long as he stays on his medication. A bit protective of the boss lady, though."

"Ms. Warren is a popular woman," Eric observed.

"She's a *good* woman," Jerry amended. "But stubborn." He shook his head. "Stubborn as the day is long."

"She's not a good manager?"

"She's the best. But a big company bought this place a couple of years ago and has been trying to change it ever since. Ms. Cindy is wearing herself out digging in her heels."

Eric kept his voice light. "There's always room for improved efficiency."

"People don't come to the Chandelier House for efficiency, Mr. Quinn. You can go down the street and get a bigger room with a better view for less money."

"So why come here at all?"

The man laughed and nodded toward the Trekkies. "We're oddballs, Mr. Quinn, and we cater to oddballs. It's a profitable niche, but Ms. Cindy can't get anyone up the ladder to listen to her."

"She confides in you?"

"Nope." Jerry grinned. "But I know this hotel—been here thirty years, and I know women—been married three times."

"The last one is a dubious credential," Eric noted, taking another drink from his glass.

"Women are the most blessed gift the good Lord put on this earth," the old man said with a ring of satisfaction. "Ever been to the altar, son?"

A short laugh escaped Eric. "No."

Jerry nodded knowingly. "But Ms. Cindy's interesting, isn't she? An attractive woman."

Eric frowned, alarmed that his interest was apparently so easy to spot. He needed to find a way to spend time with Cindy Warren, but he didn't want it interpreted as a come-on. "I barely know her."

Jerry sucked deeply on the cigar, then blew out the smoke in little puffs. "Oh, yeah, you like her all right."

Feeling warm with a mixture of annoyance and embarrassment, Eric finished his drink. "No comment."

"Mmm-hmm. Got it bad." He laughed, a low, hoarse rumble. "How long you planning to stay in San Francisco?"

A bit rankled, Eric shrugged. "My business will be over in a few days, but I'm thinking about hanging around through New Year's. Maybe visit the wine country."

Jerry studied the burning end of his cigar. "Spending Christmas alone, are you? No family?"

Eric considered lying, then decided the truth was just as simple. "My father and I aren't very close since my mother's passing a few years ago. My younger sister will be with him for the holidays."

"You and your sister don't get along either?" Instead of judgmental, Jerry sounded only curious.

"No, that's not it. Alicia is quite a bit younger than I am, and she has her own family."

The barber looked sympathetic. "Still, kinfolk should stick together, especially at this time of year."

Eric shifted on the stool, struck by a pang of longing for Christmases of his childhood. Popcorn garlands on a live tree, homemade cream candy and his father playing the piano. But Gomas Stanton had grown taciturn after his wife died, until finally Eric couldn't bear to spend holidays at home, God help him.

If this holiday turned out like the last few, Eric would call his father on Christmas Eve, only to be subjected to a diatribe about how Eric's work contributed to the fall of American capitalism. A master glassblower who had worked in a union factory for thirty-three years, his father believed a man's contribution to the world came from a hard day's work to produce a tangible good, something that could be bought and sold and owned. Eric's chosen field, business consulting, was a mystery to him. *"People like you are doing away with mom-and-pop enterprises—the kind of businesses and people who built this country,"* his father had once said. And then there was the music, always the music.

The more Eric thought about it, the better Christmas right here on the West Coast sounded. Especially if he could manage to maintain an amicable relation with one Cindy Warren. Some GMs stayed close to their hotels for Christmas. Perhaps they could ring in the New Year together. He smiled wryly. If the accident-prone woman lived that long.

"Course, you'll feel different about Christmas when you settle down with a lady," Jerry pressed on, blowing a slow stream of smoke straight up in the air. "Love's got a way of makin' holidays special, yessir."

Eric laughed. "There's no danger of me falling in love, my man, Christmas or no."

The man squinted at him. "Famous last words. I saw you two this morning, bouncing off each other like a couple of magnets turned the wrong way. I'm old, but I ain't blind."

Shaking his head, Eric set his glass on the counter and pushed away from the bar. "You're imagining things, Jer." He stood and gave the man a curt nod. "But thanks for the company anyway."

"You'd better watch your step around her," Jerry warned without looking up.

"Don't worry," Eric said dryly. "I'm not going to give Tony a reason to violate parole."

Jerry laughed. "Mr. Quinn, don't you know a pretty woman is ten times more dangerous than a hardened criminal?" He took a last puff on his cigar, then set it down with finality. "You're a goner, son. Merry Christmas."

3

"SO, WHO'S THE LUCKY GUY?" Manny asked as he rolled a section of Cindy's hair with a fat curling iron.

Concentrating on his technique for later reference, she glanced at him in the mirror of her dressing table. "Lucky guy?"

"Amy told me you had a hot date for the party tomorrow night—who is he?"

"Is nothing sacred in this hotel?"

"I think we still have a bottle of holy water from a baptismal lying around somewhere."

She sighed. "I don't have a date…yet."

"I can make a few calls."

"He has to be straight."

Indignant, Manny scoffed. "I know some straight guys—two, in fact." Then he frowned. "Oh, but they're married, and one is Joel."

Cindy sniffed. "I smell smoke."

Manny jumped and released the lock of hair, which fell limply back in place, perhaps straighter than before. "No harm done," he assured her, then clucked. "Your hair is thin."

"Thanks." She lifted her bandaged hand. "Would you like to pour alcohol on my cuts, too?"

"What the heck did you do to your hand, anyway?"

Cindy hesitated. "I'll tell you later. Maybe. Fix my hair—and hurry."

"The hairdresser should have known better than to give you all these layers," he grumbled.

"I told her to."

"Then she should have exercised her right to a professional veto."

"Maybe *you* should be our new stylist."

"Cindy, contrary to popular belief, all gay men cannot cut hair and we don't have track lighting in our refrigerators."

"So tell me again why I'm submitting to your ministrations."

Manny shrugged. "I'm simply trying to make the best of this tragedy." He released another dark lock of hair that stubbornly refused to curl. "But I'm failing miserably—your hair won't even *bend*."

"Never mind." She groaned and held up her hands in defeat. "I'll borrow a nun's habit."

"You jest, but I think there's one in the lost and found."

"What am I going to do? My mother will have a stroke when I go home for Christmas."

He scoffed. "You'll be there for what—three days? You'll live and so will she."

"I'm glad you're coming home with me," Cindy said earnestly. "She'll believe you if you tell her my haircut is in style."

"Oh, no. I'm going home with you for baked ham and pecan pie, not to play referee for Joan and Christina Crawford."

"We're not that bad," she retorted, laughing. "Just the normal mother-daughter, tug-of-war relationship. She'll think you and I are sleeping together, you know."

His forehead wrinkled. "Is that a compliment?"

"Yes!" She punched him. "And thanks in advance for saving me from the usual harangue about settling down."

''So, what's up with that?'' he asked, fluffing and spraying her hair.

''My mother?''

''No—you not settling down. Got a bad suit in the old relationship closet?''

Cindy gnawed on the inside of her cheek for a few seconds, pondering the sixty-four-thousand-dollar question. ''I can't recall any particularly traumatic experiences. On the other hand, I can't recall any particularly noteworthy ones either.'' She shrugged. ''I've never met a man who appreciates the more *unusual* things in life. You know, a guy who uses words like 'happenstance' and 'supercalifragilisticexpialidocious.'''

Manny stared.

''Okay, maybe I'm expecting too much.''

But he merely shook his head, tucked her hair behind her ears, and studied the effect. ''Nope. Don't settle, because if you're like most of my friends—male *and* female—falling in love will be an agonizing event with a man who represents everything you hate.''

She laughed. ''Don't hold back.''

''I'm serious. Oh, yeah, *now* they're giddy with newly-weditis, but right here is the shoulder most of them cried on during the courtship.'' He tapped his collarbone. ''And frankly, I'm not sure it was worth the trouble.''

Cindy held up one hand. ''You're preaching to the choir. But I am in desperate need of a day off, so I've got to find a date for the party even if I have to hire a man.''

He nodded. ''Now that's the ticket—retail romance.'' Exhaling noisily, he shook his head at her reflection. ''Sorry, Cindy, that's the best I can do. I must say, though, without all that hair, your eyes really come alive.''

She stared at the bottom layers hanging limply around her shoulders, the top layers hugging her ears. ''Thanks, but I simply can't go around looking like this.'' Cindy told herself she was *not* trying to look good in case she bumped into the man from room 1010 again.

"Just go back to the salon tomorrow and take the advice of the stylist. Their instincts are usually correct." He gave her a pointed look. "They mess up by trying to satisfy the armchair experts."

"It looks like I slept with panty hose on my head," she mumbled.

"Control top," he agreed.

She stood with resignation. "I have to get back to work—believe it or not, I have more pressing issues at hand than my coiffure." Like the wad of silk at her back that she still hadn't had time to take care of.

"Don't forget to work in some time today for manhunting."

"With this hair, I'll need an Uzi to bag a date."

"Where's that nice Chanel scarf Mommy dearest sent for your birthday?"

"The yellow one?" Cindy walked over to a bureau and withdrew the filmy strip of silk. "Here. Why?"

"Wrap it around your throat and let the ends hang down your back." He smiled apologetically. "It'll draw attention away from your hair."

She made a face, then followed his advice, checking the result in the mirror. As usual, he was right.

Manny slowly wound the cord of the curling iron. "Cindy," he said, his voice unusually serious. "You're worried about this Stanton man coming, aren't you?"

She caught his gaze, then nodded. "Among other things."

He sighed. "Just when I was starting to like this crazy place."

"We're not out of a job yet," she assured him. "But I won't lie to you, Manny—we're a company stepchild and I suspect Harmon is looking to prune the family tree."

"This scrutiny could be a good thing," he pointed out. "Maybe Stanton's people will see the potential of the old gal and headquarters will throw some improvement funds our way."

"As long as those funds don't dictate changing what makes the Chandelier House unique." She forced a smile. "Just who are you calling an old gal, anyway?"

Manny smiled, his good humor returned. "By the way, since you're on the make, there was a guy in the lobby this morning who looked like he wouldn't mind having you in his Christmas stocking."

She frowned. "Me?"

"Uh-huh. Guy named Quinn."

Cindy's pulse kicked up. "Eric Quinn?"

"You've already met him?"

Anxious to get it over with, she reached around, stuck her hand down the back of her skirt, and whipped out the pajama pants. "Sort of."

Manny's eyes bulged. "You siren, you."

"It's not what you think."

"I think those are the man's pants."

"Okay, it is what you think, but I didn't get them the way you think."

He crossed his arms. "I guess you expect me to believe you stole them?"

Cindy bit her lower lip.

His jaw dropped. "You *stole* them?"

She collapsed into a chair. "I don't believe this day."

Manny sat too. "Now you're starting to worry me."

"*I'm* starting to worry me. Every time I see Eric Quinn, I end up doing something stupid."

"Cindy, I'm dying here—what's up with the silk drawers?"

Just thinking about the incident made the backs of her knees perspire. "I went to his room to handle a simple request. Next thing I know, I've cut myself on a freaking clipboard and I'm in his bathroom washing up.''

He made a rolling motion with his hand. ''Get to the good part already.''

''His pajamas were hanging on the back of the door. They fell, I picked them up.'' She turned the pants around to show him the handprint.

Manny frowned. ''So you offered to get them cleaned?''

''Not exactly.'' She buried her head in her hands. ''I was afraid he'd think I was some kind of pervert stroking his pajamas, so I took them.''

Her friend pursed his lips. ''You run this entire hotel, and that was the best plan you could come up with?''

Cindy lifted her head. ''It sounded good at the time!''

He took the wrinkled pants by the waistband, then peered closer at the stain, tisk-tisking. ''I hate to tell you this, Cindy, but your chances of getting blood out of nonwashable silk are zippo.''

She moaned. ''Now what?''

''Beckwith's,'' Manny declared, scrutinizing the label. ''It's a men's boutique in Pacific Heights that carries this brand.''

Cindy brightened. ''Really?''

''Yeah. The man has expensive taste.''

She reached for her purse. ''Manny, I don't suppose you would—''

''Run to Beckwith's and see if they have a duplicate?''

Steepling her hands, she said, ''I'm officially begging you.''

Manny pressed his lips together and adopted a dreamy expression. ''Well, I have a few errands to run first, but there *is* this tie in their window I've had my eye on.''

''It's yours!'' she exclaimed, handing over her gold credit card. ''But I need those pajama pants before dinner.''

''Now there's a sentence you don't hear every day.''

"And—" she lifted a finger in warning. "Not a word of this outside these walls."

His mouth twitched. "Didn't you know that concierge is French for 'keeper of dirty little secrets'?" He stuffed the pants into the toiletry bag, along with the curling iron. "By the way, Amy said to stop by the front desk—she might have a line on our undercover Mr. Stanton."

Cindy perked up. "No kidding?"

"She wouldn't tell me a thing. She said she'd only talk to you."

They rode the elevator to the lobby together, then separated after Manny promised to page her as soon as he returned "with the goods." Cindy started feeling shaky again as she approached the front desk—she'd hoped that at least the tree would be installed and all the holiday decorations completed before Stanton arrived.

Amy stood with her head back, placing drops in her eyes.

"Allergies?" Cindy asked.

Blinking rapidly, Amy nodded toward the wall behind her. "I think it's the evergreen wreaths."

"Christmas is a lousy time of the year to be allergic to evergreen," Cindy noted.

"It's almost as bad as Valentine's Day."

"Are you allergic to chocolate, too?"

The rooms director frowned. "No, penicillin."

Cindy squinted. "How does penicillin—never mind." She leaned close and lowered her voice. "Manny said you might have spotted Stanton posing as a guest?"

"I think so," Amy reached into her jacket pocket and withdrew a slip of paper. "Here's his room number—you might want to check it out yourself."

After reading the scribbling, Cindy gasped. "I spoke to this man about a room change this morning. Why do you suspect he's Stanton?"

Amy sniffed, then dabbed at her eyes with a tissue. "Besides the name similarity and the fact that he's alone, he's been all over the hotel asking questions about the furniture and making notes. Plus,'' she lowered her voice, ''he's booked in his room through Christmas Eve and instead of using a credit card, he paid cash for his room deposit.''

Cindy nodded, the implications of the man's identity spinning in her head. ''Sounds like he could be our man. I think I'll drop by his room again to say hello.''

''Um, boss.'' Amy leaned over the counter and glanced at Cindy's sensible navy skirt. ''If you're going to pay him a visit, show some leg, would you?''

Her mouth fell open. ''Amy! Do you honestly think I'd resort to feminine wiles to influence the man's decision?''

Amy looked at her for a full minute.

Cindy sighed, looked around, then opened her jacket to roll down the waistband of her skirt. ''How much leg?''

CINDY SMILED BRIGHTLY as the door swung open to reveal the man still dressed in slacks, shirt and loosened tie. ''Hello again, Mr. Stark.''

Holding the same pad of paper as earlier, the graying man's eyes swam behind wavy lenses. ''Yes?''

''I'm Cindy Warren, the general manager. I spoke to you this morning about changing rooms?''

''Oh, right,'' he said tartly. ''I don't want a better view now since I'm already settled in.''

''Fine,'' she said quickly, deciding not to mention they had already booked the room she'd offered him earlier. ''I wanted to express our regret once again, and let you know if there's anything we can do to make your stay more enjoyable, don't hesitate to contact me or someone on my staff.''

''A couple of free meals would be nice,'' he said bluntly.

She cleared her throat mildly. ''I've already arranged for

a complimentary breakfast to be delivered in the morning, sir.''

He glanced over the top of his glasses. ''More than coffee and a doughnut, I hope?''

She bit her tongue. ''Yes, sir. Enjoy your stay.''

After the door closed behind her, none too gently, she backed away and frowned. If that sour man had their fate in his hands, they were all in trouble. Waiting for the elevator, she got an unwanted view of her hair in the mirrored doors and groaned. When she remembered her foolish bet with Joel, she groaned again. The doors opened and she stepped inside, lost in thought.

''Hello,'' a deep voice said.

She glanced up to find Eric Quinn smiling at her. For a few seconds, she could only absorb his good looks. She noticed a high dimple on his left cheek she'd missed before. He had changed into gray sweatpants, a loose white T-shirt and athletic shoes. She prayed he hadn't yet missed his jammies.

''Uh-oh,'' he said. ''Problems?''

''No,'' she assured him hurriedly, then smiled. ''Well, no more than usual.''

''No more injuries, I hope.''

Her cheeks warmed. ''No, no more injuries.'' She cleared her throat, searching for a new topic. ''How is your stay so far, Mr. Quinn?''

''Productive,'' he said smoothly, glancing at her shortened skirt, his gaze lingering on her legs before making eye contact again. ''And I'm Eric.''

Oh, those eyes. Her fingers tingled slightly—the clipboard had probably severed a few nerves. She scrutinized the numbers panel, trying to remember where she'd been headed. ''What's your line of work...Eric?''

''Sales.''

"What kind of sales?" she asked, for the sake of conversation.

"Oh, trinkets and…things."

She puzzled at his vagueness, then remembered the adult toy show the following week. "Are you here in preparation for the trade show next week?"

He shifted uneasily. "As a matter of fact, I *am* preparing for next week."

Which explained the condom smorgasbord in his toiletry bag. She nodded and averted her gaze, hoping she hadn't turned as pink as she felt. She was liberal, she was hip. She'd even gone to a men's nude dancing club once with Manny. So why should the thought of this man selling dildos and fringed pasties unnerve her?

"Are you going to the basement, too?" he asked, nodding to the only lit button.

"Er, no," she said, stabbing the button for the lobby. The door slid open almost immediately, and she practically fell out in her haste to flee.

Cindy didn't look back as the doors closed, but was brought up short by a sudden yank to her neck. She stumbled backward and swung around, horrified at the sight of her scarf caught in the elevator door and being dragged down the shaft. She stood frozen as the bit of silk whipped off her neck with a swish and disappeared into the floor.

Thankful she hadn't knotted the noose, Cindy closed her eyes and hit the palm of her hand against her forehead.

"Was it him?"

At the sound of Amy's voice, Cindy turned to find her employee walking toward the elevator, scratching her arms.

"Rash," Amy explained. "Do you think Stark is the man we're looking for?"

Nodding, Cindy murmured, "Could be. He's a bit contrary."

The rooms director's forehead creased. "Maybe he's not

a leg man." Then she grinned. "Or maybe he's a man's man—perhaps we should have sent Manny."

Cindy shook her head, smiling wryly. "Just let the staff know they need to be on their toes around our grumpy Mr. Stark."

Amy snapped her fingers. "Why don't you invite him to the Christmas party tomorrow night?"

She stared. "Are you insane?"

"Why not? Show him a good time."

"Let him see the staff at their most drunken, uninhibited selves?"

"Oh." Amy frowned. "You have a point, but you also need a date."

"Well, it won't be the man who has come to make mincemeat out of us," she insisted. "Besides, I don't mind playing nicey-nicey, but I certainly don't want the staff thinking I'm kissing up to this man to save my own job."

"You're right," Amy said, scratching at her neck. "I'd better get back to the desk."

"See you later." Sighing, Cindy jogged down the stairs to the basement in the unlikely event her scarf had escaped the moving parts of the shaft and had somehow floated out intact onto the floor. Nothing. Her mother's gift was probably wrapped around some critical gear, damaging the working parts of the elevator even as she stood wringing her hands.

She glanced at her watch. Three o'clock—Manny should be back within the next hour. Then she'd easily be able to replace the pajamas while Eric Quinn worked out in the health club, a vision that conjured up a sweat on her own body. Cindy called engineering again about a Christmas tree, but the nursery had not yet located a candidate.

She dropped by the crowded Trekkie trade show and skimmed the many rows of tables to make sure the spring show's bestseller, a stun gun capable of administering a dizzying shock, was nowhere to be found. The public swarmed over the trading card tables. Costumes and masks were also enjoying a brisk trade. All in all, the show had successfully attracted a sizable family crowd.

Cindy fast-forwarded to next week's adult toy show. Picturing Eric Quinn surrounded by erotic paraphernalia was enough to convince her to skip that particular exhibition.

At seven o'clock, still without a word from Manny, Cindy decided to have dinner while she waited. She descended the service stairs to the restaurant and walked through the kitchen to say hello to the staff. After a few minutes of small talk with the chef, she chose a bad table near the rest rooms and slipped off her shoes. *What a day.*

"Surely you don't intend to eat alone," Eric Quinn said behind her.

She turned to see him seated at a table a few feet away, half hidden by a silk tree. Her pulse picked up. "I don't mind."

"It's kind of silly for both of us to dine alone, don't you think?" His voice was empty of innuendo. "May I join you, Ms. Warren?"

Say yes, she told herself. He was simply a nice sex-toy salesman, looking for light dinner conversation. Besides, this way she'd be able to keep track of him until Manny paged her. "Please." He stood and carried his wineglass to her table, then gave her a tired little smile. She nodded toward the vacant chair across from her. "And call me Cindy."

"All right, Cindy." He had changed into casual brown slacks and a pale blue button-down. He settled into the chair with athletic grace, his movements triggering an awareness in her limbs.

"What do you recommend?" he asked.

A married girlfriend had once diagrammed a position she'd always wanted to try on a napkin. "The rib eye,"

Cindy said, her heart thumping wildly. *Not that she hadn't had her chances with men.*

He nodded. "Rib eye is what the concierge suggested."

"You talked to Manny?" *It was just that none of those guys she dated had particularly lit her fire.*

"Yeah—seems like a nice fellow."

"He's my right-hand man." *Oh, the restaurateur from Oakland showed the spark of a promise, but she'd been mired in hotel problems at the time and...oh, well.*

"Good help is hard to find," he agreed.

"Especially in the hospitality industry." *But* this *man—this man was one big mass of flammable substance.*

"Cindy, before we go any further," he said, his eyes merry, "there's something we need to discuss."

A sense of doom flooded her. He knew about the pajamas. He'd discovered them missing and deduced that she'd taken them. "Wh-what do you mean?" she asked, reaching for her water glass.

His smile sent a chill up her spine. "I mean a certain piece of clothing."

She gulped down a mouthful of water, choking in her haste, her mind racing. "Oh, that. Well, I can explain—"

"It's not necessary," he said, shaking his head, his smile never wavering. "You were a little embarrassed—I understand."

"Um, yes, I was, but—"

"Actually, I think your little mishaps are funny."

Irritated, Cindy squirmed. "I'm glad, but—"

"And I hope you don't mind that I consulted the cleaners around the corner," he said, reaching inside his jacket.

"Well, as a matter of fact," she said, "I've already made arrangements for a replacement, so you don't have to worry about the bloodstain." Then she stopped. Cleaners? He knew the pants were gone, but how would he know about a stain?

He frowned as he withdrew a small paper bag. "Blood-stain? You were injured when your scarf came off?"

"My scarf?" she croaked.

"Yes, your scarf." Laughing, he withdrew her yellow Chanel scarf, folded neatly. "What did you think I was talking about?"

"I thought you were talking about...my scarf, of course," she replied lamely. "The cuts on my hand—I was afraid I had gotten blood on my scarf when I tried to grab it."

"I was able to pull it inside the elevator," he explained. "But the silk was soiled, so I thought I'd have it cleaned for you." He smiled again. "I had to drop off a few shirts anyway—I hope you don't think it was too forward."

Not when I have your PJs. "Not at all," she said. "Thank you. This was a gift from my mother."

"Ah. And where is she?"

"Virginia. Along with my father and older brother."

He blinked. "Really? I'm from Virginia, too."

Her surprise was interrupted by the sound of her beeper. "I'm sorry, I'm still on call." She glanced at the number, then withdrew a small radio from her pocket and punched a button. "Yes, Amy?"

"Sorry to bother you, Cindy, but our special guest in room 620 is complaining about the room temperature."

Suspecting Mr. Stark was still testing them, Cindy asked, "Too hot or too cold?"

"Too hot."

"Check the air-conditioning personally, Amy. And take a fan with you just in case."

"Sure thing, Cindy."

She stowed the radio and smiled at Eric. "Where were we? Oh, yes—what part of Virginia?"

"Near Manassas."

"Ah. I grew up farther south on Interstate 95, near Fredericksburg."

"I've been to Fredericksburg too many times to count," he acknowledged. "Small world."

A waiter took their order and they agreed to split a carafe of white wine. Cindy relaxed somewhat, but wished Manny would hurry up and call. The wine arrived and Eric filled her glass, then his.

"Do you go back often to visit?" she asked.

Something flashed over his face. Regret? He shook his head. "My sister and I are close, but my father doesn't exactly approve of my, um, line of work."

She nodded sympathetically, but she could see his father's side, too. That your son sold sex toys wasn't exactly something to brag about. But she had to admit, the combination of Eric's good looks, the dim lights and the good wine made his occupation seem kind of...titillating.

"Do you like your job?" he asked.

She opened her mouth to say yes, but her beeper went off and they both laughed. "Excuse me," she said. Within a few seconds, she had Amy on the line again.

"Cindy, now he's complaining about the noise next door."

"What noise next door?"

"I walked up, but I didn't hear a thing."

"Walk up again."

Amy sighed. "He's kind of hateful."

"I know, but hang in there." She put away the phone. "Yes, I like my job most of the time. Working with the public has its frustrating moments."

They chatted until appetizers arrived, and Cindy found herself warming up to Eric Quinn, despite his somewhat questionable vocation. Once their fingers brushed when they reached for the wine, and Cindy felt a definite spark of sexual energy. From the slightly hooded look of his eyes, she knew Eric felt it too.

What perfect Christmas-party date material—gorgeous, gentlemanly and temporary. "Eric, I was wondering—" Her beeper sounded again, and she groaned, then laughed.

When she pushed the button, Manny's voice came on the line. "Cindy, I have what you asked for—meet me at the concierge desk."

Her heart lifted. The sooner the pajama pants incident was taken care of, the better. "I'll be there in two minutes." Then she smiled at Eric. "This shouldn't take long. I hope you don't mind waiting alone for our meals to arrive."

"Not at all," he said politely, standing when she did.

"I'll take this opportunity to put on my scarf," she said, scooping up the handful of silk. She wanted to look her best if she ever scrounged up the nerve to invite him to the Christmas party.

"Beware of attack elevators." His flirty grin sent a bolt of desire through her midsection that hastened her steps.

Eric watched her leave the restaurant. The woman was such an enigma, an irresistible mix of beauty and strength and vulnerability. And the chemistry between them was undeniable.

He drained his glass of wine. Ethically, he shouldn't become involved with her physically, at least not until after the conclusion of the study. He frowned, feeling unsettled, then glanced at his watch. He probably had time to return to his room and make a quick call to Lancaster before Cindy came back. Perhaps talking about the study would reinforce his resolve to maintain a respectable distance from the fetching general manager.

After flagging the waiter on the way out to let him know they'd both be returning, Eric strode toward the elevator.

4

"WHY ARE YOU MAKING ME go with you?" Manny demanded, trotting down the hall behind Cindy toward Eric Quinn's room.

"For a ninety-five-dollar tie," she retorted, "the least you can do is stand lookout."

"Compared to the pajama pants, the tie was a bargain."

Cindy stopped and her friend nearly barreled into her. "How much were the pants?"

Manny winced. "Three hundred and fifty."

Her knees weakened. "Dollars?"

"What can I say? I told you the man has expensive taste. What does he do for a living, anyway?"

Cindy resumed walking. "He's a salesman," she answered evasively. *And apparently, sex sells.* She stopped in front of door 1010, then draped the Chanel scarf over her shoulder to free her hands. After looking both ways, she inserted a master key into the lock.

"I could get fired for this," Manny said, his voice stern.

"I'll put in a good word for you with your boss." The door clicked open. "Give me the pants and cover me."

He handed her a small bag with handles. "What if Quinn shows up?

Heat climbed to Cindy's ears. "He's in the dining room…waiting for me."

"Ho ho ho. Dinner?"

"Don't start."

"And what if he ambles up here while you're gone?"

Cindy sighed. "I don't know—sing or something. Work with me, Manny. There's no section in the handbook on breaking into a guest's room!" Her heart thumping like a snare drum, she pushed open the door and stepped inside, where she moved quickly to the bathroom and flipped on the light. With shaking hands she withdrew both the old and the new pants. She had to give Manny credit—they were identical, all right, except the new pair looked a little too...well, new. Quickly she removed the alarming price tag, then gently twisted the garment to add a few wrinkles. With considerable trepidation, she lifted the old pair and inhaled the scent of the velvety pale blue fabric, detecting the trace of a vaguely familiar cologne.

She glanced toward the toiletry bag, then unzipped the non-condom-carrying side before she had a chance to change her mind. Cindy rummaged for cologne, smiling unexpectedly when her fingers curved around an unpretentious bottle of English Leather. Eric Quinn wore three-hundred-and-fifty-dollar silk pajamas, and used seven-dollars-a-bottle cologne? Intriguing. She squirted her father's standby fragrance into the air, then held the new pants beneath the falling mist. Satisfied, she carefully hung the pajama bottoms behind Eric's toiletry bag and checked her watch. Six minutes—not bad.

She stuffed the old pants into the paper bag and started to leave the bathroom when she heard an odd racket in the hall. Was someone belting out "Santa Claus Is Coming to Town"? Then Cindy bit down hard on her tongue— Manny's warning!

Nearly tripping over her feet, she dived for the light switch. Manny stopped singing and began conversing loudly with someone outside the door. *Please, let it be housekeeping.* Panic paralyzed her limbs as she heard a key being inserted into the lock. Manny's words were indecipherable, but his tone had elevated considerably.

In the darkness of the bathroom, Cindy could see the whites of her eyes shining back in the mirror. There was nowhere to go but…she gulped and leapt into the tub in one motion, then jerked the curtain closed in another. Feeling faint, she shrank in the corner, visualizing her career going down the drain beneath her feet.

The door opened and Manny's shaky voice reached her. "Just a little holiday entertainment, sir."

The low rumble of Eric Quinn's laugh sounded, sending sheer mortification through her body. "I didn't realize I was on the concierge level, Mr. Oliver."

Manny cleared his throat. "Could I adjust your room thermostat, sir?"

"Uh, no thanks."

"Fill your ice bucket?"

"It's full, thanks."

"Check your towels?"

"I'm fine. Excuse me, I need to make a phone call, then get back to the dining room."

"Of course, sir."

Cindy allowed herself a tiny surge of hope—maybe he wouldn't be here long.

She heard him move through the bedroom and pick up the phone. He wouldn't be able to see the door if she left very quietly. But she hesitated—what if he hung up quickly and caught her leaving? Deciding to stay put, Cindy made herself as small as possible.

She could hear his murmured voice on the phone. Cindy wondered about the person he was calling. A girlfriend? A wife? A frown pulled at her mouth. Then she pushed aside the silly response—neither the presence nor the absence of a woman in Eric Quinn's bed made any difference in her life.

What life? I'm cowering in the bathroom of a guest whose pants I stole. She broke out in a fresh sweat at the sound of Eric putting down the handset. His footsteps came closer, then to her horror, he stepped into the bathroom. Her heart lodged in her constricted throat as fluorescent light bathed the room. She clamped her hand over her mouth, biting back a gasp. What was he going to do?

Remove something from his toiletry bag, from the telltale sound of a zipper. A condom? Indignation lifted her chin. Did the man think he was going to get lucky with her? Water splashed in the sink, and Eric Quinn proceeded to...brush his teeth with the fervor of a dentist.

She felt a sliver of disappointment, but apparently Eric was in a grand mood because when the water stopped, he began whistling under his breath. Cindy strained to make out the tune and pressed her lips together when she recognized "Santa Claus Is Coming to Town."

...gonna find out who's naughty or nice...

She frowned wryly, thankful she no longer believed in Santa Claus, because she'd never been so naughty.

He tapped his toothbrush on the counter, then returned it to his bag. Her heart stopped when he folded a towel over the shower curtain rod, rattling the plastic liner. Faintly silhouetted in the harsh light, his tall figure seemed even more imposing. Would he fling back the curtain and finding her squatting in his bathtub? Just when she thought she might pass out, the room went dark and he left the bathroom. Seconds later, he exited the room and Cindy's body went limp with relief.

She sat on the edge of the tub for a full two minutes, then climbed out and crept to the main door, her muscles taut. After checking the peephole and finding the coast clear, she sucked in a breath, opened the door and stepped into the corridor.

"Well, it's about time!" Manny whispered harshly behind her.

Cindy jumped. "You scared the schnitzel out of me!"

"I was going out of my mind—what the devil happened in there?"

Heading down the hall, she lifted the paper bag. "I switched the pants."

"Did he see you?" he asked, exasperated.

"No." She stopped in front of the elevator and stabbed the button, then sheepishly turned to face her friend. "I hid in the bathtub."

He shook his head slowly. "Unbelievable."

"No," she corrected, shaking her finger, "un*repeat-able*."

Manny grinned. "Wonder what a good blackmailer pulls down these days?"

"I have to get back to dinner with Mr. Quinn." Her chest heaved as if she'd been running a marathon. She held up the bag. "Would you mind disposing of these for me?"

"Okay. So how's it going?"

She frowned. "What do you mean?"

"Supping with the quintessential Mr. Quinn."

Cindy pressed the button again. "Dinner with Eric Quinn was simply a ploy to keep tabs on him until you returned."

"No footsie under the table?"

She scoffed. "Of course not." In the elevator, Cindy selected the basement button and Manny chose the lobby. With a tissue from her jacket pocket, she dabbed at the perspiration on her forehead.

"If I didn't know better," Manny said, his voice sing-songy, "I would think you're starting to like this guy."

"Except you know better," she reminded him as the doors opened to the lobby.

"See you tomorrow." He stepped into the corridor, then turned. "And don't forget to tell Mr. Quinn the Christmas party tomorrow night is black tie."

Cindy opened her mouth to protest, but the doors slid closed on Manny's knowing smirk.

Feeling completely exhausted, she exited at the basement and hurried back to the restaurant. Eric Quinn sat at the table with his hands wrapped around his wineglass, but he stood when she approached the table.

Manufacturing a smile, she lowered herself into her seat, hoping to get through the meal without another embarrassing disaster. "Sorry for the delay." Someone had lit a votive candle in the table centerpiece, and the light from the flickering flame threw the planes of his chiseled face into relief. Either Eric had grown handsomer during her absence, or her own glass of wine was kicking in.

His eyes crinkled with a smile. "No trouble, I hope?"

"Um, no."

The waiter arrived with their entrees under domed lids, but Cindy had lost her appetite. Instead she found herself studying Eric for some sign of sleaziness, some manifestation of peddling provocative products for a living that would give her a reason to avoid his company. But she saw only a darkly gorgeous, thoroughly masculine man politely waiting for her to begin eating.

Eric gazed across the table at the ruffled Cindy Warren, trying to figure out how he could spend time with the beauty without arousing her suspicion—or his libido. "Where were we?" he asked as he raked the grilled onions off the top of his steak—not that he expected to be kissing anyone tonight.

"Virginia," she said, tucking a strand of dark hair behind her ear.

Even with the hacked haircut, the woman was stunning. Classically beautiful with large eyes, high apple cheeks and skin as flawless as glass. "Ah, yes," he said, already wanting to change the subject. Thinking about his argumentative father gave him indigestion.

"Do you still live near Manassas?"

He sliced into the rib eye, shaking his head. "No, I'm on the road quite a bit. I maintain condos here and there."

"Will you be traveling back for the holidays?"

First Jerry and now Cindy. Eric wondered if his cover had been blown and if the employees were trying to cozy up to him. "Probably not," he answered as casually as possible. "I believe you were about to ask me a question before you left the table?"

Cindy reached for her wine. "Whatever it was has slipped my mind." She fidgeted, then asked, "Is this your first time staying at the Chandelier House?"

"Yes, although I'm in the Bay area several times a year on business." When she averted her eyes, Eric wondered again if she knew why he was here. If so, there wasn't anything he could do about it now except play along. "This is a very charming place."

"Thanks. The hotel was built in the twenties, suffered through two substantial earthquakes, plus countless tremors. She's been repaired, added on to, torn down and built up again. And still, she perseveres."

Noting the affection in her voice, he said, "You speak of her more like an acquaintance than a structure."

"The Chandelier House is something of a family friend," she said wistfully. "My maternal grandfather was one of the original owners."

Surprise infused him. He hadn't been informed of Cindy Warren's personal connection. "That's remarkable. So it's no accident that you're here—" he smiled "—and running the whole show."

"Yes and no," she said between picking at the salmon on her plate. "My grandfather sold his interest in the Chandelier House years before I was born." A smile lit her face. "My mother says I take after him, although I hardly remember him at all." She sipped her wine. "Anyway, I studied hotel management in college and worked in a couple of small, independent hotels before stumbling onto this opening a few years ago.''

He played dumb. ''So the Chandelier House is independently owned?

''When I came here, it was. But about two years ago a company in Detroit bought it and thankfully, allowed me to stay on as general manager.''

''A vote of confidence for you, I'd say.''

She shrugged. ''I'm not bragging, but the Chandelier House is a special place, with special employees. It takes a certain kind of person to appreciate the, um, atmosphere.''

On cue, a crew of Vulcans filed by, in full costume. Cindy smiled. ''It's never dull.'' He refilled her glass from the carafe, but she stopped him at the half-full mark. ''I'm still on call for another hour,'' she said, an adorable blush on her cheeks.

''So,'' he said, nodding toward the Trekkies, ''are they your typical clientele?''

''Oh, no. Our typical clientele is much weirder than that.''

''Really?''

She took another deep drink of wine and nodded. ''The snake handlers were the scariest, I think.''

Eric blinked. ''Snake handlers?''

''And surprisingly, the tattoo artists were the most courteous.''

''Hmm.''

''And last year the vampires ran up an incredible bar tab, so we're looking forward to having them return in the spring.''

He leaned forward. ''Vampires, did you say?''

''Oh, don't worry—the whole staff gets tetanus boosters ahead of time.''

Eric's jaw went slack. ''That's good.''

"And, um, your people will be arriving shortly."

So, she had somehow discovered who he was. Relieved, but unreasonably disappointed at the same time, he nodded slowly. "I hope you understand why I had to be discreet."

She averted her gaze. "Yes, I can see why."

"People tend to treat you differently once they know the truth."

A smile curved her mouth and her eyelids drooped sexily. "Well, I have to admit had I not had the opportunity to get to know you, Eric, I might have been one of those people."

"I'm glad to see my line of work won't interfere with our, um…friendship."

Another wine-induced smile. "I'm an open-minded woman."

Eric's body leapt in response. Alarms went off in his ears. Was she going to come on to him in hopes of favorable treatment? "I'd rather not talk about work at all," he said, "because I hate mixing business with pleasure."

"Fine with me," she said agreeably, then turned back to her plate with more gusto.

Eric watched her with no small amount of surprise. He had worried the moment of revelation would be confrontational, or tense at the very least, but obviously he'd been wrong. If anything, Cindy seemed more at ease—happy even—that his reason for being at the Chandelier House was out in the open. He relaxed back into his chair and lifted his glass to his mouth, studying the woman before him.

She wasn't wearing the yellow scarf, but realizing how embarrassed she'd been over the elevator incident, he decided not to say anything. Eric did, however, wonder if she had any idea this was the most enjoyable meal he'd had in months.

Cindy pushed aside her plate, her eyes shining and her

lips wet with wine. Suddenly she leaned forward and confided, "I have a confession to make."

Lifting his eyebrows, he said, "Okay, but I feel compelled to warn you I'm not a priest."

She laughed, making a bubbly little sound, then hiccuped and clapped her hand over her mouth. "Excuse me," she gasped.

Eric laughed, delighted at her lack of inhibition. He pushed his own plate aside and split the remaining measure of wine between their two glasses. "So what's this confession?"

She drank deeply, then toyed with the stem. "Actually," she said, her voice tentative, "I *was* planning to ask you something earlier."

"Good evening, Cindy." A suited man walked up to the table holding two full-bellied glasses and a small beribboned bottle.

Straightening, Cindy said, "Joel. This is Eric Quinn, one of our guests. Mr. Quinn, this is Joel Cutter, our food and beverage director."

At least she was planning on keeping his identity a secret for a while longer, Eric noted. Cutter set the glasses on the table and extended a hand.

"Sorry to interrupt," the man said smoothly, "but since you're finished with your meal, I thought you might like to try a cinnamon liqueur I ordered in for the holidays."

"Sure," Cindy agreed. "Eric?"

"Sounds interesting."

Cutter poured an inch of reddish liquid into the fat goblets. "Enjoy," he said, then moved away. Cindy studied the liqueur thoughtfully, holding on to the edge of the table as if trying to orient herself. Maybe she'd had too much wine.

"Shall we drink a toast?" Eric asked, lifting his glass.

"I'm not sure," she said carefully.

"Just a taste," he said, respecting her restraint.

"Okay." She smiled, wrapping her hand around her own glass. "To Christmas."

"To Christmas," he agreed, clinking his glass to hers over the candle, then added, "May we both get what we want."

Cindy's smile faltered and her glass fell, struck the candle, then bounced across the table. The white tablecloth absorbed a second's worth of liqueur before the flame caught, setting the table ablaze. Eric reached over the flame and pushed Cindy away, catching his sleeve on fire in the process. Screams sounded across the dining room. Someone yelled for a fire extinguisher, but Eric yanked the edge of the table cloth and folded it over his arm, smothering the fire instantly.

Hovering six feet away, Cindy stared at the smoking tablecloth.

"Are you all right?" Eric clasped her elbow and gently turned her toward him.

Mortified, she blinked his concerned face into focus. "I set you on fire."

"No, you didn't—it was an accident." He held up his arm, displaying a smoke-blackened but intact shirtsleeve. "See?" He unbuttoned the cuff and rolled back the fabric. "No damage."

She still stared, astounded at her own carelessness. First the man's pajamas, now his shirt…and very nearly his arm!

"Cindy!" Joel jogged toward them. "What happened?"

"Everything's okay," Eric said. "The liqueur spilled and the candle—"

"Joel," Cindy cut in, finally finding her voice. "I'm sorry for causing a disturbance. If you'll send someone to clean up this mess, I'll sign for Mr. Quinn's dinner and see him to the first aid station."

"That's not necessary," Eric assured her, but she gave

him her best don't-argue-with-me look. He relented with a nod and an eye-locking smile that made her knees grow even weaker.

Cindy signed the meal receipt with a shaky hand, still marveling over her own stupidity. "Look, Cindy," Joel whispered over her shoulder. "Don't worry about the mess—I'm just glad you weren't hurt." He smiled sheepishly. "And I know this isn't the best time, but I'm looking for a volunteer to be Santa for the party tomorrow night."

She glanced up with a laugh. "You want me to be Santa Claus?"

"Well," her friend squirmed, "I thought it would be good for morale if everyone saw you in the holiday spirit, you know, with the review coming up and all."

She sighed. "Okay, bring the suit to the party—I'll duck out and change when it's time to give out gifts."

"Swell, and don't worry—the suit is flame-retardant."

"You're a real gas."

As Joel walked away, Cindy glanced at Eric who stood a few feet away reassuring everyone he was all right. Even if she could get up the nerve to ask Eric to the Christmas party, the man would be nuts to go—she was liable to kill him!

He joined her and they walked out together, Cindy blushing with humiliation. "I strike again," she said finally.

"It wasn't your fault," he repeated gently.

Cindy punched the elevator call button. Her body was a quaking mass of fear, embarrassment, exhilaration and confusion. When the doors opened, she chanced a glance at Eric, noticing a smoky streak marking his left cheek. Pulling a tissue from her jacket pocket, she turned toward him and reached high, then stopped in midmotion as their gazes met.

Cindy swallowed. "There's a…here." She handed him

the tissue and gestured to the black mark, then stepped away from him.

Out of the corner of her eye, she saw him stretch his neck toward the stainless panel, then swipe at the mark. ''Think we'd better choose a floor?''

Completely bereft of dignity, Cindy lifted her hand, then stopped. Choose a floor? Was he dropping a hint that he'd like to spend the night with her? Her finger started to shake, and the ten button lit suddenly. His floor.

''And for you?'' he asked.

''F-fifteen,'' she squeaked, feeling ridiculous. He wasn't dropping a hint about spending the night with her. He was probably going to call his insurance agent—or his lawyer.

''Unless you'd like to come in for a nightcap,'' he said, checking his watch, then offering an unreadable smile. ''And you never did get around to asking me that question.''

Panic washed over her. The way things were going, she'd probably go back to Eric's room and the roof would collapse, or he'd be electrocuted, or heaven only knew what else. But the man must be desperate if he was willing to entertain a firebug. Unless he was looking for someone to tie to the bed while he demonstrated S&M toys from sample cases. ''No!''

''Okay. Thank you for a wonderful dinner.''

Cindy smiled wryly. ''Despite the crash and burn?''

He revealed white teeth in a broad smile. ''Despite the crash and burn.''

His eyes were so riveting. ''I had fun, too.''

The elevator dinged and the doors opened to his floor. ''Perhaps our paths will cross again tomorrow.''

Her throat ran dry. ''Perhaps.''

When the doors closed, Cindy leaned against the wall heavily and looked at the ceiling. *Please let this day end.*

First the bad haircut, then cutting her hand, the pajama-pant mess, the scarf thing—

She straightened. Where was her yellow scarf? She closed her eyes, her mind rewinding. She remembered taking it when she left the table and she recalled tossing it over her shoulder just before she'd...

Her eyes popped open. Eric's room! Somehow, she'd lost her scarf in his room, probably in the bathroom—or in the *bathtub*. If he found her scarf, he'd know she'd been in his room, and when. Choking back hysteria, Cindy darted out of the elevator as soon as the doors opened, and fled toward the stairs.

5

CINDY ZOOMED DOWN the five flights of stairs in record time, twisting her ankle twice. Thank goodness Eric's room was at the far end of the building—with luck she could catch him before he went in. She sprinted down the hall, turned the corner and saw him standing in front of his door, inserting his key.

"Eric!"

He turned, his gaze questioning.

She jogged toward him, then slowed, suddenly realizing how out of breath she'd become.

"Cindy, is everything okay?"

Her chest heaved while she searched for an explanation. "I...I...want to...buy you...another shirt!"

His face creased in amusement. "You ran all the way back here to tell me you want to buy me another shirt? I assure you it isn't necessary. I'm not overly attached to my clothing."

A fact she wished she'd been privy to three hundred and fifty dollars ago.

"I insist. If I can borrow...a piece of scratch paper...I'll write down the brand...and your size."

He shrugged good-naturedly. "Okay, if it will make you feel better. But how about just taking the shirt?"

She massaged the stitch in her side and nodded.

"Give me a minute to change."

Panic gripped her again—she had to get in his room. "Um, Eric!"

He turned back, the hint of a smile still hovering. "Yes?"

"About that question I was going to ask."

"Yes?"

Desperate, she looked both directions, then lowered her voice. "Well, it's kind of personal."

"In that case, please come in."

As expected, he unlocked the door and gestured for her to precede him into the room. Her heart pounded at the compromising situation in which she'd managed to land herself—again. She scanned the carpet in the entranceway for her scarf, but found nothing. The darn thing had to be in the bathroom.

"Would you like a drink?" he asked.

"Um, no, I have to go to the bathroom," she blurted. Then she added, "to freshen up."

He blinked. "Be my guest."

She fled to the bathroom and closed the door behind her. Cindy glanced at her reflection, then closed her eyes. Bizarre hair and even more bizarre behavior. What must he think of her? She hurriedly searched the room, then found her scarf—surprise, surprise—in the bathtub. After tying the scrap of yellow silk around her neck in a secure knot, she fluffed her hair, brushed her teeth with her finger, then washed her hands.

When she could stall no longer, Cindy opened the door. With a deep, calming breath, she walked down the short hall to the opening into Eric's bedroom. She wasn't sure what to expect—candles, Eric reclining on the bed in a smoking jacket?—but she felt vague disappointment to find every light blazing, from the corner lamps to the night-light in the electrical outlet, and Eric standing across the room looking out the window.

Gazing at the illuminated city of San Francisco, even more spectacular than usual due to added holiday lights,

Eric mulled the unfolding situation. Of all the women in the world, why did he have to be attracted to one who not only ran a hotel, but a hotel he had been sent to terminate? And even though she said she was open-minded about the conflicts that could arise, Eric wasn't as comfortable. In fact, he was beginning to wonder if he was drawn to the woman simply because he knew deep down that she wasn't accessible. Or if she was drawn to him out of some conscious or unconscious desire to influence his decision in the coming weeks? He'd been approached before by comely employees who were under the microscope of a corporate review.

He heard a movement and turned his head to see her standing in the entrance to his room, looking nothing like a woman hell-bent on seducing or being seduced. As a matter of fact, she looked a little scared.

"Nice view," he said, nodding toward the vista.

"Mmm-hmm. If you have a chance before you leave, go up to the roof at night. Just phone the concierge desk and they'll buzz you through the security door."

"I'll do that. You put your scarf on," he noted with approval.

"Um, yes, I did." She fussed with the ends. "Well, Eric, if you'll give me your shirt, I'll be on my way."

Maybe she'd lost her nerve, or maybe she was waiting for him to make the first move. His body screamed yes, peel off her uniform and find out if she loved with as much energy as she lived. But a sexual encounter had never taken priority over doing a job to the best of his ability, so he simply unbuttoned his shirt quickly, smiling when she turned to scrutinize an unremarkable painting on the wall. Shrugging out of the ruined shirt, Eric walked toward her, glad for his father's advice to always wear a T-shirt underneath a dress shirt. "Here you go."

Visibly relieved to see his torso covered, she reached for the garment. "I'll get a replacement as soon as possible."

He inclined his head, realizing the futility of arguing. Their fingers brushed and desire surged through his chest. "Cindy."

She felt it too, the chemistry. He could tell by the confusion in her green-gray eyes. "Yes?"

He imagined himself pulling her against his chest, capturing her mouth with his, and then to his astonishment, he realized he wasn't imagining it. He tasted her breath, her lips, her tongue. Her hands curled, then splayed against his sides, her breath escaping in little sighs. Eric drank the wine that lingered in the depths of her mouth while resisting the urge to fill his hands with her body. Instead, he smoothed back her hair and tilted her face to allow him greater access. His body swelled with longing to crush her closer, but the fierce response was uncommon enough to deliver a dose of reality. Eric lifted his head and released her, attempting to check his raspy breathing.

She took a half step back, biting her swollen lips.

"I didn't mean for that to happen," he said lamely, bending to retrieve the shirt lying at their feet. "But since I've been fighting my attraction to you all day, I can't truthfully say I'm sorry."

"Fighting?" she asked softly. "Are you married?"

He shook his head, laughing. "Oh, no, I'm not married, or engaged." Then he sobered and ran his hand through his hair. "But I still have reservations about us becoming, er, involved, because of my job."

Cindy retrieved the shirt from his hand and studied the blackened sleeve for a few seconds, then she lifted her gaze. "I can get past it if you can."

Eric caught his breath at the sensation her words evoked. He'd never lacked for female company, but he couldn't remember being more satisfied to realize a woman found him attractive. So, while his mind warned that he was about to embark on a path of potential destruction, his mouth said, "Perhaps we could have dinner tomorrow night."

She laughed—not quite the answer he'd hoped for.

"Eric, the question I've been trying to ask you all evening is whether you'd like to escort me to our employee Christmas party tomorrow night."

Ridiculously pleased, he remained wary. "Have you told your employees why I'm here? I'd hate to get nasty rumors started about the boss."

She angled her head at him. "Right now I don't see a need to share this kind of information with my subordinates."

"And if it comes up?"

Cindy shrugged. "Tell the truth and let everyone deal with it."

The party, he reasoned, would be a great chance to see her interact with her staff informally—not to mention an opportunity to see how money was spent on after-hours activities. "Sounds great. Black tie?"

She nodded. "Donte's tuxedo shop is just a couple of blocks over, but I insist on paying for it. It's the least I can do." She moved toward the door and he followed.

"Well, thank you anyway, but I travel with my own tux."

She stopped, her hand on the doorknob. "Oh."

"What time is the party?"

"Eight o'clock until midnight in the lounge."

He smiled, despite the warnings going off in his head. "I'll knock on your door at fifteen of."

"A BODY WAVE?" Cindy asked, staring in the mirror. "Are you sure?"

"Sure as shootin'," Camelia, the new hairdresser, said, her animated nod sending her high ponytail whirling around like a ceiling fan. "There are only two ways to add volume to thin, straight hair like yours. One is to layer it, and it looks like you've already been down that road. Number two is a perm. You're a prime candidate for Miss Fern's Permanent Wave with Aloe, fifteen to eighteen minutes, I'd guess."

Cindy brightened. "It'll take less than twenty minutes?"

"Heck, it'll take me an hour to roll this mess, but after that, it'll be a breeze."

Cindy glanced over at Jerry who was shaving a gentleman in the other chair, but the barber kept his head down. "But what will it look like?" she asked the hairdresser.

"Nice and full," Camelia assured her. "Big, loose curls—it'll be darling, just you wait and see."

"I've always wanted curly hair," Cindy admitted, then smiled. "And I have a party to go to tonight, so I want my hair to look nice."

"They won't be looking at anyone else," the lady assured her. "Let's get started."

Cindy suffered through agonizing tugging on her hair as the zealous Camelia rolled the small sections tight enough to draw up the corners of her mouth.

She studied her hollowed eyes in the mirror, trying to recall when she had looked worse. The sleepless night she'd had after yesterday's numerous fiascos was reflected plainly on her face. Not to mention the thoughts of Eric Quinn that had haunted her all night.

She'd risen with that sick feeling in her stomach she first experienced during puberty when the cutest boy in school winked at her in algebra class. The stress of wondering what to do next paralyzed her. Oh, during high school she'd managed to shuffle a few steps further, and in college she'd stumbled over the edge, but the nagging refrain—"Is this *it*?"—always came back to haunt her.

Much as she lusted after Eric Quinn, she had the vague

sensation she was setting herself up for a huge letdown. Even though she hated to admit it, his line of work *did* bother her, the eroticism notwithstanding. Her mother's head, of course, would explode before her very eyes if she found out. And Christmas was the worst time of the year for launching a new relationship.

"Almost ready for the solution," Camelia sang. Cindy endured the eye-stinging pain of the last too-tight curler, and smiled as Camelia squirted the pungent-smelling liquid across the helmet of rollers. "We'll let it soak in and I'll check the curl in a few minutes."

The peal of Cindy's beeper sounded and she punched a button on her radio. "This is Cindy."

"Hey, it's Amy—can you come up to the lobby?"

Cindy glanced in the mirror. "I'm a little indisposed at the moment. Is this an emergency?"

The rooms director's voice floated to her in a scratchy whisper. "That annoying Mr. Stark is here swearing there's a rat in his room. He insists on seeing the general manager."

Cindy rolled her eyes heavenward. "Take him to the break room and get him a cup of coffee—decaffeinated. I'll be right there." She turned and smiled apologetically at the hairdresser. "Can you wrap a towel around my head or something? I'm needed in the lobby."

Camelia frowned, unfolding a bright green towel. "You can't be gone too long, now, you hear?"

"Ten minutes, tops," Cindy promised.

She trotted to the lobby, one hand on the towel and her eyes on her feet, hoping to get through unnoticed. A split second later, she collided with a large body and landed on her rump, sliding three feet on the marble floor before coming to a halt. She instantly recognized the feet and bit back a curse. At least the towel remained intact, but she couldn't imagine how silly she looked to Eric—this time.

"Good morning," he said, the laughter clear in his voice.

"Morning," she mumbled, refusing to look up.

"Are you all right?"

She nodded, causing the curlers to rattle beneath the towel.

"I'm sorry, Cindy, I didn't see you coming, although now I can't imagine why."

"Everyone's a comedian."

He squatted down and angled his head until their eyes were on a level plane. "Would you like a hand?"

The man was just plain gorgeous. "A round of applause is exactly what I had in mind," she said miserably.

Eric laughed and her sick stomach flipped over. "Here." He reached for her hand and she reluctantly accepted his warm grasp, allowing herself to be pulled to her feet. Devastating in gray slacks and a plum dress shirt, he surveyed her turban. "Is this a West Coast thing?"

"I was interrupted in the salon," she explained, thinking the green towel was the perfect complement to her undoubtedly scarlet face.

"Then I guess I'd better let you go," he said merrily. "We're still on for tonight?"

"You mean you still want to?" she asked wryly.

"See you then, swami."

Well, at least the man had seen her at her worst—she hoped. Cindy rushed to the break room to find Amy fussing over a scowling Mr. Stark. She stepped forward, wondering how many times her name already appeared on his reports. "Mr. Stark, I'm Cindy Warren, the general manager."

"We've met twice before, Ms. Warren," he said with agitation. "I'm not senile."

She swallowed a retort while Amy escaped without a backward glance. "My apologies, Mr. Stark. Of course you aren't. Amy told me you saw a, um, rodent in your room?"

"It was a rat." He straightened his conservative burgundy tie. "What's wrong with your head?"

Her cheeks warmed. "I was in the salon, sir."

The man's bushy gray eyebrows rose. "You were having your hair done while on duty?"

Cindy squirmed. "I'm almost always on duty, sir. I rarely leave the hotel, so I work in personal services when I can."

"You look like the rest of those fruitcakes walking around here in costume. What kind of freak show are you running?"

She bit the inside of her cheek to calm herself. He was testing her again. "I'm sorry if any of our guests make you uncomfortable, sir, but I assure you, their role-playing is a harmless hobby." She inhaled deeply. "Now, about the um, animal you saw in your room. I'll send someone from maintenance immediately, and I apologize profusely for the incident."

His chin jutted out. "I think I'm entitled to some kind of compensation for my ordeal."

Cindy maintained her friendly smile. "I agree, Mr. Stark. I'll instruct the front desk to deduct one night's stay from your bill. I hope this incident doesn't ruin your visit with us."

He harrumphed and, jamming a hat on his head, strode toward the door. "The prune Danish this morning already did that."

Cindy winced as she realized she'd forgotten to change his breakfast order. Then, remembering her hair, she sprinted back to the salon, where Camelia stood tapping her foot. "You're ten minutes late."

Cindy dropped into the chair. "Is my hair ruined?"

"Let me check—the curl isn't permanent until I put on the neutralizer."

The woman unrolled a curler and to Cindy's delight, the

lock of hair sprang back to her head in a spirally curl. She threw Jerry a triumphant smirk in the mirror. He simply shook his head.

Camelia frowned. "The curl's a little tight."

But to Cindy, who'd never had curly hair, there was no such thing. "I love it!"

"Okay," the woman said, breaking open the bottle of neutralizing solution. "Curly it is."

WHEN SHE OPENED THE DOOR, Manny only stared. "Oh… my…God."

Her worst fears were confirmed. "It's horrible, isn't it?"

He reached to touch it, then pulled back. "It's like that awful wig Jan Brady wore when she wanted to be different."

"Except it's orange!"

He looked sympathetic. "It does appear that the permanent leached the color a bit."

She burst into tears. "What am I going to do?"

Manny put his arm around her and walked her toward the dressing table. "There, there, it's not that bad. What happened?"

"I got a perm," she wailed. "Then I had to handle a problem and the solution stayed on too long."

"What did Jerry say?"

"He isn't speaking to me." She dropped onto the padded stool and tearfully glanced in the mirror at her friend standing behind her.

He reached into her brassy, stiff hair tentatively. "Good grief, Jimmy Hoffa could be in here." His nose wrinkled. "And pew."

"I didn't know it was going to smell so bad, either," she moaned.

"Better stay away from open flames tonight, or you'll spontaneously combust."

She sniffed. "I take it you heard about the little incident in the restaurant last night."

"I caught it on Joel-SPAN this morning."

"I toasted Eric Quinn's shirt."

He tisk-tisked. "Cindy, I know you want to see this guy naked, but don't you think destroying his wardrobe one garment at a time is a little too obvious?"

She scoffed. "Who says I want to see him naked?"

"Okay, maybe I'm projecting, but you do seem to lose control when he's around."

She stuck out her lower lip. "You're supposed to make me feel better."

He gestured wildly to her eight-inch-high hair. "You're not giving me much to work with here."

Cindy brightened a smidgen. "Well, at least I have a date for the Christmas party." Then her shoulders drooped. "Of course that was before the perm."

"Ah, but *after* the fire," Manny pointed out. "So at least we know he doesn't scare easily. Just in case, better wear the Donna Karan."

"You think? The slit's a little high."

"With this hair, you'd better rip it another six inches."

"Is there any hope?"

He clucked and tried to get his hands around the mass. "You can gel it for a wet look this evening, but for now we'll have to strap it down. Where's your scarf?"

Cindy opened the top drawer and handed him the Chanel scarf. "Remind me to tell you *that* story later. Look at this mess—as if I didn't have enough to worry about today."

"Problems?"

"Did you hear that Mr. Stark-Stanton reported a rat in his room?"

"Any truth to it?"

"Maintenance found some half-eaten food under the heat register, but no rat."

"He could have planted the vittles."

"Exactly. I'm getting tired of these little tests." She sighed. "And engineering said the nursery bumped us down on the list for Christmas trees. At this rate, we might get one by New Year's."

Manny jammed his hands on his hips. "Can I use your phone, dear?"

She pointed into the bedroom. "The handset isn't working in here, but try the one on my nightstand."

"Back in a jiff."

While he was gone, Cindy wrapped her scarf around her head in different configurations. After a few minutes, she admitted defeat and considered wearing the scarf as a veil so that no one would recognize her.

Manny returned with a satisfied look on his face. "The tree will be here in an hour."

Cindy gaped. "How did you do that?"

Shrugging, he said, "Connections. I simply called the nursery, dropped a few names and told them if they didn't deliver a fabulous tree today, I'd sic the gay Mafia on them." He snapped his long fingers. "They'd never get flowers wholesale in this town again."

She grinned. "Manny, where would I be without you?"

He emitted a long-suffering grunt. "In *Glamour* magazine with a black strip across your eyes and a big 'Don't' by your picture." Smoothing her hair back from her face, he fastened the mop into a fat ponytail, then reached for the scarf. "So tell me about this Quinn fellow who has you whipped into such a lather."

Injecting as much innocence into her voice as possible, she said, "He's a salesman."

"So you said. What kind?"

"Hmm?"

He sighed, exasperated. "What kind of salesman?"

Cindy decided to confess, since Manny would find out

anyway. She cleared her throat. "Adult entertainment articles."

His hands stopped. "Sex toys?"

She squirmed. "You make it sound so tawdry."

"If the stiletto boot fits, wear it."

"Well, somebody's got to sell the stuff."

He held up both hands. "Hey, I'm grateful, but that doesn't mean I trust him with my best friend."

She smiled and elbowed his thigh. "You're just a big old softy."

"Keep it to yourself, would you? I have an image to uphold." He leaned down. "So do you think you could get me some free samples?"

"I have a box of stuff under the bed that Sam gave me to preview for the trade show—you're welcome to sift through it."

"I'm there."

ERIC STEPPED THROUGH the door of Sammy's and claimed a seat at the bar. A tent sign by an ashtray announced the bar would be closed to guests after eight to accommodate a private Christmas party. The piano bench was stacked high with decorations. He extracted a cigarette from his pocket, suddenly realizing he'd begun smoking about the time he'd become too busy to play the piano.

He ordered a Canadian beer from a glowering Tony and lit his cigarette, frowning after the first drag. He really needed to quit—the damn things didn't even taste good anymore.

"Those things'll kill you." A middle-aged suited man with thick glasses slid onto a stool next to him and plopped a limp fedora on the bar. "Got an extra?"

Eric slid the pack of cigarettes toward him. "Help yourself."

The man ordered a Scotch from Tony, then lit a cigarette. "Thanks. Reginald Stark."

"Eric Quinn."

"Glad to know you." He glanced around, taking note of the group of Trekkies glued to the TV set in the corner. Frowning, he leaned close. "I think you and I are the only people in this hotel who aren't in costume."

Eric laughed. "I'm here strictly for business. You?"

Stark shrugged. "I'm an antique dealer, here on a shopping trip. I always stay in older hotels and keep my eyes open." He took a drag on his cigarette and exhaled sloppily in Eric's direction. "Sometimes I get lucky and stumble across things the hotel is ready to throw out or sell for next to nothing."

"And have you found any good stuff here?"

"Nah," the man said. "Oh, the furniture is great, but not what I'm looking for at the moment." He laughed, a dry hacking sound. "This place is kind of pricey, but I've discovered that if you complain enough, you can usually get some freebies."

Eric experienced a pang of sympathy for the staff who had to deal with people like Mr. Stark, day in and day out.

The irksome man expelled a cloud of smoke, glanced side to side, then murmured, "You got any money, Quinn?"

Eric reached for his wallet. "I can spot you a ten if you need to cover your tab."

"No, man. I mean do you have any *real* money? I have an investment opportunity."

Eric shook his head. "I'm not interested in the latest multilevel marketing scheme."

Tobacco fumes hung thick around the graying man's head. "It's not like that. I happen to know where there's a fortune in plain sight, waiting for someone to jump on it."

What a con man. Eric put out his own cigarette.

"You don't believe me? Okay, I'll tell you because you look like a man of honor." Stark glanced around surreptitiously again. "It's the chandelier."

Eric frowned. "The chandelier?"

"Yeah, that huge one in the lobby."

"I remember," he said. "What about it?"

"Worth a fortune, that's what." The man reached into his pocket and withdrew a ragged page torn from a book. "See for yourself."

His curiosity piqued, Eric studied the page which featured an aged black-and-white photo of a chandelier, with a small amount of text beneath. "French lead crystal. This says that three chandeliers were produced, but only two are accounted for."

Stark nodded, then pointed toward the lobby. "I think the third one is hanging right in plain sight."

Dubious, Eric said, "The chandelier in this photo looks different."

"From what I can tell, there's a piece missing in the center, but the rest of it's the same."

"But this page says it's worth over seven hundred thousand dollars."

"That's from an old book," the man said, puffing on the cigarette. "Probably worth a cool million now."

Eric's heart rate picked up. "And you're telling me that no one knows about this?"

"I don't think so."

Eric squinted, trying to remember the hotel's balance sheet. To his recollection, the fixtures category hadn't seemed inordinately large, but it was something to look into.

"The way I see it, if you've got, say, five hundred Gs, we can make the hotel an offer."

He blinked. "If *I* have five hundred Gs?"

"Sure. I have a party interested in buying it, but I need

up-front purchase money. I'll split whatever we clear with you.''

The man was a total scam. Eric shook his head and handed back the dog-eared page. "Sorry, buddy. I'm not biting.''

Stark stuffed the paper into his pocket, then drained his drink. "Your loss, pal.'' Slapping a bill on the bar, the man stood and snuffed out the cigarette. "Thanks for the smoke, anyway. See you around.''

Eric watched as the man left, wondering if he'd actually find someone dumb enough to give him five hundred thousand dollars. Still marveling over the man's gall, he signaled Tony and was settling his own tab when the guy who'd given them the Christmas liqueur at the restaurant sauntered over, extending a hand. "Joel Cutter. We met last night. Quinn, isn't it?''

Eric nodded and shook his hand. "No crises today?''

Cutter grinned. "The day's not over yet. I hear you're coming to the party with Cindy.''

Eric cut his gaze to Tony the bartender, who was frowning at the news. "Strictly as friends,'' he assured them both, pushing aside the memory of their kiss. Thankfully, a ringing phone distracted Tony.

"Cindy's a great gal,'' Joel said warmly. "She certainly loves this place—to the point of neglecting her personal life, if you know what I mean.''

Eric nodded pleasantly, wondering if Joel was singing his boss's praises because he knew Eric's true identity. He hated second-guessing those around him, but speculating about ulterior motives was part of his job.

"Joel!'' Tony hung up the phone and reached behind him to untie his waist apron. "Problem in the lobby— Cindy needs all available staff, pronto.''

"Is Stanton here?''

Joel's question caused Eric to jerk his head involuntarily.

So Cindy hadn't yet told them who he was. And it sounded as though the staff expected his arrival to be traumatic.

"It's not Stanton," Tony said, bringing his stout, muscular body from behind the bar. "The Christmas tree just arrived, and the delivery men have it wedged in the front entrance."

Joel glanced at Eric. "What did I tell you about the day not being over?"

Eric pushed away from the bar. "Think you'll need an extra hand?"

"Come on." Joel trotted toward the door. "If not, we can always use an eyewitness."

6

CINDY MASSAGED THE ACHE at the base of her neck, not quite sure if the pain stemmed from the hairdresser's brutal rolling job, her skinned-back ponytail, or the stress of seeing a twenty-five-foot Christmas tree wedged in the double-door entrance of the hotel.

Beneath the massive shimmering chandelier, chaos reigned in the lobby. Guests snapped pictures, some posing in front of the spectacle. Employees stood around with their hands in their pockets, gazing first at the giant blue spruce, then at her, expectantly.

The top half of the tree lay inside the lobby, the bottom half sprawled across the sidewalk plus one lane of the busy street in front of the hotel. Manny stood outside, his long arms waving wildly as he gave the delivery crew a tongue-lashing. Cindy had sent a woman from security out to direct traffic around the tree trunk—and to make sure Manny didn't kill anyone.

"Ms. Warren, how am I supposed to leave this place?"

Cindy closed her eyes and groaned inwardly, then turned to face an impatient Mr. Stark. "I apologize for the inconvenience, sir. There is a side exit past the elevators."

"I decided I'd better go out and buy a rat trap," he said contrarily.

Thankfully, Cindy spotted Amy hovering in the background, a white filtering mask over her allergic nose and mouth. She signaled her rooms director who came forward with something less than a spring in her step. "Amy, please arrange for a complimentary cab to meet Mr. Stark at the side entrance and take him wherever he needs to go.''

The man's bushy-browed frown lessened, but only slightly. Amy led him away, explaining that he might be part of a growing medical phenomenon known as Christmasitis—people who are grumpy around the holidays who, in fact, are experiencing physiological sensitivity to Christmas trees, angel-hair...

''What happened?''

Joel skidded to a halt beside Cindy, followed by Tony, Samantha in a yellow, caped uniform, and to her consternation, Eric. Oh, well, she wouldn't want him to wait more than a few hours before seeing her in yet another jam. Cindy sighed. ''The plastic netting around the tree split open when they had it halfway through the door, and now with the branches fully extended, they can't budge the thing.''

Joel stared at her. ''I meant what happened to your hair.''

Resisting the urge to pinch him, she snarled, ''I had it done.''

Sam squinted. ''It looks kind of...orangey.''

''It's the glare of the fluorescent lights,'' Cindy said through clenched teeth.

''Your head has a real nice shape,'' Tony offered.

She smiled tightly. ''Thanks, Tony.''

''Do you have a plan?'' Eric asked, his expression amused.

''I was considering shaving my head and borrowing one of Sam's costumes.''

''I was talking about the tree,'' he said, the corners of his mouth twitching.

''Oh. No.'' She glanced around the group. ''But the floor is officially open for suggestions.''

Her staff assumed identical blank expressions. Eric walked closer to the tree, stroking his jaw with his thumb.

Hugging her clipboard, she followed him, self-consciously smoothing a hand over her wiry hair. "What do you think?"

After a few seconds, he gave her a half smile. "I'd call the maintenance department and see if they can remove the panels around the door to widen the opening."

"Great idea," she agreed. "I already called, and they can't."

His smile flattened. "Oh. Well, you could cut the tree in two and use just the top."

"But then we'd be left with a mighty short Christmas tree for this mighty big lobby."

He shrugged. "It's just a tree. It'll be up for what—three weeks. Then it will wind up being mulch in somebody's yard."

Cindy blinked at his unexpected Scrooginess, evidence of a definite chasm within his family. The sad realization made her own comments about dealing with her mother seem petty, triggering a stab of remorse. She made a mental note to call home later.

Her expression must have betrayed some of her thoughts, because Eric straightened and laughed softly. "Of course, that's only my opinion."

She wagged her finger as if he were a child. "You need a big dose of Christmas spirit." Turning, she addressed Joel. "Round up every pair of gloves you can find. Sam, drag Manny in here, would you?"

"What are we going to do?" Tony asked.

Looking back to the tree, Cindy lifted her chin. "Let's try to hold down the branches one by one and push it inside. Even if we break a few, we'll still be better off than if we cut the tree in two."

She slid a smile toward Eric and paused, mesmerized by his incredible ice-blue gaze. This man turned all her peaceful, orbiting atoms into crazed, overcharged ions. Cindy swallowed. Tomorrow she would write an apology note to her high school science teacher for saying she'd never use that stuff.

Joel returned with a bundle of work gloves and passed them around. The self-appointed team leader, Manny waved his arms for silence, then pulled on his gloves as precisely as a surgeon. "Okay, everybody, we can get through this if we work together. Remember to use your legs, not your back. I know you'll feel like you want to push, but wait until I say."

Many employees and several guests pitched in, stepping into the branches and grabbing hold. Eric positioned himself amongst the tangle of towering limbs opposite Cindy, by chance or design, she wasn't sure. From her vantage point, she could see the lower part of his face, see him smile and his lips move as he spoke to a young man next to him. And in that instant, surrounded by cool air swirling in through the open doors, Cindy decided that Eric Quinn would be an easy man to fall for.

She quelled a little thrill of anticipation by wrapping her fingers around a sturdy branch the width of a soda can…not that she was looking for a phallic substitute. She sighed— might as well drop a note to her psychology teacher too.

Amy handed Manny an extra filter mask. He pulled it over his mouth, then squatted by the door, wrapping his hands around a branch. "Okay, take a deep breath and push on three. One…two…three!" With the nursery workers pushing from the outside and everyone else pushing from the inside, the tree inched through the doorway.

"Easy now," Manny yelled. "Easy, don't let her turn."

Cindy kept her gaze averted from Eric as she threw her weight behind her section of trunk, but she was so aware of him she could scarcely concentrate. In less than six hours, she would be spending the evening on the arm of the sexiest man she'd met in ages. And he had a great sense of humor, good taste in clothes, a decent job.

Okay, maybe *decent* wasn't the right word. Stable. After all, what could be more stable than a career in sex?

"One last push!" Manny yelled. "Here she comes!"

With a collective grunt, they shoved one more time and the tree whooshed through the door and into the lobby, sliding easily across the marble floor. Cheers and applause broke out, and relief washed over Cindy—the tree would be set up by the time cranky Mr. Stark-Stanton returned.

Laughing, Eric pulled off his gloves. "Why do I feel like passing out cigars?"

Cindy decided he really should laugh more often. Her heart danced a crazy little jig. Despite the uproar around them, she felt strangely secluded with this man who had affected her so in such an alarmingly short period of time. She seized on a neutral subject. "Speaking of which, how goes the decision to quit smoking?"

"I'm okay as long as I keep my hands busy," he said with the barest smile.

Cindy swallowed. So much for neutral. Over his shoulder she noted the arrival of the two tree decorators. Feeling flirtatious, she lowered her voice. "What if I told you I had something to keep your hands and your mouth busy at the same time?"

He looked around them. "I'd say we're in public."

"Okay." She shrugged. "The tree decorators are here, so I'd better get back to work."

"Hey." He laughed, grasping her arm as she halfheartedly started to leave. "All right, I'm curious."

Cindy angled her head at him. "You also have a very dirty mind." She reached into her pocket, pulled out a pack of Sweet Tarts, then handed it to him with a grin. "Ta-da! The quitting smoker's secret weapon. Use it wisely, grasshopper." Cindy sobered slightly, then said, "If our paths don't cross again, I'll see you tonight. Thanks for helping with the Christmas tree.''

He nodded slowly. ''Thanks for the dose of Christmas spirit.''

Fingering the package of candy, Eric watched her cross the lobby and greet two men, obviously gay. They embraced Cindy, then touched her hair with concern. He smiled—she'd been harboring a permanent under that towel this morning. Actually, he found the reddish highlights in her hair attractive. In fact, he couldn't imagine anything she might do to herself that would diminish her beauty.

Eric maintained a calm exterior while his insides thrashed with sensory overload. He couldn't rationalize the urge he felt to keep her within eyeshot—hell, he could barely *acknowledge* the urge, much less explain it. Away from Cindy, the arguments against spending time with her stacked up neatly, but in her proximity, those arguments tumbled with alarming ease.

Workers were building scaffolding and tying ropes up and down the massive trunk in preparation for hoisting the evergreen next to the magnificent staircase. Eric's gaze traveled to the dazzling chandelier hanging high above everyone, thinking for the first time how much his father would appreciate the craftsmanship of the glass. Perhaps he would send him a postcard of the chandelier with a quick note to let him know his son was thinking about him. Mysteriously buoyant, Eric made his way back through the lobby.

THE REST OF CINDY'S AFTERNOON passed in a merciful blur. She spot-checked the installation of the towering spruce, then left the somewhat flaky decorators to their own devices after they promised her ''a masterpiece'' by morning.

She also arranged for Mr. Stark to enjoy a night out at the theater, gratis. At least the play would keep the man occupied while the employees drifted in and out of the Christmas party. She swung by Sammy's to make sure preparations were under way. Joel waved to her from the other side of the room and gave her a thumbs-up. Jerry stood on a ladder where the piano used to sit, hanging an armful of lights.

Cindy walked over, struck by affection for the elderly man who always pitched in, in any area of the hotel. "Are you still mad at me?" she asked, looking up at him.

Without glancing down, he grunted. "It's your head of hair to ruin, I reckon."

She sighed. "Okay, okay, I should have left well enough alone. It'll grow out."

"No, it'll *fall* out."

"Maybe," she conceded. "But I have it on good authority that my head has a nice shape."

At last he laughed and sat down on top of the stepladder, shaking his head. "You look like you got your head caught in a rusty commode and you're still able to charm the birds out of the trees."

She shot him a wry smile. "So glad we've made up. Where's the piano?"

"They moved it around the corner to the Asteroid Room to get it out of the way. Hey, I found a sprig of artificial mistletoe—do you think I should put it up?"

She shook her head. "Just last week I received a memo prohibiting mistletoe at company Christmas parties."

"Never listened to 'em before."

"I think I'd better this time," she said. "Nix the mistletoe."

He climbed down the ladder slowly. "Afraid you'll be caught under it, are you?"

"No!"

He grinned. "Afraid you won't be?"

"I won't dignify that question with a response."

"Bringing that Quinn lad, aren't you?"

"Jerry, he's hardly a lad." Then she narrowed her eyes. "Besides, how did you know?"

"Camelia told me when I walked into the salon this morning."

"But I didn't even *meet* her until she gave me this dreadful perm!"

He shrugged. "She said Stan, the shoeshine man, told her."

Cindy shook her head. "Unbelievable." She threw up her hands, defeated. "Well, at least she's working out."

The old man grimaced.

"She's not working out?"

"You keep scarin' them off with your hair disasters."

Cindy looked up at the ceiling. "Now what are we going to do for a hairdresser?" She cut her gaze to Jerry, then smiled sweetly. "You know, Jerry, if you'd agree to wait on female customers, your tips would probably skyrocket."

He held up one brown, weathered hand. "Oh, no. Men, give 'em a few snips here and there, clip the eyebrows, mustache and the occasional bushy ear, and they're happy. Women? No, thanks."

"I guess I need to call personnel to arrange for another temp."

Jerry glanced at his watch. "You'd better pick up the pace if you're going to get all duded up for the party."

She pretended to be hurt. "How long do you think I need?"

He gave her a rare one-armed hug. "Build in some time to relax, okay? Try to forget about this old hotel and have a good time tonight with your young man." Then he held up the mistletoe and grinned, revealing large, perfect teeth. "And I'll try to find someplace appropriate for this."

Cindy punched him playfully. "You're determined to get me into trouble. I'll see you tonight."

But Jerry's words stirred up the anticipation she'd suppressed all afternoon. She tied up a few administrative loose ends, distracted to the point of craning for a glimpse of Eric as she moved through the hotel.

At six o'clock, she returned to her suite and grabbed an apple. Then, sinking onto her bed, she wistfully dialed her parents' number. Janine Warren answered on the first ring.

"Hi, Mom. How's everything— Nothing's wrong, Mom. In fact, I'm going to a party tonight and I had a few minutes— Hmm? Yes, I have a date. He's a very nice man who happens to be a guest— What? Of course he's not married. Yes, he told me—huh? Eric Quinn. No, with a *Q*, not a *K*. Guess what?… No… No… No. He's from Virginia, can you believe— Manassas…Manassas…Ma-nassas. Right. Virginia. Right. So how's everything? He's a salesman. What kind? A successful salesman, Mom. So how's everything? Right, Christmas Eve. No, Mom, Manny is just a friend, he doesn't care that I— As a matter of fact, they *have* met. Oh, look at the time! I have to get ready for the party. I will. Okay, I will. Say hello to Daddy for me. Love you, too. Bye-bye…okay, bye-bye…okay, bye-bye."

Cindy replaced the handset with a sigh, then bit a chunk out of the apple. "I'll know I'm grown up when my mother lets me finish an entire sentence," she mumbled. But she had to admit it was comforting to know her mother still fretted over her. She would probably be the same kind of mother. Cindy stopped in midchew—mother? It was definitely time to stop thinking and get ready for the party.

Her stomach was so full of butterflies, it fairly flapped. She undressed slowly, then turned on the shower and let the water run over her fingers until it warmed.

With trepidation, she unfastened her hair, not surprised when the coarse, reddish mass instantly vaulted toward the ceiling. Manny had instructed her to wash her hair twice to diffuse some of the curl and most of the odor. Resigned, she stepped under the water and lathered the rat's nest carefully, unused to the shortened length and springy texture. After dousing her hair with thick conditioner, she soaped her body, then went for the big shave—both the bottoms *and* tops of her legs.

She rinsed, then wrapped her hair in a towel. The flashlight from her nightstand was required to locate her special-occasion matching body lotion and perfume in the depths of her vanity cabinet. After slathering her slight curves with moisturizer and stepping into a robe, she finally dredged up the nerve to remove the towel from her head.

The tight curls clung to her head haphazardly, brassy in color even when wet. Cindy moaned and reached for the cosmetic bag Manny had given her with various picks, gels and a little black thing that looked like a tiny hammock. She smoothed out his page of written instructions and drew a calming breath.

Thirty minutes later she had managed to pull out most of the tangles with a wide pick, but by then the mass stood around her head like some kind of exotic hat. She worked the gel through her wild tresses, then slicked it back into a low ponytail according to Manny's drawing. The little hammock, she discovered, was called a snood, a fancy name for a ponytail net. She fastened the snood in place, then turned sideways to critique her handiwork in the mirror and smiled. It didn't look half-bad.

She turned back to the vanity mirror and frowned. Her face was another story. She hadn't arched her eyebrows in ages and next to her perm-lightened hair, they looked darker and more severe than usual. "Glam up the eyes," Manny had told her. She fished tweezers and an eyelash curler from a cluttered drawer, then pulled her magnifying mirror closer. With grimacing plucks, she thinned her wayward eyebrows, begrudgingly acknowledging her greenish eyes were her best feature.

Carefully, she positioned the eyelash curler to tackle her long straight lashes, and squeezed the handle. The phone in her bedroom rang, startling her, and her hand jerked. She gasped as searing pain zipped across her eyelid, then jumped up to answer the phone, covering her stinging eye with the heel of her hand.

"Hello?"

"Cindy, this is Manny. You have a delivery—shall I bring it up?"

"What kind of delivery?" She wiped at the involuntary tears running down her cheek.

"Let it be a surprise."

Glancing down at the eyelash curler, she frowned at the number of lashes stuck to the little rubber pad, then froze. "Yes, Manny bring it up." Cindy slammed down the phone, dread washing over her as she stumbled back to the vanity table. She pressed her face close to the mirror, then gasped. Funny—she'd never realized how much eyelashes, or the lack of them, contributed to the overall balance of a person's face. The top of her left eye was nearly bald in places.

She groaned, then threw up her hands. She'd simply have to call Eric and cancel. Obligation dictated that she attend the party, but she couldn't face him with only half her lashes on one eye. Then she chewed her bottom lip—maybe it wasn't so noticeable. A knock at her door interrupted her panicked scrutiny.

Cindy secured the sash around her robe and jogged to the door. After a quick check of the peephole, she swung open the door to find Manny sporting a smashing black tux with a silver cummerbund and bow tie, and holding a small vase of exquisite flowers with a card tucked among the blooms. She smiled. "What on earth?"

"I didn't check the card, but I suspect they're from your dashing date." He handed her the vase and followed her inside the room. "Hey, your hair looks great."

"You sound surprised," she said, setting down the fragrant mixture of white roses and lilies. "By the way, love the tux."

"Thanks. Was I right?"

Cindy read the card, a zing of pure pleasure coursing through her at Eric's neat handwriting. *Thank you in advance for an engaging evening. Eric.*

"Well, is his note naughty, or nice?"

Scoffing at his implication, Cindy said, "Nice, of course."

He made a face, then he leaned forward, squinting. "Cindy, your eye." His jaw dropped. "What happened to your eyelashes?"

She sighed. "So much for it not being noticeable."

"Let me guess—eyelash curler?"

Cindy nodded miserably.

"A dangerous tool in the hands of a nervous woman," he observed.

"I'm not nervous."

He gave her a pointed look.

"Okay, I'm a little nervous—my hand jerked when the phone rang. What am I going to do?"

"They'll grow back."

"I mean about tonight!"

He tilted his head to one side. "Got any falsies?"

She frowned. "Are we still talking about eyelashes?"

"Yes."

"Then no."

He turned and strode back toward the door. "Put on the rest of your makeup—everything but the eye stuff. I'll be right back."

After he left, Cindy buried her nose in the flowers, then

dropped onto the stool at her vanity. *An engaging evening.* He didn't seem the type to copy words from some generic book at the flower shop. Eric was a sincere and forthcoming man. After all, he obviously suspected his vocation might turn her off, yet he'd been up front with her.

Cindy smoothed foundation over her skin, then applied blush and rummaged for the brightest red lipstick in her makeup case. As Cindy drew on the rich color, she remembered in vivid clarity the pressure of Eric's lips against hers the previous night. She closed her eyes and relived the taste of him, the sensation of his hands holding her face…a shudder traveled her shoulders and she knew the hair on her neck would have stood straight up were it not plastered down.

She had to admit, the man captivated her at a time when she'd have bet she couldn't be distracted from the goings-on within the hotel. The presence of the notorious Mr. Stark-Stanton hadn't consumed her the way she'd feared, although she would continue to do her best to placate the difficult man.

Keeping a near-bald eye on the clock, she stepped into the fitted long black gown. Cindy checked the top half of her dress in her vanity mirror, then climbed on her bed to check the bottom half. "Someday I'll invest in a full-length mirror," she mumbled, jumping down to slide her feet into suede pumps.

She slicked clear polish on her short nails, which had dried by the time Manny knocked on the door again. He strode in and whipped a package of false eyelashes out of a bag.

"I don't have time to put on false eyelashes," she said in exasperation. "Eric will be here in fifteen minutes!"

Manny, slightly out of breath, lifted his hands high. "Okay, if you want to get nose to nose with this guy with nothing to bat at him as he unlocks the door to his room—"

"You don't think he'll ask me to go back to his room," she gasped, then added, "do you?"

He laughed and gestured toward the vase. "*Hello?* Do these flowers say 'I'll settle for a goodnight kiss' to you? No. More like 'I want to devour you, my pet.'" He plucked a white rose from the vase, clenched it between his teeth, and wagged his eyebrows.

"Do you honestly think so?" She nibbled on a freshly painted nail.

Manny pursed his lips and nodded, then broke off the rose and motioned for her to turn around.

"So," she said sheepishly as he inserted the flower in her hair, "how long does it take to put on falsies?"

"Sit down and give me five," he said, ripping open the package and pulling out a tiny bottle of something clear. "Your dress is fab, by the way."

"Thanks." She eyed the flimsy semicircle of lashes warily. "I've never worn these things before."

"You'll get used to them in no time."

Cindy gave him a questioning look.

"So I've been told," he added.

She flinched throughout, but true to his word, Manny quickly patched the gap in her lashes quite convincingly. She tested the subtly heavier eyelid with a few blinks, then grinned and pulled him down for a quick peck on his cheek. "Thank you." A knock sounded at the door, sending her heart into her throat.

"I'll stall Mr. Quinn for a few minutes while you finish your eye makeup," Manny assured her. "And don't forget your glass earrings."

Her hands started shaking. "I'm a nervous wreck," she said. "Any last-minute advice?"

Her friend gave her a wry smile. "Try not to destroy any more of the man's clothing tonight when you undress him."

7

ERIC FELT LIKE A TEENAGER picking up his date for the prom. He had to acknowledge, however, that his anxiety about developing an attraction to Cindy Warren had increased tenfold since the tree incident in the lobby. The woman moved him...it was an unsettling sensation.

During the afternoon, he'd stumbled onto more disturbing aspects of the hotel operation. On the two floors with the most conference-room space, there were three bathrooms marked Men, Women and Other. Scary. And instead of the conference rooms bearing regal names, they were dubbed the "Phenomenon Room" and the "Dimension Chamber."

A quick look at the balance sheet had revealed the chandelier was booked at a legitimate-sounding twenty-eight thousand dollars. So why had he penned on the postcard to his father: *Dad, wondering if you can help me dig up information about the chandelier in this photo—possibly French, nineteen-twenties? I'll call you soon.* And why did he feel as if every minute spent with Cindy Warren would suck him deeper into a quagmire of right and wrong?

The door opened and his anxiety turned to puzzlement. Manny, not Cindy, stood in the doorway. "Hello," he ventured.

The blond man smiled tightly. "Cindy will be ready in a couple of minutes. Come on in."

Bemused, Eric followed him down a short hallway to a

surprisingly spacious sitting room tastefully decorated in a celestial motif of blues and golds.

"Have a seat," Manny invited, making no move to sit himself.

"Thanks, I'll stand," Eric replied, once again wondering if the concierge was smitten with his boss. Closer scrutiny revealed a red lipstick mark on the man's cheek, eliciting an unreasonable stab of jealousy in Eric. Did Cindy have romantic feelings for her employee? It didn't seem likely considering the way she'd responded to his kiss last night, but what if she was just trying to butter him up after all? Questions chewed at Eric, renewing his resolve to resist her charms, especially in light of the troubling revelations about how business was conducted at the Chandelier House.

Manny glanced over Eric's tux and pursed his lips. "Nice threads."

"Thanks," Eric said with a nod. "Yours, too." The subject of clothing reminded Eric of the bizarre incident he'd been meaning to report, but he hadn't wanted to bother Cindy. He lowered his voice. "Listen, Mr. Oliver—"

"I'm ready."

Cindy floated down the hallway toward them, her beauty taking Eric's breath away. The black dress covered her gleaming shoulders and neckline modestly, but hugged her curves, confirming his earlier suspicions of what lay beneath the plain green and navy uniform she wore—a shapely bust, trim waist, flaring hips. A mid-thigh slit revealed a long, lean leg encased in shimmering black stockings. Eric's body hardened, reminding him again of a high-school date.

Their gazes locked and his tongue grew thicker. Translucent, faceted earrings hung from her small ears like huge raindrops. With her hair skimmed back from her face, her lovely features were brought into relief. Her green-gray eyes shone luminously, set off by thick dark lashes. She winked, surprising him, and he smiled in return. Her bee-stung red lips curved into a shy smile. Eric couldn't take his eyes off her, and his tongue refused to budge. She, too, seemed hesitant to speak.

"Cindy received your flowers," Manny injected. "She loves white roses, don't you, boss?"

Cindy nodded, but didn't otherwise acknowledge the presence of her concierge. Eric spotted her pulse jumping at the side of her slender neck.

Manny cleared his throat. "Well, I guess I'll be leaving you two chatty kids alone. Don't mind me, I'll show myself out."

Eric heard the shuffle of the man's footsteps, and the click of the door closing behind him. After a few seconds of heavy silence, he murmured, "Hi."

One side of her mouth went up. "Hi, yourself."

"You look…great."

The other side of her mouth joined the first. "That's the look I was aiming for."

He swallowed. "I like your—" *body* "—earrings."

She touched one lobe, setting the glasslike bauble into sparkling motion. "Thank you. The flowers are beautiful." She turned her head slightly to show him the rose in her hair. "And thank you for the nice card."

"You're very welcome."

"I guess we'd better get to the party."

Eric moved toward the door, his steps faltering when she turned to retrieve an evening bag from the breakfast bar. He devoured the sight of her bare back, imagining the sensation of running his hands down the indentation of her spine. Promising himself some unimaginable treat in the morning for resisting her tonight, Eric opened the door and kept his eyes averted as she preceded him into the corridor. As if sharing his awkward awareness, she moved down the hall beside him, staring straight ahead.

Since Cindy, too, seemed quieter than usual, Eric decided the long ride down the elevator might be a good time to casually broach at least one topic niggling at him. "Cindy, when we were moving the tree this morning, I was noticing that amazing chandelier—is it valuable?"

She raised her lovely shoulders in a slight shrug. "The chandelier holds sentimental value to everyone who works here, I suppose."

"So it's not a particularly historic piece?" he pressed gently.

"I guess the chandelier is an antique, even though it's a reproduction."

"A reproduction?"

Cindy nodded. "I was told the original crystal fixture came from France. Allegedly, three were delivered to the States in the twenties—one to our hotel, one to a hotel in Chicago and the other to a department store in Beverly Hills." She smiled sadly as the doors slid open to the lobby. "But during the Second World War, all three chandeliers were replaced with glass replicas, and the originals donated to help the war effort." She smiled and led the way toward Sammy's. "Sorry to burst your bubble, Mr. Quinn."

She was teasing him by using the name under which he'd registered. He played along—after all, she probably didn't want to slip and use the name Stanton in front of her employees. "It still makes for an interesting story." He extended his arm to her as they reached the entrance to the bar, already alive with moving bodies and Christmas music. "What happened to 'Eric'?"

She smiled as she tucked her arm inside his. "Shall we, Eric?"

They walked down the two steps at the entrance, and heads turned. More than one set of eyebrows raised, telling Eric they were not used to seeing their boss on the arm of a man, or at least not on the arm of a stranger. He scanned the room for Manny, and as he suspected, the blond man, unaccompanied, had already captured them in his unwavering gaze.

The room glowed with strand upon strand of Christmas lights. A DJ sat on the elevated stage, surrounded by stacks of music selections. Tall speakers were currently blaring "Jingle Bell Rock." He estimated two hundred people in sparkling dresses and fancy suits studded the room.

Cindy was soon swept up in a circle of employees, meeting spouses and shaking hands, introducing him simply as Eric Quinn. He asked what she wanted to drink, then excused himself and approached the bar. Jerry, dashing in a charcoal-gray suit and red tie, occupied a stool in the middle. Eric shouldered in next to him, then shouted their drink orders to Tony who was managing the open bar.

"Did you come alone, Jerry?"

The old man nodding, smiling. "Yep."

"I thought you were married."

"I said I'd *been* married," the barber corrected, then his mouth split into a wide grin. "I'm between wives right now."

"Ah."

"Do you and Ms. Cindy have big plans tomorrow?"

Confused, Eric frowned. "Tomorrow?"

Jerry nodded his graying head. "Since you're the reason she has the day off and all, I figured you'd be spending it together."

Eric laughed. "Excuse me?"

"She didn't tell you? Joel Cutter bet Cindy she couldn't get a date for the party and if she did, he'd cover for her tomorrow." Jerry slapped him on the back. "She must have wanted that day off mighty bad, son."

Piqued, Eric frowned. Cindy had invited him as part of a wager?

"Ah, don't get all down in the mouth about it, son. I'm sure she likes you a bit, too."

Producing his best casual shrug, Eric said, "We're just two people at a party having a good time. No big deal." He collected the mixed drinks and headed back to Cindy. Approaching her, Eric experienced another pull of sexual longing. She was a beauty, all right. And smart. And sexy.

And off-limits, he reminded himself, swallowing a mouthful of cold rum and cola to cool his warming libido. And although at times he would have sworn he detected a glimmer of interest in her eyes, perhaps her invitation to the party had more to do with the silly bet than with influencing the man who held her livelihood in his hands. The thought cheered him. Then he frowned—either explanation ruled out the possibility that she was just plain interested.

When Cindy lifted her head to see Eric threading his way back to her, she acknowledged a thrill of excitement. He handed her a Fuzzy Navel and winked, warming her with his intense gaze. She sipped her drink, a feeling of bonelessness overtaking her. Given the chance, she just might seize the moment and spend one night of abandon with this gorgeous man.

"Hey," he said, leaning close, his eyes dancing. "What's this I hear about a bet?"

Heat suffused her cheeks. "B-bet?"

His mouth twitched. "Yeah, word has it that my going rate is a day off with pay."

Tingling with embarrassment, Cindy pressed her lips together. "It was just a harmless bet between friends."

"And what was the wager?"

"If I won, Joel would cover for me tomorrow."

He pursed his lips. "And if you lost?"

She sighed. "Joel would get my parking spot for a month."

"And I thought you actually liked me."

"Oh, I do—" She flushed. "I mean, believe it or not, I actually forgot about the bet."

He grinned. "In that case, I'm sure Joel will be glad to hear—"

"Wait!" she cried, laughing. "I need the day off tomorrow."

"In that case," he said, capturing her hand and leading her toward the center of the vacant dance floor, "let's dance and discuss *my* compensation."

Her heart thudded at the touch of his hand against hers. "I'm not a very good dancer," she protested.

"Just follow my lead," he said smoothly, spinning her into a slow waltz to "I'll Be Home for Christmas." Other couples joined them.

Supremely conscious of his hand at her waist, grazing the bare skin on her back, Cindy kept as much distance between herself and Eric as possible, stiffly following his footwork.

"Relax," he said, drawing her closer. "This is supposed to be fun."

"I think it's the song," she quipped.

"Does it make you sad?"

"'Stressed' is a better word. My mother can be a little intense."

"Such a shame," he said lightly, "that you can't choose your family like you choose your friends."

Suspecting a deeper issue lurked in his words, Cindy smiled. "I'm sure parents feel the same way occasionally about their kids."

He laughed suddenly. "You're probably right." Distracted by the conversation, she involuntarily moved closer to his body. Eric took up the slack immediately, his hand splaying across her bare lower back. "Now, about tomorrow," he whispered.

"What about tomorrow?" she asked, fighting the urge

to lower her head on his shoulder. He smelled so good, damn him. He moved with such grace. And his feet were so intriguingly huge.

"Since I'm the reason you'll have the day off, I think the least you can do is spend some of it with me."

Secretly thrilled, Cindy pretended to relent with a sigh. "And what did you have in mind?"

"Sleeping in."

She missed a beat and stepped on his foot.

"Ow!"

"Sorry, I told you I'm not a very good dancer." She couldn't be sure he meant he wanted to sleep in *with her*.

"So we'd have to get a late start," he said, picking up where he left off.

"I have Christmas shopping to do. Not exactly the most *engaging* pastime."

He smiled wide. "The company will be engaging. You'll be shopping all day?"

"No. I thought I'd walk the Golden Gate Bridge—it's invigorating and the view is great because there's no fog this time of the year."

"Sounds wonderful. I have some shopping to do myself, and in all the times I've been to San Francisco, I've never seen the Golden Gate."

Suddenly nervous, Cindy stalled. "Did I say the view was great? I meant to say 'gray.' Blah. And the bridge is not really golden, you know. Kind of rust-colored. Actually, there's no gate, either. Come to think of it, the bridge isn't all that special."

"I believe you're trying to talk me out of going," he said in a low voice, winking at her for what seemed like the hundredth time. "Which is very naughty, considering I'm the reason you're getting a day for fun and frolic."

The song changed to the upbeat "Rockin' around the Christmas Tree," and Cindy allowed him to swing her into a fast waltz, laughing with every dip. After a few spins, she started feeling the alcohol bleed through her system. "I'm getting light-headed."

"If we stop now, I'll have to find something else to keep my hands busy."

At his whispered words, Cindy's breasts tingled. "Okay, one more song." She had the deliciously dangerous feeling she was spiraling out of control, but she couldn't deny she was enjoying the ride. He alternately brushed his body close to hers, then away for a spin. At last the song ended and everyone applauded.

"You're a very good dancer," she remarked as they walked off the floor.

"I haven't danced in ages," he said, almost to himself. "My kid sister used to make me jitterbug with her in the kitchen." With a blink, he seemed to return to the present. "You're pretty light on your feet yourself." He winked.

There was that wink again—maybe he was getting drunk, she thought, concern creasing her forehead. The last thing she needed in her life was a man who sold sex toys and had a drinking problem. Then she chastised herself—this was only a potential fling, not a relationship. And she could relax her standards a bit for a fling.

They stopped by the buffet and piled their plates high with quiche and sausage balls and fruit, then joined Manny, Samantha and Sam's date seated around a table. Eric excused himself to go and get fresh drinks.

Samantha, stunning in a long green dress, had invited a Trekkie friend who apparently thought "black tie" meant the type of tennis shoe laces to be worn. Manny looked incredibly bored.

"Cheer up," she whispered.

"Easy for you to say," he muttered back. "You're getting laid tonight."

Her mouth dropped open. "I am not."

"I'll betcha Mr. Quinn thinks you are."

"Simply because I danced with him?"

"No. Because you've been winking at him every twenty seconds."

"What are you talking about?"

"How are the lashes?"

The *winking*. "Oh, my goodness, Manny—you're right. I've been winking at him nonstop. He probably thinks I'm being fresh."

Manny smirked. "I'd say 'fresh' would be a safe understatement."

"Knock it off, here he comes."

"So, Cindy, how's the Christmas tree in the lobby progressing?" Sam asked.

"The decorators said they'd be finished by morning."

"That's great. Oh, and how are things going with our difficult Mr. Stark?"

Cindy sighed. "I made sure he'd be off the premises tonight. I hope he doesn't have any other bizarre room experiences to report." She smiled at Eric as he rejoined them. Sam's date pulled her to the dance floor.

"I heard the tail end of your comment," Eric said, popping a grape into his mouth. "And speaking of bizarre, I've been meaning to mention a rather strange incident."

"What?" Cindy asked. Manny leaned forward.

"This is going to sound crazy," Eric said, shaking his head, "but I think someone stole a pair of pajama pants from my room and replaced them with a new pair, same color, same brand."

Cindy swallowed hard, refusing to look at Manny. "Really?"

"Yeah, sounds nuts, huh?"

"Insane," Manny agreed, nudging her knee.

"The thing is," Eric continued slowly, "the pants were a gift—probably expensive, too—but I never cared for them." He laughed. "The pervert who took them obviously wanted something worn, but little did he know, he didn't have to replace them."

Now you tell me. "Eric," she said, playing with the end of her napkin, "if these um—pajama pants, did you say?"

He nodded.

"If these pajama pants are the same color and same brand, what makes you think they're not the same pair?"

"Because," he said simply, "my initials were monogrammed on the pocket."

"Your initials?" she squeaked.

He bit into a tiny quiche, nodding. "Odd, huh?"

"I might go as far to say 'warped,'" Manny declared. "Desperate, sick, disturbed—"

Cindy gouged him in the ribs. "If there's anything the hotel can do—"

"I'm not looking for compensation," Eric said. "I just wanted you to know you might have a weirdo on the loose."

She conjured up a watery smile. "Thanks for the tip."

The hours slipped away. She drank and ate and danced with Eric until she was giggly and exhausted—and more turned on than she could have imagined. Her apprehension increased as the minutes ticked away. Surely they would share another good-night kiss, but what if he suggested more? Should she explore the unbelievable chemistry she detected between them? She smiled at him and, feeling languid, rubbed her foot against his leg.

In the middle of telling a funny story, Eric jerked, then cut his eyes to her.

"Hey," Manny said sternly. "Hands on the table, Cindy."

Everyone laughed, and to her astonishment, Eric actually blushed. Suddenly Joel appeared. "Eleven-thirty, Cindy. Ready to play Santa Claus?"

Cindy blinked. "Santa Claus?"

"Don't you remember? You said you'd do it the other night after you set one of my tables on fire."

Cindy stared, her memory sliding around. "Oh, yeah, I did say something about being Santa." *When I presumed I'd be coming alone.*

"Follow me," he said. "The suit's in the back."

Just when she thought she'd get through the next few hours with a scrap of dignity. She glanced at Eric, and he winked. Propping up her lazy eye with her index finger, Cindy sighed and slid out of her seat.

"No way," she said, looking at the outfit.

Joel lifted his finger. "Ah, ah, ah. You already said you would, boss."

"But *you* said I'd be wearing a Santa suit."

"This is a Santa suit."

"Joel, it's a long-sleeved mini-dress with fur around the edges."

"Well…it's red."

She crossed her arms.

"And look, there's a pair of black boots with it."

"They're thigh-highs!"

"And the hat—don't forget the hat," he said, dangling a red stocking cap with a white ball on the end.

"Who bought this ridiculous getup?"

A tolerant expression came over his face. "The lady who runs the gift shop came across it in a clearance catalog. I don't think she realized what she ordered. She paid for it out of her own pocket."

Cindy sighed, her shoulders dropping. "If you're trying to make me feel like a dog, it's working." Joel smiled triumphantly. "You'd better be glad I've been drinking," she declared. "And I am *not* wearing those boots."

"Okay, okay. The thing looks a little big for you," he

said, holding up the red dress. "At least it won't be skin-tight."

She yanked it out of his hands and pointed toward the door. "Scram."

"I'll get the gifts ready—everyone is going to love this!"

"Ho, ho, ho," she mumbled, waving him out of the supply room. She shimmied out of her dress, then hung the black gown on a hook next to a mop. The fuzzy white hem fell just below her knees, the furry cuffs down to the tips of her fingers, and the dress bagged around the waist. Spotting a wide plastic black belt on top of the preposterous boots, she wrapped it around her middle and cinched up a couple of feet of fabric.

Feeling like a complete fool, she set the cap on her head, and flipped the white cotton tip over her shoulder. At a tap on the door, she took a deep breath and stepped outside. Joel stood holding a bulging red velvet bag, grinning ear to ear.

Cindy lifted a finger. "Not a word."

He pressed his lips together and handed her the bag.

Eric watched for Cindy's return, but he heard the roar of laughter before he actually saw her. When she came into view, he grinned and joined the ranks of those around him. She didn't look nearly as amused to be wearing the baggy red dress, obviously made for a much taller, more buxom Santa. She was a good sport, though, and made the rounds, passing out envelopes to all her employees while the DJ played "I Want a Hippopotamus for Christmas."

From the good-natured ribbing she received, it was apparent to him that Cindy's bubbly personality made her popular with the employees. Unfortunately, in his experience, well-liked managers were not always the most efficient, because they let personal relationships influence their decisions. He swallowed a large mouthful of his drink.

Which was precisely why he had to maintain a proper distance from Cindy, at least until he finished his job at the Chandelier House.

Of course, he acknowledged wryly, if he recommended that the hotel be sold, or that Cindy be replaced, that personality of hers might undergo a quick change from bubbly to boiling.

When she stopped at their table, Cindy made sheepish eye contact, then handed Manny and Sam identical envelopes. "You're in luck this year. You get the same gift regardless of whether you've been naughty or nice."

"Speaking of nice," Eric remarked, toying with the cotton ball on the end of her cap, "love the outfit." A vision of her wearing nothing but the hat flashed through his mind.

"I wanted to make sure no other woman at the party would be wearing the same dress," she said with a mock-serious face. "I'm almost finished. Will you still be here when I get back, or are you completely humiliated?"

He laughed. "I'm completely humiliated, and I'll be here when you get back." Sam and her date hit the dance floor again, leaving him alone at the table with Manny. Eric's gaze strayed to Cindy as she finished passing out the envelopes, and his body swelled in…anticipation.

"Cindy's a gem," Manny said crisply, interrupting his musing.

Eric started, then turned to the concierge and nodded. "She's quite a lady."

Manny leaned forward. "Just so you know, she told me why you're here." His tone was even, his expression serious. "Normally I couldn't care less what a person does for a living, but in this case, it matters because Cindy matters. You'll be leaving in a few days and Cindy's the one who will have to deal with the fallout." The blond man pursed his mouth, then said, "Cindy means a lot to me, sir. I don't want to see her get hurt."

Rubbing the condensation off his glass, Eric pondered the man's words. He heard the wisdom, but hated the implication. "I don't want Cindy to be hurt any more than you do."

"Good," Manny said, pushing away from the table. "At least we see eye to eye on one point. Good night."

"Manny." Eric pushed himself to his feet. "If you wouldn't mind waiting a few minutes, would you stay and give Cindy my apologies? I think I'd better call it a night."

"No argument here," the man said curtly. "Merry Christmas, Mr. Quinn."

Eric didn't miss the dig, calling him by his registered name. "Yes, merry Christmas, Manny." Funny, he thought as he left the bar, this was the first time he could remember ever wishing he was anybody but himself.

8

"GONE?" CINDY BIT her lower lip, trying to hide her disappointment.

"He said to tell you he was sorry," Manny said. "But he had to call it a night."

She plucked at the neckline of the black gown she'd changed back into. "Well, after all, it was just a date. You know, to show Joel."

Manny clucked. "You like this guy, don't you?"

Grimacing, she rolled her shoulders. "I don't know. It's hypocritical to make my living off people like Eric, then hold his profession against him. But I have to admit it does bother me that he makes a living selling plastic rear ends. How does a man like Eric find his way into that industry?"

"Maybe he was a porn star."

Her eyes bulged. "You think?"

He shrugged. "He's got the looks for it."

"Oh, my God, you're probably right. I might as well put a casket by the phone for my mother to fall into."

"It was just a thought, Cindy. Don't bury her yet."

She sighed. "It's just that otherwise he seems so... perfect."

"Well, trust me," Manny said, "no man is perfect."

She squeezed his shoulders. "You are."

He grinned. "Well, excluding me, of course. How about I walk you back to your room?"

Cindy sighed, looking around the deserted bar. "No, but thanks anyway. I'm going to check a few things in the back, then go to bed." She managed a smile. "At least I get to sleep in tomorrow."

"Hey," he said softly. "Are you okay?"

She nodded. "Sure."

"If this guy breaks your heart, I'll break his nose."

"Not a chance," she assured her friend. "I'll see you tomorrow." But as she watched Manny leave, Cindy acknowledged that she had been looking forward to talking to Eric alone, even if it was only during the few minutes' walk back to her room. Even if he only shook her hand good-night...well, okay, she would have preferred a grinding, full-body kiss, but beggars couldn't be choosers.

If truth be known, she was hurt that he hadn't said good-night. Wasn't it just her luck that the first man in years she was attracted to couldn't conjure up enough desire for her to even make a lousy pass?

Cindy picked up the sack of extra gift certificates she would give out tomorrow to those who missed the Christmas party. She slung the bag over her shoulder, then waved to the team of cleaners who had emerged to put Sammy's back in order. She stepped into the corridor, paused, then turned in the direction of the stairs. After climbing fifteen flights, she reasoned, she'd be so tired, she wouldn't lose a minute's sleep thinking about Eric Quinn.

Just as she grasped the door handle, the strains of music reached her ears. Cindy stopped and cocked her ear. Someone was definitely playing the piano that had been moved from the bar. Curiosity won out and she followed the tinkling sound down the long hall to the Asteroid Room.

Part of a larger ballroom, Asteroid by itself was roomy enough to host a dinner party for a hundred guests. She opened the door silently to find the room cast in darkness. The unmistakable melancholy notes of "I'll Be Home for Christmas" wafted out, and the pianist wasn't half-bad. The piano had been pushed to the far corner of the room with its back to the door, obscuring the identity of the player.

Intrigued, she crept closer, recognizing the soft glow spilling around the sides of the piano as candlelight. The player missed a note, but covered well. Cindy's heart pounded as she circled closer, squinting when she recognized the outline of a man. Then she gasped and the pianist stopped abruptly, his head swinging around.

"Eric!" she exclaimed softly. "I heard the music and I…I mean, I had no idea you were in here or…geez, you're really good."

His tuxedo jacket lay folded over the top of the piano, and his bow tie hung down the front of his open-throated shirt. A half-burned candle sat on the ledge above the keys, casting soft light over the ivory and his long-fingered hands. His chuckle reverberated in the room. "I haven't played in years. I found the piano and…well, I didn't mean to disturb anyone."

"Play as long as you like," she said quickly, walking backward. "Good night."

"Cindy."

She stopped.

"I'm sorry I bailed on you at the party."

"It's fine," she said. "Really."

"I had a good time."

Her heart lifted slightly. "So did I."

He looked as if he wanted to say something else, then he cleared his throat and gestured toward the keys. "Any requests before you go? Trying to keep my hands busy, you know."

"Well," she said, lowering the red sack of envelopes to the floor, "I've always been partial to 'Blue Christmas.' How's your Elvis impersonation?"

Laughter rumbled from his throat. "A little rusty."

"Okay—you play, I'll sing." She walked to the piano.

He slid over on the padded bench and smiled broadly. "Have a seat."

Cindy settled onto the seat next to him, keeping a safety zone of a few inches between them. He started playing and she sang, *"I'll have a blue…Christmas…without you."* He leaned his ear closer as if he couldn't hear her, so she belted out, *"I'll be so blue…thinking…about you."*

He grinned. "You're really terrible."

"I know. *Decorations are great…on a green—"*

He stopped playing. "I don't think those are the words."

"Those are too the words."

"Decorations of *red* on a green Christmas tree."

"You play and I'll sing."

"Okay."

"Decorations of red…on a green Christmas tree…won't mean a thing, dear—"

He stopped playing. "Won't *be the same,* dear."

She motioned for him to keep playing. *"If you're not here with me.* Harmonize—this is where the girls go 'ooh-ooh ooh-oohwoo'."

He laughed so hard he could barely play and finally Cindy succumbed, too. Their shoulders brushed, triggering a bolt of awareness through her. Eric's fingers tripped over the keys lightly, playing the song with a honky-tonk swing. Cindy sang to the end, then yelled, "Big finish—everybody sing!" and Eric crooned the last refrain with her. Cindy clapped and whistled while he tinkled out a resounding finale. "You're amazing!"

A self-deprecating laugh escaped him. "You *must* be inebriated."

Feeling dreamy, Cindy leaned on her elbow and faced him, struck by his strong profile in the semidarkness. "I mean it. The fact that you can put your hands on these keys and make recognizable sounds is remarkable. Did your mother teach you to play?"

"No," he said quietly, still playing a soft, ambling melody. "My father. *He* was amazing." Respect colored his voice. "Couldn't read a note of music, but he could play the most complicated concertos by ear." The melody he played took on a haunting quality. "I was never as good as he was—never wanted to be. I enjoyed playing for my mother and my sister, and to impress girls." He laughed softly. "It made my dad nuts that I didn't love playing as much as he did."

"You argued?" she probed gently.

"More times than I can count," Eric admitted, his gaze still on his fingers. "I wanted to make money, lots of it, instead of winding up teaching piano lessons out of my home."

"Is that why you aren't close?"

"There are other reasons, but yeah, basically, it boils down to my old man being disappointed in the way I make a living."

Cindy resisted the urge to ask why he didn't just sell pianos. Eric was a grown man and undoubtedly knew his choices and the ramifications of those choices. "You should call him," she said simply.

"It always turns into a disagreement." He suddenly stopped playing, plunging the room into eerie silence. "You know, the first sales bonus I received on my first job was for four thousand, six hundred and thirty-eight dollars, and twenty-five cents." He glanced up and caught her gaze, his expression rueful. "I went to the piano store in the mall and blew the entire check on the nicest piano I could afford and had it delivered to our house for Christmas, for my dad."

"That's the most incredible thing I ever heard," she said, tearing up.

"Except he didn't want it." Eric laughed sadly. "He told me I was materialistic and didn't know what was important in life. That was over fifteen years ago, and that damned piano is still sitting in the family room, pushed up against the wall. To my knowledge, it's never been played.''

Cindy brought her fist to her mouth as the tears welled in her eyes. ''When was the last time you saw your father?''

''Last spring I went home for my niece's birthday. I stopped by to see him for a few minutes. It wasn't pretty.''

She shook her head. ''He must love you very much to have reacted so fiercely to your choosing, um—'' she searched for a euphemism ''—a business career over music.''

One side of his mouth lifted. ''I suppose that's one way of looking at it.'' Then he straightened, obviously ready to change the subject. ''Last call for requests.''

Her head still spun from his revelations. ''Play *your* favorite Christmas song.''

He smiled, a welcome transformation. ''That's an easy one.'' He played a dramatic opening, then launched into a bluesy ''Santa Claus Is Coming to Town.'' ''Bring it home, Cindy.''

She sang loudly, bumping his shoulder until he moved with her side to side. *''He's making a list, and checking it twice, gonna find out who's naughty or nice, Santa Claus is coming to town!''* They finished the song in rollicking style, laughing and clapping.

''That was fun,'' she declared.

''I'm glad you came to investigate,'' he said, lowering the wooden key cover. He picked up the votive candle as if to blow it out, then stopped. ''Well, well.''

Cindy glanced up, and her pulse leapt. Hanging from the top of the piano was Jerry's mistletoe. *Thank you, Jerry, wherever you are.*

Slowly Eric set down the candle, then turned toward her,

his expression unreadable. "It would be a shame to waste the mistletoe, don't you think?"

Cindy pursed her lips and nodded. "A l-low-down d-dirty shame."

He leaned closer, his gaze riveted on hers. "You look beautiful tonight."

Her throat constricted. "Well, technically, it's tomorrow."

Eric brushed his lips against hers lightly. "Then you look beautiful tomorrow." He tilted his head and Cindy closed her eyes just as his mouth covered hers. At first his lips were firm and gentle, cautious and sweet. But when she offered her tongue, he deepened the kiss with a groan. She leaned into him, her skin tingling for his touch.

He tasted of rum and grapes, he smelled of English Leather and starch. Her breath caught in her chest, until she had to break the kiss and gasp for breath in a decidedly unsophisticated manner.

He glanced away and swallowed. "I guess we'd better get going."

She nodded, struggling for composure.

Eric stood and shrugged into his jacket, then picked up the candle. Cindy rose on shaky knees, then followed him out of the room, picking up the red sack of envelopes. In the corridor, Eric blew out the candle and set it on a banquet table. "I'll walk you to your room," he said, taking the sack from her.

"That's not necessary."

"I know, but it's the least I can do for skipping out on you."

"Oh, I'm sure you had your reasons," she said congenially.

"I did." They strolled toward the elevator. "At the rate we were going, I was afraid I'd end up asking you to spend the night with me."

Cindy tripped, and he grabbed her arm. "And you were afraid I'd say no?" she asked nervously.

"No," he said with the barest hint of a smile. "I was afraid you'd say yes."

Smooth line. "Eric," she asked as the elevator arrived, "do you have any experience in the film industry?"

A look of puzzlement came over his face. "Film? No, why?"

"Just wondering," she said happily, pushing the button for her floor.

He seemed so relaxed on their walk to her room, Cindy's awkwardness evaporated. He'd obviously liberated himself by deciding not to ask her to spend the night with him. After she unlocked her door, he set the red sack inside, brushed her cheek with his lips, and said, "Good night, Cindy. Thank you for a truly engaging evening."

Remembering her intent to seize the moment, Cindy touched his sleeve, her heart thudding. "Eric, did you leave the party because you're still worried about how I feel about your, um, job?"

He considered her words for a few seconds, then nodded. "That's part of it."

She slid her hands up the lapels of his jacket. "Then maybe this will alleviate that part of it." Curling her fingers around the back of his neck, she pulled his mouth down to hers for a slow, sensual kiss. His arms immediately encircled her, his hands splaying against her naked back and pulling her against him. She felt his hardening desire for her and her body responded in kind. Next week her job would be on the line, this week she deserved a little fun.

She drew back and looked into his ice-blue eyes. "Eric, spend the night with me."

He swallowed, then ran his hand through his hair.

She held up one hand. "I'm going into this with my eyes wide-open."

"Cindy, are you absolutely certain?"

In answer, she grabbed him by the lapel of his jacket and dragged him inside.

Once he passed the threshold of her suite, Eric blocked out all the reasons why he shouldn't spend the night in her bed and concentrated on all the reasons he should. His mind shut down and his body took over.

They stumbled through the hallway, tugging at each other's clothing in the near darkness. They shed their shoes in the sitting room, his jacket in the second hall, his pants in the doorway of the bedroom. Cindy fumbled with her zipper and Eric obliged, standing behind her, his breath catching as he reached around and slid his hands over her flat stomach. The dress whooshed to the ground, then she turned in his arms, naked from the waist up.

Standing in the window light of her bedroom, she was simply breathtaking. Slender and long-limbed, her breasts firm and round like two peaches waiting to be plucked from a shapely tree. He wrapped his arms around her waist and pulled her against him, reveling in the feel of her. She pulled at the hem of his T-shirt and soon the hindering garment joined the others scattered about.

Eric was drowning in his desire for her, undoubtedly fueled by the fact that he shouldn't have her. But she felt so damned wonderful next to him, her skin as smooth as the ivory keys of his chosen instrument. He swung her into his arms and carried her to the bed, lowering her gently. Taking ragged breaths, he rolled down her stockings, overcome by the sight of her lying beneath him, clad only in teeny black bikini panties. She arched her back, pushing her breasts in the air.

Eric practically dived into the bed. He wanted to make love to her leisurely, but she reduced him to the likes of an inexperienced teenager, hungry for every inch of her, and unsure where to begin. His raging erection strained against the front of his boxers, but he knew he'd come undone if he felt her bare skin against his arousal. He kissed her mouth hard and nipped at her neck, then stroked her nipples, playing her until the music of her moans reached his ears.

Rolling her beneath him, he lowered his mouth to a perfect breast, and laved the plump nipple while she drove her hands through his hair. Her body, her moans, her scents drove him blind with need. He pushed her flimsy panties down her thighs, swallowing hard at the sight of her tangled dark nest. He groaned and gritted his teeth for control.

She tugged at the waistband of his boxers and he hesitated only because he knew it would be over soon if she unleashed him. Then with a frustrated moan, he stilled her hands.

"What's wrong?" she gasped against his chest.

Embarrassment coursed through him. So determined was he not to let the night end this way, he'd left protection in his room. "I seem to be a bit, um, unprepared for the moment."

Sudden realization dawned. "You mean a rubber?"

He cleared his throat. "Yes."

How odd—she figured he carried condoms like business cards. Her desire-drugged mind raced. Of the pack of twelve she'd bought years ago, eleven were still buried somewhere in her bathroom cabinet, but she'd never trust them. Then she remembered the box of sex samples under the bed. Cindy hesitated, embarrassed at the thought of rifling through the box of torrid toys in front of Eric. A second later she realized that not only would he recognize every trinket, but he would probably be able to rattle off the product code. And what better way to prove to him that she was okay with his line of work? "I might have one."

Eric brightened considerably.

Sliding out of bed, Cindy knelt and pulled the suitcase-size box from under her bed. She opened the lid of the carton, recalling with jarring clarity the diversity of the products she'd given a perfunctory glance.

"Wow," Eric said, standing behind her.

She rummaged through the bounty, and not wanting him to know how inexperienced she was with the tricks of his trade, handed him the products she thought might be useful.

"Coconut body liqueur…textured condoms…" She held up an interesting-looking battery powered device and raised her eyebrows in question.

Eric shrugged and added it to the pile.

"Chocolate flavored whipped cream…crotchless panties?"

Eric passed on the whipped cream, but fingered the minuscule panties. "Maybe later?" he asked.

She nodded and bent back to her task.

Suddenly Eric was kissing her neck, and rubbing his hard chest against her bare back. "Um, Cindy," he whispered. "Don't you think we have enough equipment for the first go-around?"

She smiled lazily. "Get the lamp, would you?"

"No way," he said, pulling her back to the bed. "I want to see you."

"And I," she breathed, pushing down his underwear to free his erection, "want to see you." She took in the size of him, then bit her lip, covered him back up and shook her head. "I don't think it'll fit."

His laughter filled her ears, apparently pleased with her assessment. "I'll stop whenever you say."

But of course she didn't stop him. She lay trembling against him like a virginal coed, wanting him so much it frightened her. They broke the seals on the flavored potions and proceeded to paint and consume each other's bodies until they both panted with restraint. She wrestled with the condom package until he took it from her and opened it, then handed the condom back to her. With shaking fingers, she placed the condom over the oozing tip of his straining shaft.

"The other way," he prompted with a smile.

She glanced down to find that yes, indeedy, she had the thing flipped. "Oops," she said, knowing her cover was blown. She wasn't a sophisticated sex kitten—she couldn't even roll on a condom.

"Let me help," he said, putting his hand over hers, pinching the top of the condom. "I have a feeling," he said with a groan as her hands encircled him, "I'm going to need extra breathing room."

He eased her back to the pillows and settled between her knees, covering her like a big, warm blanket. Her body sang with exhilaration from the feeling of his skin against hers. The light hair on his chest teased her breasts as his hands entwined with hers above their heads. With the moment of reckoning near, Cindy had nearly lost her capacity to speak. Instead, she let her body converse with him, responding to his kisses, nips and caresses with expressive shudders, contractions and yielding.

"Ladies first," he whispered, then began making love to her with his hand, his arousal branding her thigh throughout. Within seconds, he had her straining against him, moving with a slow, probing rhythm. Months of pent-up sexual energy and the heady presence of the man above her sent her quickly over the edge with shameless abandon. Their moans mingled as she slowly descended.

He withdrew his powerful hand and she instantly felt his shaft at the door of her desire. She ran her hands down his back, clutching his buttocks, inviting him inside. He advanced slowly, his heart thrashing against hers, his teeth clenched. Her knees opened slowly to give him full access and he filled her with one long moan. Cindy threw her head back and arched into him with ecstasy, crying aloud. He slipped his hands under her hips, undulating into her body with agonizing slowness and shocking depth.

She clawed at his back, matching his rhythm, tightening around him instinctively to draw the life fluid from him. Their rocking tempo increased to a frenzy of movement and sounds. Cindy sensed his approach and when he shuddered his release, swelling emotion pulled her over with him. He cried out, his face a mask of pleasure-pain, then lowered his face to her neck.

Gasping for breath, Cindy stroked his back softly and felt an odd stirring in her chest. Stark fear forced her to lighten the moment. "I'm glad you changed your mind about spending the night," she murmured.

His deep laugh rumbled against her neck. "So am I." He propped himself up on his elbow and smiled devilishly. "And the night is young."

Cindy's toes curled with anticipation. "Now about that gadget with the battery pack…"

CINDY HOVERED between sleep and consciousness for long, languid minutes. Imbedded into the fluffy mattress, her body ached pleasantly. Slowly she opened her eyes, although her left one felt a bit sticky. The events of the previous evening flooded over her. Eric still slumbered, facing her and breathing shallowly through his mouth. Awake, he was gorgeous, but asleep, the man was a god.

When she remembered the way he had held her, a warm, fuzzy tingle spread over her limbs. Their familiarity staggered her. She turned on her side to watch him. Tender, fun, sexy. She sighed. If only Eric's job was more… ordinary. Of course, she reminded herself, his vocation explained why such an eligible man remained eligible. Apparently, all the good ones were either taken or made their living selling blow-up dolls.

She wasn't sure why she was complaining. She should

be grateful that her uneasiness about the man's job kept her from falling head over heels in love—

Cindy jerked back. Love? Manny had once said love was best saved for cashmere and Dom Perignon. Pain exploded in her head, reminding her of how much she'd had to drink at the party. And coconut body liqueur did not contribute to a fresh morning mouth. She lifted a hand to her tingling scalp, only to encounter a tangle of wiry hair. Groaning inwardly, Cindy wondered how scary she must look right now.

Keeping an eye on Eric, she slid out of the bed and limped across the carpet, wincing at her stiff muscles. She wore the yellow crotchless panties, and they had found their way into uncomfortable crevices. Their clothes were strewn from chair to chair, and all surfaces in between. Bottles of flavored potions littered both nightstands and the memory of their consumption brought warmth to her cheeks. And a nurse's cap from the sampler case hung over the edge of a lamp shade—now *there* was a week's worth of journal entries.

She yanked a short terry robe from the bench at her vanity and pulled it around her, then leaned forward for a glimpse in the mirror. Cindy gasped, covered her face with both hands and peeked through her fingers.

Her hair sprang in indiscriminate directions. Medusa with a serious case of bed head. A strip of eyelashes stuck to the center of her forehead like some kind of weird tattoo. She plucked at it, managing to loosen one end.

Before Cindy could decide what to do first—dive into the shower or simply leave—the phone rang. Eric stirred. Cursing under her breath, she lunged to the nightstand on her side of the bed and pounced on the phone. It was only eight-thirty, for heaven's sake, and this was supposed to be her day off!

"Hello," she snapped, turning her back to the bed and walking as far across the room as the cord would allow.

"Um, good morning?" Manny sounded sheepish.

"This had better be good," she whispered sharply, cupping the mouthpiece.

"You're not alone?" he asked, his voice tinged with concern.

"As a matter of fact, no, I'm not."

"Oh, brother. Quinn isn't warming your sheets, is he?"

"That's none of your business."

"I totally agree, but I have a bit of news that you might find, er, eye-opening."

She turned to look back at the bed. Eric lifted his head and glanced around the room, then smiled when he saw her and rolled onto his side to watch her. Instantly, her nipples pebbled and her thighs twitched with the memory of his weight on her. "What is it?" *He's married, he's a felon, he has seven children in Iowa.*

Manny cleared his throat. "Well, I hadn't gotten around to disposing of his pajama pants yet—I thought I might cut them up, you know, maybe make pillow covers or something out of the fabric."

Eric lifted himself with flexing biceps and piled the pillows against the headboard. The nubby blanket slid down past his waist, but he didn't seem to mind. And neither did she.

Her heart thrashed in her chest. "I don't care what you do with them," she told Manny sweetly. "But I do wish you would get to the point."

"I found his monogram on the pocket, Cindy, and I did some checking. The man in your bed is Eric Quinn, all right—Eric Quinn *Stanton*."

The air left her lungs. Her vision narrowed to the handsome man lounging on her bed, fragrant from her body's scents, smug with the knowledge that not only had he duped the naive general manager, but he'd bedded her, too. Humiliation crashed over her, with mortification close on its heels. A hot flush singed her skin from feet to forehead.

"Cindy, are you there?"

He'd lied to her. Lied in order to get next to her, to win her over, to blackmail her—who knew the extent of his motivations? Of all the unmitigated gall. She had a good mind to take those inflated gonads of his and give them a hearty twist. The phone slipped out of her hand and she took one determined step toward the bed, her muscles propelled by calm fury.

Eric absently watched the phone fall to the carpet, completely distracted by Cindy's approach. He swept her tousled appearance with a smile and lustily wondered if she'd be willing to fulfill his morning urges like she'd fulfilled him last night. He hated to push, but the woman was addictive. Her sex sampler kit had been a delightful surprise. Without a doubt, they were horizontally compatible. He smiled. For a few seconds last night, he could have sworn they levitated off the bed.

"Did you sleep well?" she asked from across the room.

He nodded contentedly against the pillow, then glanced behind her. "Don't you need to hang up the phone?"

"No."

A smile crept up his face. She obviously didn't want the phone to disturb them again.

"You're pretty good," she said quietly, stepping closer.

His allowed himself a sliver of pure male satisfaction. "I'd like to think we were good together."

She sauntered closer, her hips swinging. "Oh, I guess I should take some of the blame—I mean credit—for what happened."

Something in her too-seductive expression set off warning bells. "More role-playing?"

She stopped by the bed, then leaned over slowly and opened the drawer in her nightstand.

"Nurse and doctor again?" he asked, craning his neck.

Still reeling from last night's adventures, he couldn't imagine what she could be springing on him now. "I'm open to just about anything," he pressed on nervously.

But when she withdrew her hand, he blinked, because she held a can of *mace.* "Except pain," he said, sitting up straighter. "I am not into pain."

Cindy's expression turned lethal as she aimed the can directly at his melting manhood. "The only game going on here, *Mr. Stanton,* is the one you've been playing, and it stops now."

Baffled, Eric pressed his back into the mound of pillows. "I don't know what you're talking about."

Her eyes narrowed. "Are you or aren't you Eric Stanton?"

He blinked. "Of course I am."

"Don't lie to me—huh?" She straightened slightly.

"Yes," he declared hotly. "I'm Eric Stanton!" Had she lost her mind?

Her mouth tightened and the can shook. "You aren't even ashamed enough to try to deny it?"

Astounded, Eric felt his jaw drop. "Why should I deny it? You've known my identity almost from the beginning."

Now *she* looked amazed. "What?" And angry. "How dare you? All along you led me to believe you were Eric Quinn, adult toy salesman. Get out of my bed and get the *hell* out of my room."

Incredulity settled in even as he made small, methodical moves to extract himself from her bed. He spoke slowly, keeping his eye on the nozzle of the mace can. "Adult toy salesman? Where did you get a cockamamie idea like that?"

"From you, you…you shyster!"

"Shyster?" Eric backed out on the opposite side of the bed, suddenly wondering if she was unstable. All too aware of his nakedness and glad to have the bed between them, he held up one hand and laughed softly. "Cindy, put down the mace, okay?"

"You'd better start making tracks, Stanton."

"I have to get dressed."

"Ten seconds, then I start spraying every appendage you've got."

"Cindy—"

"Ten...nine—"

"Wait!" He stooped to grab his pants, then jerked them on as he stumbled across the room.

She followed him, taking aim. "—eight—"

"I don't understand," he protested, grabbing clothes as he trotted through her bedroom. "Last night we—"

"—seven—"

"—had incredible sex—"

"—six—"

"—many times, in fact—"

"—five—"

"—and now—" He jogged backward through the hallway, shrugging into his tuxedo shirt.

"—four—"

"—you're ready to—" Eric passed through the sitting room in a blur.

"—three—"

"—disable me!" He backed up against the door, half dressed, his arms full of clothes. "Can't we discuss this?"

"—two—" She assumed a firing stance.

He whipped around and undid the dead bolt and chain with lightning speed.

"—one."

"I'm gone!" he shouted, throwing open the door and

diving headfirst into the corridor. He landed with a thud, followed by the sound of her door slamming.

Eric raised on his elbows and groaned at the smarting carpet burns on the undersides of his arms. He heard a noise and turned his head to see two white-haired women standing in the hall, staring.

He smiled tightly and pushed himself to his bare feet, then gathered up his tux jacket, his boxer shorts and one sock. ''Morning, ladies.'' Stepping aside, he gave them a friendly nod as they passed, wide-eyed.

When they rounded the corner, he cursed, feeling like a pervert. Mystified and irate, he walked back to Cindy's door and rapped loudly. ''Cindy, open the door. Dammit, Cindy,'' he whispered harshly through the door. ''At least give me my shoes.''

But apparently, she was not in the same generous mood she'd been in last night when she'd—oh, hell. Eric set off in the direction of the stairs, painfully stubbing his toe on the carpet. When he heard the sound of her door opening, he turned back, relieved she had changed her mind about talking to him. He barely had time to duck before one large hard-soled shoe bounced off the wall behind him. The second shoe clipped his shoulder, then her door slammed again.

Confounded, Eric stuck his sockless feet into the stiff shoes, and shuffled toward the stairs, dragging his pride behind him.

9

AFTER GOING TO THE TROUBLE to make a pot of coffee, Cindy passed on her morning dose of caffeine since she already had the shakes. She clung to the full mug anyway, taking comfort in something she could actually get her hands around, unlike her current predicament.

A fresh wave of self-castigation kept her rooted to the stool at the breakfast bar. She craved a long, numbing shower, but she couldn't bear to go back into the bedroom, to see the remnants of her lovemaking with…that man. And to think she'd actually flirted with the idea of falling for him. She gritted her teeth, trying to banish the memory of the intimate things she'd done with him and *to* him. And the "Box o' Sex Toys" she'd unveiled, trying to impress the "trinket man" when all the while…

She groaned, blinking back tears. How could she have been so stupid? The man had come to study her staff, to scrutinize her operation, to test her professionalism, and last night she'd played "Santa and the naughty elf" with him. When she thought of the ridiculous props she'd worn, entering the witness protection program actually seemed liked a viable alternative to facing Eric Stanton—or her staff.

What would her employees think of her cavorting with the enemy? Would they label her a traitor? And how fast would word spread to headquarters? Panic seized her anew. Had Eric Stanton already reported what undoubtedly seemed like lascivious behavior toward guests? Perhaps she'd been too hasty to eject him from her room, sans a shower and his shoes.

At the sound of a discreet knock on her door, Cindy inhaled deeply, summoning courage to face Eric if he'd returned. She smoothed a hand over her haphazard hair, not that it helped—or mattered—then padded to the door, her heart pounding. She looked through the peephole, nearly collapsing with relief to see Manny's grim mug staring back at her. "Are you alone?" she called.

"Yes. Are you?"

She swung open the door, then nodded miserably.

Manny sighed. "I couldn't hear everything on the other end of the phone, but it sounded bad. Is the receiver still off the hook?"

She shrugged. "I forgot about the phone."

"Sorry to have been the bearer of bad news," he said as he moved inside.

To her horror, she welled up with tears. "Oh, Manny, I couldn't have dreamed up a worse nightmare."

"I should have figured it out," he said, pulling her into a comforting hug.

"*I* should have figured it out," she exclaimed. "I should have realized Eric wasn't hanging around just to spend time with me."

Manny frowned. "Hey, don't sell yourself short. And don't waste time dwelling on what you can't change."

She inhaled deeply and raised her chin. "You're right. I have to get a grip and concentrate on damage control."

"Attagirl."

She exhaled. "Want some coffee?"

He checked his watch. "Sure, I've got a few minutes left on my break."

"Okay," she said, pouring the hot liquid into a cup for her friend. "Let's go over what *we* know he knows about the hotel and about me."

"Well, for starters, he knows we're shorthanded in the salon."

She frowned, then nodded.

He ticked off the items on his fingers. "He watched you stab yourself with a clipboard, the scarf incident in the elevator you told me about and the fire in the dining room."

Her confidence started to slide.

"He was there when the tree got wedged in the front door, plus he came to the party last night, watched everyone get drunk and saw you dress up like a Christmas Playmate to pass out gifts."

She slouched on her stool.

"He knows something strange happened to his pajama pants. And let's not forget," Manny said, then jerked a thumb toward her bedroom.

She closed her eyes. "Oh, God. Don't remind me."

"By the way," he said lightly. "How was it?"

Cutting her gaze to him, she considered lying, then sighed. "Un-freaking-believable."

He grinned. "Really?"

"I think I passed out once."

"Darn."

"Yeah, it's a shame he turned out to be a conniving, lowlife, corporate scumbag who came here to dig up dirt on me."

"Well, how did he act this morning? Was he sorry?"

She scrunched up her face. "No, the jerk had the nerve to act surprised—he said I'd known his identity all along."

"But didn't he tell you he sold adult toys?"

She nodded, then stopped, replaying their elevator conversation. "He said he was in sales, and when I asked him what kind, he answered 'trinkets and things.'"

A frown wrinkled Manny's forehead. "And from that comment, you assumed the man sold X-rated playthings?"

Cindy scoffed. "No. Then I asked if he was here for the

trade show next week, and he said something like 'As a matter of fact, I *am* preparing for next week.'"

Manny sighed. "Except he really meant he was preparing for his ream team to arrive at the Chandelier House for a good going-over."

"Well, *now* I know that, but with the condoms and all—"

"What condoms?"

She rubbed her temples. "When I was in his bathroom washing up, he told me to get a couple of bandages out of his toiletry bag. I unzipped a pocket, and out fell enough contraceptives for China."

"Which is interesting, but not particularly incriminating."

"It was other things he said," she insisted, then snapped her fingers. "He told me his father didn't approve of his line of work."

Manny shrugged. "Another blanket statement."

"But there's more!" The words tumbled out as she remembered them. "Last night we were talking about convention groups and I said something about the adult toy people—no, wait, I said 'his people' would be arriving shortly."

He held up his hands. "His people *will* be arriving shortly."

"Then he said he was glad I knew what he did for a living and hoped I understood why he had to be discreet."

"Bingo! From that point on, he thought you knew he was Stanton."

She gaped. "But if I knew he was Stanton, why would I have invited him to the party?"

"To butter him up, ply him with liquor."

Nodding in dismay, she said, "He did say that people tended to treat him differently once they knew the truth about him." She felt the blood drain from her face. "He said he was glad to see his line of work wouldn't interfere with our 'friendship.'"

"And you said?"

She stared at him. "I told him I was open-minded."

Manny drained his cup and set it down with finality. "Well, at least now we know how the mix-up occurred, and that Stanton didn't bed you under false pretenses."

"No, he simply thought I knew who he was and would sleep with him anyway."

He shrugged. "Probably not the first time it's happened to him."

She stopped, suddenly remembering the questions he'd asked about the chandelier. Nausea clutched her stomach. How much had she divulged?

"I'd better get back to work," he said, pushing away from the bar. "The decorators are supposed to have unveiled the tree by now. Will I see you later?"

She nodded numbly. "I'm going to call a quick staff meeting as soon as I shower and do something with my hair."

"In that case," he said with a wink, "I'll see you in the spring." Manny gave her forehead a sympathetic rub, then placed her wayward false eyelashes in the palm of her hand.

Cindy sighed. "I guess I'd better get used to wearing these things."

Manny tilted his head. "Don't you have a pair of reading glasses somewhere?"

She sniffed and nodded, cheering slightly. "Good idea. Maybe they'll hide my black circles, too."

He touched his thumb to a loose tear, then smiled. "Just you wait. Stanton will be gone by Christmas and you'll forget this ever happened."

Touched, Cindy watched Manny leave, then leaned heavily against the wall. "Gonna find out who's naughty or nice," she whispered.

ERIC TOWELED HIS HAIR DRY, mulling over the events of the last few hours. If he understood the scene in Cindy's room this morning, she had been under the impression that he was some kind of adult toy salesman. Admittedly, he'd first told her he was in sales, but how she had concocted the rest of the story was beyond him.

His best guess was that someone on her staff—probably the concierge—had discovered his identity and called to deliver the news, not realizing he occupied her bed. On the other hand, if Manny had designs on Cindy for himself and suspected Eric had spent the night, the timing of the phone call might simply have been a bonus.

Regardless, the misunderstanding meant one thing— they'd slept together and he alone had known it would pose a conflict of interest. Last night's justification that Cindy also knew the ramifications now fell flat. He should have conducted himself like the professional he was reputed to be.

Eric finished dressing, still stupefied over how he had let himself be drawn into Cindy Warren's bed. He'd been propositioned by women more beautiful and more determined, but never had he succumbed to temptation during an assignment. Eric cursed—he was getting sloppy.

Feeling like a heel, he slowly rehung his rumpled tuxedo in the closet. He had to talk to Cindy, to try and explain…what? That he had assumed she was the kind of woman who would sleep with the man sent to evaluate her and the hotel? He sighed, then looked down as something crunched under his shoe. He knelt and picked up two broken pieces of one of Cindy's earrings which must have gotten tangled in his clothing. Not surprising, considering their frantic progress to her bed.

Regret washed over him. Fortunately, the break along the narrow part of the long translucent teardrop appeared to be clean. Perhaps a jeweler could repair it. He hoped so—it was the least he could do to make up for his behavior last night.

He'd promised Lancaster an update call this morning, but considering what had transpired, he needed to clear his head and decide what to do next. He had compromised his objectivity and the trust of the general manager, not to mention the trust of a "good woman," as Jerry had called her. Great, just what he wanted for Christmas—guilt.

Flashes of their lovemaking plagued him. She had pushed buttons he hadn't known he possessed. Oh, the silly games were fun, but when he closed his eyes, what he remembered most was the total abandon on her lovely face as she climaxed with him buried inside her. At the ripe old age of thirty-six, he was no sexual novice, but no woman had ever bared her vulnerability to him that way. For a few seconds, she had passed complete control of her body and soul to him. She had trusted him, only to discover this morning that he wasn't the person—or the man—she'd thought him to be.

And she was right, of course. He wasn't a lovable man— hell, his own father preferred not to have him around. He had no business entertaining thoughts of spending time with Cindy Warren. She ran a hotel for misfits, ignoring corporate policies and making a laughingstock of what could be a stately property. He and Cindy Warren might be in perfect harmony between the sheets, but when it came to business, they were way off-key.

He wrapped the broken earring in a tissue and tucked the package inside his shirt pocket. Cindy didn't answer her phone, and he couldn't think of an appropriate message to leave, so he simply hung up. Perhaps he would catch her in the lobby and talk to her before she left the hotel.

Opting for the stairwell so he could smoke half a cigarette on the way, Eric slowly descended to the lobby. His temples throbbed with a nicotine headache, and his lower back hurt from either the strange mattress or the high-spirited ride he'd given Cindy the Naked Elf last night on a trip around the world. He gritted his teeth and snuffed out the cigarette. Hell's bells, what had he gotten himself into?

From Mr. Oliver's rigid posture behind the concierge desk, he assumed the man had indeed placed the ill-timed wake-up call.

"Good morning, Mr. Stanton," the blond man said in a crisp tone, confirming his suspicion. When Eric neared, the man leaned forward and whispered, "I ought to punch your damn lights out."

Eric blanched at the man's verbal attack, then angered. "Mind your own business, Oliver."

"We had an understanding last night when you left the party."

Eric chewed the inside of his cheek. "Cindy made the pass."

Manny scoffed. "She didn't know who the hell you were!"

"Well, I thought she did."

The blond man looked disgusted. "So is this standard procedure for you, Stanton?"

"I'm going to overlook that comment because I know how much you care about Cindy." Eric clenched his teeth. "Now, have you seen her?"

Manny's mouth tightened. "Yes."

When he didn't elaborate, Eric asked, "Where can I find her?"

The man's blue eyes gave away nothing. "I believe she's taking a day of vacation."

"So she's already left the hotel?"

"Can I help you, Mr. Stanton?"

He turned to find Cindy standing five feet away, looking more composed than he felt at the moment. Dressed casu-

ally in a pair of slim jeans, white turtleneck and a man's
boxy plaid sport coat, she looked like a coed. She'd stuffed
her too-curly reddish hair under a green velvet newsboy
hat, but a few strands had managed to escape down her
back. The round wire glasses were new, and flattering. No
one would have guessed this serene-looking woman had
spent the better part of last night naked and writhing beneath, beside and on top of him.

"May I help you, Mr. Stanton?" she repeated coolly.

Eric walked toward her, stopping at a professional distance. Striving for a level tone, he said, "Cindy, I'd like a
private word with you."

"Sure," she said, surprising him. "Except it will have
to wait until after my staff meeting." She glanced at her
watch, then gave him a polite smile. "I'll be back in fifteen
minutes—perhaps I can address your concerns then." She
signaled Manny, then strode toward the elevator.

Not sure what he expected, Eric stood rooted to the spot.
"Ms. Warren," he called.

She turned.

He suddenly wanted to see her smile again. "I thought
you were due a day of fun and frolic."

Her expression remained unmoved. "Something came
up," she said simply, then kept walking.

Watching her retreating back, Eric experienced a foreign
twinge…loss? He coughed and thumped his chest, deciding
that smoking on an empty stomach had given him heart-
burn. He wheeled in the opposite direction and went in
search of coffee, pondering Cindy's impending staff meeting.

…*Twenty-four, twenty-five, twenty-six.* Cindy stopped
counting her steps at the elevator and began counting the
seconds until the car arrived. In her pocket, she'd clicked
the end of an ink pen in quick succession so many times,
she'd practically worn out the button. Counting always

helped calm her, and if ever she needed a soothing ritual, it was now. In five minutes she would admit to her staff that not only was Mr. Eric Stanton on the hotel premises, but she'd unwittingly ensured him anonymous access to her employees. As for the access she'd given him to herself, well that was beyond belief or understanding.

"Goodbye, Ms. Warren."

She spun to see Mr. Stark approaching her, suitcase in tow. Stifling a groan, she painted on a smile. "Are you leaving, Mr. Stark?"

"Yes, headed home earlier than I'd planned." He tipped his hat. "Thanks for the great tickets last night. The rat incident aside, I must say, I enjoyed my stay."

"That's wonderful," she said tightly.

He folded a business card into her hand. "If you ever decide to remodel, give me a call and I'll take some of this junk off your hands."

"I'll do that. Have a nice trip home." As soon as he disappeared toward the door, Cindy flipped over his card. Reginald Stark, Antiques. She grimaced.

Manny walked up just as the elevator doors opened. "Perfect performance," he murmured. "Don't let Stanton know you're rattled."

"Rattled?" she said airily, stepping inside. "Who's rattled?"

"Here," he said, handing her a new ink pen. "For when the one in your pocket falls apart."

She shot him a grateful smile, then sighed. "Do you want to hear the worst part about last night? I lost one of my earrings."

"Did you check the bed?" he asked dryly.

"Yes, smart aleck, I did. It's not in my room. I think I might have lost it when I put on that stupid Santa dress at the party. I checked the bar, but no luck."

"Joel and I will look for it," he soothed.

"I think this might be the worst week of my life," she said as they approached the meeting room. "Do you think the staff will stone me?"

"They'll come around when they realize he hoodwinked you, too."

"Oh, now I feel better."

"Don't torture yourself. This was all one big misunderstanding. If he was good in bed, count your blessings."

"Unless this affects his review of the hotel in a bad way. Talk about performance anxiety."

"So call corporate human resources and tell them what happened—you thought he was a guest."

"And then everyone in the home office will think I'm seducing guests on a regular basis."

"That's ridiculous, Cindy. My goldfish get more booty than you do."

"*I* know that and *you* know that, but extended abstinence is difficult to prove." She glanced around, then lowered her voice. "Especially after Mr. Stanton and I set land records for speed and endurance last night." She groaned. "Manny, I don't know what it is about this man, but just when I think I can't do anything more idiotic around him, I amaze myself."

With her heart pounding, she walked into the boardroom and greeted her staff already seated around the table. She decided to stand, eyeing the distance to the door in case she needed to make a quick getaway.

"This must be important," Joel piped up, "considering you're supposed to be off today after bringing a *real, live date* to the party." A titter traveled around the room, stopping at Manny, who studied the ceiling tile.

Her cheeks flamed with memories of just how alive Eric had been last night—and just how much she'd wanted to kill him this morning. Still, she dredged up a wry smile. "I am planning to do my Christmas shopping later, but, um—'' She cleared her throat. ''First I want to discuss a personal matter with you.''

Amy, sporting a white breathe-easy strip on her red nose, leaned forward. ''Is everything okay, Cindy?''

She nodded vaguely, glanced at Manny, then plunged ahead. ''I b-believe most of you met the gentleman who escorted me to the party last night.''

''Oh, my God,'' Sam said, leaping to her feet. ''Eric proposed, didn't he?''

The room erupted while Cindy nearly swallowed her tongue.

''You're getting married?'' Joel exploded. He began clapping and hooting.

Approaching hysteria, Cindy waved her arms. ''Wait!''

The door in the back of the room opened and to her abject horror, Eric Stanton walked into the melee.

Manny silenced the room with a two-finger whistle.

Everyone turned to stare at Eric.

He indicated the door. ''I'm sorry to interrupt. I knocked.'' Edging closer, he said, ''I have a feeling I'm the reason this meeting was called.''

Unable to maintain eye contact with him, Cindy nodded, practically numb. ''You might as well come in.'' She waved everyone back into their seats, her mind spinning.

Joel frowned. ''So are you and Eric getting married or what?'' He yelped in pain and jerked back, eyeing Manny directly across the table.

She wished for something sharp to throw at Joel, then gripped the edge of the table. ''First of all,'' she said with deadly calm, ''I'm not getting married anytime in the foreseeable future. And second—'' She inhaled and swept an arm toward Eric. ''Everyone, may I introduce Mr. Eric Quinn *Stanton*.''

He stepped up and glanced around the group, falling short of a smile. ''Good morning. As you have previously been briefed, my review team and I will be conducting a routine study of your operations at the request of your parent company. I met most of you last night. Hello to the new faces.''

Jaws dropped. Eyes bulged. Adam's apples bobbed. She watched as incredulity transformed to confusion, then accusing gazes swung back to her.

''Ms. Warren didn't discover my identity until—'' He caught her gaze and she silently begged him not to say ''this morning'' with all its lewd connotations. ''Until a short while ago,'' he finished.

Cindy glanced back to the group. ''As we discussed, the rest of Mr. Stanton's team will be arriving soon, but on Saturday instead of Monday. According to my schedule, they will be on the premises for five days, leaving on Wednesday the twenty-third.'' She looked to Eric for confirmation.

He nodded.

''Until that time,'' she continued, ''I'm sure you will extend every courtesy to Mr. Stanton as he directs the review.'' She herself had certainly gone above and beyond the call of duty. Cindy picked up her clipboard to signal a welcome end to the meeting. ''That's all I have. If you haven't met Mr. Stanton, please introduce yourself before you leave.''

Cindy walked around to the other side of the table to avoid Eric and glanced at her watch.

''Ms. Warren.''

At the sound of his voice, she stopped. And so did everyone else. Cindy turned back to find Eric flanked by a few of her employees, apprehension clear on their faces. ''Yes?''

On dark eyebrow raised slightly. ''You said we could have a word after the meeting.''

Damn. "I'll be in the lobby near the Christmas tree." She made a hasty exit without waiting for his response.

Amy trotted up next to her on the way down the hall. "I'm sorry, boss."

Cindy frowned. "Why are you sorry?"

"If I hadn't pinpointed Mr. Stark as the corporate spy, you might have suspected Eric before you—" She broke off abruptly.

Cindy sucked in a breath. As far as she knew, only Manny was aware that Eric had spent the night in her bed, and she planned to keep it that way. "Before I what?"

"Before you asked him to the party," Amy finished, looking sorrowful. "Don't blame yourself, Cindy. He used you to get close to us."

Her friends scrambled to assure her they didn't blame her. When they arrived at the lobby, Amy slipped away. Joel started to make his escape too, but one of his two beepers sounded.

He pushed a button and lifted the radio to his mouth. "Joel here, what's up?"

Manny's voice crackled over the tiny speaker. "Trouble at the Christmas tree—you'd better get here quick. And bring Cindy."

Cindy strode toward the front entrance with Joel right behind her. Her steps faltered as they rounded the corner. "What the—?"

Black. The blue spruce was dressed in black from top to bottom. Black ribbons, black ornaments, even a black star on top. Horrified, Cindy could only stare. Guests passed by and winced.

Joel gasped. "Who ever heard of black Christmas decorations?"

"Get the decorators back here," she ordered, then pointed to a knot of people gathering on the sidewalk, some with signs. "And security. Looks like we've got a picket forming. We just may have offended every religious group in the city.''

"Oh, Stanton will love this," Joel muttered.

"I'll cut him off and take him out the side entrance," she offered, handing him her clipboard.

"You're a trooper," Joel said, clapping her on the back.

"I'm an idiot," she mumbled as she clambered back to the elevator to wait for the man she never wanted to see again. As she lingered, Cindy evaluated her situation and concluded she was definitely up the creek without a paddle. But she didn't have long to berate herself. Eric stepped off the elevator and nearly smiled when he saw her. Gloating, no doubt. She swallowed the pride she had left—less than a mouthful—and offered him a flat smile. "Have you eaten breakfast?"

His forehead wrinkled slightly, then cleared. "No."

"I thought we could walk to a diner to have that word in private."

He pursed his lips, evoking thoughts of her mouth on his. Cindy shook off the memories, thinking tomorrow would be easier since she wouldn't be reminded of their lapse every time her sore muscles moved. "Fine," he said, sweeping his arm toward the front entrance.

"Um, the side exit is closer," she said, moving in the opposite direction.

"HAM, HASH BROWNS, two biscuits, gravy and a side order of grits." Cindy handed the menu to the waitress with a nod. "I'm starved."

Amused, Eric tugged on his ear—he couldn't deny they had worked up an appetite. "I'll have the same."

When the waitress left, he lifted his coffee cup. Where to start? He wished he knew what she was thinking, but she'd barely spoken a word to him during the stroll to the restaurant, despite his best attempt at small talk. She looked so fetching in her little green hat and scholarly glasses, Eric wished he could strip away the murky circumstances and carry her back to her disheveled bed. He splashed coffee over the edge of his cup. "Cindy, we obviously need to talk."

"Me first," she said, unsmiling, then cleared her throat. "Mr. Stanton—"

"I'm Eric, remember?"

She gripped her coffee cup with those wonderfully familiar hands. "Maybe," she said evenly, "but you are not the person I thought you were."

His set his jaw, and nodded in concession.

"Mr. Stanton," she began again, her voice stronger. "Let me start by saying that I'm not in the habit of…of fraternizing with male guests. In fact—" she dropped her gaze "—last night was the first such incident." She returned her gaze and lifted her chin before she continued. "I have no excuse for my behavior, but I sincerely hope you won't hold my regrettable lapse in judgment against my staff."

Eric pursed his mouth. Regrettable?

"That's why," she said, pressing on, "if you feel obligated to report this incident to headquarters, I'm asking you—" she hesitated, then wet her lips "—no, I'm *imploring* you to wait until the review of the hotel has been completed. If I'm removed as GM now, employee morale will suffer and the profit margins on holiday events might be compromised. I want the Chandelier House to present as healthy a bottom line as possible."

His respect for her ratcheted up yet another notch. "Ms. Warren, I have no intention of bringing this, um, awkward situation to the attention of anyone at Harmon, although it had crossed my mind that you might be the one filing a report."

Her forehead wrinkled. "Me?"

"Yes. Especially if you thought I might threaten to divulge or withhold certain details about the operation of the hotel unless you, er, you know."

"Slept with you again?"

He nodded.

"Would you?"

For the first time he wished he was more of a people person, more intuitive, because her greenish eyes were clouded with emotions he longed to decipher. "No," he said quietly. "I'd never blackmail my way into your bed."

Her mouth twitched, but she remained silent.

"Which brings me to why I wanted to talk to you," he continued. "I'm sorry I misled you into thinking I was someone else. For the sake of discretion when I'm undercover, I'm usually vague with personal details, but I don't deliberately try to deceive people I'll be working with, especially not the general manager. I truly thought I had already blown my cover." He sighed. "And I've never indulged in this kind of liaison before either."

She studied her hands, then lifted her gaze. "I owe you an apology for accusing you of tricking me. In hindsight, I jumped to wrong conclusions based on that vague information."

"I'm sorry you're embarrassed—"

"Please," she cut in. "Let's stick to how this situation will affect your handling of my hotel and staff."

"Okay," he agreed, having slammed into the personal brick wall she'd erected. "I have two propositions—" He stopped and laughed uncomfortably. Cindy didn't even blink. "Um, make that two *solutions* I want to put on the table."

She nodded, unsmiling.

"First, I can remove myself from this project entirely—"

"I like that one."

Eric sighed with resignation. He couldn't blame her for

being angry, but he didn't want her to make a decision that might adversely impact the hotel. "Except, I have a sneaking suspicion that if the review is delayed, some executive at Harmon looking for a promotion is going to ax the Chandelier House without a fair shake."

"Why?" she asked, spreading her hands. "We've maintained a healthy margin, no thanks to Harmon. They're pocketing our earnings and doling out nickels and dimes for expansion and repair."

"The hotel is bad for their image," he said bluntly. "You're familiar with Harmon's strategy to cater to the corporate traveler—your guest demographics are way off the chart."

"So let them sell us," she said, pounding her fist on the table. "We'd be better off in the hands of someone else."

"Cindy," he said, resisting the urge to cover her hand. "It's not that simple. If Harmon puts your hotel on the block, they'll do it piece by piece—first the antique furniture, then the fixtures, then the building itself. And chances are, the building could be bought for the land alone and the structure bulldozed."

She inhaled, then exhaled noisily. "And the alternative?"

"I stay on the project and if the books are as healthy as you say, I could at least present Harmon with a fair business case for keeping the hotel. A positive review won't keep them from selling, but it will at least make a divestiture more difficult to justify."

"That's it?"

He locked his gaze with hers and spoke sincerely. "I can't make any promises."

A scoff escaped her lips. "You mean my best hope for saving the hotel is for you to stay and perform the review?"

"In my opinion, yes."

"And what if you screw me?" One corner of her mouth lifted, but her eyes remained flat. "Again?"

Eric squirmed, knowing he'd put them both in an ethical position more awkward than any position they'd conjured up in her bed last night. "Cindy, I'm not in the business of wrecking people's lives."

"That's not what I've heard."

The remark hit him like a sucker punch, but he didn't flinch. "You'll have to trust me on this one."

Her mouth tightened. "It looks as though I have no other choice, Mr. Stanton." She pushed herself to her feet, her face pinched and pale. "I guess I won't stay for breakfast. I lost my appetite. And since I'm going to be forced to see you for the next few days, Mr. Stanton, I think I'll take this opportunity to avoid your company."

"Cindy—" he said, half standing and putting his hand on her arm.

She pivoted her head to stare at his hand, which he removed after a few seconds of silence. Cindy slung her purse over her shoulder, then walked away.

CINDY DIALED THE NUMBER twice, hanging up both times before the phone could ring on the other end. With a heavy sigh, she leaned her head back on the comfy chair and stared at her bed. With no effort, she could picture Eric lying nude amidst the covers, his rakish smile beckoning her. She closed her eyes, allowing herself the sinful pleasure of reliving the more vivid sensations of their love-making before the inevitable, crushing return of humiliation and self-reproach roused her from her daydream.

Resigned, she picked up the phone and redialed the number, almost hoping no one would answer. But when her mother's voice came over the line, Cindy acknowledged a decidedly juvenile sense of comfort she hoped she'd never outgrow.

"Mom? Hi, how's everything—hmm? Oh, the party was fine—what? Well, the date didn't turn out exactly—no, Mom, he didn't take advantage of me, in fact—huh? No, I doubt if we'll be going out again—the Donna Karan. Yes, the black one. My hair? Well, I've been doing some experimenting—oh, no, I like it. Hmm? A little shorter—no, it's not ruined. Everyone around here is talking about it. So how's everything—Eric…Eric Quinn. Right, with a Q. No Quinns in Manassas? Well, it's a big place—Mom, it doesn't matter because he was only—what? Ham will be fine. No, Mom, Manny is not Jewish. No, you don't have to buy him a gift—size large will be fine, I think. Right. I just called to say hello—yes, Christmas Eve. Uh-huh. Uh-huh. My love to Dad…Love you, too. Okay…Okay, bye-bye… Okay, bye-bye."

Cindy replaced the phone and shook her head, then smiled warmly, her spirit on the mend.

10

"I'M SORRY, MR. STANTON," the jeweler said, shaking his head. "I can't fix it, and there's no way I can find a replacement."

Eric's shoulders drooped. "When I left it here two days ago, the woman said it would be no problem."

"Again, I'm sorry, but my wife didn't realize, and neither did I at first, that this earring isn't glass—it's vintage crystal."

Irritated, Eric scrubbed his hand over his face. Cindy hadn't exactly warmed up to him in the last couple of days, and he was hoping the gift would help repair their strained relationship. *Like the piano you gave your father?* He squashed the unsettling thought.

The jeweler turned the pieces over in his hand, his expression regretful. "Beautiful piece—looks like it might have come from a chandelier."

He stopped and squinted at the man. "A chandelier, did you say?"

"Uh-huh. Now *that* would be some piece, a chandelier made from this caliber glass."

Eric poked his tongue in his cheek, his mind spinning with possible scenarios. After securing the broken pieces in his pocket, Eric left the shop and found a pay phone. He punched in a number slowly, feeling a stab of longing when a familiar voice came over the line.

"Pop? It's Eric."

"I know that," his father snapped. "I only got one son, you know."

Eric bit his tongue, then asked, "How are you doing?"

"Bored to damned death—not that you care."

"Pop, that's not true—"

"I got your postcard from San Francisco. You out there hacking up another company?"

"No," he answered patiently. "Dad, did you get a chance to check out the chandelier on the postcard?"

"Sure—recognized it right away. It's a French design— *A Merveille.*"

"A merveille," Eric murmured. "'To perfection.'"

"Right. I did a little research. This particular model was custom-made in the twenties—the three originals took months to make. It was copied in lesser materials quite a bit in the forties and fifties. And the chandelier on the post-card appears to be a good copy, except for a missing piece, probably broken."

Eric's pulse picked up. "Tell me about the missing piece, Dad."

"The original had a small spiral of crystals hanging from the center."

From which at least one pair of earrings had been fash-ioned? "Do you have any idea what the original might be worth?"

"I wrote it down—one point three million."

Eric clutched the edge of the phone booth. "Really."

"Uh-huh. But the copies are only worth between twenty and thirty thousand. Not chump change, but not enough to retire on. Why the sudden interest in a light fixture?"

"Just trying to estimate a book value," Eric lied, to gain time. "Dad, I need a picture of the original chandelier."

"Christmas is only a few days away. Can't you get the book then?"

Eric pinched the bridge of his nose. "Actually, I need

that photo right away, and I, um…I'm not going to make it home for Christmas this year.''

There was a brief pause on the other end. ''Why not?''

Because I don't want to argue with you the entire visit and hear about how much money I wasted on that damned piano. ''Something came up at work.''

''Okay by me, but Alicia and the kids will be disappointed.''

''I'll call her and try to plan a visit after New Year's.'' He sighed. ''Will you send the book?''

''Sure. What's the address?''

Eric pulled out Cindy's business card and read the hotel address to his father, thinking it sad that two of the people he cared about most would just as soon not be around him. Then he stopped. Cared about most?

CINDY HELD HER HEAD BACK, looking straight up at the tree. ''I think you're right,'' she said to Manny. ''Those veil-decorations are definitely melting.''

Her friend scoffed. ''A Middle Eastern theme—aren't those addle-headed decorators aware that most people in the Middle East don't celebrate Christmas? In fact,'' he said flatly, ''maybe I'll move there.''

''Oh, don't be such a Scrooge,'' she said lightly. ''We've managed to have a decorated tree for—what? Four whole days now. Have Amy call the decorators and tell them to take off everything but the lights—that way it'll still be festive when the rest of the review team arrives today.''

''You're nothing if not optimistic,'' her friend noted. ''Speaking of the review team, I haven't seen Stanton lurking around today. Wonder where he slept last night?''

She offered a rueful smile. ''As long as it wasn't with me, I couldn't care less.''

''Just checking,'' he said, his low voice rich with innuendo.

"What's that supposed to mean? I've gone out of my way to avoid that man these last few days." She'd even resisted the urge to hand-deliver the shirt she'd bought to replace the one she'd burned.

His pale eyebrows shot up. "My point exactly."

"I don't want anyone thinking I'm...I'm, you know."

"Still infatuated with him?"

Her jaw dropped, then closed. "Not *still*...not ever!"

"That's what I meant," he said smoothly.

"Well—" Flustered, she scrambled for words. "I take issue with the term 'infatuated.'" Her arm flailed of its own volition. "Being infatuated implies the existence of...some type of emotional involvement, of...of some kind of personal attachment. Anything between me and Stanton was purely physical."

"Just a one-night stand," Manny said, nodding.

A frown pulled down the corners of her mouth. "Right."

He smiled and exhaled noisily. "What a relief to hear you say that. I can't imagine a worse match than you and Eric Stanton."

"Right." She worried the inside of her cheek with her tongue. "What makes you say that?"

He scoffed. "Cindy, you're so fun-loving, and he's so...*anal*."

A fond memory of him playing the piano washed over her. "Eric has his less serious moments."

"And you value tradition, people. That man won't lose a wink of sleep worrying about the employees here."

She worked her mouth side to side. "But he said he'd try to help us make a case to Harmon."

"Why would he do that? Harmon is paying him untold dollars to oversee this review because of his hard-ass reputation. And you think that Stanton is going to help us because he's undergone a sudden change of heart?" He gave her a dubious look. "This is the same man, Cindy, who climbed into your bed knowing he'd be evaluating you on job performance. What makes you think you can put your faith in him now?"

Hurt stabbed her from all sides. "You're right." Deep down, she'd known all those things about Eric—so why did hearing the words aloud bother her so much?

He handed her a plastic bag he'd been holding.

"What's this?"

"*Stanton's* jammies."

Her eyes widened. "Why did you bring them back?"

Manny shrugged. "I don't know—I couldn't bring myself to throw them away, and it seemed icky to hang on to them."

"Icky?"

"Another word for 'I don't want this on my conscience, girl.'"

She clamped the bag under her arm. "Like I don't have enough on mine."

"Well, I feel better about giving back the pants knowing that Stanton doesn't mean anything to you."

She swallowed. "Thanks. I have to go. I have an appointment with our new hairdresser in the salon." She held up a finger. "Don't say a word."

He made a zipping motion across his mouth with his finger, turned on his heel and headed back to the concierge station.

Cindy turned toward the salon, anticipating a few minutes of peace and quiet to mull her recent restlessness.

"Whew, that perm really stripped your color," Matilda, the new hairdresser, said emphatically. "Let's try shade number twenty-eight B, chocolate coffee."

Cindy settled into a salon chair, frowning in puzzlement.

"Dark brown," the woman clarified.

"Ah. Good—back to my original color." She glanced at

her hair in the mirror. "Is it safe to color so soon after perming?"

"I'll apply a conditioner first."

"Okay, you're the expert...aren't you?"

Matilda nodded, while in the background, Jerry shook his head.

"Just match my eyebrows as closely as you can," Cindy declared, ignoring the barber. How hard could it be to open a bottle of dye and pour it on?

"Okeydokey."

At least her hair would be back to its normal color by the time she met the review team. While the stylist painted on goopy hair dye with a brush, Cindy's thoughts strayed to pending catastrophes. She longed for the days when they weren't enslaved to a corporate master, when they didn't expend so much energy watching their p's and q's. "How much longer?" she asked the hairdresser.

"Time to rinse," the woman said, yanking Cindy's head back into a sink and nearly drowning her in her attempt to wash away the residue. After a knot-raising towel dry, Matilda plugged in a blow-dryer.

Except when she flipped the switch to the hair dryer, the lights blinked, then went out, pitching the salon into total darkness. "Did I do that?" Matilda cried.

"I don't think a hair dryer could do this," Cindy said. The low-watt generator lights came on. "It would take a huge power draw, something like a..."

"Like a Christmas tree?" the woman asked.

"Yeah," Cindy said, nodding, then gripped the arms of the chair. The Christmas tree—had the decorators added more lights once they stripped the melting decorations?

She launched herself out of the chair and fled for the lobby.

"POWER FAILURE," Eric murmured, grasping the rail along the three-story staircase landing. He immediately wondered

if Cindy was at the source of the calamity and smiled to
himself, surprised that the mere thought of her evoked that
odd twisting feeling in his chest. Guilt, probably. He held
a small pair of binoculars through which he'd studied the
chandelier hanging a few yards in front of him for a good
fifteen seconds before everything went black.

Emergency lights came on, supplementing the thin day-
light streaming in around the front entrance. Eric had a
fairly good view of the activity in the lobby. Newly erected
scaffolding held a dozen workers, some of whom had been
removing items from the tree while others had been adding
strands of lights. Someone with a pronounced lisp yelled
for everyone on the scaffolding not to move. A knot of six
guests came through the front door, dressed professionally
and pulling sleek suitcases. His team, he noted, cursing the
bad timing. Eric descended the long stairway in the semidarkness.

As expected, Cindy came flying onto the scene, almost
literally, since she sported some kind of cape that flapped
behind her. Her hair sprang wild and wet around her. Eric
approached his team, shaking hands and explaining the recent turn of events. With a start, he realized he was becoming numb to the hotel's minidisasters. Within a few
minutes, Cindy had coordinated an evacuation of workers
on the scaffolding and announced that the electricity, which
was off in a two-block radius, would be restored soon.

He waved to get her attention and gestured her over. She
resembled a drowned cat with her huge greenish eyes and
her wild, wet hair that looked almost…no, it was probably
just the low lighting that made it look purplish. From the
gray cape he assumed she'd been "salonus interruptus"
when the blackout occurred.

"This is Ms. Cindy Warren," he said to his team, "General manager of the Chandelier House." That she occa-

sionally moonlighted as Nurse Lovejoy, he kept to himself. "Ms. Warren, meet the Stanton & Associates review team members who have been assigned to evaluate your property."

She blanched, then recovered quickly as she exchanged greetings with his stoic-faced team. "We apologize for the inconvenience," Cindy said with a big smile. "Lights are being rounded up as we speak so that everyone can find their way around the hotel. Ah, here we are. Eight lights over here, please."

From a box, a young man passed out pale cylinders to the group, then moved on. Eric studied the object in his hand, frowning.

"Ladies and gentlemen..." A voice he recognized as Samantha Riggs's came over a bullhorn. "We are providing all guests with a combination glow-in-the-dark flashlight/vibrator, batteries included, compliments of Readynow, one of our vendors for the adult entertainment trade show that will begin on Monday. If you're still visiting with us at that time, we invite you to drop by the show. Oh, and please bring photo ID."

Eric shot Cindy an amused glance as she stared at the contoured flashlight cradled in her hands, closed her eyes and mouthed something heavenward. He suppressed a smile. "Ms. Warren, I was hoping you'd join us for dinner in the restaurant, say around seven? Hopefully the lights will have been restored by then."

She nodded and smiled shakily. "We can hope, can't we?"

"IT'S PURPLE," SHE MOANED, looking in the mirror.

"'Eggplant' sounds so much more fashionable," Manny declared.

"Why does this keep happening to me?"

"It's a conspiracy, Cindy. What did the hairdresser say?"

"By the time I got back to the salon, Jerry had sent her home."

"Hmm. And did Jerry have any advice?"

"He gave me a paper sack to wear on my head. I asked for plastic so I could suffocate myself."

"You have to admit it's very trendy. Some people would pay top dollar for this look. It's not half-bad, actually."

"Manny, I'm supposed to have dinner with Stanton and the rest of the review team in one hour. I look like one of the Spice Girls."

"Is this just a shmoozy meeting?"

"I think so, although Eric mentioned he wanted to talk to me afterward."

"Uh-oh."

"Relax. He said it was about the hotel, although he didn't give me any specifics." She gave him a wry smile. "And with my wet head and wearing that plastic cape, I was in such a hurry to get out of there, I didn't question him."

"I heard the rest of the review team arrived during the blackout."

"When else? I'm sure they were very impressed with my getup, not to mention the vibrating hostess gifts."

"Oh, well, it can't get any worse."

"Please don't *say* that."

"At least the lights are on now."

"Which is a good thing, else no one would be able to see our totally bare three-story Christmas tree."

"That's the spirit."

"Do you think the green hat is too casual for dinner?"

"Yes." He picked up a lock of her wine-colored hair. "Don't you have a dress this color?"

She nodded.

"How about a head wrap? Blue would be nice."

"I don't have a blue scarf."

"Hmm." He pursed his mouth as if an idea had struck him.

"What?"

"Where are the jammies?" He spied the paper bag in a nearby chair and pulled them out.

"Oh, no." Cindy held up her hands. "I am *not* going to dinner with Eric wearing the pajama pants I stole from him wrapped around my head."

But his hands were already at work. "Think of it as a three-hundred-and-fifty-dollar scarf. Fold under the waistband, hide the stain, tie the legs in back, tuck, tuck, tuck, and *voilà!*"

She opened her mouth to protest, but he guided her face to the mirror. She looked…good, exotic even. Creating a four-inch strip around her hairline and ears, the makeshift scarf held the curly purple hair away from her face, forcing it to spill up and over the pale fabric. "Dammit, Manny, how do you do that?"

"Resourcefulness," he said, snapping his fingers.

"But what if he recognizes it?"

"If he were gay, I'd say don't risk it. But straight, hungry, horny and under low lights—are you kidding?" He laughed. "Besides, this is *too* perfect."

Frowning, Cindy looked at her reflection and let out a sigh. "I don't have a good feeling about this."

11

STANDING NEXT to the long dinner table, Eric lifted his hand in a final wave as the members of his review team filed out of the restaurant. Strange, but he hadn't noticed before what incredibly dull company his associates were. Of course, he suspected the hours had dragged because he was longing to talk to Cindy alone. She'd chosen the seat farthest from him, so he hadn't been able to engage her in conversation. "Thanks for agreeing to stay awhile longer."

She nodded curtly, her expression guarded, as it had been each time he had caught her gaze throughout the meal. "You wanted to talk to me about a hotel matter?"

When she started to reclaim her seat, Eric's mind raced to come up with a venue that would offer privacy without the connotation of either of their rooms. "How about if we go up to the roof to take in that great view you told me about? I hate to admit it, but I'm dying for a smoke."

She pressed her lips together, hesitating.

"And I don't want to risk our conversation being overheard," he added.

Her eyes narrowed slightly. "I thought you said you wanted to discuss the hotel."

"I do, but I believe you will appreciate the privacy."

Concern furrowed her forehead. "I'll need to stop by my room to get a jacket."

"You can use mine," he offered. "I won't keep you long."

In answer, she picked up her bag and walked to the hostess station, where she signed for their meal. Eric couldn't stop himself from devouring the swell of her hips beneath the thin fabric of her slim burgundy dress. Her hair, which was actually an odd, lovely contrast to her green eyes, would take a little getting used to, but—

What was he thinking? He wouldn't be around long enough to get used to *anything*. Spending the night with Cindy would undoubtedly be a fondly recalled memory, but little more. Once he put a little space between him and the Chandelier House, he would recover his edge.

"You made a good impression on the team," he said with sincerity as they strolled toward the elevator.

She laughed softly. "With the utter chaos surrounding my introduction this afternoon, I had nowhere to go but up."

He waved off her concern. "I told everyone they'd get used to seeing you like that."

"Gee, thanks."

Eric laughed. "I meant, they'd get used to seeing you in the middle of things, taking charge, no matter what."

She turned wary eyes his way. "That's my job, Mr. Stanton." She walked into the elevator car, claimed a front corner and depressed the top floor button. Her posture remained uncompromising.

Hating the formality, the distance and the awkward tension, he watched the floors light as they climbed. Strange, how they had gone from being strangers to acquaintances to lovers, and now back to mere acquaintances.

They reached the top of the building in short order. Cindy removed a handheld radio from her bag and asked the operator to notify security that the silent alarm for the roof door would be tripped. Eric followed her down a hallway, up a flight and a half of stairs, and through the heavy metal door covered with warning stickers.

Cindy looked forward to the openness of the roof after

being in close confines with Eric for the past few hours. A gusting breeze enveloped her as she stepped outside, the December chill raising gooseflesh on her skin, despite the long sleeves of her dress.

She shivered involuntarily, then started when Eric's jacket appeared around her shoulders. The warmth from his body still emanated from the silky lining, and the faint scent of English Leather drifted up to tease her. "Thank you," she murmured, then stepped away from the stairwell enclosure toward the center of the roof.

"Nice," he observed, scanning the view.

She had to agree. At this height, the world was a soothing mixture of calm silence with faint undertones of traffic far below. The wind sent the ends of her hair skimming across her face and dancing in the air. She patted the pseudo-scarf, experiencing a stab of alarm that it seemed much looser. Oh, well, the wrap seemed intact for now, and Eric had told her the discussion wouldn't take long.

Her heart pounded in her ears, drowning out the wind. The only reason she could think of for his wanting to talk in private was to rehash the impact of their night together on the review, and she didn't want to talk about it again. Wasn't it enough that the encounter was never more than a few seconds from her mind anyway?

She tried to distract herself by absorbing the wonderful view, which remained breathtaking no matter how many times she made this pilgrimage. A myriad of lights from homes, cars and Christmas decorations, studded the landscape in three directions as far as one could see. To the west, of course, lay the bay, offering its own nighttime spectacle.

"Beautiful," Eric said, turning to look at her.

Despite the circumstances, Cindy found it difficult to make eye contact with the man and not be affected. Not only was he undeniably handsome, but she also knew intimate secrets about the powerful body standing little more than an arm's length away. The awareness of their physical compatibility pulled at her like a vacuum. "Mr. Stanton," she said hurriedly, "I need to get to bed early tonight."

The words hung in the air between them.

"Alone," she amended quickly, then stopped and took a deep, calming breath. "Maybe you'd better just dive right in… Into whatever you wanted to talk about, I mean." To cover her growing uneasiness, she smiled cheerily into the stiff breeze and rambled on. "You know, I'm so glad we've been able to get past that little indiscretion and move on to building a business relationship based on—" she spit out a hank of hair that the wind blew against her mouth "—mutual respect."

Eric nodded, his expression unreadable. Then he stepped forward and reached for her. Terrified at the zing of desire in her stomach, she held up both hands to ward him off. "Stop right there, buster." Her body responded shamelessly even as her indignation ballooned. "How dare you lure me up here under the guise of business when all you had on your mind was…was copping a feel!"

He halted, his eyes wide.

Hurt loosened her tongue, making her want to give pain in return. "Haven't you ever done it on a roof, Mr. Stanton? Does it turn you on? Didn't I give you enough material the other night for a few weeks' worth of locker-room talk?"

He frowned and nodded toward his jacket. "If you're finished, there's something in the left pocket, wrapped in a tissue. I believe it's yours."

Slightly deflated that he hadn't brought her to the roof to feel her up after all, Cindy reached into the pocket and withdrew a wad of tissue.

"Careful," he warned.

She gently unfolded the tissue, at first confused by the bits of glass winking in the moonlight. Then she sucked in a breath. "My earring," she said softly, wincing when she saw the two pieces.

His tie whipped in the wind, curling around his neck. "It must have fallen into the pocket of my tux or gotten hung on my clothes somehow," he explained. "I stepped on it accidentally. I'm so sorry."

"That's all right." But she could hear the hurt in her own voice.

"I wanted to have it repaired, but the jeweler told me he couldn't replace it."

Her head jerked up. "Jeweler?"

"He told me it wasn't glass, as I'd thought, but vintage lead crystal."

She met his gaze, looked away, then glanced back, her knees weakening. "Um, yes, as a matter of fact, it is crystal."

"He also said it probably came from a chandelier."

"Did he?" Stuffing the broken earring into her purse, she walked past him and over to the shoulder-high concrete edge, her mind spinning.

"He told me an intact chandelier made out of this crystal would be extremely valuable." She could tell from his muffled voice that he stared at the opposite horizon. How perfectly symbolic, she realized.

Cindy wet her lips, blinking against the wind, which was much stronger here on the perimeter of the roof. "I suppose it would be," she said over her shoulder. She gasped as the scarf fell slack against her hairline and a leg of the pajama pants whisked in front of her face, riding the wind like a flag. She snatched the leg and straightened, using both hands to try to repair the damage.

Eric still stood with his back to her, hands on his hips. He obviously didn't know how to broach the next question, which made Cindy a nervous wreck. How much did he know? How much should she tell him?

The head wrap fell around her neck. She panicked and whipped it off in a motion she knew would leave burn marks on her throat. Holding the garment in front of her in a ball, her mind raced. Her purse was too small. She had no pockets of her own. He still had his back to her. Her heart thudded.

"Cindy."

She held the wadded-up pants over the edge and dropped the bundle, then spun and gave Eric her seemingly undivided attention as he crossed the small distance between them. "Yes?"

"Did that earring come from the chandelier hanging in the hotel lobby?"

"The earrings were p-passed down in my family," she said quickly.

"And I remember you saying that your grandfather was one of the original owners of the Chandelier House, isn't that right?"

She inclined her head. "You have a good memory." *Dammit.*

He stepped closer, then pinned her down with his gaze. "Cindy, *did* that earring come from the chandelier hanging in the lobby?"

"Eric," she said, laughing softly, "I'm not an expert on chandeliers."

"No," he said quietly. "But my father happens to be."

She swallowed. "Your father?"

"He's a retired master glassblower. I sent him a picture of the chandelier. According to his research, if it's an original French *A Merveille,* it's worth a fortune."

"I can't recall what the chandelier is worth," she said, her voice sounding high-pitched even to her own ears. "But I'll make sure someone in accounting gets that information to you."

"I checked the books," he said calmly, "and I don't

think they're right. Cindy," he said, stepping even closer and leaning forward, "I'm giving you one more chance to tell me everything you know about that chandelier. If you don't, I'm going to call Harmon, tell them my suspicions, and suggest the piece be appraised."

She evaluated her options—including jumping—but none of them seemed viable. Finally she angled her head at him. "And how do I know you won't call Harmon anyway?"

His mouth tightened. "You don't."

She sighed and turned back to the view. Eric joined her, resting folded arms on top of the concrete wall. Wetting her lips, Cindy said, "My grandfather loved this hotel. He said the chandelier symbolized the greatness, the uniqueness of the place. While he was still part owner, he had the center piece removed from the chandelier and commissioned these earrings for my grandmother. I inherited them, along with the wonderful story about the three original chandeliers being sold for the war effort and replaced with glass copies."

With a soft laugh, she said, "I honestly didn't suspect the one in this hotel might be one of the originals until after Harmon bought the Chandelier House."

"What made you suspect it wasn't a copy?"

"I had a chance to visit the hotel in Chicago where one of the other two *A Merveille* originals once hung. That chandelier had an extra central spiral that our chandelier doesn't. Out of curiosity, I made the trip to Hollywood and the copy there also has the center piece."

He shrugged. "So maybe the center piece was removed from your copy to make it look like the original."

She smiled, her lips dry and tight. "My thoughts exactly—until I poked around in my grandfather's personal journals. At the last minute, instead of donating the chandelier, he made a hefty cash donation to the war effort, an amount that exceeded the value of the original chandelier at the time. The copy was hustled away on the black market, and no one was the wiser.''

He shook his head slowly. ''That's an amazing story.''

''And sad,'' she noted. ''That cash donation drained my grandfather's resources and he ended up selling his interest in the hotel, even though he continued to love the place. He wrote that it was his secret, knowing the magnificent chandelier reigned over the place in his absence.''

''And why didn't you notify someone?''

''Because I knew Harmon would probably sell it to the highest bidder and replace it with a cheap copy, if they replaced it at all. And our talk the other day at breakfast only reinforced my resolve to keep quiet.''

''Cindy,'' he said quietly. ''That piece should be in a museum.''

She frowned, turning to face him. ''It belongs here.''

Eric shook his head. ''It's not right, Cindy. Harmon owns that chandelier and they should be told how much it's worth.''

She stared at him. ''And you're going to tell them?''

He sighed and held up his hand. ''I didn't say that—I need to think things through.''

''I'm trusting you.'' To her horror, her eyes filled with tears. ''I'm trusting you to look past the capital gain and do the right thing, Eric.'' She looked up at him, hoping for reassurance, but saw only indecisiveness in his expression.

Cindy turned and gripped the top of the cold concrete wall. She hated needing something from him…hated feeling so vulnerable…hated thinking she could be responsible for over two hundred employees losing their jobs. ''It's my fault,'' she whispered. ''I brought all this trouble on the hotel. I should have conformed to the corporate mandates. Now we'll be sold or closed and the chandelier will be lost, too." Cindy brought her hand to her mouth to stem a humiliating sob.

"Hey," he said softly, turning her to face him. She inhaled deeply to regain her composure, loath to meet his gaze. "Cindy, don't take this review personally—you did what you thought was best for your employees. It won't be your fault if Harmon decides to divest the Chandelier House."

She looked into his eyes, aware of the warmth of his hands on her arms, even through the fabric of his coat. "You mean if *you* decide, Eric?"

He faltered, then nodded curtly. "It's strictly business, Cindy."

"How can you do this?" she asked, searching his face. "Don't you care that a few words from your mouth can change the lives of so many innocent people?"

His head dipped until their eyes were level. "We both have a job to do. We can't let emotion interfere."

She looked into his eyes, frustrated that with everything on the line, he could still have such a physical impact on her. His mouth mesmerized her, too vividly bringing back the memory of his lips on her body. Let emotion interfere? He taunted her. She lifted her chin. "That's not the way I operate, Mr. Stanton. The Chandelier House is more than an entry on a profit-and-loss statement. If I could afford to, I'd buy this place myself."

His expression softened and he lifted one hand to smooth her unbound hair back from her cheek. "And if I could afford to, I'd buy this place for you." As if in slow motion, Eric pulled her to him and wrapped his arms around her, tucking her head beneath his chin. Enclosed in his warm coat and strong embrace, Cindy closed her eyes and relaxed against him. Gradually, the comforting hug gained momentum. Eric ran his hands up and down her back and she folded her arms around his waist, delaying the moment she'd have to release him.

Eric drew back slightly, cupped her chin in his hand and lifted her mouth to meet his. She inhaled deeply just before their lips touched, because she wanted the kiss to last a long time—through the night, past the review and into the new year. His mouth moved on hers with an aching sweetness. He flicked his tongue against her teeth and gave her his own breath when she needed air. Her knees buckled and she fell against him, moaning and straining for his touch.

Eric moved his mouth to her neck, nipping at the sensitive curve until waves of desire set every nerve ending on edge. His hands moved inside the jacket, cradling her hips with one large hand, supporting her back with the other. Effortlessly he lifted her against him, sliding her down oh-so-slowly over his chest, his stomach, his swollen arousal.

"Cindy," he whispered. "You make me want to do crazy things, like make love to you right here."

"We shouldn't," she murmured, more for herself than him. Yet she felt herself succumb to the titillating temptation of making love with him under the stars, with the wind whipping over their bodies. She massaged his erection through his slacks, eliciting a frustrated groan from Eric.

He pulled up her dress and slid his hands inside her panties, grasping her bottom and rubbing her against him. Teasing her nest from behind, his fingers urged her to open and give him better access. With a sigh she leaned into him, gasping when he inserted his fingers into her wet folds. The angle of his probing drove her wild and within seconds, they adopted a rhythm, him thrusting, her sliding back to meet his hand. The cool air on her exposed skin, and the sounds of his encouraging whispers billowed her higher and higher, until she trembled around his fingers in a shuddering pinnacle.

He showered her face and neck with kisses, caressing her body with both hands, murmuring her name. Wanting to pleasure him and since her legs were still weak from her own release, Cindy lowered herself to her knees and unfastened Eric's belt. With his help, his monster erection was soon freed. A little intimidated by the size of his shaft, she trailed kisses and licks up and down before tentatively taking the tip into her mouth.

Eric plowed his fingers into her hair and threw his head back as a long moan escaped from his lips. She advanced carefully, taking him into her mouth with utmost care, grasping the base with her hands and falling into a slow tempo of massage. He could have been in agony or ecstasy from the sounds of his groans, but he let her set the pace. She stroked and devoured him while the wind whisked between them. At last he gasped her name, warning her of his impending flood, giving her time to retreat if she desired.

Suddenly a floodlight lit the sky, illuminating Eric's head and shoulders above the concrete wall. He jerked around. "What the—?"

Cindy froze, then dragged herself to her feet, struggling to rearrange her clothing. Eric did the same, under considerably more duress. She glanced over the edge straight into a beacon of blinding light.

"Stop!" the head of hotel security bellowed through a bullhorn. A crowd of several dozen had gathered on the sidewalk. "For God's sake, don't jump! The police are on their way!"

"What the devil is going on?" Eric growled.

She stared down at the street. "I think *he* thinks there's someone up here going to jump."

"Believe me," he said, running a hand through his hair, "I'm tempted to jump, just to wring that idiot's neck!"

"Pete!" she yelled down through cupped hands. "Nobody's going to jump!"

"Cindy? Is that you?"

"Yeah, Pete, it's me."

"What happened to your hair?"

She looked for a brick to drop, but seeing none, yelled, "Call the police and tell them it was a mistake. I'll be right down."

"Okay." He sounded dejected.

The light was extinguished, plunging them back into semidarkness. "I have to go," she said, the impact of her lapse suddenly dawning. "Or else someone will come for me."

"Hey," he said quietly, pulling her close for a quick kiss, "I was about two seconds away from coming for you."

But the tawdry way she'd behaved shamed her. Her hands started trembling. They'd groped like frenzied animals, with no emotional involvement—at least not on his part. With a sinking feeling, Cindy realized that somewhere between "What's wrong with long, straight hair?" and "I was about two seconds away from coming for you", she'd fallen for Eric Quinn Stanton.

"I have to go," she said forcefully, breaking his embrace and shrugging out of his coat.

A frown marred his smooth forehead. "What's wrong?"

"Nothing," she said coolly, feeling like the world's biggest fool. "Like you said, we both have a job to do." She turned and strode toward the door, mortified by her heart's revelation in light of all that had transpired.

What was it Manny had said? *Falling in love will be an agonizing event with a man who represents everything you hate.*

Manny…right again, dammit.

MANNY LOOKED in the plastic bag she held open, then gaped at her. "You threw the pajamas off the top of the building?"

She shrugged. "How was I to know they'd snag on someone's window? Security thought there was a man on top of the building getting ready to jump."

"Little did they know there was a man on top of the building who was *being* jumped."

"Hardee-har-har."

"Where did you get these?"

"I filched them from security—it took me four days of sneaking around to find them."

He looked at her as if she was insane. "Okaaaaaaay. I'm almost afraid to ask where you're headed now."

"To the furnace room," she declared. "I'm going to burn these things so they can't get me into any more trouble." Her stomach rolled with queasy fear. "Stanton said he'd give me a preview of the final report this afternoon at four. And although it doesn't seem likely that I'll have yet another catastrophe before he leaves, I'm trying to limit the possibilities."

"At least the tree is taken care of."

"Right. What could be more harmless than plain old candy canes?" She checked her watch. "Got to run—I'm due at the salon."

Manny clucked. "What else could you possibly have done to your hair?"

"I'm getting it fixed this time. New stylist."

He shook his head. "You never learn, do you? Besides, I've heard a lot of people say they think the color is cool."

Cindy nodded. "Complete strangers have stopped me to ask about my hair, but I just don't think I can live with it."

"You or your mother?"

"Both."

He fidgeted. "Cindy, are you nervous about the report?"

"Sure," she admitted shakily, "but I'm trying not to worry about it." Trying not to worry about losing her job, or the chandelier being sold, or the entire hotel being auctioned off, or being in love with Eric, or why bubbles form in leftover glasses of water.

Manny patted her hand. "You're doing a bang-up job here and if Stanton and his people can't see it, they're blind."

"Thanks."

"And I hate that man for putting you through the wringer."

She gave him a careful little smile. "Don't blame Eric, Manny. Everything I'm going through, I brought on myself." And to her mortification, her eyes filled with tears.

He brought his hand to his head in a helpless gesture. "Oh, God, you're in love with him, aren't you?."

She nodded, wiping her eyes. "A fact I am not proud of," she added. "But don't worry, I'll be over him by New Year's." She tried to laugh it off. "Besides, I may have a change of heart when I hear his report this afternoon."

"He's a fool if he doesn't realize how lucky he is."

She sniffed and gave him a grateful squeeze. "Thanks. I'm glad you're going home with me for Christmas."

"Me too. Speaking of which, I have to run a couple of errands early tomorrow, so I'll meet you at the departure gate."

Falling in love with Eric Stanton—how stupid could she be? she thought morosely as she tramped downstairs to the furnace room. A corporate hack with no real ties to his family, and no appreciation for the things in life that were really important, like preserving the integrity of the Chandelier House.

Using a mitt, she opened the door of an aged furnace and stuffed the pants into a bed of coals, gratified when they caught instantly and began to burn. She watched the tiny white monogram of EQS fold in on itself, then disintegrate. Then she made herself a note to turn in a security report for Eric's missing pants, just in case he checked her paperwork.

At the salon, Cindy did a double-take at the line of men, women and teenagers waiting to get in. "There she is," yelled one. "That's the exact color I want!"

Confused, Cindy walked in to find Matilda furiously working on clients in three separate chairs. "You're a hit," she told the woman, amazed at the crowd.

"No, you're the hit," the hairdresser said. "Most of these people are here for exotic coloring jobs because they saw your hair."

She touched her purplish tresses. "Really?"

"Yep. We could make a fortune specializing in coloring, head shaving and stuff like that."

With their clientele, Cindy couldn't believe they hadn't thought of it before. She grinned. "That sounds terrific."

"Great. Oh, Jerry is waiting for you in the back."

"Thanks." Cindy wound her way to the back where Jerry had staked out a small sink. "I owe you big for this," she said, sitting down.

He snapped the cape, then draped it around her shoulders. "It's my Christmas present to you," he said with a smile, then raised an eyebrow. "Even if you have been naughty."

She frowned. "Don't believe everything you hear."

He leaned down, his gaze boring into hers in the mirror. "And what if it's something I see with my own eyes?"

Glancing away from his knowing expression, she said, "I have no idea what you're talking about."

He shrugged. ''You make a good couple, you and the Stanton lad.''

She shook her head, but recognized the futility of arguing. ''Jerry, did you have any idea that Quinn was Stanton?''

He nodded. ''I knew that day in the salon when you first cut your hair.''

''He told you?''

''Nope—I just knew.''

She sighed. How like Jerry to sit back and watch people just to see what unfolded. She shot him a lethal look, but he simply spun her away from the mirror and picked up a pair of shears, chuckling beneath his breath.

12

ERIC SCANNED THE REPORTS each of his review team members had provided on every aspect of running the hotel from linen inventory to customer service to leaving Sweet Tarts on the pillows. The phrase "unconventional, but effective" appeared over and over. In all, his associates had confirmed his conclusion that the Chandelier House was a finely tuned nuthouse with a profit margin Harmon could only dream about for some of their "pet" properties.

Unfortunately, the Chandelier House didn't score well on Harmon's predetermined checklist for the corporate direction. So, although he'd composed several pages about the viability of the property, the crux of his recommendation had to answer one question: Did the Chandelier House meet the profile of a future Harmon property?

Eric tossed down his pen and crossed his arms. The answer was obvious to the point of hilarity, but Cindy's pleading green eyes kept getting in the way. In a weak moment, he considered the scenario of recommending that Harmon keep the property—his reputation would be compromised, they would think twice before retaining him again and they would likely go against his recommendation in any case. And even if Harmon did keep the hotel, they'd forever be pressuring Cindy and her staff to conform—or more likely, replace her with a more corporate-minded general manager.

He stroked his chin, frustrated because never before had he labored over the delivery of such a logical directive. The words he'd spoken to Cindy on the roof kept haunting him.

If I could afford to, I'd buy this place for you. He couldn't afford to, but he had the contacts to assemble investors who could, and possibly the clout with Harmon to convince them to sell the property intact instead of piece by piece. Resigned but considerably cheered, he typed up the report on his laptop. At least he'd be able to walk away from this assignment knowing he'd treated all parties fairly.

Fairly? What a joke. He'd bent over backward...for the sake of Cindy Warren.

But could he walk away? Definitely. He had no business diddling with the comely woman—if he needed proof, he had to look no further than the disconcerting report he'd just prepared. His team had left this morning, and tomorrow was Christmas Eve. He'd decided to fly to Atlanta and spend a few days looking for a condo. The Southeast was pleasant this time of year, and New Year's in Atlanta was hard to beat.

And he was bound to find some Southern belle who could take his mind off Cindy Warren. She'd spent the night with him, then ignored him for days, then spilled the beans about the chandelier and begged him to keep a million-dollar secret. Then the next thing he knew, they were both half-naked on the roof and howling at the moon. Had she participated only out of hope he'd keep quiet about the chandelier? And after they'd been interrupted, she'd decided to play hard to get again. To keep him on a chain? Hot, then cold, then hot and cold again. Was that her game? If so, then...then...

Then it seemed to be working.

Gritting his teeth, he typed in a half page of text about the chandelier, then changed his mind and deleted it. Eric cursed and slumped back in his chair. He'd vowed never to let a woman get in the way of doing a good job, and he never had—until now. Falling for Cindy had scrambled his brain.

He jerked his head up. Falling?

Eric pounded his hand on the desk, then attacked the keyboard again, typing furiously. After a few minutes, he absently patted his pocket for his cigarettes, then remembered he couldn't smoke in his room. Begrudgingly, he grabbed a package of Sweet Tarts and popped a couple, then resumed typing.

Falling for an eccentric, soft-hearted, nostalgic, crazy-haired woman who would have him in knots every day of his life? He hit the caps button, then typed N-O W-A-Y.

MANNY SQUINTED, tilting his head from side to side. "Your hair really looks wonderful. You should have cut it sooner."

Cindy lifted a hand to her short, wavy, blessedly dark brown locks, then punched him in the arm. "Now you tell me!" She was happy to spend a few minutes clowning with her best friend—especially now, when her stomach churned over the impending meeting with Eric. Laughably, she was more nervous about facing Eric Stanton the man than Eric Stanton the hotel mutilator.

Fifteen minutes before the appointed time she headed up to the boardroom, wanting to appear calm and collected when Eric arrived—for once. She turned on the lights and made herself a cup of hot tea, then assumed the authority seat at the end of the table, facing the door. She gulped her tea, trying to drown the butterflies in her stomach, but only managed to dribble on her best white blouse. She swore, then buttoned her jacket. For five minutes she practiced her busy, on-the-edge-of-her-seat pose for when he came in, and her jaunty-hair-toss-and-ease-back-in-the-chair-confidently maneuver for when he sat down. Then she raised her seat four inches and lowered the one to her right by four inches to give herself a feeling of superiority.

At the sound of approaching footsteps, she quickly assumed the pose, scrutinizing a memo she'd memorized. A light rap resonated through the room. She glanced up and, ignoring the catch of her heart at the sight of him, she waved Eric in, then immediately looked back to the memo and jotted a note in the margin.

"Do you need more time?" he asked, lowering himself, to her consternation, into the chair to her left instead of her right.

"Um…no," she said after an appropriately occupied pause. She closed the folder and set down her pen, then carefully tossed her hair and slid back in the chair. Except the chair tilt didn't lock. A leisurely split second passed during which Cindy experienced that sick feeling of knowing she was going over backward. Her eyes bugged and her arms flailed as she fought desperately to regain her balance, but to no avail. Eric lunged for her, but he couldn't move fast enough to keep her chair from slamming against the floor.

Her head bounced twice, but the rest of her seemed to be okay, thanks to the death grip she'd maintained on the arms. She sat in the chair perfectly aligned, apart from the fact that she was looking at the ceiling.

Eric's face appeared over her, tight with concern. "Are you okay?"

"I'm fine."

An amused smile broke over his face as he helped her up. Burning with humiliation, she leaned against the table and gingerly touched her forehead. She felt light-headed, but then again, she *was* down a few pounds of purple hair.

"No wonder it tipped over," he said, inspecting the chair. "Someone raised it too high and threw off the center of gravity." He pushed her power chair aside and replaced it with the one she'd lowered. "Try this one."

She cursed silently, but her head hurt so much, she

dropped into the proffered seat, not caring when she sank so low his knees were at her eye level.

Eric knelt and peered into her face. "Are you sure you're all right? Can I get you a glass of water?"

"No, thanks," she mumbled. With her luck she'd probably drown herself. Cindy caught the fragrance of his strong soap, and she noticed he'd nicked his square chin while shaving. She wanted him. She loved him. She despised him. "Let's just get this over with."

He studied her face, his eyes guarded, then he nodded abruptly and reclaimed his seat. She looked up at him from her dwarfed position, her heart thudding. Eric opened a leather portfolio and read aloud. "This document serves as the official report from Stanton and Associates concerning Harmon Hospitality property number eighty-five, the Chandelier House, located at—" He stopped and pursed his mouth, closed the portfolio, then slid it toward her. "You can read it at your leisure, Cindy. I'll hit the highlights."

From his close body language and hesitancy she didn't have to guess the contents. "Go on."

He pressed his lips together, then said, "My final report contains a recommendation that Harmon sell the Chandelier House. I'm sorry. Professionally, I had no choice."

She sat immobile, struck by a profound sense of sadness. Aside from the fact that her beloved hotel would likely be quartered and auctioned, Eric simply didn't get it. Some things were worth more in sum than the total of their parts, market price be damned.

He pointed to the portfolio. "Overall, the review team found this property to be well-run. The hotel's worst distinction is being purchased by Harmon in the first place. It's all in my report if you care to read it."

Cindy swallowed carefully. "Perhaps later."

Eric folded his hands and leaned forward. "In case

you're wondering, I didn't disclose the alleged history of the chandelier.''

She smiled tightly. ''But when the hotel is put up for sale, unlike when Harmon stole the place two years ago from a group of granny investors, every last spoon will be appraised.''

He conceded her point with a nod. ''I decided the only way I could make an objective business evaluation was to proceed as if you hadn't told me.''

''But I did,'' she said slowly. ''I *did* tell you the story of the chandelier, so it *should* have influenced your decision. The history of this hotel should be preserved, especially when you consider that the Chandelier House is well into the black.''

''For now.''

''What's that supposed to mean?''

''That in five years role-playing groups and vampires and tattoos might be out of vogue.''

''So? Other special-interest groups will emerge.''

He threw up his hands. ''The long-term customers Harmon needs to cultivate are large and midsize corporate—''

''You made your point, Mr. Stanton.'' Cindy fought to maintain her composure. ''This meeting is over.'' She spun around in her low chair, turning her back to him and biting back tears of disappointment.

She heard him push away from the table and walk across the room. A few seconds of silence passed and she thought he must have left quietly. Then he spoke from the doorway. ''Cindy.''

She looked at him over her shoulder. ''Yes?''

''I'm sorry if I ruined your Christmas.''

Egotistical S.O.B.—at least he'd be easy to get over. ''Mr. Stanton, you don't have that much power in my life.''

From the squaring of his jaw, she knew she'd scored a

point. "Then let me say it was very nice, um, working with you, despite the misunderstandings."

She blinked.

"And just one more thing," he said.

She waited.

"Your hair looks nice." Then he walked out.

Cindy laid her aching head back on the chair and wished for the hundredth time that she'd never heard of Eric Quinn Stanton.

Her beeper sounded. Massaging the knot on the back of her head, she punched a button on the handheld radio. "Cindy here."

"It's Manny. Can you stand one more Christmas tree crisis?"

A groan started deep in her chest and eased out. "How could five thousand candy canes possibly be hazardous?"

"If hordes of street people are shaking the tree to knock down the candy."

"I'll be right there."

ON THE WAY TO SAMMY'S for a stiff drink, Eric heard a commotion in the lobby and investigated the noise. The sky rained candy canes. Teams of shabbily dressed people were grabbing up the candy and stuffing it in bags, hats and pockets. The limbs within reaching distance were picked clean. Four large men hugged the trunk of the tree, taking turns shaking it to dislodge the stubborn hangers-on.

Eric shrank to a secluded corner to watch. As expected, the newly shorn general manager arrived on the scene in record time, dismantled the tree-shaking team, and ordered maintenance to erect scaffolding—again. The remaining candy was to be removed and placed in a bin just inside the entrance, free for the taking.

She'd done it again, he acknowledged. Danced into a crisis and handled it beautifully, dousing tempers and making everyone happy. As he watched her, Eric once again experienced the swelling in his chest he'd begun to associate with seeing and thinking about Cindy Warren. She was a delightful woman—witty, charming, beautiful and honest. Her employees loved her.

And he loved her.

With a jolt, Eric admitted he had indeed fallen for the wrong woman at the wrong time. Some of her most irresistible qualities—eccentricity, aplomb and chutzpah—were the very ones he knew would eventually drive him stark raving mad. He needed order in his life. He liked being surrounded by practical, predictable people.

Which was why he and his father couldn't get along, he supposed. His father was unconventional. He preferred the process of making music and art to owning it. If his father had a choice, he would rather have been the creator of the chandelier than the heir to its value. That philosophy had been behind the hurtful things he'd said when Eric had purchased the piano so many years ago.

Eric watched as Cindy surveyed the workers and, apparently satisfied that her instructions were under way, slowly climbed the sweeping staircase. Dressed in her standard green uniform she seemed unremarkable, but he knew better. He knew that beneath the sensible skirt lay a pool of desire he craved more than he could ever have imagined. And what about the heart that beat beneath the buttoned-up jacket? Did she have any feelings for him other than malice? It was just as well, he decided, that their jobs had hindered their physical involvement before emotional barnacles started forming.

She stopped at the top of the stairs and wrapped her hands around the railing. Then she simply stared at the magnificent chandelier. Eric wondered what could be going through her mind—was she thinking of her grandfather? Of all the employees and guests who had walked through those double doors? She waved as the maintenance men carried away sections of the impromptu scaffolding. The street people and a few guests lined up to take candy canes from the bin set near the entrance. The tree, tall and naked and completely abandoned, flanked the staircase, swaying slightly.

Swaying?

Eric emerged from his hiding place, his steps quickening. He glanced up and saw the expression on Cindy's face. She, too, suspected something was wrong. ''The tree is falling!'' she screamed, shooing stragglers with animated gestures. ''Get out of the way, the tree is falling!''

He pulled back a few spectators, then watched in stunned amazement as the tree leaned, then gained slow momentum on its way down. The top branches grazed the chandelier, sending it rocking violently. Eric dragged his gaze from the scene to look for Cindy. She stood on the landing, her hand over her mouth, her eyes riveted on the swinging chandelier.

The gigantic tree landed with a fantastic whoosh, sprawling across the lobby in a spray of needles. Remarkably, no one had been in its path. But Eric knew spraying crystal would not be so kind. ''Everybody down!'' he yelled. And sure enough, with a sickening twist of metal, the magnificent fixture spun loose and fell on top of the tree, splintering into thousands of pieces.

13

CINDY OPENED HER EYES, practically swollen shut after a night of endless crying. It was Christmas Eve morning, and she'd never felt so miserable in her entire life.

She'd thought the meeting with Eric would be the lowlight of the day, but the falling Christmas tree and the crashing chandelier had outdone that horrible meeting. Luckily the tree broke the fixture's fall, but she wasn't sure how or if the chandelier would ever be completely restored. For the time being, the remnants had been carefully gathered and stored in countless boxes.

Eric was one of many who had helped with the cleanup last night, but she'd been careful to stay as far away from him as politely possible. If her overwhelming grief for the shattered chandelier had an upside, it was the fact that it numbed her to the biting sadness of knowing Eric was not the man she'd thought him to be—the kind of man who could love her, eccentricities and all, the kind of man who wanted to build and preserve people and places and things, not tear them down in the name of corporate cloning.

She dragged herself to the edge of her bed, her head spinning with the events of the last several days. Her life had gone from upbeat and fairly stable to downtrodden and perhaps *living* in a stable if she lost her job. And her heart...well, maybe she'd get a new one for Christmas. An unbreakable one.

On impulse, she picked up the phone and dialed her parents' number.

"Hello, Mom? Merry Christmas—hmm? No, we'll be there in a few—what? I've got a bit of a cold—no, I don't have a fever—Mom, I need some advice…Mom, are you there? Good, well, remember the man from Manassas? Right, with a Q. Well, actually, it's an S…''

ERIC STRODE into the health club and absently climbed on a vacant treadmill, surprised when he realized that Manny Oliver was running on the neighboring machine.

The blond man had a muscular build, tall and lean. Sweating profusely, he nodded curtly at Eric, then checked the display monitor and slowed down.

"Getting in your workout early," Eric observed.

"Got a plane to catch in a couple of hours," Manny explained, his tone not overly friendly.

"Going home for Christmas?"

"Yeah," the man said, "with Cindy."

Eric balked—so she *was* having a relationship with her concierge? The realization shocked him because she didn't seem the type to…not that it was any of his business. He'd been battling guilt all morning over not seeing his family for Christmas. Now his heart squeezed painfully as he imagined Manny and Cindy sharing a good old-fashioned holiday. He increased the speed of the machine to a brisk jog as intense jealousy pulsed through him. "I hope the two of you have a nice Christmas together," he managed to say.

Manny's eyes never left his own display. "Well, Mr. Stanton, I'd say you sort of nixed that now, didn't you?"

Eric didn't miss the thinly veiled hostility. "Look, I didn't realize you and Cindy were involved."

Slowing to a walk, Manny shook his head, smiling ruefully. "Cindy and I aren't involved, Stanton."

Eric's heart lifted, surprising him. Then remembering the man's comment about him ruining their Christmas, realization dawned. "I guess Cindy told you about my recommendation to sell the Chandelier House. I'm sorry, but that's my—hey!" Manny pushed him from the machine with one strong shove. "What the hell are you doing?" Eric thundered.

The blond man's face was a mask of calm disgust. "Cindy told me everything in the final report was positive, you jerk. Sounds like she was trying to spare me." He scoffed. "You're a chickenshit, Stanton. You don't deserve her, and she doesn't deserve what you've put her through, professionally *and* personally. Excuse me, sir, but I'd better leave before I pop you in the mouth and lose my job."

Dumbfounded, Eric watched the man walk away, wiping the sweat from his wide shoulders. A slow revelation crept over him, shaming him. Manny was right. He *was* afraid to reach out to the people in his life he cared about—Cindy…his father.

His mind spun with scenarios. Harmon would collect insurance money for the booked value of the chandelier. Even restored, the piece would never be as valuable as before, except to Cindy. A smile crept up Eric's face. He just happened to know a bored glass expert who might be willing to tackle the painstaking process of rebuilding the precious antique. Perhaps the project would also give him and his father the time to repair their own bruised relationship.

But first, he had to talk to Cindy and tell her how he felt. Desperate times called for desperate measures. "Oliver!" Eric called. "Wait up."

The concierge stopped, his towel draped around his neck. "Stanton, I really don't want any trouble."

Eric ignored him, rushing to explain what he had in mind.

Manny shook his head and started to walk off. "That's crazy, man."

"I know it's crazy," Eric said, following him and throwing his hands in the air. "But our entire relationship has been crazy." He pushed his hand through his hair. "This ordeal has thrown me for a loop." He knew he was rambling, but he couldn't stop. "I mean, when you think about it, it's pure happenstance that our paths even crossed."

Manny stared at him. "Happenstance?"

A flush climbed his neck. "You know—luck, serendipity."

"I know what it means, it's just that—never mind." Manny sighed. "If this backfires, Cindy's going to kick both our asses."

CINDY CHECKED HER WATCH, scanning the crowd for Manny. He'd promised he wouldn't be late, but where was he?

"Last boarding call," the gate attendant announced.

Unbidden tears welled in her eyes when she realized that on top of everything else, she'd miss spending Christmas with someone she really cared about. She picked up her carry-on bag and shuffled toward the gate, looking over her shoulder one last time. No Manny in sight.

As she sidled down the crowded aisle, she steeled herself to hold her tears until she at least found her seat. Then she'd have several hours to purge before arriving home. She had to admit she was anxious to see her mother. Their phone call this morning had been such a turning point in their relationship. Her mother had actually listened and sympathized, woman to woman.

The seat next to her sat vacant, dashing her hopes that she'd somehow missed Manny in the crowd. Cindy stowed her bag, then dropped into her seat, exhausted.

"Hi."

Cindy rolled her eyes upward, then froze. "Eric?"

Devastating in dark slacks, red sweater and a sport coat, he smiled, looking...tentative?

She straightened in her seat. "What are you doing here?"

He stretched overhead to stow the familiar black leather toiletry bag. "I bought the seat next to you."

Her heart squeezed. "Manny sold you his seat?"

"Yeah," he said, lowering himself into the vacant spot. "Well, maybe traded is a better word." His mouth stretched into a wry smile. "He's on his way to Atlanta."

She nodded slowly. "He used to live there and still has friends in the city." Still, she was hurt that he hadn't informed her of his change in plans. She took a deep breath, wondering how she'd get through the next few hours. Determined to make the best of the situation, she smiled. "I guess this means you talked to your father."

"As a matter of fact," he said cheerfully, "I did. Things are going to be much better between us, I think."

"That's great," she said, and meant it.

The intercom beeped and the captain informed the cabin that due to heavy runway traffic, their takeoff would be delayed for forty-five minutes. A series of groans rose from the passengers, including Cindy. The flight couldn't be over soon enough.

"Well, perhaps that will give us time to talk," Eric said.

Cindy cut her eyes over to him. "Talk?"

From the pocket of his coat, he withdrew a small package wrapped in silver metallic paper and red string ribbon. "This is for you."

She gaped, her heart pumping. "For me? Why?"

"Open it," he urged.

With trembling hands, she uncovered a slim box imprinted with the name of the finest jeweler in the city. She raised wary eyes to Eric, but he nodded for her to lift the lid.

She did and gasped. Two perfect diamond teardrop earrings lay against the black velvet, winking back at her in breathtaking splendor. "Oh, my goodness," she exclaimed, swallowing hard. She traced the outline of one with a trembling finger, then turned to him, shaking her head. "Eric, I can't accept these."

"But I ruined your other pair."

"That was an accident."

"Okay, then I love you."

"And besides, these are much too expensive—" Cindy stopped and wet her lips. "You what?"

"I love you," he whispered. "I talked Manny into trading tickets so I could spend Christmas with you. And you wouldn't believe the strings I had to pull to do it." He leaned toward her and captured her lips in a sweet kiss, but Cindy, too stunned to respond, sat stone-still. He pulled back, his expression clouded with disappointment. "I messed up, didn't I? I'd hoped you had feelings for me, too." He laughed softly. "Other than animosity." He sighed and fell back in his seat. "Manny warned me you'd whip us both for this stunt."

Her body stung with jumping sensations—happiness, fear, confusion. "Eric," she said carefully, closing the lid of the box. "I am in love with you." At the hopeful look in his eyes, she added, "But it takes more than love to make a relationship last. Basic values, similar goals, family ties." She smiled tentatively. "Remember, I'm going to be out of a job soon."

Eric grasped her hand and proceeded to tell her of his hopes for buying the hotel. Cindy listened with dawning joy, her heart soaring. "And I can't think of a better person to run the whole show," he said with a smile. Then he added, "as long as you don't fraternize with the male guests."

He claimed another kiss and Cindy warmed to him, moving closer, re-familiarizing herself with his taste. When the kiss ended, she frowned slightly. "You give me a pair of unbelievable diamond earrings and I'm supposed to fall into your arms?''

His eyes crinkled with merriment. ''Is it working?''

''Absolutely.''

He studied her face, smiling at her short halo of dark hair. ''I think I fell in love with you the moment that woman cut your hair.''

She leaned on the armrest, propping up her chin with her hand. ''Then I guess it's a good thing I didn't take your advice. Are you ready to meet my family?''

''Yes. Are you ready to meet mine?''

She bit her bottom lip. ''I think so. Do you think your dad will like me?''

''The woman who got me playing the piano again? I'd say that's a safe bet.''

Reeling from sheer bliss, Cindy sat back in her seat. Within a few hours, the most miserable Christmas Eve of her life had turned into the happiest.

Eric reached into his pocket and withdrew a slightly crumpled sheet of paper.

''What's that?''

''When I checked out, the reservations clerk gave me a copy of the security report on my 'switched' pajama pants.''

Her pulse kicked up slightly at the mere mention of the problem pants.

He pressed his lips together, almost smiling. ''Cindy, this report has your signature on it.''

''That's because I filed it.''

''Really?'' He leaned forward. ''How did you know the color of the pants?''

She almost panicked, then relaxed and swallowed. ''W-well, I remembered seeing them hanging behind your toiletry kit when you offered a bandage for my hand.''

He nodded and glanced back to the sheet. ''And this note

about the monogramming on the pocket, how did you know that?''

She meant to laugh softly, but it came out sounding somewhat tinny. ''Don't you remember? You told me and Manny at the Christmas party that your initials were on the pocket.''

His forehead wrinkled slightly. ''Funny, but I don't remember mentioning the specific letters.''

She manufactured an animated shrug and gave him a thousand-watt smile. ''I assumed the monogram was your full name, EQS.''

''Really?'' he asked, his eyebrows high.

''Uh-huh.'' She nodded uncontrollably.

''And how did you know the monogram was—'' he referred to the report '' ''—straight across the pocket edge'?''

Perspiration moistened her upper lip. ''Um, a lucky guess?''

''Ah.'' He folded the sheet of paper and stuffed it inside his jacket pocket. ''Just one more thing, my dear,'' Eric said, tipping up her chin with his finger. ''How is it that you happened to know the *color* of the monogrammed letters?''

She bit her lip, her mind racing. Then she smiled and leaned forward, running her finger down Eric's nose seductively. ''I have an idea,'' she said. ''Why don't we go to the lavatory and finish what we started on the roof the other night?''

He grabbed her finger. ''I think you're trying to change the subject.''

''Is it working?''

''Absolutely.''

Clasping his hand, Cindy jumped up, and trotted toward the bathroom with him in tow. After they jammed themselves into the tiny cubicle, Eric laughed. ''You,'' he said, shaking his head, ''are very naughty.''

But when her lower lip protruded in a pout, he grinned, kissed her hard, then leaned his forehead against hers and whispered, ''Which is what makes loving you so very nice.''

CHRISTMAS FANTASY

Janelle Denison

TEDDY SPENCER'S two good friends, Brenda and Laura, could always be counted on for a good time, especially when it came to marking a special occasion. It was the perfect excuse for them to get wild and crazy, and although Teddy considered herself the more reserved of the trio, after a few mai tai's that feisty, rebellious side of her personality—the one her parents hadn't been able to tame—usually made an appearance.

After spending the past hour and a half at a subdued birthday dinner with her parents at the local country club, and listening once again to her parents' favorite speech lately—that she was getting older and needed to settle down like the rest of her siblings had—Teddy welcomed the opportunity to let loose with her friends. She was on her second mai tai, and thoroughly enjoying herself, even if Brenda had embarrassed her by swiping the deejay's microphone and announcing to everyone in the Frisco Bay Bar that it was Teddy's twenty-sixth birthday. Teddy had thought that fairly obvious by the half-dozen balloons attached to her chair and the I'm-the-birthday-girl pennant Brenda and Laura had insisted she wear, but Brenda had a way of coaxing everyone to join in on the fun.

If that hadn't been embarrassing enough, having fifty pairs of eyes watch her open presents from Brenda and Laura brought a warm flush to her cheeks. The gifts had included an array of skimpy lingerie, not to mention other sensual delights. The single men in the room had issued wolf whistles, and Teddy found herself overwhelmed by invitations to model the silky, provocative underwear.

The bartender delivered the chocolate cake Laura had smuggled to him earlier and, as Brenda lit the single "26" candle, the deejay played "Happy Birthday." Everyone in the lounge chorused the traditional song just for her.

It was all in good fun, and just what Teddy needed to take a break from the stress she was under at work, and make her forget about her parents' quest to diminish the independence she'd worked so hard to gain over the past few years. She knew her mother and father meant well. Unfortunately, their views of what was important to her, and for her, varied drastically from her own.

Determined to enjoy the evening, she pushed aside those troubling thoughts. As the lounge settled back to its normal din, and she was able to relax without being the center of attention, Teddy shook her head at her friends. "You two are outrageous."

As if Teddy had just issued a compliment, a grin brightened Laura's classical features. "Yeah, we are outrageous, aren't we?"

"And damn proud of it, too," Brenda added, her eyes dancing with mischief. "Heck, there's no telling what we might do next."

Teddy lifted an eyebrow at the insinuation in Brenda's voice, but her friend merely feigned innocence. Suspecting something was up, but unable to guess how they could possibly top the evening so far, she glanced at her cake...and frowned at the inscription they'd chosen.

"Happy birthday and congratulations?" She looked from one friend to the other.

Brenda nodded. "We're combining your birthday and your senior graphic design promotion all together."

Teddy smiled, genuinely touched. "That's sweet of you, but I haven't gotten the promotion yet." Whether she did or not wouldn't be decided for another two and a half weeks, just after the new year.

Laura gave Teddy's knee an encouraging pat. "See how much faith we have in you?"

Teddy wished she had that much faith in herself. It wasn't that she wasn't qualified for the job—she'd double majored in graphic design and had a master's degree in business administration, not to mention being an exemplary employee. It was her boss, Louden Avery, who was making her advancement within Sharper Image Advertising so difficult.

"Come on, Teddy." Brenda nudged her with her elbow. "Blow out your candle and make a wish."

Teddy absently toyed with the ruby and diamond band on her left-hand ring finger. It bothered her that she felt forced to wear a ring to discourage Louden's subtle interest in her, and back up the claim that she had a steady boyfriend. But it was the only thing she could think of. Taking a deep breath, she blew out the single flame and hopefully secured her future. Her wish was simple. She wanted that promotion, awarded to her on her own merit.

"Wow," Brenda breathed dreamily. "If I had to make a wish, he would be it."

Teddy followed her friend's line of vision to the entrance of the Frisco Bay, and caught her breath at the sight of a gorgeous hunk making his way through the Tuesday-evening crowd. Every woman in the establishment was staring at him—for two very good reasons. One, his mere presence was captivating, and two, his unusual attire stood out conspicuously against all the power suits filling the trendy bar. He was the epitome of a cowboy, from the beige Stetson on his head, to the pearl-snap western shirt covering a wide chest, to the chaps and worn jeans that molded to trim hips and muscular thighs, all the way down to his scuffed leather boots. He looked as if he'd just stepped out of the Wild West, though he didn't appear to be uncomfortable in the ultra-urban setting, surrounded by a crowd of Ivy League patrons.

He sidled up to a vacant spot in front of the bar and ordered a drink. While he waited for the bartender to return, he scanned the people in the lounge as if searching for someone. Annoyingly enough, the brim of his Stetson cast shadows over the upper portion of his face, but Teddy caught a glimpse of chiseled features, a well-defined mouth and dark brown hair that curled over his collar at the nape of his neck.

He turned his head her way. Even though she couldn't see his eyes because of that damn hat, she got the distinct impression he was looking directly at her. The corner of his mouth kicked up ever so slightly in an I've-got-you-now kind of smile. Her skin warmed and tightened, and something deep within Teddy fluttered with awareness. It was a sensation unlike anything she'd ever experienced.

She forced her gaze from him and drew a stabilizing breath. "Wow is right," she murmured in agreement, and was a little surprised that she'd spoken her thoughts out loud.

Laura issued a reciprocating sound of appreciation and turned to look at Teddy. A sassy grin curved her lips. "What do you think, birthday girl? Would you like to take a ride with that cowboy?"

Laura's question made all kinds of images spring into Teddy's mind. She thought of leather, the scent of hay, the jangling sounds of spurs and the fun she'd have if he'd let her ride... Suddenly, what he stood for had become more erotic than she cared to admit.

"He's kind of out of place, don't you think?" she said nonchalantly, trying to keep her friends, the bloodhounds that they were, at bay. "San Francisco isn't known for its ranches. Maybe he's lost."

"Maybe he's looking for a good time." Brenda wiggled her

eyebrows lasciviously. "I'm sure it gets awfully lonely out on the range."

As casually as possible, Teddy slid her gaze back to the cowboy, hoping he'd moved on to peruse another woman, considering any one of the ladies in the lounge would have killed for a smidgen of his attention. But no, he was still staring at her, and as she watched, he tipped his Stetson, then reached beside him for the glass that the bartender had delivered. He saluted her, and took a long drink of the dark liquid that looked like whiskey.

Her own mouth went dry, and she reached for her mai tai. The cool, sweet-tangy mixture did little to extinguish the heat spreading through her.

"Didn't you once say you wanted a cowboy of your own, Teddy?" Brenda asked.

Teddy was startled that Brenda remembered that crazy night nearly six months ago when they'd sat at this very table and spun fantasies about the men in the lounge—imagining who they could be beneath their Armani suits and executive image. At the time, Teddy had wanted a cowboy, because it bucked convention—or rather her parents' stuffy standards.

"We were just fooling around, and I think I had one too many mai tais." Setting her drink back on the table, Teddy waved a hand in the air. "It was just a fantasy, Brenda."

Laura leaned toward Teddy, a meaningful glimmer in her eyes. "Well, honey, fantasy is about to become reality."

Suspicion twisted through Teddy as her two friends exchanged a covert look. "What are you guys up to?"

"Hey, cowboy," Brenda called out. "We've got a birthday girl over here who has a thing for cowboys. Do you think you could oblige her?"

Teddy's jaw dropped, and her face heated in mortification. Before she could recover from her shock, her fantasy man moved away from the bar and strolled lazily toward them.

"I'll certainly do my best," he drawled in a deep, rich voice that carried across the room and snagged a good amount of attention. The women he passed looked on with envy and longing, not that her cowboy noticed. His gaze was trained on her, and the smile curving his mouth was pure, unadulterated sin.

Closer and closer he came. Teddy's heart tripled its beat, and a mixture of excitement and apprehension warred within her. "Are you nuts?" she whispered to Brenda.

"Naw." Brenda winked at Teddy. "Laura and I wanted to do something special for your birthday. He's all yours, at least for the next twenty minutes."

Teddy blinked. "I don't understand..."

Laura gave her a jaunty grin. "It's all very simple. Just enjoy yourself, and the fantasy."

Teddy wanted a better explanation than that, but there wasn't time to ask. Her fantasy was standing beside her chair. Hesitantly, she glanced his way, and found herself eye level with a pair of sinewy thighs wrapped in soft leather chaps that molded to his lean hips and strong legs, and profiled what made him impressively male. She forced her gaze higher, taking in a body honed to masculine perfection—virile, sexy and scrumptious enough to send her pulse racing.

It was a long climb up—she estimated his height well over six foot—but the trek was extremely enjoyable. By the time she reached her cowboy's face and saw the warm, private smile flirting with the corners of his mouth, she felt breathless.

And then she saw his eyes for the first time. They were a striking green, with gold flecks that mesmerized and seduced. He had ridiculously long, dark lashes, and she had the fleeting thought that his eyes alone could tempt a woman to shed her inhibitions, and anything else he might request.

He touched his long fingers to the brim of his Stetson in a brief caress that had her thinking about those hands of his, and how they'd feel against her skin. It was a maddening, and totally inappropriate, thought, considering she didn't know him at all, but if this was her fantasy, she intended to enjoy it to its fullest.

"Care to dance, darlin'?" he asked, the perfect gentleman.

She melted just a little, and speech suddenly became a difficult task. "I, uh..."

Brenda lifted Teddy's hand toward the cowboy and winked at him. "She'd love to dance, and anything else you might be inspired to do."

"It would be my pleasure," he murmured huskily.

Uneasiness rippled down Teddy's spine, putting her feminine senses on alert. What would be his pleasure? she wondered, feeling as though she was in the middle of a conspiracy.

What were Brenda and Laura up to?

A warm hand clasped hers, pulled her to her feet, and she found herself being led to the dance floor, which was currently vacant. That didn't seem to bother her partner, who gave the deejay a brief nod. As if on cue, the young man put on a slow, country ballad and announced into his microphone, "This one is for you, Teddy."

If that dedication wasn't perplexing enough, the soft, crooning voice drifting from the speakers totally bewildered her. In all the times she'd come to the Frisco Bay in the past two years, not once had she ever heard a country song. The deejay played rock and roll, and on occasion, a slow tune by a popular soft-rock artist. If you wanted country music, you went to the Silver Spur.

The plot was getting thicker and thicker...

Like a man accustomed to taking the lead, her cowboy smoothly pulled her against him, aligning their bodies intimately. One arm slipped around her lower back, keeping her from attempting to put any distance between them, and his other hand held hers loosely to the side. Very hesitantly, because she really had no choice, she lightly rested her free hand on his biceps...nice, strong, muscular biceps.

She kept her gaze averted, focusing on the crowd of on-lookers over his shoulder, while valiantly trying to distract her body's response to the man who held her so provocatively.

It was no use. Through the silk of her blouse and the cotton of his shirt, she experienced the crush of his hard chest against her soft breasts that had suddenly become achingly sensitive. And there was certainly no way she could dismiss the subtle pressure of his belly against hers, or the arousing friction of his leather chaps scraping against her thighs where the hem of her skirt ended. It was like being charged head to toe with an electrical shock.

She'd danced with plenty of men through the years, but none had ever ignited such an instantaneous blaze of heat, or made her so aware of herself as a woman.

It was thrilling, incredibly sexy and unnerving.

As he moved her in a circle on the dance floor, she caught sight of her friends. Brenda grinned and gave her a thumbs-up, and Laura snapped a picture of her and the cowboy.

Cringing at their enthusiasm, she cast a surreptitious glance at the man she was dancing with, only to find him staring at her, his eyes taking on a smoky moss hue. She felt the stroke of his thumb along her spine, the press of his large palm against the small of her back, and shivered. His warm breath fluttered a silky strand of hair near her cheek, and she caught an odd scent. She'd expected to inhale the strong odor of whiskey from his drink. Instead, she encountered the delectable fragrance of root beer, which made something curl deep within her. The man drank root beer, of all things! Briefly, she wondered if he tasted as sweet and warm as he smelled.

Clearing her suddenly dry throat, she pushed the forbidden thoughts aside and forced herself to break the silence between them. "This is, um, incredibly awkward. My friends can be a bit wild, and I'm sure they put you on the spot." She licked her bottom lip nervously. "Dancing with me really isn't necessary."

He blinked lazily, a slow sweep of those gorgeous lashes. "Darlin', I find it hard to refuse a woman's fantasy, especially on her birthday."

She detected an underlying insinuation to his words, but wasn't quite sure what he meant by that cryptic remark. She wasn't quite sure she wanted to know, either. Deciding to make the best of the two minutes left to the song, she introduced herself. "I'm Teddy Spencer."

There was a bit of mischief in his eyes, as if he knew a secret and she didn't. "Austin McBride," he offered. "And it's a pleasure to meet you, Teddy."

There was that word again, *pleasure*. This time, though, the way he rolled it together so seductively with her name caused a flurry of sensations to erupt within her. It tickled her belly and spread out toward her thighs and breasts. Her reaction was crazy, confusing and exhilarating in a very unladylike way.

You're shameless, Teddy, her good-girl consciousness taunted. The wicked, bad-girl part of her was beginning not to care.

She gave him an upswept look, along with a flirtatious smile she hadn't used in what seemed like years. There was an undeniable chemistry between them, though reserved on his part, and it made her feel daring, and a little reckless.

She slid her hand up his arm, until her fingers touched the soft strands of hair lying against the collar of his shirt. She had the sudden urge to take off that Stetson of his so she could see his face. But knowing how inappropriate that would be, she held herself back.

"So, Mr. McBride," she said, surprising herself with the throaty quality of her voice. "Are you really a cowboy?"

"As real as it gets in San Francisco, I suppose." He followed that up with a private, playful wink.

She lifted an eyebrow, intent on finding out more about this mysterious man. "I take it you're not from around here, then?"

He expertly moved her to the slow beat of the music, dancing with her as if they were the only two in the bar. "As a matter of fact, I am."

She regarded him with a combination of curiosity and speculation. "I wasn't aware of any ranches in the area."

The corner of his generous mouth quirked, but he didn't comment. "So, it's your birthday, hmm?" he asked, smoothly changing the subject.

She rolled her eyes. "Trussed up like I am with this silly pennant, it's kind of difficult *not* to know it's my birthday."

He smiled, his eyes shimmering with warmth and a scampish spark. "Well, your friends got you a very special present."

At that moment the song they were swaying to ended, and before she could take in what he'd said, or politely excuse herself from his wonderfully solid body, he maneuvered her four large steps back, until the curve of her knees hit a lounge chair someone had put out on the dance floor. Wide-eyed, she tumbled into the cushioned seat. Startled on more levels than one, she frantically sought out her two friends.

She found them, but quickly realized neither one would be any source of help. Both Brenda and Laura wore goofy grins. Laura lifted her camera, and a bright flash momentarily blinded Teddy, but she had no problem hearing Brenda yell, "Take if off for her, cowboy!"

A flush of mortification burned Teddy's cheeks as she realized she'd been set up. New music blared out of the speakers, an upbeat, rock-a-billy tune that encouraged her cowboy to move his hips in such a provocative fashion, it took her breath away.

Belatedly, she realized his intent and attempted to escape while there was still a chance. "I really don't think—"

He leaned forward and braced his arms on either side of her chair, crowding her between hunter-green tweed and an unyielding wall of masculinity. "No, don't think at all," he agreed in a teasing drawl. "Just sit back, relax and enjoy your fantasy, darlin'." Lifting his hand, he withdrew the beige Stetson from his head and settled it lightly on the crown of hers. "And here's a little something to remember me by."

Oh, God. Backdropped by thick, luxurious, dark brown hair, his eyes seemed greener, sexier, if that were even possible. But her muddled mind only had a handful of seconds to register that fact before he straightened, ending her hypnotic state of fascination.

Then he stepped back, and while his hips moved rhythmically to the beat of the music, he grasped the sides of his western shirt and ripped open the pearl snaps securing the front. Teddy gasped, and the women in the Frisco Bay went wild—of which Brenda and Laura were the loudest and most unrestrained in their cheering. The men in the establishment looked on with idle amusement.

Despite a fond wish to be anywhere but sitting in the middle of the dance floor with a gorgeous man stripping for her, she found herself totally mesmerized by Austin McBride. Fascinated by his eat-'em-up eyes. Stunned by his breathtaking smile. Enthralled by his incredible body.

It had been a long time since a man had captured her interest so thoroughly.

With a wicked grin, he turned around and slowly shrugged out of his shirt, letting the cotton fabric slide down his arms to reveal a smooth, powerful-looking back that sloped to a trim waist. There wasn't an ounce of fat on her cowboy that she could tell—even that nice, cute butt of his was all firm muscle as he gave it an enticing wriggle that had the women screaming for more.

Yanking the shirt from the waistband of his faded jeans, he tossed the garment over his shoulder, and it landed right in the middle of her lap. The material was warm against her stocking-clad thighs, and smelled earthy and male. She had little time to register that before he tugged on the sides of his chaps and the Velcro holding them on gave way. Those, too, came sailing her way, the soft leather draping across her legs like a lover's caress.

Though the low-slung jeans he wore had a well-worn look about them, they were snug enough to mold to his narrow hips and the long, muscular length of his thighs and legs. The soft-looking material was creased and faded in all the right places, and even a little threadbare in the most intriguing spots, she noticed, as he slowly, sensuously, rolled his hips to the tempo of the music.

His long fingers settled on the heavy belt buckle cinching his waist, and Teddy's stomach bottomed out. But she couldn't look away. With a lazy flick of his wrist, the leather strap slipped from the buckle, the movement slow and somehow erotic. Leaving the belt on and hanging open, he moved close enough for her to reach out and touch the tight muscles rippling along his belly. The dare in his eyes was unmistakable—he expected *her* to take off his belt!

Someone in the crowd let out a shrill, wolf whistle, followed up with, "Go for it!"

Austin grinned, obviously used to such enthusiastic displays. "You heard the lady," he drawled encouragingly. "Go for it."

And so Teddy did. Grasping the metal buckle, she gave it a tentative tug. Austin gyrated his hips at the same moment, and the belt slid from the loopholes on his jeans and into her hands. The strip of leather was warm and supple against her palm, inciting naughty thoughts that shocked even herself. She groaned at her runaway imagination, grateful that no one could hear her over the noise in the bar. The music pulsated, the beat seemingly as raw and primitive as the man before her.

She expected him to strip off his jeans like most male exotic dancers did, but he made no attempt to remove that last barrier of clothing. Instead, he danced for her wearing nothing but his formfitting jeans and a sinfully wicked smile. But, oh, this provocative teasing was so much more arousing than watching him strip down to a skimpy G-string, which would have spoiled the illusion he'd created. This teasing glimpse gave her enough to stir her imagination and incite future cowboy fantasies.

It was apparent Austin McBride knew exactly how to stimulate a woman's senses, and he used that knowledge to his advantage. He rocked his honed body to the beat of the music, giving her time to take in his bare chest, dusted with a light sprinkling of dark brown hair. Unable to help herself, she followed that trail down to where it whorled around his navel, then disappeared into the waistband of his jeans. And when he turned, giving her a view of his backside, the muscles across his shoulders bunched, and his tight bottom and sinewy thighs flexed with the easy, rhythmic movement of his body.

He was truly a work of art.

She licked her dry lips, suddenly feeling as though someone in the establishment had kicked up the temperature ten degrees. Her face was warm—hell, her entire body was prickly with fever—and her breathing was deep and labored.

When her gaze lifted back to his face, his eyes were filled with a combination of sultry heat, immense charm and forbidden enticement. It was all a well-orchestrated act. She knew that, so why did she experience such an inexplicable connection between them, one that went beyond immediate sexual attraction to something deeper and mystifying in that man-woman way?

Not soon enough to suit her embarrassment, the music ended and her fantasy was over. She glanced over at Brenda and Laura and narrowed her gaze. Brenda grinned outrageously and blew at the tip of her finger as if it were the smoking end of a gun—*too hot* was her unmistakable message—and Laura waggled her fingers at Teddy impishly.

No doubt about it, Teddy was going to kill her two best friends.

AUSTIN McBRIDE INWARDLY cringed as the Frisco Bay broke into a roar of raucous cheers, whistles and applause, and tried not to let his growing discomfort show. It was an odd sensation to find himself uncomfortable in what should have been a very familiar, and routine, situation.

However, three months ago, at the age of thirty, while standing center stage wearing nothing more than a tight pair of pants with a roomful of women going crazy with lust, Austin had come to the conclusion that he was getting too old, and certainly less assertive and brazen, to be taking his clothes off in public. As owner and founder of Fantasy for Hire, he'd made the decision to retire his outrageous costumes, and let his younger and more energetic employees handle the exotic, and sometimes outrageous, fantasies women requested.

Tonight had been the exception. Taking off his clothes had been a necessity, not a choice. Don, one of his most requested strippers, had called Austin on his cell phone to tell him that someone had sideswiped his car, and although he was physically okay, he wouldn't be able to make his seven o'clock appointment at the Frisco Bay. That gave Austin a little over an hour to scramble to find someone to fill in. The two guys he managed to get hold of didn't have the requested cowboy costume on hand—but Austin did. Deciding it would be simpler to take care of the engagement himself since time was so limited, he'd donned his western attire, all the while swearing this would be the very last time he fulfilled a woman's fantasy outside of a bedroom.

Tonight's incident only served to shore up his decision to put Fantasy for Hire on the market for a new owner. In the past six years his shoot-from-the-hip venture had increased beyond his wildest expectations, expanding from two part-time employees to nearly a dozen young men who were willing to fulfill a woman's twenty-minute fantasy for ample compensation.

Austin had been amazed by the popularity of his business. Fulfilling fantasies, it seemed, was a very profitable commodity. Fantasy for Hire was so inundated with requests that he was turning away more customers than he had fantasies available.

Despite the fact that the business cut into too much of his personal life of late, it was hard to complain about Fantasy's success. The company had served its purpose in supplementing his income to help pay for the school loans and bills he'd accumulated while embarking on another venture in commercial landscaping nearly four years ago.

His second business and ultimate career choice, McBride Commercial Landscaping, was finally lucrative and self-sufficient. Now, Austin wanted a life. One that didn't include costumes and games, or bringing fantasies to life for hundreds of faceless women who clung to the illusions he displayed. He'd discovered the hard way that women found it difficult to separate him from the part he played. Once he performed for a customer, he couldn't be sure if she wanted him for himself, or the private fantasy he'd created for her.

That's why he'd established his own personal rule a few years ago, after being used for one woman's particular fantasy. The customers he performed for were off limits, no matter how intriguing the woman. And he found Teddy Spencer plenty fascinating, from the sleek cut of her silky blond hair that brushed her shoulders with a slight under-curl, to her big brown eyes that combined wholesomeness with a heady dose of sensuality, to those shapely killer legs extending from the hem of her short, teal-colored business suit. Her cream-hued blouse was pure silk, and although it was buttoned primly enough, he could see the faintest outline of lace shaping her full breasts. She was a dynamite package of sophistication and casual elegance, a distinct kind of demeanor shaped by old money and ingrained from birth. Those obvious signs should have warned him off, but the awareness that had leaped to life between them while they'd danced was still too fresh in his mind.

Once the noise in the bar lessened, she lifted his shirt toward him with a wavering smile on her lips and the color of roses staining her smooth cheeks. "I, um, guess you'd like your clothes back?"

Her tentative question made him smile. The way she so easily blushed was refreshing—an endearing, old-fashioned quality he didn't see very often these days. "It is getting a little drafty in here." He took his shirt from her, and slipped into it. He didn't bother to snap the front closed—it was a little late to worry about a "no shirt, no service" policy.

Grasping her hand, he helped her to her feet. The touch was simple, an everyday, gentlemanly gesture, but when his fingers slid against her soft palm he heard her breath catch and saw something in her eyes flare. Incredibly, his body flashed a reciprocating heat that spiraled low in his belly.

For the first time in years, Austin thought about mixing business with pleasure, until he saw the ruby and diamond ring staking a claim on her left hand. A woman didn't wear a sparkly ring on that finger unless she was taken.

It was too bad, but just as well—considering the only thing he had in common with her fantasy cowboy was his love of outdoors. Take off all the western trappings, and he was just a simple, hardworking, blue-collar city man. Hardly a match for her.

"You were a great sport," he said, distracting himself from the attraction racing between them.

She groaned, the sound rife with chagrin. "As if I had a choice." She shot her two friends an I'm-going-to-get-you-for-this kind of look.

He grinned. "Happy birthday, Teddy." Lifting her hand to his mouth, he brushed his lips over the back of her knuckles. A fleeting touch as soft as a butterfly's wing. The gallant kiss wasn't a service he normally provided for his customers, but he couldn't stop the urge to give her one last thing to remember this evening by. "It really *was* my pleasure."

He let her go, leaving her speechless, and gathered up the rest of his things. He'd taken two steps off the dance floor when she exclaimed, "Oh, your hat!"

He turned back around, and because she'd closed the distance between them, he tipped back the Stetson on her head with a flick of his finger. "I meant it when I said it was yours to keep. Compliments of Fantasy for Hire, and your girlfriends." He gave her one last wink. "It's up to you to explain to your boyfriend where you got it."

She appeared startled by his last comment, but he didn't give her time to respond. The gig was up. No more pretenses. Back to real life.

He headed toward the entrance of the Frisco Bay, and he didn't look back.

He never did.

2

SHE COULDN'T STOP thinking about him.

Teddy leaned back in her office chair and flicked her finger along the corner of the white business card that stated simply, Compliments Of Fantasy for Hire. With a soft sigh, she stroked her thumb over the bold, black raised letters of Austin McBride's name embossed on the left-hand corner. Beneath that was the business phone number, which was permanently etched in her mind.

She'd found the rectangular card as she'd set the Stetson on her bedroom dresser when she'd gotten home last night after her impromptu birthday bash. It had been tucked into the thin leather band around the crown, and since Laura and Brenda had insisted she wear the hat the entire evening, she hadn't discovered it until later.

The card certainly wasn't an invitation to call, not unless she wanted a repeat performance from Austin, which she didn't. She recognized the business card for the piece of advertisement it was—referrals and word of mouth went a long way in making a business successful—so why had she slipped the card into her purse this morning instead of leaving it at home with her birthday Stetson?

She couldn't stop thinking about him.

It was a pitiful excuse, but there it was. She reminded herself that she couldn't afford a distraction like Austin McBride, fantasy extraordinaire, not when she was so close to achieving the goals she'd set for herself. Goals that included a solid, steady career and complete independence from the overbearing family that still hadn't recovered from the shock that she'd broken off her engagement to the affluent Bartholomew Winston two years ago. Her plans didn't include a man, especially one who fulfilled women's fantasies on a regular basis.

She had to stop thinking about him. That's all there was to it, she decided. Opening the middle drawer of her oak desk, she set the card on top of the other business cards stacked neatly in a small partition in the left-hand corner.

"Out of sight, out of mind," she muttered, doubting those six words would be able to make her forget her gorgeous, green-eyed cowboy.

"Is that problem with your sight and mind going to affect your performance on the World Wide Travel account?"

Startled by the intrusion, Teddy pinched the tip of her index finger in her desk drawer just as it closed. Wincing, she glanced up and gave the man approaching her desk a barely tolerable look. Louden Avery, her boss and creative director at Sharper Image, considered himself above the courtesy of knocking or announcing his presence.

He strolled into her office as if he owned it, his pale blue eyes missing nothing, not the remnants of a half-eaten lunch that attested to the extra hour she'd worked without compensation, or the files and sketches on her desk that she was currently devoting time to, or even what she wore. The latter was the worst, because he took his time about it. By the time he finished his deliberate perusal, her jaw ached from gritting her teeth.

Keeping in mind that he was her boss, she summoned a pleasant smile she was certain didn't quite reach her eyes. "Contrary to what you might have heard, my sight and mind are sound."

"That's good to know," he replied with calculated mildness. "I wouldn't want anything to impair your chances of getting that promotion."

"The only thing that could hurt my chances is if someone more qualified than myself come along." After all, they both knew she had the experience, along with a degree that gave her a distinct advantage over Fred Williams, the colleague she was up against.

Louden merely smiled. Rounding her desk, he propped his hip on the corner nearest her, unmindful of the papers resting on the edge. Bracing his left forearm on his thigh, he leaned toward her, though his gaze was busy taking in the project laid out in front of her. "How is the preliminary sketch coming on the World Wide Travel logo?"

"Just fine." Louden liked to feel superior, and she had no doubt that his position on her desk had been chosen for such a purpose. She forced herself to look up at him, determined to meet his gaze. "It'll be on your desk first thing in the morning, two days before deadline."

"My, aren't you efficient." Using a slim finger, he turned the sketch she was working on toward him, taking in the rough draft of a globe with connecting W's, the initials the travel agency had requested. "And so talented, too. It would be a shame to see all this creativity go to waste."

His mocking tone chafed her nerves, but she didn't let it show. "Since you weren't expecting the project on your desk until Friday, is there some other reason you stopped by?"

He stared at her for a long moment, obviously not caring for the way she was trying to dismiss him. "According to my secretary, you haven't RSVP'd for the Christmas party, which is this Saturday. Certainly you weren't going to miss the biggest bash of the year?"

She resented the sanctimonious way he chastised her. She hadn't planned on attending the party, mainly because she didn't relish the thought of having any outside-of-the-office contact with Louden, but he was making it difficult to refuse.

"I've been so busy, I forgot to respond." The excuse was

handy, and served its purpose. "Consider this my confirmation."

"For one or two?"

Uncomfortable with the direction of their conversation, her mind grappled for another convenient excuse...and came up blank.

His pale gaze slid pointedly to the ring on her finger. "Two," she said quickly. "There'll be two of us attending the Christmas party."

Surprise registered in his eyes, and was quickly replaced by skepticism. "Ah, we finally get to meet the elusive boyfriend."

What had been an innocent white lie to keep Louden at bay was now becoming a tangled mess. He hadn't pressed her, accepting the fact that she had a boyfriend in the beginning, but as the months wore on, she suspected he had his doubts. This was the first time he'd made any direct reference to his suspicions.

"What's his name?" he asked casually.

She stared at Louden, her mind freezing. "Uh, excuse me?" The phrase bought her some time, but not much, she knew. She hadn't thought to create a name for her fictitious boyfriend.

"Your boyfriend," he repeated slowly. "He does have a name, doesn't he?"

"Well, yes, of course he does." *A name, Teddy. Pick a name!* At the moment she couldn't even think of one of her three older brother's names!

"Then what is it?" he persisted. "My secretary needs it for the place settings. We can't have just *anybody* finagling their way into the party."

Teddy's chest hurt and her head swam. When she finally realized that she was holding her breath, she let it out in a rush. "Well, maybe I should check with...him. We'd talked about the Christmas party, but quite honestly, he didn't actually say yes, so we probably should discuss it further." She offered Louden a placating smile.

Louden's eyes narrowed slightly, and a smile curled the corner of his mouth.

Very casually, he picked up her hand, the one with the diamond and ruby band, and ran his finger over the embedded jewels. She tried not to visibly shudder at his touch.

"You know, Theodora," he said, deliberately using her full name as a way of maintaining his superiority. "For a woman who claims she's committed, you sure do have a hard time remembering the simplest things about your beau. Maybe he's not as important as you'd like everyone to believe."

She yanked her hand from his grasp. "That's ridiculous."

A pale eyebrow lifted, expressing those doubts.

Desperation coiled within her, and she seized the only name in her mind. "Austin," she blurted.

He looked taken aback by her outburst, and somewhat confused. "Pardon?"

She summoned as much confidence as she could and injected it into her voice. "My boyfriend, his name is Austin." The threads of her white lie were taking on a decidedly black cast. Hell, since she'd incriminated Austin this much, she decided to go all the way and worry about the consequences later. "Austin McBride."

Sliding off the edge of her desk, Louden straightened and glanced down with enough arrogance to make her uneasy. "Well, I suggest you give him a call and find out for certain if he'll be attending the Christmas party with you. My secretary needs a firm head count by the end of today."

Teddy watched Louden leave the office, and knew she'd backed herself into a corner. What she needed was her own personal fantasy man, a fake boyfriend who would establish territorial rights so Louden Avery would back off and see her as a professional, someone well qualified for that promotion. Austin McBride, fantasy for hire, was the man to help her accomplish that goal.

Drawing a deep breath, and hoping Austin could be persuaded to be her date for an evening, she reached for the phone and dialed the number she'd memorized from his business card. The line connected and rang, then a recorder clicked on.

"You've reached Fantasy for Hire," Austin's voice came over the line, just as deep and rich as she remembered. The sexy, masculine tones spread warmly through her, touching places that had been untouched for too long. "Leave a message and I'll get back to you as soon as possible." A long beep followed.

"Hi, Austin," she said, just as Louden walked back into her office, a file folder in his hand. Their gazes met from across the room, the interest in his eyes enough to tell her he'd heard her greeting. She had no choice but to finish her message to Austin.

She hadn't counted on having an audience, and had only planned to leave a brief, impersonal message for Austin to return her call. Louden's unexpected presence changed all that, forcing her to make up a believable monologue as she spoke.

"It's, uh, Teddy," she continued, while her mind latched on to an idea. "I'm calling about the Christmas party this Saturday. Have you decided to go? Since you're not home, I guess we'll talk about it tonight. We're still on for drinks, right? I'll see you at seven at the Frisco Bay." She dropped her voice to a husky pitch, lowered her lashes coyly for Louden's benefit and added, "And later on tonight I'll wear that adorable Stetson you gave me for my birthday, as long as you promise to wear your chaps."

She hoped that last intimate reference would serve a dual purpose—to give Louden the impression that she and Austin were, indeed, intimately involved, and to leave no doubt in Austin's mind who, exactly, the caller was. Austin didn't seem the type to forget a woman's name, but she wasn't taking any chances. The Stetson would identify her, if her name failed to spark his memory.

Whether or not he showed up to meet her was a whole other issue.

Her face burning at her brazenness, she hung up the phone, hoping Louden would mistake the heat scoring her cheeks as a lover's glow.

Setting the file in her in-box on the corner of her desk, he stared at her for a long moment, making her uncomfortable. Even after hearing her one-sided conversation, he still didn't believe her. She could see the doubt in his expression, could detect his skepticism in the set of his rigid posture.

Wanting to deflect his suspicion, she pasted on a smile. "He wasn't home, but go ahead and tell Janet to add two more to the guest list."

"Are you sure about that?" he asked, too quietly for her peace of mind.

She suspected his question went much deeper than her certainty about the party. "I'm sure. Go ahead and put Austin's name down as my date. He'll be there. I can be very...determined when it comes to something I want." She shot one of his double-edged comments right back at him.

"Sometimes, determination isn't enough," he retorted meaningfully.

"He'll be there." She wished she felt as confident as she sounded. Truth was, she feared Austin would hear the message on his answering machine and write her off as a nutcase.

"Very well, then. I look forward to meeting the elusive Austin McBride."

She folded her hands on top of her desk and met his gaze levelly. "He's looking forward to meeting you, too."

"WHERE HAVE YOU BEEN? You were supposed to be home an hour ago."

With a large, flat box tucked under one arm and his other wrapped securely around a green plastic container holding a small, wilting Douglas fir tree, Austin maneuvered his way through the front door of the old Victorian home he and his older brother, Jordan, had inherited when their parents died fourteen years ago. For the past eight years he'd occupied the house by himself, ever since Jordan had moved to Los Angeles to pursue his architectural career. Eight years of coming and going as he pleased, without worrying about accounting for his whereabouts.

Some habits, especially Jordan's protective instincts toward his little brother, died hard. Jordan had always been the dependable, levelheaded one of them, but then he'd had the responsibility of raising a sixteen-year-old hellion thrust upon him when he, himself, should have been tasting freedom at the tender young age of eighteen. A huge obligation like that tended to make a man out of a child fairly quickly, and Jordan had taken the role of guardianship very seriously. Too seriously, Austin thought, refraining from the urge to remind his brother that he was a big boy and had proven that he could take care of himself.

Pushing the door closed with his shoulder Austin shoved the potted fir into his brother's hands, giving him no choice but to take the plant.

"Well?" Jordan persisted, following Austin into the adjoining living room where he put the Douglas fir on the corner of the brick hearth. "Where have you been?"

"You haven't even been home a week and already you're starting to sound like a wife, big brother." Setting the package on the settee that had once belonged to his great-grandmother, Austin cast an amused glance Jordan's way. "A wife is the last thing I need in my hectic life."

Jordan shoved his fingers through his thick, dark brown

hair and grimaced. "Sorry," he said, releasing a deep, frustrated sigh. "It's been a long, boring day. And you did say you'd be home at four, and it's after five."

Austin's gaze touched on the fifty-year-old grandfather clock in the corner of the room and noted the time. "Hmm, so it is."

Despite his brother's annoying habit of keeping tabs on him, Austin experienced a bit of sympathy for Jordan. After giving an L.A. architectural firm eight years of loyalty, and being promised a partnership in the firm, he'd been bypassed when they'd promoted a relative instead. Jordan had been used and lied to, and if there was anything he abhorred, it was dishonesty. Two weeks ago he'd quit the firm, packed up his belongings and moved back to San Francisco to reevaluate his life.

In Austin's estimation, Jordan had too much idle time on his hands. And until his brother decided which direction he wanted to take with his career, Austin pretty much resigned himself, and his life, to his brother's scrutiny.

Jordan was still waiting for an answer. Austin liked making him suffer—goading his brother had always been a favorite pastime, one he'd missed over the past eight years. Shrugging out of his sports jacket, he draped it over the back of the settee. Then he went to work loosening his restricting tie.

"I'm late because I had an afternoon appointment with a client that ran longer than I'd expected," he told Jordan as he pulled the tie from around his neck and added it to the jacket. "But I got myself a signed contract for a landscaping project I bid on a few weeks ago for a new restaurant. The job came in at a little less than fifty grand."

"That's great." Jordan's hazel eyes brightened with pride and genuine excitement for Austin's success. "Congratulations."

"Thanks." Austin was still feeling the elation of having

outbid the other landscaping companies. This one project, coupled with half a dozen other smaller projects he'd been awarded recently, would keep a steady paycheck coming in. "And after that, I picked up the Christmas present I was supposed to get last night."

Jordan flicked his finger at the big, fat red bow topping the package wrapped in bright holly paper. "Ah, and who might this be for?"

Austin watched Jordan pick up the box, and knew from experience what was coming next. "It's for you, and don't shake it—"

The order came too late. For all Jordan's seriousness, he had an insatiable curiosity, which included trying to guess what his gifts were. The contents of the box rattled as he gave it a brisk jostling, and his eyes lit up like a little kid's.

Austin's stomach pitched as he imagined the delicate, expensive pieces belonging to the specially ordered model of the Bay Bridge breaking into minuscule segments. "Dammit, Jordan," he growled as he grabbed the box and rescued the collector's edition from Jordan's abuse. "I'm serious. It's very fragile."

A grin quirked Jordan's mouth. "What did you do, get me a set of wineglasses?"

"Very funny." Austin put the gift next to the potted fir.

Jordan came up beside him and cast a hand at the withering tree. "And please don't tell me you're going to try and pass this off as a Christmas tree. It's pathetic, Austin."

"That's why I chose it." Austin smiled and shrugged. "It needed a home, and we couldn't celebrate our first Christmas together in years without a tree."

"So you picked the scrawniest one you could find?"

"I didn't think we'd need anything big and elaborate, considering it's just the two of us."

Jordan shook his head at the sad state of the tree. "I hope it holds up for the next week."

"A drink of water, a string of garland, and it'll be fine." Austin turned toward Jordan and cuffed him on the shoulder. "And for what it's worth, I'm glad you're home for the holidays."

Jordan returned the sentiment with a smile. "Yeah, me, too."

"So, any important calls today?" Austin asked as they headed into the kitchen. Opening the refrigerator, he snagged a can of root beer for himself and popped the top.

"That depends on how you define 'important.'" Jordan's tone turned rueful. "I overheard a message on your Fantasy for Hire line that was certainly interesting."

Austin was used to customers leaving odd messages and requests on that line. When you were in the business of fulfilling fantasies, you got some doozies. Though Jordan was aware of the basic operation of the business, his mind was still boggled by the appeal of Fantasy for Hire, and the outrageous requests he'd been privy to the past week.

Jordan smirked. "You must have made quite an impression last night at your cowboy gig."

The can of soda stopped midway to Austin's lips, and he lifted an eyebrow at his brother. "What makes you say that?"

Jordan's grin broadened. "The very personal message someone left on the Fantasy for Hire line for you."

Interest piqued, Austin set his soda on the counter and headed into an adjoining room that had once been a dining room. Now, it was a no-frills, makeshift office for Fantasy for Hire, consisting of an old, scarred mahogany desk and a battered metal file cabinet. The surface of the desk was cluttered with order forms, and a large appointment book opened to the month of December. Judging by all the fantasies filling it, it certainly *was* the month for giving.

The phone, with an answering machine and fax attached, sat on one corner of the desk. A digital display indicated he had eight messages waiting for him. He sighed. So much for relaxing after a long day at McBride Landscaping—it looked as if he'd be spending the next hour or so returning calls and scheduling his guys.

He rewound the tape, wondering who'd left the message Jordan seemed so amused with. The only thing he could think of was that the women who'd hired him for Teddy's cowboy fantasy had been disappointed with his act. According to the description he'd given them when they'd placed the order, they'd been expecting a blond-haired, blue-eyed cowboy. If they'd been dissatisfied with him or his performance, he'd refund their money.

"Oh, by the way," Jordan added as he stepped into the office behind Austin. "You've got a seven o'clock appointment tonight."

Austin jerked his gaze to Jordan, certain his brother was joking. Seeing that he wore his serious, older-brother expression, Austin's hopes for a peaceful evening dwindled even more. "I told you last night I wouldn't be performing anymore, not unless I absolutely have to."

"You performed last night," Jordan pointed out.

"That was due to circumstances beyond my control. I had no choice."

"You don't have much choice for tonight, either." Jordan displayed no sympathy for Austin's plight. "You were specifically requested."

Frustration coiled through Austin, and he dragged a hand along his jaw. "I thought you said you didn't want to have anything to do with the business, including taking calls during the day."

"I don't, and I didn't." A humorous sparkle entered Jordan's eyes as he pushed his hands into the front pockets of his pleated trousers. "I heard the message while the caller was leaving it. Seems that filly you played cowboy for last night took a hankering to you. She requested a repeat performance for tonight."

"Teddy?" The name, which had invaded his thoughts all day, slipped from Austin's lips almost involuntarily.

"Teddy..." Jordan repeated the word as if testing it, then nodded. "Yeah, I believe that's what she said her name was."

Easing himself into the chair behind the desk, Austin frowned. Despite the chemistry that had charged between them, Teddy didn't seem the type to brazenly pursue a man, especially when a ring on her finger indicated she was committed to another. Then again, he could have pegged her all wrong. It wouldn't be the first time he'd been led astray.

Punching the play button on the recorder, he listened to four requests for fantasies before her voice finally drifted out the phone's speaker.

"Hi, Austin," she said, then hesitated a few moments before continuing. "I'm calling about the Christmas party this Saturday. Have you decided to go? Since you're not home, I guess we'll talk about it tonight. We're still on for drinks, right? I'll see you at seven at the Frisco Bay."

Though her voice was strong, he grasped another thinly veiled emotion in her tone. *Desperation.*

She continued in a sexy, husky voice, "And later on tonight I'll wear that adorable Stetson you gave me for my birthday, as long as you promise to wear your chaps."

The recorder beeped at the end of her message, and Austin hit the stop button before the next caller could speak. He sat there, feeling both confused and fascinated by what he'd heard.

Jordan chuckled. "If that isn't a line to inspire fantasies, I don't know what is."

Austin silently agreed with his brother's comment, considering the provocative images that had leaped into his mind, of Teddy wearing nothing more than the Stetson he'd given her, and a head-to-toe flush tinging her skin. Oh, yeah, he was certainly inspired. And intrigued. More than he'd been in years.

But beyond the sexy innuendo of Teddy's final remark, there was more to her words than a flirtatious come-on. Though she'd spoken in an enticing tone of voice, he didn't get the impression that she was asking for a personal fantasy. On the contrary, he got the feeling that her entire message was a setup of some sort, and that last line had been her way of prompting him to remember who she was.

As if he could forget.

When he'd arrived home last night, he'd been keyed up from the performance and that rare, inexplicable connection he'd experienced with Teddy Spencer. And though he'd tried, he hadn't been able to shake his mental image of her soft smile and those incredibly sensual brown eyes that had shown him glimpses of shyness, and the potential to be a little reckless. She was off limits, for so many reasons, but his mind had a hard time accepting that fact. Despite his best efforts to maintain his professionalism, she'd taken a hot shower with him, then continued to distract him while he'd attempted to concentrate on an estimate he was preparing for an upcoming landscaping bid. She'd so totally consumed his thoughts that he had no choice but to abandon the figures and call it a night. And that's when he'd done the unthinkable—he'd taken her to bed with him and succumbed to the most erotic dreams he'd had since puberty.

And damn if he didn't wake up hard and aching, and wanting her.

Suddenly, the familiar stirring started again, deep in Austin's belly. He drew a deep breath, gradually released it and firmly focused on the present situation. He knew nothing about a Christmas party, or a date for drinks tonight. She'd left no phone number, no way of contacting her to find out what her strange message was all about.

Remembering the silent plea he'd detected in her voice, he found he couldn't bring himself to stand her up.

"So, what's this about a Christmas party this Saturday?" Jordan asked, his expression curious. "Do you think maybe she needs a guy to play Santa Claus?"

Austin curbed the impulse to let out a hearty *ho, ho, ho*. As amusing as he found Jordan's suggestion, gut instinct told him Teddy's request had little to do with needing a Santa for hire.

"I haven't the slightest idea what she's talking about," he admitted, then allowed a slow, devilish smile to form. "But I do intend to find out."

3

HE WAS LATE. Either that, or Austin McBride had no intention of meeting the woman who'd left such a brazen message on his answering machine. Despite how much Teddy was depending on Austin to help her out of her predicament, a part of her wouldn't blame him if he didn't show.

Feeling anxious, Teddy glanced at her wristwatch for the fourth time in the past ten minutes and made the decision that she'd give Austin until 7:30 p.m. before she resigned her post in the Frisco Bay.

While she waited, she sipped her sparkling water and looked over the patrons in the lounge, most of whom she knew as regular customers of the bar. Thanks to Brenda's and Laura's outgoing personalities, Teddy was now acquainted with many of the men on a first-name basis. She'd even politely turned down a date or two from a few of the single males present tonight. Luckily, the men who frequented the Frisco Bay were out looking for a good time, no strings attached, and didn't seem to take rejections personally.

As the minutes ticked by, Teddy found herself perusing the guys in the bar tonight, sizing each one up as a potential date for Saturday's party should Austin not show. None sparked her interest. Certainly none compared to Austin McBride's gorgeous looks and charisma. His confident appeal was precisely what she needed to convince Louden that he could never measure up.

"Hey, Teddy," a female acquaintance sitting at a nearby table called. "Isn't that your cowboy?"

Every female head in the establishment turned toward the entrance of the Frisco Bay to get a glimpse of last night's attraction. Teddy included.

Relief at seeing him mingled with a heady dose of awareness that prickled along the surface of her skin. "Yeah, that's him."

There was no trace of the cowboy who'd come calling the previous evening, but then Austin didn't need a western costume to accentuate that athletic body of his. A dark brown knit shirt showed off his broad shoulders and molded to a muscular chest and flat belly. The khaki pants he wore weren't nearly as tight as the jeans he'd donned last night, but they looked just as good, in a more polished, urban sort of way.

What the women in the place recognized, Teddy suspected, was Austin's head-turning features, that tousled thick brown hair that made a woman want to run her fingers through the warm strands, and those striking green eyes that flirted and seduced with a simple sweep of those long, dark lashes.

"Is he back for a repeat performance?" another woman asked hopefully.

"Not a public one," Teddy replied, startled by the spurt of jealousy she felt. She certainly had no claim to Austin McBride, but that thought didn't diminish the fact that she didn't want to share him with the dozen other women in the bar who were anxious to see him shed his clothes.

Eyebrows rose curiously, and Teddy reached for her drink, refusing to elaborate on her comment, though it was true. Austin's performance would be a private affair, one he'd be keeping his clothes on for.

He found her sitting at the bar and headed in her direction, carrying himself with a relaxed self-assurance that was at once appealing and unwavering in confidence. Oh, yes, Teddy thought breathlessly. Austin was exactly what she needed to convince Louden that he was overstepping boundaries. Austin came across as the type who wouldn't tolerate another man infringing on his territory.

Her stomach fluttered as his gaze locked on hers, making her feel as though she was the only woman in the place—certainly the only woman he was interested in, despite the hungry looks and moist-lipped smiles being cast his way by the other women in the bar. The intensity with which he focused on her was a good indication that he could convince anyone that he was her devoted lover.

By the time he reached her, Teddy knew she wouldn't be able to find a better man for the job than Austin McBride. He was *the one*.

"Hi," she said, gracing him with a smile she hoped didn't look too enthusiastic.

She'd saved the padded stool next to her for him, and he slid into the vacant seat, his own smile adorably contrite. "I'm sorry I'm late. I had a scheduling conflict I had to resolve that took longer than I'd anticipated."

"Lots of fantasies to fulfill, hmm?" she teased.

For a moment he appeared harried, then covered up that fleeting glimpse with something resembling reluctant resignation. "More than I can handle."

Considering Austin epitomized a woman's fantasy, she wasn't at all surprised that his services were in demand. "Well, I'm just glad you showed up," she said gratefully. "After that message I left on your answering machine, I was certain you'd think I was a nutcase."

"Not at all." He braced his forearm on the bar, humor dancing in his eyes. "I was intrigued by your message, to say the least. So was my brother."

Her heart flipped at the thought of another McBride brother as gorgeous and charming as this one. Before she could ask Austin if his brother was in the business, too, Jack, the bartender, sidled up to their seats from across the mahogany surface of the bar, recognition glimmering in his eyes. Drying a beer glass, he grinned broadly at Austin.

"So, what will it be, cowboy?" Jack asked in a feigned western drawl. "The regular?"

"That would be great." Austin tossed a five-dollar bill toward Jack with a comment to keep the change before Teddy could offer to pay for his drink. "Make it on the rocks this time."

"You got it, just so long as you keep your clothes on tonight." Jack set a glass with ice in it on the pouring pad in front of him, then used a spigot to fill the glass with a dark, fizzing liquid. "It took me hours to settle the women down after you left last night. Since you've walked in, the crowd has gotten a little restless."

Austin's gaze slid to Teddy, irresistibly warm and sexy. "My business here tonight is all pleasure."

She shivered at the deep, rich timbre of his voice, and that flirtatious smile that tempted and teased. He seemed totally unaware of the interest he was generating, unaware of all the eyes and ears tuned into them. Teddy, on the other hand, grew increasingly uncomfortable with everyone's scrutiny. What she needed to ask Austin wasn't something she wanted up for public speculation.

"Would you mind if we took that table in the corner so we can have a little privacy?" she asked.

If he was surprised by her request, he didn't show it. "Not at all."

Grabbing her purse and drink, she led the way, nearly jumping out of her skin when he settled his hand lightly at the base of her spine. It was a common gesture, yet with Austin his touch had a decidedly possessive air to it. Not to mention enough heat to penetrate her tightly knit sweater and make her feel branded.

Once they were seated next to each other, he glanced at her and smiled. "So, what can I do for you, Teddy Spencer?"

The answers that filled her mind were shameless, and she gave herself a firm mental shake that knocked those naughty thoughts out of commission. "I have a problem, and I'm hoping you can help me out."

"In what way?"

Currently, her problem seemed to be her inability to think straight while those sexier-than-sin eyes were trained on her. "I need a fantasy..." Startled that such a reckless request could tumble from her lips, she grappled for another line. "I mean, I need a fiancé..." She groaned at her blunder, felt the rising warmth in her cheeks, and didn't trust herself to speak further.

His grin turned a bit more wicked, giving her the distinct impression he was enjoying her slip of the tongue. "The fantasy I could help you out with, since I have plenty of experience in that area, but I'm afraid being your fiancé is out of the question. I hardly know you."

The humorous note to his voice made her relax. She leaned back in her chair, wiped her damp palms on her black denim jeans and decided to try again. For all her business savvy with clients, she was beginning to sound like a bungling idiot with the one man who could help her pave the way to a smooth future with Sharper Image.

"Let me try this again," she said, drawing a deep, calming breath. "I need someone to pose as my steady boyfriend and escort me to a party."

He stared at her, the enjoyment of the previous moment fading from his expression. "I don't run an escort service."

The disapproving edge to his voice was enough to alert her she'd crossed a professional line with him. "Of course you don't," she amended hastily. "I never meant to imply that you did, but isn't it at all possible that I could hire you for a few hours? You do hire out by the hour, don't you?"

The words, once they were out, sounded like an indecent proposal.

He shook his head, his dark hair gleaming from the low lights in the lounge. "I'm really sorry," he said, his voice filled with genuine regret, "but I can't help you out. I make it a rule never to mix fantasy with reality."

She found his comment odd, but didn't have the time to worry about what, exactly, he meant. She bit her bottom lip, realizing she had no choice but to put her pride on the line.

Taking a swallow of her sparkling water to ease the dryness in her mouth, she met Austin's gaze. "I'm embarrassed to have to admit this, but I told my boss that my boyfriend's name is Austin McBride."

Austin's dark eyebrows rose in surprise, and a grin quirked the corner of his mouth. "Really?" he drawled.

She held up a hand, certain he was writing her off as a basket case. "I know what you're thinking—"

"You have no idea," he murmured, his low, amused voice stroking along her nerves. Seeing the mischievous glint in his eyes, she decided maybe she *didn't* want to know what he was thinking.

Hopelessness settled over her. Could this meeting get any worse? she wondered, dragging her hand through her loose hair to pull it away from her face. She'd failed in her attempt to proposition Austin for an evening, and even her humiliating admission about blurting out his name to Louden hadn't swayed him.

As much as she hated to admit it, she needed Austin McBride. Her career at Sharper Image depended on him. Only he could knock Louden down a peg or two. And having Louden witness the sexual chemistry between them would be a bonus, too. One night, five hours max. A few tender touches and intimate glances, and once the Christmas party ended they'd go their separate ways.

It was the perfect arrangement.

But first, she had to convince Austin. "Maybe I should explain my situation from the beginning, so my request for your services makes sense."

"Please do." After taking a drink of the dark liquid in his glass, he reclined back in his chair, clasped his hands over his flat stomach, and regarded her with rapt curiosity.

She glanced around the lounge to make sure they didn't have an audience, and was relieved to find the excitement caused by Austin's appearance had subsided. Returning her attention to the man next to her, she forced her thoughts on business. "I started with Sharper Image, the company I'm currently working for, a little less than a year ago. I was hired as a layout assistant, and within six months was promoted to a graphic designer position with my own accounts."

"Do you like your job?"

Austin's unexpected question threw her concentration off stride and the genuine interest he expressed warmed her. Nobody ever asked her about her job, whether she enjoyed it or hated it. When she'd enrolled in college, her brothers and parents hadn't taken her goals seriously, and wrote off her dream of becoming a graphic designer as a hobby. They'd hoped her engagement to Bartholomew Winston would settle her down, but that brief period in her life had only served to make her realize how important her independence was to her, and how badly she wanted to make it on her own.

The disappointment of their daughter embracing a career over marriage was still a sore spot with her parents. Talking about her job and how much she relished the mental stimulation and challenges wasn't something the older Spencers encouraged when she visited, and so Teddy had learned in order to keep peace, she kept quiet.

"I love my job," she told Austin, taking advantage of his interest. "Especially the creative freedom I have as a graphic designer. I design letterheads, logos, brochures and develop advertising strategies for businesses and corporations. I've got a flawless record with Sharper Image, and my reviews have been glowing. Recently, the position of senior graphic designer became available. Considering my experience, degree and performance the past year, I'm a prime candidate for the promotion."

She paused for a moment, making sure she still had Austin's attention. "This is where it gets tricky. Louden Avery, who is my boss and creative director over my department, sees me as a candidate of an entirely different sort. Ever since I started at Sharper Image, he's made a few comments that leave me feeling uncomfortable. A few months after I was hired, I told him I had a steady boyfriend, thinking he'd lose interest. He backed off for a while, but it hasn't lasted."

Austin's gaze flickered to her left hand, which rested on the armrest nearest him. "So, you don't really have a boyfriend then?" he asked, looking back up at her.

She recalled the odd comment he'd made last night, about having to explain the Stetson to her boyfriend, and realized the ring on her finger had given him the wrong impression. "No, no boyfriend. The ring is merely a diversion, but it's losing its credibility. When Louden pressured me about bringing my elusive boyfriend to the Christmas party and demanded a name, yours was the first one I came up with."

He smiled. "I'm flattered."

Hope bloomed within her. "Flattered enough to stand in as my date Saturday night?"

Indecision touched his expression, and before he could succumb to his reservations, she reached out and grasped his hand, stopping just short of dropping to a begging position in front of him. She was desperate, yes, but she didn't want everyone in the Frisco Bay to witness her despair. "One night, Austin, please? I'll pay you enough to make it worth your while."

A young woman at a nearby table turned and looked at

them, shock and curiosity brightening her eyes. Belatedly, Teddy realized how incriminating her words had sounded.

Teddy glared until the woman turned back to her own companion. So much for being discreet! Before the night was over, word would probably spread through the Frisco Bay that Teddy Spencer had propositioned her cowboy. She hadn't said what that one night entailed, but knew the other woman was thinking along the lines of sex. When Teddy returned her gaze to Austin, silent laughter glistened in his eyes.

"Please," she begged in a low whisper.

"Let me get this straight," he said, leaning forward so he could brace his forearms on his knees. In the process, he switched the position of their hands, so hers was enveloped in the warmth of his. "If I decided to do this, you'd expect me to act like your steady boyfriend?"

She nodded eagerly and dampened her bottom lip with her tongue. "Yes."

His fingers drew lazy, sensual patterns on her palm, sending scintillating tremors up her arm. That frisson of awareness settled in the tips of her breasts, tightening her nipples into hard, sensitive peaks. "And give everyone the impression that we're intimately involved?"

The sensations he was evoking were as intimate as anything she'd ever experienced. He stroked softly between thumb and index finger, a skillful caress that made her pulse race. "Ahhh, yes," she managed to say, though she sounded as if she was out of breath. "The, um, more people that think we're intimately involved, the better."

The corner of his mouth kicked up in a seductively wicked smile that matched his deep, rich voice. "You want Louden Avery to have no doubt in his mind that we're a couple well and truly committed."

"Exactly." Unable to stand his provocative caresses any

longer she gently withdrew her hand from his. "One night should do it, as long as you think you can be convincing."

"Oh, I don't think that'll be a problem." On him, confidence was an incredibly sexy thing. "I specialize in fantasies. I have a feeling this performance will come naturally."

Judging by the thrum of desire that had just shimmered between them, she suspected he was right. She flashed him a cheeky grin. "Well, I don't expect you'll have to take off your clothes for this performance."

He smiled. "You don't know how relieved I am to hear that."

"So you'll do it?" she asked anxiously, needing to hear him say yes.

Instead of the positive response she anticipated, he grew serious, studying her intently. "Why is this so important to you?"

Teddy resisted the urge to throttle him. The man certainly wasn't an easy sell, though she had to admit it was nice to know he wasn't in it just for the money. It was as though he cared, and it had been a long time since someone had cared enough to listen to her.

"I want that promotion, and I want it awarded to me on my own merit. I've worked hard and I deserve that position without having to compromise my morals. Since Louden is making the process so difficult, proving to him that I'm in an intimate relationship will put an end to his pursuing me."

He tilted his head, his gaze kind, but concerned. "And you think if Louden believes you're unavailable, that will make him judge the candidates for the position fairly?"

The doubt in his voice was unmistakable, but she refused to dwell on it. "That's what I'm hoping. I'm the most qualified for the position, but I refuse to submit to Louden's tactics to get it."

She saw him wavering despite his concern, and panicked. She couldn't lose him now! Giving in to that damned vulnerable emotion named desperation, she dug into her purse, withdrew her leather checkbook case and wrote a check for his services in the amount of one thousand dollars before he could refuse her.

Tearing off the signed voucher, she pushed it across the small cocktail table toward him and lifted her chin in sheer determination. "If that isn't enough for your time, I'm willing to pay more."

Austin glanced at the check, noted the staggering amount she'd offered, and realized how deeply her tenacity ran. She wasn't making him a reckless, frivolous offer—she was proving she'd take whatever risks necessary to secure her future.

He wasn't comfortable accepting that much money, even though it appeared Teddy Spencer could easily afford it. She didn't even bat an eye at the amount she'd written on the check. Although she came across as very down to earth in attitude, her well-bred sophistication couldn't be hidden beneath a pair of black jeans and a Christmas red sweater that outlined perfect breasts. The cut of her hair was a shoulder-length classic, the kind of style that fell softly around her face and made the best of her naturally elegant features. Flawless half-carat diamonds winked in each earlobe, an exquisite, but understated touch. And she had the moves of wealth, too, walking and gesturing with a grace that was refined and private-school polished.

On a distant level, those particular signs made him uneasy, but he didn't know enough about Teddy to make any assumptions. He only had tonight's encounter to judge her by, which had given him a mixture of fascinating contradictions to sort through.

Confidence radiated from her, yet he'd detected touches of vulnerability, too, as if she had to struggle to maintain that hard-won self-assurance. That quality he understood and identified with—he'd grappled with similar emotional challenges after his parents died. He'd only been sixteen, and it had taken him years, along with Jordan's guidance, for him to finally understand the security he'd lost. His landscaping company gave him the financial stability he sought, but he was still searching for that emotional connection that offered the deep solidity he craved.

"Is it enough?" she asked, her voice quiet, but firm with purpose.

Picking up the check, he studied it, deciding the name Teddy suited her much more than her stuffy given name, Theodora.

He shifted his gaze back to her and smiled. "Actually, this amount is a bit high, considering I don't have to take my clothes off."

The fingers she'd knotted in her lap relaxed and the tense set of her shoulders eased. "Then consider it an easy night. And I'll pick up any other expenses you might incur." She stuffed her checkbook back into her purse and began issuing instructions, as if fearing any lapse in conversation might give him a chance to come to his senses and refuse her proposition. "The Christmas party is a black-tie affair, so you'll be expected to wear a tuxedo. I can set up an appointment for you to see my tailor, who also rents tuxedos—"

"Actually, I already have a tuxedo," he said, interrupting her. She blinked at him in surprise, and he grinned. "It's quite a common fantasy."

"Oh, of course." Her face now becoming a shade of pink, she ducked her head and rummaged through her purse to retrieve a pen and notepad. "Cocktails are at six-thirty, so you can pick me up at six. Here's my address, home phone number and my number at the office if you should need it."

He listened to her ramble on, waving a hand in the air while giving him verbal directions to her condominium complex. He watched her mouth as she talked, enjoyed the way she used her tongue to sweep across her lush bottom lip and wondered what it would be like to kiss her. The urge to find out what she tasted like was strong, and his body tightened in response.

She placed a hand on his arm, her light touch severing his erotic daydreams. "I can't thank you enough for agreeing to this." She looked out of breath, which is what he suspected ended her rambling—the need for oxygen.

Diamonds and rubies sparkled on the hand resting on his arm. That ring might have dissuaded her boss's advances, but in the process, the band also gave every other man she met the impression she was unavailable. He found Teddy's motive for wearing the ring very interesting, and wondered if it served a dual purpose for her.

He met her gaze and gave in to curiosity. "Tell me something, Teddy. You're a beautiful, classy woman. You must have been able to find a date for Saturday, someone you might know who could have convinced Louden that you're off the market. So why me, a total stranger?"

She hesitated. Deep reservation passed over her features, along with a flash of defiance, adding yet another dimension to her already intriguing personality. "I don't want anything complicated," she told him. "And since we really don't know one another, our transaction can be strictly business. One evening, then we go our separate ways."

She made it sound so easy, but he was beginning to think the situation wasn't so cut-and-dried. Certainly pretending to be Teddy's lover had enormous appeal, but his interest went beyond a single night of flirtatious overtures and provocative glances.

He found Teddy attractive, sexy, vivacious and full of secrets he wanted to discover. Despite the fact that he had little time for a relationship in his busy life, he wanted Teddy Spencer. He wanted to see if the heat between them was as electrical as it felt, wanted to kiss her and feel her come alive in his arms as she had in his dreams last night...

"Well, it's getting late," she said abruptly, and reached for her purse. "And I need to get up early in the morning."

"So do I." He stood, and while he waited for her to follow suit, he folded her check and put it into the front pocket of his pants. He still wasn't sure what to do with the money, but he'd already decided that Saturday night was going to be his treat. It would be his pleasure to be Teddy's lover. "I'll walk you to your car."

They left the bar together with the stares of the patrons following them out the etched-glass door. Outside, the air was December chilled, and the parking lot was barely illuminated by two streetlights. He followed her to a sedate white Honda Accord, parked in a shadowed area of the lot.

Standing by the driver's side, she turned to face him. "I guess I'll see you Saturday night." She thrust out her hand. "Thanks again."

She was so polite, and so determined to keep their agreement on a business level. He had other ideas. Slipping his hand into hers, he tugged her closer. The unexpected movement caused her to waver off balance. She put her hand out to catch herself, and her palm landed on his chest. She gasped, a sexy little intake of breath that warmed his blood and told him her attempt at formality had just slipped a serious notch.

Her luminous brown eyes were wide and searching. "Austin?"

Her voice trembled, not with protest, but with the thrum of desire. Slipping his fingers around her wrist, he stroked his thumb over the wild pulse beating at the base of her palm. Her skin was soft and warm, and when he took a deep breath, he inhaled a subtle, floral fragrance that awakened something hot and primitive within him: *The need to make her his.*

"You know," he murmured, his tone vibrating with low, husky nuances. "Since we'll be pretending to be lovers, there's something we should get out of the way before Saturday."

"What's that?" she asked, her voice a whisper of anticipation.

"Our first kiss." He lowered his head, and experienced a heady rush of excitement when she automatically tipped hers up to meet him halfway. Inches away from claiming her mouth, he hesitated, drawing out the moment to marvel at her acquiescence. He hadn't even touched his lips to hers, but they were parted and ready. Her breathing was eager and expectant, turning him on and making him think of the needy, purring sounds she'd make if he ever had the pleasure of making love to her.

She didn't play coy, didn't shy away from the blatant sexual energy between them. She didn't try to suppress something as basic and natural as desire and he liked that about her. The awareness had been building all evening, in subtle ways, and both of them were ready for the culmination of all that smoldering tension.

Closing the breath of space separating them, he dropped his mouth over hers, and didn't even have to cajole his way past her incredibly soft lips. His tongue glided deeply, sought and found hers, and tangled playfully. The kiss was slow and silky, soulful and honey-sweet. He took his time exploring, tasting and seducing, until leisurely sweeps of his tongue were no longer enough to satisfy the deep, vital hunger gripping him.

He needed...*more*.

She gave a soft, frustrated moan that echoed his own growing impatience, and the hand on his chest curled into a tight fist. Heat coiled low in his belly and spread outward, ruthlessly reminding him just how long he'd gone without the softness of a woman's body to ease his more baser needs.

He didn't want any woman but Teddy. Teddy with her soft, sexy sighs and incredibly generous mouth...

In a flash he was hard and hungry and feeling more than a little wild. And reckless enough to take their encounter one level higher.

Keeping his mouth slanted across hers, he maneuvered her a step back so she was crushed between her car and his body. A gasp caught in her throat, then rolled into a seductive moan when he released her wrist and gripped her hips in his hands, pulling her intimately closer, if that was at all possible considering their bodies were fitted as tightly as a man and woman could get...from breast, to belly, to thighs.

Blood pounded in his ears and rushed along his nerve endings. Her hands slid up his chest and around his neck, then her fingers delved into his thick hair, urging him to give more. His mouth opened wider over hers, and that's when the tenure of the kiss changed, turning demanding, erotic, and so wet and hot he knew if they didn't stop he was going to spontaneously combust.

He broke the kiss, and she whimpered in protest.

"Damn," he muttered, trying to regain his composure. He hadn't meant for things to get so out of control, never expected her to be so soft and giving. Taking a deep, calming breath that did nothing to ease the racing of his heart, or diminish how much he wanted her, he glanced down at Teddy.

She looked stunned, a little disoriented and completely aroused.

Tenderly, he ran his knuckles down her soft cheek and traced the line of her jaw with a finger, slowly drawing her out of her sensual trance. "At least no one at the Christmas party will doubt the chemistry between us." He couldn't help the masculine satisfaction in his voice, or the pleased grin curving his lips.

She visibly swallowed and gave him a shaky smile. "That's exactly what I'm counting on."

4

"I CAN'T BELIEVE you let him kiss you." Teddy frowned sternly at her reflection in the bathroom mirror as she chastised herself for surrendering to Austin's kiss three days ago outside of the Frisco Bay. The fact that she'd thoroughly enjoyed Austin's advances and openly participated in that sensual embrace was another issue she'd lectured herself on, all to no avail.

"Well it wasn't *me* who instigated that kiss," she argued with her twin image as she dusted blush lightly across her cheekbones.

A mocking smile curved her evil twin's mouth. "You certainly didn't do anything to stop him, now, did you? In fact, I distinctly remember you kissing him back with shameless abandon. You didn't even try to resist him."

"Fine!" Teddy's cheeks heated, making the blush she'd just applied unnecessary. Tossing her cosmetics into the bathroom drawer, she lifted her chin, meeting her own gaze defiantly. "I wanted that kiss, okay?" She'd wanted much more than just his lips on hers, but she wasn't about to admit *that* out loud.

Drawing a deep, steady breath, she swept her hair into an elegant chignon, allowing a few wispy curls to escape around her neck and face. "Tonight, you're going to behave yourself, Teddy."

She rolled her eyes at herself. "Of course I'm going to behave myself! This is a business deal, nothing more." She pushed rhinestone-studded pins into the mass of hair at the nape of her neck to hold it in place. With a decisive nod of her head, she ended the absurd discussion and headed into the adjoining bedroom.

Her reflection followed, appearing in her dresser mirror, taunting her.

Glaring, she slipped out of her robe, leaving her scantily clad in black lace panties. Ignoring her image, she retrieved a pair of smoke-hued, thigh-high stockings from her lingerie drawer, lifted a slender leg onto the edge of the bed and rolled the hose up her calf to her thigh. She snuck a peek at her alter ego in the mirror and experienced a prick of annoyance at the perception glimmering in her eyes.

"What?" Teddy demanded haughtily, securing the other stocking.

"Business deal, hmm?" her reflection murmured. "What about Austin posing as your lover? He's going to touch you, pretend intimacy..."

Teddy's breasts swelled and tightened at the thought of enduring Austin's amorous advances. Gritting her teeth in frustration, she grabbed her black slip dress from where she'd laid it on the bed, carefully shimmied it over her head and wriggled the clingy fabric over her hips. She adjusted the rhinestone straps holding up the snug bodice and criss-crossed along her bare back.

Reaching for her diamond stud earrings, she slipped them into her lobes, then backed up to get a full-length view of how she looked for the Christmas party. Elegant, yet sophisticated and confident. Precisely the self-assured look she wanted to achieve.

She gave herself an approving nod. "Just keep your mind on that promotion, Teddy, and off your gorgeous date, and you'll be fine."

"Good luck," her twin smirked. "Considering you melt when the guy just looks at you, you're gonna need it."

She jammed her hands on her hips and scowled. Before

she could issue an argument, a knock sounded at the door, and her stomach rolled...with nerves, anticipation and a bubbling excitement that didn't bode well for her peace of mind. Squelching the flurry of butterflies taking flight in her belly, she hurried out of the bedroom to the condo's front door. One glance through the peephole at the gorgeous man standing in the hallway and her heart rate skyrocketed while her knees turned to mush.

Willing a calm composure, she opened the door, momentarily dizzied by the enticing spice cologne drifting her way. Her gaze took in his tailored tuxedo, deriving immense pleasure from the way the suit complimented a body she knew to be virile and incredibly honed. The dark color accentuated his chiseled good looks and gave him a mysterious air. She dabbed her tongue along her dry lips, fantasies aplenty leaping to mind. It wasn't hard to imagine him stripping off that jacket for some woman, releasing the black bow tie, ripping off his shirt...

An amused smile curved his mouth, reaching his warm, moss-green eyes. "Hi," he murmured, pulling her from her inappropriate thoughts.

"Hi," she replied, unable to help the husky quality of her voice. The man simply made her feel breathless, reckless and too aware of herself as a woman. The sensation unnerved her, because she couldn't afford that kind of distraction.

She cleared her throat. "You look..." Scrumptious, sexy, to-die-for. All apt descriptions, but she settled for, "great."

Flirtatious eyes appraised her just as thoroughly as she'd assessed him, lingering appreciatively where the black dress dipped to reveal a swell of cleavage, then downward to the hem that ended just above her knee. The journey upward was just as lazy, and just as arousing to her senses. "So do you."

Promotion, promotion, promotion. The chant ran through her mind like a litany.

"Come on in," she said politely, stepping back to let him enter. She closed the door, then followed him into the adjoining living room. "I just need a few more minutes, and then I'll be ready to go. Make yourself comfortable."

Just as she would have turned to escape to her bedroom for a last-minute lecture, he reached into the front pocket of his trousers and withdrew a piece of paper. "Before we leave, I wanted to give this to you."

She eyed the yellow slip he held toward her. "What's that?"

"A receipt for my services."

"Oh." Tentatively, she took the proof of payment, not sure she wanted a reminder of her desperation.

"And I hope you don't mind," Austin continued, "but I donated the thousand dollars to the Children's Hospital in your name."

Startled at his announcement, she lifted her gaze to his face, noting his earnest expression. "Why?"

His broad shoulders lifted in a casual shrug. "Because I thought the money would be better spent on people who need it. And besides, it is the season of giving."

"Yes, it is," she agreed, overwhelmed by his generosity, and his sincerity, when most of the men she knew would have pocketed the money without a second thought. She folded the receipt and tucked it into her purse on the countertop separating the living room from the small kitchen. "Thank you. That was incredibly thoughtful and selfless."

His easy, charming smile dismissed her compliment. "Tonight is on me. Merry Christmas, Teddy."

Touched by his gesture, she closed the distance between them, wanting to express her own gratitude with a chaste, affectionate kiss on the cheek. At the last moment, he turned his head slightly, and her lips brushed his in a soft, infinitely gentle kiss. Her eyes momentarily closed at that tender touch, a rush of warmth suffused her veins and her lips parted on a sigh.

Austin didn't take advantage of her unconscious offering. His mouth hovered above hers, his breath warm and scented with mint as it caressed her lips. Desire twisted through Teddy, sharpening her senses. He didn't touch her, didn't initiate a deeper kiss, like the one she yearned for, yet her body sizzled with awareness.

Heart pounding, she slowly lifted her lashes. Her gaze collided with the unmistakable heat in his eyes—a hunger that told her she was playing with fire, and if she was bold enough to close the inches separating their lips, he'd be happy to oblige her, and more.

She considered the temptation, anticipated the pleasure and weighed the consequences of involving herself with this man who was proving to be more of a distraction than she'd counted on. Deciding she couldn't allow her attraction to Austin to interfere with her goals, she abruptly stepped back, severing the moment. But the magnetic pull was still there, shimmering in his eyes, tugging her toward the promise of sexual satisfaction, and something deeper and more intimately connected.

The ache within her intensified.

"I'll, uh, be ready in a few minutes," she said quickly, then retreated down the hall. Enclosing herself in her bathroom, she pressed her back against the door, took deep breaths to still her racing pulse and didn't dare look in the mirror for fear of encountering her evil twin again.

"Promotion, promotion, promotion," she chanted like a prayer.

AUSTIN STROLLED around Teddy's modestly decorated living room while he waited for her to return, unable to wipe the smile from his face. There was something incredibly sexy about Teddy when she was flustered. Add to her appeal her generous, straightforward personality and that little black dress she was wearing, and he was finding himself hard-pressed to resist her.

Judging by that near miss they'd just had, it appeared she was struggling to suppress the same craving for him. And if a little kiss made her nervous, he wondered how she was going to handle the evening, with him making sure everyone at tonight's party went home with the impression that he and Teddy were intimate. Surely she realized that illusion meant more than stealing a kiss or two?

He looked forward to those stolen kisses, those subtle caresses. And he was hoping by the end of the night she'd realize that there was something very personal and real between them.

That was the main reason he'd donated the money she'd paid him. Not only was he uncomfortable taking such a huge chunk of change for something he wanted to do, but also, he absolutely refused to be a paid escort. Donating the check to a good cause seemed the perfect solution, for him to keep his conscience intact, and to take away Teddy's excuse that she couldn't mix business with pleasure.

Tonight, he was her date, accompanying her to the Christmas party of his own free will. Pleasure was the fundamental purpose of this evening, and he planned to make sure Teddy experienced her fair share.

The phone on the countertop rang, breaking into Austin's thoughts. He glanced down the short hallway toward her bedroom, wondering if Teddy was available to pick up the line.

The phone pealed again, loud and insistent.

"Teddy?" he called, and got no response. Figuring she was in the bathroom, he decided to do her a favor and take the call, just in case it was important.

He lifted the cordless receiver to his ear on the third ring. "Hello?"

Silence greeted him.

He frowned. "Hello?" he said again, more assertive this time.

"Hi, uh, is Teddy there?" a female voice tentatively asked.

A girlfriend, Austin guessed, and could only image what the other woman was thinking. "Yes, she is, but she's busy at the moment. Can I take a message?"

"Who is this?" the voice queried.

Austin hesitated. He had no idea how many people thought Teddy was seriously involved, especially considering she wore a ring all the time. So he decided to stick with the story he and Teddy had come up with.

"This is Austin McBride, her boyfriend."

"Her boyfriend?" The woman sounded genuinely delighted. "I didn't realize Teddy was seeing someone. Isn't it just like her to keep something like this a secret from the family?"

Her family? Austin cringed. "Could I ask who is calling?"

"This is Teddy's sister-in-law, Susan," the woman said, introducing herself in a bubbly tone. "Have you and Teddy been seeing each other for long?"

Austin glanced down the hallway, hoping to see Teddy coming to his rescue. No such luck. "We've been friends for a while," he hedged. *Three days, at least*, he mentally justified. "And just recently started dating." How recent, he wasn't going to elaborate on.

"Wow!" Susan released a gust of light laughter. "The rest of the family is going to be thrilled. Teddy hasn't dated since her breakup with Bartholomew." She paused as if realizing she'd revealed too much. "Uh, she did tell you about Bart, didn't she?"

Austin could feel himself being ensnared in a trap of his own making, and wasn't sure how to escape. "Oh, absolutely," he replied, certain he was sinking in way over his head.

"Her parents still haven't gotten over the fact that she'd throw away a great catch like Bart to pursue a career. But for as long as I've known Teddy, which is going on ten years now, she's always been the rebellious one in the family. Not that I blame her, considering how stifling her parents and brothers have been," Susan added wryly.

All Austin could manage was a quick nod, because Susan-the-talker didn't give him a chance to respond to her steady monologue.

"Don't get me wrong," she continued. "I love my husband and the rest of the Spencer clan, but they are a bit old-fashioned in their thinking. It took me years to knock some sense into Teddy's brother and make him realize that I'm an independent woman, who doesn't need to be coddled. Teddy has been trying to prove the same thing to her family, but they just don't seem to understand how important it is to Teddy to make it on her own, without the influence of Spencer money or connections."

Austin's stomach bottomed out, and old bitter memories threatened to swamp him. So, Teddy did come from money, as he'd suspected. He couldn't help but wonder how someone blue collar like him might fit into her group of Ivy League friends and family. Not well, as he'd learned from experience.

"So, in some ways, I'm not all that surprised that Teddy has been keeping you all to herself. When I was dating Teddy's brother, Brent, I was the one subjected to the Spencers' scrutiny. It wasn't fun."

Austin pinched the bridge of his nose with his thumb and forefinger. As fascinating as he found Susan's rundown on Teddy's family, he didn't like hearing this stuff secondhand. Or maybe he just didn't care for what he was hearing, period.

"Well, Susan," he managed to break into the conversation

when the woman finally took a breather. "Is there some kind of message I can pass on to Teddy for you?"

"Oh, of course!" She laughed brightly. "Here I am, talking your ear off, and I'm sure Teddy is waiting on you. Tell her that Christmas Eve dinner next week is at six, and to be on time. I think she shows up late just to annoy her mother." Humor, and understanding, followed up that statement.

Austin grinned at Teddy's display of defiance, and jotted down the message on a notepad situated near the phone. "Will do."

"You will come with her, won't you?" Susan asked hopefully.

Austin's insides clenched tighter. "I don't think I'll be able to make it," he lied. Not only was he certain he wouldn't fit in with the Spencer clan, he didn't think Teddy would appreciate him tagging along to meet Mom and Dad. "I have other plans."

"Surely you can make the time to meet Teddy's family, even if it's just to stop by for a few minutes?"

Was it his imagination, or was there an underlying disapproval in Susan's words, like what kind of guy was he if he couldn't even make the effort to meet his girlfriend's family? He felt like a schmuck, yet it was his own fault for allowing the fabrication to stretch so far. But how was he to know who knew Teddy's secrets?

The excuse did nothing to ease the twinge of guilt he experienced. "I'll see what I can do," he compromised. Hopefully, Teddy would be able to smooth out the mess he'd made of things.

"Great." Enthusiasm infused Susan's voice. "It was nice talking to you, Austin. I'm looking forward to meeting you."

"Uh, same here." He disconnected the line before anything more could be said. Hanging his head, he shook it in dismay.

Hell, what had he done?

"I heard the phone ring while I was in the bathroom." Teddy's voice drifted from down the hall as she approached the living room. "Did you catch the call, or did the answering machine pick it up?"

"Don't I wish," he muttered.

"Excuse me?"

Straightening, he faced her, just in time to see her drop a lipstick tube into her small black beaded purse and snap it shut. During her absence she'd put on a pair of heels, lengthening those eye-turning, shapely legs of hers. She looked like a million bucks.

The irony of that assessment wasn't lost on him. "That was your sister-in-law, Susan."

Teddy came to an abrupt halt in front of him. "Oh?"

He thrust his hands into the front pockets of his trousers. "And she's now under the assumption that I'm your boyfriend."

"Oh, no," she groaned.

"I'm sorry, Teddy," he rushed to apologize, not that his own regret could make up for any damage he'd done. "I had no idea who you told about your 'significant other,' and it came out before I found out who she was."

He expected her to be angry, or at the very least upset, but she appeared more worried than anything. "Oh, it's not all your fault. I adore Susan, but even if you hadn't said you were my boyfriend, she would have come to that assumption on her own. Everyone in my family wants me to find a decent man and settle down." The disgust in her voice was evident.

He didn't get that impression from Susan, but then again the other woman had been quite enthusiastic about Teddy being in a relationship again. Family dynamics were a curious thing.

"I'll just give her a quick call and explain our one-night arrangement." Startled by the sound of her own words, she amended hastily, "I mean, set her straight about our business deal."

So, she was back to *business*, was she?

Teddy reached for the phone, tucked it next to her ear and punched in a series of numbers. With a forced lightness, she added, "The last thing I'd want is for my entire family to think I'm seriously involved with someone. They'd be all over you like piranhas, picking you apart, piece by piece."

Her analogy wasn't a pleasant one, but it served to remind him of where they stood with one another—on opposite sides of the tracks. There was no way her family would approve of a guy who fulfilled women's fantasies, and was struggling to maintain a landscaping business.

A frown creased Teddy's forehead, and with a deep sigh, she set the phone back into the cradle. "The line's busy." She gave her gold watch a quick glance. "I'll have to catch up with Susan later. We need to get going."

Picking up her black shawl from the couch, she settled it over her bare shoulders and headed for the door. Minutes later, they were in Austin's black Mustang, following Teddy's directions toward the Bay area.

Silence filled the interior of the vehicle, except for the low volume of mellow music drifting from the speakers. Austin glanced briefly Teddy's way. She sat in the passenger seat, staring out the window, quiet and subdued. Reserved even. Was she mulling over the conversation he'd had with her sister-in-law? Or was she more worried about the Christmas party ahead?

"So, who is Bartholomew?" he asked, voicing the one question that had been on his mind since Susan mentioned him.

"I'm gonna strangle Susan," Teddy muttered darkly.

A grin quirked the corner of Austin's mouth. "Pardon?"

"Bartholomew Winston is a past mistake," she said succinctly, without looking at him. "And one I'd rather not talk about."

The resentment in her tone was unmistakable. "All right," he conceded, now even more curious about this mystery man of her past, and what had happened between them.

Again, silence reigned. As Austin exited the freeway and neared the hotel where the Christmas party was being held, the more tense Teddy seemed to become. He no longer suspected that her uneasiness stemmed from Susan's call. It was all about the promotion she was up for—if Louden fell for their little game.

Tonight would tell.

Pulling the Mustang under the valet awning, he put the car in park and turned toward Teddy. He touched her knee, his fingers rasping along her silky stockings, and she jumped in response. She jerked her luminous gaze, now filled with anxiety, to his, but the slight tremble he felt where his fingers lay idly against her thigh told him she was very aware of him, and the intimacy of their situation.

He tilted his head, regarding her with genuine concern. "Hey, you okay?"

She moved her leg out of his reach, dislodging his gentle touch. She gave him a smile that appeared more like a grimace. "Sure, I'm fine," she said in a tone too bright and chipper.

He stared at her for a long moment. Beneath all that forced cheerfulness, there was something incredibly vulnerable about her—not that he'd expect an independent career woman like Teddy to ever admit to such an emotion. No, she wanted to be strong and confident, and in control. A part of him understood that. Respected it, even.

"Teddy," he whispered, wishing she'd ease up and relax around him. Otherwise, Louden Avery would know he was a fraud, and that revelation would defeat Teddy's purpose. But before he could express his concerns, a young man opened her door and offered a gloved hand to help her out of the car.

Austin sighed, gave his vehicle over to valet and met up with Teddy on the curb. Settling his palm on her lower back, he ushered her through the automatic glass doors that whooshed open for them. She stiffened, but didn't protest the hand resting so familiarly where her spine ended and the curve of her bottom began. There was nothing inappropriate about the way he touched her, yet he got the distinct impression that she would have preferred he didn't.

Knowing she was forcibly resisting what was between them, irritation gripped him. She was nervous, he acknowledged that, but she was giving off the wrong kind of vibes if she expected everyone to believe they had something going on. He wasn't sure what to do about her remoteness, but his mind mulled over various ideas.

They followed the signs for Sharper Image's party through the lush, expensively decorated lobby to a glass-enclosed elevator that shot straight up to the thirty-second floor and overlooked the bay. Stepping into the lift behind Teddy, Austin pressed the only button available that would take them to the tower's ballroom.

The elevator, dimly lit inside to make it easier to look outside, slowly made its ascent, giving the occupants plenty of time to admire their surroundings. The evening sun had set almost an hour ago, but nightfall allowed them to appreciate the expanse of water beyond, and the twinkle of lights from the boats coasting along the ocean. A quarter of the way up, they had a breathtaking panorama of the Bay area.

The atmosphere was romantic, made more so by the intimate four-by-four cubicle that confined them. Teddy didn't seem to notice, or appreciate, the ambience. She stood at the brass bar lining the thick glass enclosure, her gaze lost on something off in the distance.

"Nice view," Austin commented, in an attempt to strike

up a conversation. Standing behind her, the view *was* fantastic—she had a nice bottom that deserved a lingering glance.

"Hmm," was Teddy's noncommittal response.

He rubbed a finger along his jaw and tried again. "It sure is an awfully long ride up. The possibilities of what a couple could do with all this time is endless." He didn't disguise the sexy innuendo in his voice.

"Hmm." His suggestive comment didn't faze her.

Frustration nipped at him. If he couldn't even shock her into acknowledging him, then they were in for a disaster of an evening.

Finally, the right idea came to him, the shock value of which would either set her off, or wind her down. He was hoping for the latter result.

Reaching back to the button panel, he pressed the red one marked Stop. The elevator came to a slow, whirring halt somewhere between the lobby and the thirty-second floor.

She spun around, panic etching her features. "Oh my God! We're stuck!"

A lazy, unrepentant grin kicked up the corner of his mouth. "I deliberately stopped the elevator."

Her jaw dropped. "You what?"

He knew she'd heard him, so he didn't bother wasting precious time by repeating himself. Instead, he closed the distance between them and braced his hands on the brass railing on either side of her hips, trapping her between the cool glass and his solid body.

A small, stunned gasp escaped her lips, and her body immediately grew rigid. "What are you doing?" she demanded.

His grin widened at her haughty tone, but it certainly didn't deter him. Moving closer, he pressed his thighs against hers, and pushed a knee between her legs to keep her in place. "You know, if you don't relax and shake off that tension that has been building since we left your place, we're never going to convince your boss that we're lovers."

Teddy dampened her bottom lip with her tongue, then released a long breath. "You're right," she admitted, and clearly expected him to release her.

Not totally convinced of her acquiescence, which he suspected was an act for his benefit, he kept her pinned right where he had her. The shock value was about to increase. "What do you think, Teddy, should we start the party off with a bang and give your co-workers something to talk about?"

Even in the dim light illuminating the interior of the elevator, he could see the suspicion in her gaze. "What do you mean?"

He caressed the back of his hand down her soft cheek, strummed his fingers along her neck, watching as her deep brown eyes darkened with the first stirrings of desire. "How about a quickie at eighteen floors up overlooking the bay?"

She gasped in wide-eyed astonishment, then a burst of laughter bubbled up from her chest. "You're outrageous!"

He chuckled along with her. "You have to admit that the thought is thrilling...maybe just a little bit."

She glanced down at their position, and he wondered if she realized what a perfect support that brass bar behind her would be. It would be just a matter of lifting her dress, removing her panties, unzipping his pants and letting her sit on that sturdy bar with her back braced against the window as he slid inside her and she wrapped her legs around his hips...

He nearly groaned at the erotic image, and knew she was thinking the same thing by the way the pulse at the base of her throat fluttered.

She swallowed hard, and managed a slight shake of her head. "Austin..."

He conceded to the warning in her voice, but the erection

straining the front of his trousers wasn't nearly so coopera-
tive. "Okay, making love here and now might be a bit too
scandalous, but how about necking? That's pretty harmless." Before she could object, he skimmed a hand along her
hip to her waist and stroked her belly with his thumb
through the silky material of her dress. "I want to kiss you,
Teddy," he murmured huskily as his head dipped toward
hers. "Will you let me?"

Her chin lifted, bringing her lips closer to his. "We
shouldn't."

He smiled. "Maybe we should, to help get rid of all that
tension."

She pulled back a fraction and frowned at him. "I'm perfectly fine."

"Yeah, that's why you get skittish every time I touch you,"
he said wryly. "Just enjoy the evening, Teddy. Have fun with
the charade. When I touch you, flow toward me..." Lifting
his hand, he smoothed it down her spine in a luxurious caress. She softened, her back arching until her lush breasts
brushed his chest. Even through his starched shirt, he could
feel her tight nipples, and it nearly drove him crazy. Keeping
his thoughts centered and focused on her, he lowered his
mouth near the side of her head. He breathed in that floral
fragrance that was uniquely hers, and his senses spun.
"When I whisper in your ear, close your eyes and think of
something sexy, so it looks as though I'm murmuring
naughty things to you, even if I'm just asking you to pass the
salt."

She let out a long breath, and he pulled back just far
enough to look at her face. Her eyes were closed, her expression soft and slumberous, certainly relaxed. Her body followed suit, growing pliable beneath his slow caresses. "Can
you do that, Teddy?" he asked.

Her lashes lifted, revealing a need as strong as the one

coursing through his veins. "Yeah," she whispered, her voice sultry-soft in the darkness of the elevator.

"Good." He marveled at his ability to remain so calm when his hormones were clamoring for something more elemental. "And how about that kiss? Can I have it?"

Seemingly seduced by all that had come before, she lifted a hand, sifted her fingers through the hair at the nape of his neck and brought his mouth to hers. "Yes," she murmured, and gave him a deep, hot, tongue-tangling kiss more potent than any aphrodisiac.

Passion rose swiftly to the surface, shattering his control. He gripped her hips and rocked urgently against her, swallowing her gasp when his thigh moved upward and pressed against sensitive flesh.

He had to have her. His palm touched her silken thigh, the same moment a shrill ring filled the small cubicle, vaguely penetrating the fog of desire that had settled over him. By the second ring, Austin realized the emergency phone in the elevator was the annoying culprit.

Reluctantly dragging his mouth from Teddy's, he reached behind him, managing to grasp the receiver without moving away from her. They were both breathing hard from their erotic encounter, and he had to take a deep, steady breath before speaking.

"Yes?"

"This is security," a gruff voice came over the line. "Everything okay up there?"

His gaze locked on Teddy's, noting the combination of amusement and arousal glowing in the depths of her eyes. Feeling incredibly daring, he trailed a finger along the rhinestone strap holding up her dress, down to the dip of cleavage swelling from the bodice. "Just taking a little time to enjoy the fabulous view."

Teddy let out a giggle at his double-edged comment, and she slapped a hand over her mouth to contain her laughter, her eyes sparkling. He managed, just barely, to contain his own chuckles.

"Keep the elevator moving, buddy," the security guard grumbled, sounding put out. "We've got a crowd of people down in the lobby waiting their turn."

Hanging up the phone, he flipped the Stop switch, and his stomach dipped as the elevator glided upward. "We still have a long way to go," he said, coming back to her with a wicked grin. Framing her face between his palms, he murmured, "Where were we?"

He didn't wait for her to answer, but resumed the kiss that had been interrupted with as much enthusiasm as before. Mouths met, lips parted and tongues entwined silkily. No resistance, just a mutual hunger that spiraled and tightened between them.

He kissed her with deep thoroughness, wanting to brand the moment in her mind forever. And in return, he was equally seduced. She was soft, provocative and sweeter than honey. He wanted to taste her skin to discover other flavors and contrasts, ached to run his tongue across the breasts crushing against his chest. He wanted to be anywhere but in a roomful of people, making polite conversation and pretending to be Teddy's lover.

He wanted to be the real thing.

Too soon, he ended the sensual embrace, but the thrum of desire remained.

"Damn," he whispered as he rested his forehead against hers, his body inflamed and his mind fogged. "Are you sure you don't want to ride the elevator back down and try a quickie?"

She groaned, and when he lifted his head, he saw that she was smiling. And much more languidly than before. Her rich brown eyes shone bright with passion, her cheeks wore a rosy hue, and her lips were swollen from their shared kiss.

Male gratification flowed through him. He'd achieved his

goal. Not only did Teddy Spencer appear to be a woman well satisfied, but her tension had abated.

She blinked, and as if finally coming out of some drugging trance, her gaze blossomed with worry. Her fingers fluttered to her hair, which Austin had been careful not to touch. "Oh, God, I probably look a mess!"

Grinning, he adjusted her shawl to cover the shoulder it had slipped from during their interlude. "You look beautiful. A little tousled, but certainly convincing."

"I can't believe we did that!" she admonished gently.

He stroked his hand over her bottom, and felt her shiver. Her uninhibited response pleased him. "And just think, we've got the whole evening ahead of us." He winked at her.

The elevator came to a slow, smooth stop at their final destination, a soft *ping* announcing their arrival. Knowing they only had seconds to compose themselves before they greeted the entire staff of Sharper Image, Austin straightened his tuxedo jacket, then at the very last moment slid his hand possessively into Teddy's.

The insulated doors whooshed open and a dozen curious eyes clamored to sneak a glimpse of the couple who had stopped the elevators midway up to the thirty-second floor. Austin watched eyebrows rise, grins split across surprised faces and murmurs of disbelief and amusement filter from one person to another.

Austin's mouth curved into a roguish grin, purposely adding fuel to the rampant gossip that would no doubt circulate during the Christmas party and establish him as the man in Teddy's life.

5

TEDDY HELD her head high and stepped from the elevator with Austin, intensely aware of everyone's inquisitive stares, and the disheveled way she looked after her interlude with Austin. With Austin gently squeezing her hand and offering silent support, she felt surprisingly confident, and reckless in a purely feminine sort of way. As nervous as she'd been about tonight, Austin had erased a good portion of her anxiety with humor, charm, and hoards of sex appeal—the latter of which had her female colleagues giving the good-looking man at her side a thorough, effusive once-over.

Back off, girls, he's taken.

Tonight, Austin was *her* fantasy for hire, and she planned to enjoy the evening, as he'd suggested. The more comfortable she was around Austin, the more convincing they'd be as a couple.

After introducing him to the group of single females obviously waiting to meet him—and watching as he dazzled everybody with his sexy smiles and irresistible personality—they decided to mingle. Over one hundred and fifty employees were present, from mail-room clerks to the top brass, all decked out in their holiday finery. She searched for Louden, but in the crush of people she didn't see him.

The mood was festive, with a hired band playing upbeat Christmas tunes during the cocktail hour. Being that this was Teddy's first company Christmas party, she was highly impressed with the show Sharper Image put on.

The ballroom was elaborately decorated for the Christmas season, with garland, holly and mistletoe aplenty. Eight-foot noble firs, gaily decorated in sparkling lights and pretty ornaments, scented the room with traditional pine. Centerpieces of bright red poinsettias and tapered cream candles adorned each table, and lacy snowflakes sprayed with a shimmering incandescent powder hung from the ceiling, giving her the illusion of being in a winter wonderland. The effect was enchanting.

Teddy made sure she introduced Austin to as many people as she could, from the CEO of the company to the front-end receptionist, and watched in amazement as he effortlessly established a male camaraderie with the men, and beguiled the women, while making it apparent, with an affectionate glance, an intimate comment, that he was completely devoted to her. During the moments when they were alone, he'd touch her possessively, run his fingers over her bare back and down her spine, keeping her body in a constant state of awareness. More daring, he'd lean close and murmur bawdy comments and jokes in her ear that caused her to blush, laugh out loud, and made them look as though they shared intimate secrets.

Teddy found herself so wrapped up in his attention, even she had to struggle to keep from blurring the lines between reality and fantasy.

"Would you like something to drink, sweetheart?" Austin asked. He'd spent the past five minutes charming two women Teddy worked with, and as much as she didn't want to be alone with the duo answering a barrage of questions, she *was* getting thirsty.

She gave him a warm, private smile for her co-workers' benefit. "I'd love a wine spritzer."

His large, hot palm casually slid over her hip to her waist, pulling her close to brush his lips across her cheek. A tremor of response rippled through her, and her breath quickened.

Striking green eyes glittered with devious pleasure when they met hers again, testimony that the rogue was relishing every minute of their performance. "I'll be right back, so don't go far."

As if her weak knees would allow her to wander off!

Barb, Sharper Image's payroll clerk, sighed wistfully, not bothering to conceal her lust as she watched Austin walk away. "What an absolute doll he is, Teddy."

"Mmm," Karen, an accounts rep, agreed, shaking her head in wonder and envy. "Where have you been hiding him all this time?"

"I, well, uh..." Teddy grasped a ready excuse while absently twisting the diamond and ruby band on her finger. "Austin's work keeps him incredibly busy. It's a wonder *I* get any quality time with him."

Barb scoffed at that. "Come on, Teddy, the guy is crazy for you. From what I've seen tonight, not to mention the rumor circulating about a little incident in the elevator, he doesn't come across as a man whose been too neglectful."

Fire burned Teddy's cheeks.

"I have to agree," Karen said, her eyes sparkling merrily over the rim of her champagne glass as she took a sip.

Knowing there was no sense denying what both Barb and Karen wanted to believe—what she, herself, needed them to believe—she didn't bother to correct their assumption. "Would you two stop, already?"

"We're just jealous," Barb admitted good-naturedly. "He's personable, totally into you, and has a body to die for. And he's probably rich to boot."

Teddy didn't think Austin wallowed in wealth, but she imagined his "Fantasy" services kept his bank account amply filled. "Oh, he does quite well for himself."

"What does he do, anyway?" Karen asked curiously.

Panic raced through her, pumping up the beat of her heart until she could hear it drumming in her ears. Good Lord, they hadn't discussed a respectable occupation! "He's a...broker." Well, he definitely qualified as such, she reasoned, considering he solicited his services, and those of his other employees.

"Oh," Barb said, looking suitably impressed. "Like an investment broker?"

"Uh, yes," Teddy said, going with the suggestion because nothing else sounded better. Feeling herself flounder in unfamiliar territory, she searched frantically for Austin, and found him over at the service bar talking to the vice president of the company while he waited for their drinks.

In an attempt to divert the conversation before she complicated the situation further, she turned back to Karen. "So, I hear you're planning a surprise baby shower for Catherine Johnson in Marketing after the new year. What can I do to help?"

A few moments later, Austin finally returned. He handed her the wine spritzer, then took a sip of his own drink, which looked suspiciously like root beer. Grateful for the interruption, she told Karen and Barb that she'd get the rest of the details on the baby shower next week at work, and quickly maneuvered Austin in the opposite direction before his cover was blown. Finding a secluded, unoccupied arbor decorated in colorful twinkling lights and Christmas greenery, she finally stopped and faced him.

He waggled his dark eyebrows at her. "Eager to find a dark corner to have your way with me, eh?" His voice was low and tinged with all kinds of wicked innuendo.

Her stomach dipped, but she resolutely ignored the sensation. "No, I—"

He abruptly cut off her words with a kiss that happened so spontaneously she didn't have a breath of a chance to stop those tantalizing lips from covering her own. Gaining her equilibrium, she jerked back, nearly spilling her wine spritzer down the front of her dress.

"Austin!" she admonished, not exactly shocked at his audacity, considering how bold he'd proven to be. But still, they'd given the employees at Sharper Image plenty to gossip about without giving them a public display, too!

"What?" He blinked at her, a picture of little-boy innocence. "You're standing under the mistletoe, and anyone watching would expect any self-respecting boyfriend to take advantage of the situation."

Skeptical, she glanced up at the arbor they stood under. Sure enough, a sprig of mistletoe dangled above her head.

Without permission, he came back for a second sampling, this time curling his long fingers around the nape of her neck and using his thumb to tip her chin up and keep her mouth firmly locked beneath his. He parted her lips with one silken stroke of his tongue, and she tasted heat, and the sweet flavor of root beer.

Losing all sense of time and place, she gave herself over to his soft, compelling kiss. The man stole her sanity, made her want things she'd convinced herself she didn't need in her life and threatened her hard-won independence. He made her feel too reckless, and entirely too needy.

Desperate to pull the situation back into perspective, she placed a hand on his chest, feeling the strong, steady beat of his heart beneath her palm. To anyone watching, the gesture looked like an affectionate caress, but he immediately picked up on her cue. Or maybe it was her panic he sensed.

With a low growl that reverberated deep in his chest, Austin lifted his head, his eyes glowing with unsuppressed hunger. "I suggest we finish this later, when we don't have an audience."

Certain that intimate comment was meant for their viewers' ears, she nodded, the only intelligible gesture she could manage at the moment.

"They have got to be the most romantic, in-love couple I've ever seen," Teddy heard some woman say from behind Austin.

They'd certainly fooled everyone, she thought with a grimace. Hopefully, Louden would be just as convinced.

Arm in arm, they strolled away from the arbor. "You're an investment broker," she whispered in a low voice to Austin, and nodded sociably at an older couple who were smiling at them.

"I am?" Amusement threaded Austin's voice.

"As of ten minutes ago, you are."

"How about I own my landscaping business instead?"

She shook her head at him, dismissing his offbeat suggestion. "No, I was thinking more along the lines of something upscale and respectable."

"Respectable?" he echoed, his voice losing that humorous edge of moments before.

Her face flushed. She hadn't meant to insult him. "Well, yes," she hedged. "Saying you're an investment broker is more respectable than announcing you're a fantasy for hire. You weren't around, we hadn't discussed an occupation, and it's the first thing I thought of."

He shrugged, and accepted her choice of career. "Okay. After all, this is *your* fantasy."

She frowned at him, and his choice of words. "No, my fantasy was a cowboy. This is strictly business."

Annoyance flitted across his handsome face, and just when she suspected he was going to issue an argument of some sort, the man she'd been dreading all evening finally approached them. The tension Austin had worked so hard to obliterate quickly spread through Teddy's body, tightening muscles and tingling nerves.

Dressed in the prerequisite black tie, Louden exuded confidence and professionalism, which Teddy supposed appealed to the higher-ups in the company. Louden couldn't have climbed the corporate ladder as high as he had without competence and some personable qualities. What the directors didn't realize, though, was just how poorly he handled employee relations.

Pale blue eyes scrutinized Austin lazily, but Teddy wasn't fooled by his complacent behavior. Even if he was suspicious, he certainly wasn't going to let it show in front of her, or anyone else.

"Hello, Louden," Teddy greeted, trying to maintain a semblance of courtesy.

"Theodora." Louden inclined his head at her and smiled pleasantly. "You look quite lovely tonight."

Ignoring his compliment, she pulled her shawl tighter around her shoulders. "Louden, I'd like you to meet my boyfriend, Austin McBride."

Louden turned his attention back to the man at her side, and Austin extended his hand toward her boss. Their hands clasped in a firm handshake, and Teddy caught an undercurrent of silent rivalry. Austin was clearly staking a claim, and Louden was sizing up the competition.

"Nice to meet you," Austin said, his tone cordial.

Louden didn't return the sentiment. "So, we finally get to meet the man in Theodora's life. Can't say I've heard a whole lot about you. Other than that ring on her finger, Teddy's been keeping you a secret."

"Well, she certainly hasn't kept you a secret," Austin replied meaningfully.

Something dark sparked in Louden's gaze, but he didn't respond. "You must be very proud of her. Theodora has proved herself to be quite a valuable asset to Sharper Image in the nine months that she's been working for the company."

"The woman constantly amazes me with her talent and dedication." Austin slipped his arm around her waist and pulled her close in an open display of support and tenderness. "I'm hoping to see her promoted to that senior graphic design position, where she can really exercise that creative mind of hers."

Teddy discreetly nudged Austin in the side. The man was pouring the praise on a bit thick.

"I'd really like to see her promoted, too, but I have the difficult task of weighing both candidates' proficiency for the

position and convincing my superiors of their competence."
He sighed, as if the selection process was a burdensome one.
"Needless to say, it's been a tough decision."

"I'm sure you'll select the most qualified person for the
job." Austin's words were cool, but very calculated.

Louden's expression was just as shrewd. "Without a
doubt."

The band announced that dinner was about to be served,
and for everyone to find their seats before the buffet began.

"If you'll excuse me, I see a few people I'd like to say hello
to before I sit down," Louden said. "You two enjoy the evening, and I'll see you in the office Monday, Theodora."

Once they parted ways with Louden and headed toward
their designated table, Austin asked, "Is there a reason why
he calls you Theodora when everyone else calls you Teddy?"

"To annoy me, and to make sure I keep in mind his position of authority." The only other person who used her formal name on a regular basis was her prim-and-proper
mother, and her brothers when they wanted to antagonize
her. "Speaking of which, I'd appreciate it if you didn't directly challenge Louden like that."

Austin clasped Teddy's elbow to escort her through the
throng of people. "Yeah, well, someone needs to knock that
guy down a peg or two. He's too cocky for his own good, and
I don't like the way he looks at you."

She bristled, feeling her defenses rising. For too many
years she'd endured coddling and protecting from three
older brothers who'd treated her as a weak, vulnerable female. She'd despised every minute of it. That Austin felt
compelled to shelter her as well provoked a bit of rebellion,
especially when she'd struggled for so long to break free
from her family's stifling habits.

"Being my bodyguard isn't your job, Austin," she said emphatically. "All I need you to do is back up the ring on my
finger. I'm more than capable of fighting my own battles in
the boardroom."

His mouth thinned ruthlessly. "Are you?"

"Yeah, I am." She resented the insinuation that she couldn't look after the situation herself. "I want this promotion on my own merit. My work record proves I'm qualified for the job, more so than my opponent."

Austin didn't look convinced. "Do you honestly believe that introducing your boyfriend is going to stop this slimeball from making future moves on you? Guys like Louden don't stop at minor obstacles like boyfriends. He wants to be in control, and he won't stop until he gets what he wants, which seems to be you. The only way he'll leave you alone is if you press charges."

Teddy's stomach churned as she sat in the chair Austin pulled out for her at their table, but she refused to dwell on his accurate assessment of Louden. "Don't worry, he'll leave me alone," she said, wishing she felt more confident than she sounded.

Austin let the subject drop as they joined the others at the table. Teddy made introductions to the people who hadn't yet met Austin, and valiantly tried to shake off the black mood Louden had cast over them and the evening.

Minutes later, they stood in line at the buffet table, plate in hand. Dinner was a selection of salads, rich side dishes, fancy breads, chicken in a mushroom-and-wine sauce, and prime rib. A quarter of the way down the buffet, Teddy glanced up to find Janet, a buxom redhead who worked in her department as Louden's secretary, staring purposefully at Austin from the opposite side of the smorgasbord. Janet was extremely loyal to Louden, and that alone made Teddy mistrust the woman.

Austin must have sensed the intensity of the other woman's gaze, because he looked up, too—which was all the invitation Janet needed to launch into conversation.

"You look so familiar," she said, tilting her head so her thick mane of curly auburn hair tumbled over her shoulder and lay enticingly just above the breasts straining the too-tight bodice of her spandex dress. "Have we met before?"

The question was harmless, yet an awful premonition made Teddy's stomach dip.

"I don't believe so," Austin replied with a smile, and pressed his hand to Teddy's spine to keep her moving along the buffet line.

Janet managed to stay aligned to them, eyeing Austin with too much interest as she put a croissant on her plate. "I keep imagining you in a police uniform. Are you a cop?"

The spoonful of scalloped potatoes Teddy scooped up missed her plate and would have landed on her shoes if it hadn't been for Austin smoothly intercepting the entrée with his own plate.

"No, I'm a broker," Austin said to Janet without missing a beat. Taking the spoon from Teddy's unsteady fingers, he ladled a small portion of the potatoes onto her dish and murmured, "Be careful, honey, or we're going to have a mess on our hands."

The meaning behind Austin's words wasn't lost on Teddy. She struggled to keep a cool composure when all she could envision was the possible scandal should Austin be exposed. Her reputation at Sharper Image would be tarnished, and no doubt she'd kiss that promotion she'd coveted goodbye.

Austin's answer didn't seem to appease Janet. Ruthless determination gleamed in her eyes. "I was so certain you were a cop."

"You must have him mixed up with someone else you've met," Teddy interjected quickly, desperate to end the interrogation.

"Maybe, but I've got a memory for faces." Janet's gaze flickered dismissively from Teddy, to Austin, scrutinizing him one last time as she waited for the chef to place a slice of prime rib on her plate. "It's going to drive me nuts until I place where I've seen you." The slight curve to her mouth suggested she found Austin a mystery she intended to solve.

Teddy let out a tight breath as they finished their trek through the buffet and headed back to their table. "Tell me she wasn't a Fantasy for Hire customer," Teddy said, knowing her wish was a futile one.

"Unfortunately, I do remember her, though she's not the one I fulfilled the fantasy for," Austin replied wryly. "It was at a bachelorette party a few months ago, and the bride-to-be was marrying a cop, thus my costume. That redhead was more enthusiastic about my performance than the bride."

Teddy groaned at her bad luck. "Hopefully, Janet won't figure out the connection."

"I think as long as I keep my clothes on, we might stand a chance," he said, winking at her.

A burst of dry laughter escaped her throat, but his playful remark didn't completely reassure her.

Clothes or no, Austin McBride had a body and face that most women wouldn't soon forget.

THE CHRISTMAS PARTY was winding down, and Austin loathed for the evening to end, especially since he had Teddy right where he wanted her—in his embrace, dancing close to a slow Christmas ballad that comprised the band's last set.

Despite the fantasy of playing Teddy's lover, he'd enjoyed being with her and wondered if he'd see her again after tonight—no pretenses, just as a man and a woman strongly attracted to each other. The thought appealed to him immensely.

It went against his work ethics to pursue a client, but he'd thrown that restriction out the window the moment he'd agreed to accompany Teddy to her party. The stakes had somehow turned personal for him, his interest in Teddy Spencer stretching beyond business, yet he had no idea where he stood with her.

Before they parted ways, he intended to find out.

He glanced down at the woman in his arms, and found Teddy frowning, her troubled gaze trained on something beyond the parquet dance floor. Following her line of vision, he discovered her watching the redhead they'd encountered at the buffet table a few hours ago, who stood near the service bar conversing with Louden. She'd yet to approach them again, and Austin fervently hoped, for Teddy's sake, that the other woman's curiosity, and tenacity, fizzled. As for Louden, he'd kept his distance as well, but there were times throughout the evening when Austin had caught the man eyeing Teddy in a way that made Austin feel territorial.

"What's on your mind, Teddy?" he asked, surprising himself with just how much he wanted to know about this woman who seemed such a paradox.

She pulled her gaze from the pair, and smiled up at him, a lazy curving of her mouth that attested to her relaxed state. "A cop, hmm?" she murmured, revealing exactly where her mind had ventured. "What's your specialty at Fantasy for Hire?"

"I don't really have one," he admitted, rubbing his thumb over the hand he held against his chest. "Women's fantasies vary, and are very personal. I've been a lifeguard, a UPS deliveryman, a biker. It all depends on the woman, and what turns her on."

The hand resting on his shoulder moved upward, until her fingers touched the hair curling over the collar of his shirt. Her body flowed against his as they swayed to Bing Crosby's "White Christmas." "I bet you look just as good in leather pants as you do in chaps."

"Ah, your fantasy," he murmured. Pressing his palm low on her back, he slid a thigh gently between hers, making their position more intimate, more arousing. "How did I do in terms of fulfilling it?"

She gave him a sultry, upswept look that had him thinking inappropriate thoughts, considering they were still in a public place, surrounded by a dozen other dancing couples.

"You certainly lassoed my attention," she admitted in a sexy, cowgirl drawl.

He felt ridiculously pleased with her confession. "So, what is it about a cowboy that turns you on?"

She gave his question some thought as they danced, her expression soft, her dark eyes luminous. "They're rugged, but chivalrous, which makes them appealing." She shrugged, her gaze meeting his daringly. "And there's just something about chaps on a man that I find incredibly sexy, not to mention the sound of spurs on a wooden floor."

A slow, spiraling heat spread toward his groin. "I'd wear spurs for you, cowgirl," he whispered huskily, honestly.

Her breathing deepened, and through his tuxedo shirt he could feel her breasts swell, and her nipples tighten against his chest, tormenting him.

She touched her tongue to her bottom lip, and as if deciding their conversation was becoming too hot and provocative, she turned the subject back to him. "So, what compelled you to fulfill women's fantasies?"

If she expected an exciting, sensational answer, she was going to be sorely disappointed. "Outstanding loans that needed to be paid."

She nodded in understanding. "And do you enjoy the business?"

"I had more fun when I was younger," he said, thinking back to the inception of Fantasy for Hire, and how a simple vision to earn extra money had exceeded his wildest expectations. Back then, he'd been enthusiastic, enjoying the excitement of each gig. "Now that I've hit thirty, I find I prefer conducting business with my clothes on."

She grinned, and he thought about mentioning his flourishing landscaping business, which had become his main focus, but Teddy's next question didn't allow him time.

"How does your family feel about your profession?" she asked curiously.

"My mother and father are both gone. They died when I was sixteen."

She appeared startled, and immediately regretful. "I'm

sorry to hear that. Losing your parents at such a young age must have been extremely difficult."

"Yeah, it was." His mother and father had been good people, very much in love, and totally devoted to their two sons. Their death had shaken up his young world, and if it hadn't been for Jordan's guidance, he very easily would have become a juvenile delinquent. "My brother, Jordan, and I still miss them."

The band announced the final song of the evening, and Bing's tune segued into another ballad without a lapse. Some of the couples dispersed, but Teddy didn't show any signs of wanting to go, so he continued to hold her close as the music played.

Her gaze shone with genuine interest, solely focused on him. "So it's just the two of you then?"

"Yeah. All we have is each other." Austin found he liked talking to her, liked even more that she'd let down her guard to indulge in personal conversation—the getting-to-know-you kind of exchange that real lovers shared. "Jordan is older than me by two years. He raised me after our parents died."

She tilted her head, looking soft, and beautiful, and very much at ease. "And how does big brother feel about you taking your clothes off for women?"

Austin chuckled, the sound swirling warm and intimate between them. "It's definitely not his cup of tea. Jordan is an architect, and has always been a conservative sort of guy, but he's always been very supportive of me and the choices I've made."

"That's great." Her voice held a wistful quality that reached her eyes. "I wish *my* brothers were that way. Heck, I'd kill for a little support and encouragement from my parents, too."

Austin thought briefly about what her sister-in-law, Susan, had divulged, but still couldn't believe Teddy had ventured into her career alone, without having someone to share each step of success with. "Your family isn't at all supportive of what you're doing?"

She shook her head a little sadly. "Nope. I'm the youngest girl with three older brothers, which is the kiss of death itself. Then there's my mother, who is from the old school, and believes a daughter should be raised to be a proper wife and hostess to her husband. She was horrified when I went to college to get my degree, and I know my father was disappointed, too."

Austin's hand rubbed small soothing circles at the base of her spine, and he could feel the rasp of her silky stockings against his slacks. He ignored the flash of heat that touched off a deep, inexplicable hunger for her, and steered his concentration back to their conversation. "Why can't you do both, have a successful career and be a wife? Women do it all the time."

A wry look crossed her features. "The two don't seem to mix well for me. Remember Bartholomew? Well, I almost did the deed with him, and luckily came to my senses before I became a clone of my mother. That's another incident my parents have yet to forgive me for." Her gaze conveyed an unmistakable reckless defiance. "I'm not ready to settle down yet. I've got goals to attain, and quite frankly, after being stifled for more years than I care to recall, I like my freedom and independence."

"Maybe you just haven't found the right man yet."

"I'm not looking for a man, remember." With a sassy grin, she reminded him of that vow with a wave of her left hand in front of his face. That sparkly ring of hers flashed, backing her claim. "Staying single is so much easier and less complicated."

"But a lot lonelier." His voice was quiet, but his words were powerful enough to touch the vulnerability behind her independent facade.

Their gazes connected, hers filled with unspoken affirmation. Even though he knew she'd never admit to being lonely, he suspected that the world she'd created for herself didn't keep her warm at night, or bolster her spirits on a bad day. What she needed was someone who believed in her and her aspirations, someone who supported her unconditionally, and didn't try to clip her wings.

It was clear to him that she was out to prove something to her parents, and herself. And possibly even to Louden. He didn't begrudge her the success she strove for, only hoped that her single-mindedness didn't keep her from enjoying other aspects of her life.

"I suppose you want a wife, kids, and the whole bit," she said cheekily, avoiding the deeper issue he'd unintentionally provoked.

"Sure I do." And the older he got, the more he wanted that kind of security. That big Victorian he lived in by himself got far too quiet at night, giving him too much time to think about how a special woman might fit into his life. Finding her was another matter, especially when Fantasy for Hire robbed him of any spare time. "When the right woman comes along, I've got an open mind about marriage. And I want a big family, too. I love kids."

She gave a shudder, but he knew she was exaggerating by the teasing sparkle in her eyes. "I get my fill of kids with my eight nieces and nephews. One night with them, and I'm completely wiped out."

He lifted an eyebrow, wondering how much of that statement was truth, and how much she'd tried to convince herself of.

The final song ended, bringing the Christmas party to a close. Slowly, reluctantly, he let her move from his embrace. A sense of loss filled him—there were no more excuses to postpone the end of the evening. And judging by the slant of their conversation, he pretty much ascertained that no further invitation was forthcoming from her lips to see him again.

She'd made it clear that her job was her priority, that a real man in her life was something her parents wanted, but she had no time or desire for. He wasn't going to push the issue...at least not much.

On the drive back to Teddy's place, Austin had plenty of time to mentally plan his strategy to sway Teddy into giving them another chance, another date, one that wasn't tangled up with lies and pretenses. Just them. And their attraction for one another.

He wondered if he stood a chance against her restricting goals, wondered if he was being foolish for wanting to pursue something that might be all one-sided. And then there was the issue of her family, and what they expected of Teddy...and of a boyfriend.

Meeting their expectations would be impossible, but at the moment none of that mattered to Austin, not when his chest ached at the thought of never seeing Teddy again. Not when he wanted this woman so badly that physical need coalesced with strong emotion.

After parking the Mustang at the curb, he insisted on walking Teddy to her condo. She wrapped the shawl around her in an attempt to chase away the midnight chill, but her teeth began to chatter. Slipping his tuxedo jacket off, he draped it over her shoulders, and she snuggled into the warmth.

She smiled up at him. "Thanks." Her voice held a slight quiver, but he wasn't sure if it was from the cold, or if she was nervous.

"I had a great time tonight." He'd especially enjoyed their elevator ride up, and slow dancing with her—both opportunities had been private, and incredibly enlightening.

She rolled her eyes. "Between Louden, and Janet, it was certainly interesting, if anything."

He smiled. "I think everything went well. We established a believable relationship, so hopefully Louden will back off like you hope."

She held up crossed fingers for luck. "As long as Janet

doesn't remember you as a cop who strips, we'll be in good shape."

Taking the house key from her grasp, he unlocked the door and opened it for her. She handed him back his jacket, started to step inside, then turned around before she cleared the threshold. A light from the living room behind her illuminated her slender form and tipped her upswept hair with gold. Even in the shadows, her eyes shimmered with regret.

"Well, I guess this is goodbye," she said softly, and offered him a slight smile.

The last thing he wanted to say was goodbye. "Not just yet."

Reaching into the pocket of the tuxedo jacket draped over his arm, he withdrew the sprig of mistletoe he'd swiped off their table as they'd left the party. The greenery was crushed, but still in working order. Her rich, chocolate brown eyes widened as he braced his arm on the doorjamb and dangled the mistletoe above her head.

His stance was lazy, deceptively so, and he grinned wickedly, declaring his intent. "I believe you and I have unfinished business to attend to."

6

SHE SHOULD HAVE said no. She should have resisted. But Teddy didn't stand a chance against the seductive pull of Austin's darkened gaze, or the knowledge that this man made her feel restless, needy sensations no other man had ever evoked.

Reckless desire caused her pulse to race. The promise of pleasure glimmering in his sexy eyes touched off a quiver of anticipation deep in her belly. And because she knew he'd make good on that silent vow, she impetuously decided that one last, parting kiss to remember him by wouldn't hurt anything.

His warm fingers brushed along her jaw and curled around the nape of her neck, urging her to meet him halfway, persuading her to participate and give as much as she took. She swayed toward him, too eager to taste him, too anxious to experience the heady thrill of having his mouth on hers.

His head lowered, hers raised expectantly. His lashes fell slumberously, she closed her eyes and waited. His mouth skimmed hers gently, teasing her unmercifully. Her lips parted with a soft, inviting sigh, and he gradually deepened the kiss, slowly, seductively, cajoling her tongue to mate with his, and offering his own in return.

The kiss was incredibly erotic, a lazy, tantalizing possession of the senses. It inflamed and stimulated a depthless passion, and there was nothing she could do but surrender.

Abandoning all coherent thought, all common sense, she

tossed her small purse somewhere behind her in the condo, twined her fingers into the thick strands of hair at the back of his neck and opened her mouth wider beneath his and whimpered, a silent plea for him to ease the ache building within her.

He answered with a deep, dark growl that reverberated in his throat, and with her face framed between his palms and her mouth anchored firmly beneath his, he guided her backward, into the darkened entryway, kicking the door shut behind them. A cool whoosh of air caressed her stockinged legs as he dropped his coat at their feet. Pushing her against the wall, he dragged the shawl from her shoulders to join his jacket, and pressed his hard, muscular body against hers, the urgency in him undeniable. Her knees threatened to buckle, but he wedged a leg between her thighs, and she felt the swell of his erection against her belly—thick, hot and pulsing. The male heat of him surrounded her, engulfed her, sparking a liquid fire that settled low in her stomach.

His breathing roughened, and his heart hammered as frantically as her own. She identified with that out-of-control need, and it frightened her as much as it thrilled her. Her head spun, her mind whirled, and the crazy momentum didn't show any signs of slowing.

He continued to kiss her, wild, greedy, insatiable kisses she returned with an enthusiasm that should have shocked her, but didn't. Like a thief, he pilfered and ravished. Like a willing captive, she succumbed and yearned for more.

He obliged her, sliding his fingers into her hair and gently dislodging the rhinestone pins securing the strands. He found each clip, untangled each one and dropped them to the carpeted floor until her hair tumbled around her shoulders in a tousled mess. He crushed the silky tresses in his hands, massaging her scalp, her nape, and then her shoulders.

Finally, he freed her lips, and she moaned as he touched

his open mouth to her throat, stroking his soft tongue across the pulse point at the base. And then he bit her sensitive skin, gently, just enough to cause another rush of excitement. She was so distracted by this new, delicious sensation that she was unaware of him slipping his thumbs beneath the thin straps of her dress and dragging them down her arms until she felt the fabric covering her breasts give way.

She gasped at the shock of cool air against her heated skin, felt her first bout of modesty as he lifted his head and looked his fill. His eyes burned with hunger, his gaze ravaged. She shivered, but didn't move. Nor did she protest when he licked the tips of his fingers and slicked them over her nipples, drawing them into tight, aching points. But she groaned, long and low, when he lowered his mouth and laved those tender crests with his tongue, then drew her into the hot depths of his mouth.

Biting her lower lip to keep from crying out, she pushed her fingers into his hair, brazenly holding him close as he leisurely lapped and suckled and nuzzled. He worked his wet mouth from one breast to the other, his tongue, lips and teeth teasing her with devastating thoroughness. The pleasure was dizzying, and frustrating, and in an attempt to soothe a sharper, more intimate ache, she clamped her thighs against the one riding high between hers and arched into him.

A harsh, aroused sound hissed from Austin, and he buried his face at the side of her neck, his breath hot and moist against her flesh. "Teddy..." he whispered huskily, his voice raw with a want so urgent it invaded every cell of her being. His palms slid down her sides to grip her hips, and rocked her rhythmically against that treacherous thigh of his, building the pressure. "All night I've thought about the taste of you, the feel of you. It's not enough. Not nearly enough."

Passion fogged her mind, short-circuiting rational thought. "Not enough," she echoed the sentiment, turning her head to the side to give him better access to the column of her throat.

His tongue touched the delicate shell of her ear, making her skin quiver, and his hands roamed lower, beneath the hem of her dress. Questing fingers rasped against the stockings covering her legs, her thighs...higher still. "I want to make love to you."

Yes, her body screamed, her feminine nerves already spiraling toward that release. All it would take to send her over the edge was the touch of his fingers against slick folds of flesh, the seductive caress of his mouth on her breasts. The elemental need to make love to this man mixed with something deep and soul-stirring, overwhelming her with emotions she'd severed herself from years ago.

Panicked that he could make her feel so much when she'd been content to be alone, she pressed her palms to his chest, pushing gently, but firmly. "Austin, we can't do this."

He immediately stopped his seduction, slowly withdrawing his hand from beneath her dress, leaving her aroused, and very disappointed. The rhinestone straps of her dress slid back up, and the bodice covered her breasts once again.

Concern etched his features, and he brushed her hair away from her face, his gaze searching. "Hey, you okay?"

No. She was scared, and confused, but admitting either defeated the purpose of all those years she'd struggled to build her confidence. "This is happening too fast."

"We can take it slow," he said, his deep, rich voice still holding the vestiges of desire. Bracing an arm against the wall at the side of her head, he skimmed his knuckles down her cheek in a feather-light caress. "As slow and easy as you need it to be."

Her skin tingled at the thought of how good slow could be with this sexy fantasy man. "Impossible, when I unravel when you just look at me, and I melt when you touch me."

Like now, those insidious fingers of his were causing all kinds of havoc with her libido.

A roguish grin curved his mouth, and he looked pleased with that revelation. "No, slow doesn't seem to apply to the attraction between us," he agreed. "But I'm not just talking about sex, Teddy. I'm talking about us."

She swallowed, hard, trying to keep her rising wariness at bay. "Us?"

"Yeah," he murmured, trailing that treacherous finger along her jaw to her lobe, eliciting a deep, dark shiver that made her body feel like warm molasses. "You. Me. A slow building relationship. *Us.*"

She shook her head, feeling crowded, and not just because his body surrounded hers. Emotionally, he was slipping under her skin, forcing her to reevaluate her personal life, and she didn't care for what she was discovering. Moving around him, she put some distance between them, shoring up her fortitude. "There is no 'us.'"

"There could be." When she didn't respond, the set of his jaw turned determined. "You honestly believe there isn't something between us worth pursuing?"

She rubbed the slow throb beginning in her temples, and chose her words carefully. "I can't afford any diversions right now, Austin." Her voice implored him to understand. "Not when I'm so close to getting everything I've worked so hard for. And I can't allow great sexual chemistry to distract me when I need to stay focused on my job." She'd only wanted a date for the evening, her own personal fantasy for hire. When had things become so complicated? "Besides, you and I have different goals, and certainly opposite visions of the future."

"Not as much as you might think," he said, ruthless intent in his gaze. "Or maybe it's just easier for you to believe that."

Anger flared within her, that he'd touched on part of the truth—a truth that made her too vulnerable. She was scared of taking personal, emotional risks, for fear of being stifled. It had taken her years to establish her independence, to gain the self-confidence to stand on her own, and there were always those niggling doubts that she couldn't mix business with a relationship and find an equal balance. In her experience, the latter always won.

She grasped a stronger argument. "You fulfill women's fantasies, for crying out loud! How opposite is that?"

He jammed his hands on his lean hips and sighed, sounding as weary as he was beginning to look. "It's just a job, Teddy, and it isn't who I am. Fantasy for Hire was a means to an end. It isn't my entire life."

There was more. She could see it in his eyes. But she didn't want to hear anything else, didn't want to give him a chance to sway her decision. "As much as I want you, I can't do this right now. I don't have time in my life for a relationship, and that's not fair to you."

He stepped toward her, so genuine and understanding. "Teddy—"

She held up a hand to stop him, knowing his touch to be a powerful persuasion. "Please, Austin," she beseeched him. "Don't make this any more difficult than it already is. You're a great guy, and you deserve better than what I can offer you, which is nothing permanent." She bit her bottom lip, acknowledging on some feminine level that she wished she could be the kind of woman he wanted, but she wasn't cut out for marriage, and babies, and all those other things that tied a person down and restricted their freedom.

He stared at her for a long, intense moment, his green eyes darkening with resignation. "All right," he finally relented, and swiped his jacket from the floor. "You win, Teddy."

It wasn't a joyful victory. Her throat burned, and her chest hurt at the thought of never seeing him again. She opened the door before she changed her mind. "Thank you, Austin. For everything."

"The last thing I want is your gratitude for something I *wanted* to do." Just as he passed through the threshold, he stopped and turned back around, his chiseled features expressing deep regret. "Good luck on your promotion, Teddy. I hope you get everything you want."

She was certain the double meaning ringing in his words had been unintentional on his part, but it was there nonetheless, haunting her, forcing her to think about what her desire for that promotion might have cost her. She found the thought disturbing.

And then he was gone, leaving only the warm, male scent of his cologne lingering in the entryway, and a horrible sense of loss blossoming within her.

Leaning against the wall for support, she slid down until she was sitting on the carpeted floor, her knees upraised. Dragging a hand through her tangled hair and trying not to think about how much she enjoyed being with Austin, she let out a deep breath that did nothing to ease the new tension banding her chest.

Her gaze landed on the cluster of mistletoe he'd used to seduce her, and she picked it up, holding the sprig of Christmas spirit in the palm of her hand. Her throat tightened, and a piercing pain wrenched her heart.

Damn Austin McBride anyway, for making her realize just how cold and lonely her life was, for making her question everything that was important to her—everything she'd struggled to attain without the support of anyone.

She'd sacrificed so much to prove her own self-worth to her family, to herself. But this sacrifice was hurting more than she'd ever imagined.

AUSTIN STOOD beneath the hot, stinging spray from the shower. He'd spent a restless night tossing and turning in bed, caused from frustration, confusion and a healthy dose of annoyance that Teddy Spencer had, in effect, brushed him off.

Well, not brushed him off, exactly, he amended as he braced his hands on the tiled wall and dipped his head beneath the invigorating jet of water to rinse his soap-slick body. But her brand of rejection stung nonetheless. He'd served his purpose in aiding Teddy in her plight to dissuade Louden, and she'd never promised him anything beyond last night. He'd *known* that. He'd followed through with Teddy's plan with his eyes wide open, knowing it was all an act. So why did he return home last night with his stomach in knots and a keen sense of disappointment riding him hard?

The answer came easily. Despite knowing Teddy had expected nothing more from him than a performance, he couldn't help feeling used on some basic male level. The unpleasant sensation was one he'd experienced before, and he'd have thought he'd learned from that brief encounter with a woman who'd taken advantage of him for her own self-centered motivations. Diane certainly had her own agenda when she'd pursued him. Too late, he'd discovered that her interest had been for the fantasy he created for her— that of a part-time plaything to keep her occupied when she was bored with her wealthy life and friends. Emotional involvement hadn't been part of her plan—just an exciting affair that abruptly ended when he no longer served a purpose in her capricious life.

Despite that lesson learned, he'd wanted to believe Teddy was different, that her ulterior motives wouldn't cloud what seemed so obvious and right between them.

He'd been wrong.

Swearing at his stupidity, he turned off the water, grabbed the thick navy towel hanging over the stall and scrubbed it over his damp hair and wet body.

"She did you a big favor, buddy," he muttered to himself as he stepped from the shower. "And she's definitely all wrong for you," he continued as he trekked naked into the bedroom, where the early-morning sun was just beginning to seep through the second-story bedroom window to warm the hardwood floor.

Grabbing his favorite pair of soft, faded jeans, he pulled them on and concentrated on all those wrongs, mentally ticking them off in his head: her wealthy family, who wouldn't approve of him, her job being more important than a relationship, and her admitted unwillingness to balance the two.

He finger-combed his thick, damp hair away from his face, and tried not to grimace at the less-than-refreshed reflection in the mirror—he looked tired, haggard and as irritable as a provoked bear. "You have every reason to be grateful that she didn't allow things to progress further than they had last night," he told himself, pivoting toward the bedroom door.

But as he headed downstairs, he found it difficult to be gracious about Teddy's rejection when he'd tasted the need and hunger in her kiss, and in the way her body had responded so openly and honestly to his touch. There had been nothing calculated about her soft groans as he'd caressed her breasts, nothing fabricated about the sensual way she'd arched toward him for more.

Letting out a deep breath to erase those arousing thoughts that would surely haunt him for months to come, he entered the kitchen. Jordan, who'd always been one to be up bright and early, flipped down the corner of the Sunday sports section and glanced at Austin. A slow grin spread across Jordan's face as he homed in on his brother's cantankerous disposition.

"You look like hell this morning, little brother." Humor threaded Jordan's voice and creased the corners of his eyes.

Austin gave a noncommittal grunt in response. Of course, Jordan looked neat and orderly and ready to begin the day, his knit shirt pressed, and his jeans crisp and a vivid shade of blue, which indicated they were fairly new. Austin barely contained a disgusted snort. Didn't his brother ever dress for anything but success?

Jordan's grin increased. "And you should be plenty rested, considering I heard you come in just a little after midnight."

Jordan's insinuation that Austin's evening plans hadn't ended as he'd personally hoped rankled. Crossing the cool tiled floor, he opened the cupboard and brought down a bowl and a box of cereal, then withdrew a carton of milk from the refrigerator. "I thought I'd outgrown you waiting up for me long ago."

"Oh, I wasn't waiting up." Jordan folded the section of newspaper neatly, and laid it aside. "I was awake, in bed reading. Even if I wasn't, the way you stomped up the stairs and slammed your bedroom door would have woken the dead."

He grimaced as he carried his breakfast items to the table. "Sorry," he said, genuinely contrite. Sitting across from Jordan, he poured Cap'n Crunch into his bowl and added a generous amount of milk. Jordan looked on disapprovingly at the sugared cereal, which Austin had eaten for breakfast since the age of eight.

Jordan believed in a healthy start to the day; Austin wasn't about to sacrifice his favorite cereal for the scrambled eggs, wheat toast and cantaloupe his brother preferred. "I guess I'm still not used to having someone else in the house."

"I figured as much." Jordan shoveled scrambled eggs onto his buttered wheat toast and took a bite while considering Austin through curious eyes. "Dare I ask how things went last night?"

Austin tried for a nonchalant shrug and failed miserably. "Depends on whose point of view you want."

"How about hers?" Jordan asked, slicing his cantaloupe into precise wedges.

"Great." Unequivocally, Austin was sure. There was little

doubt in his mind that everyone at Sharper Image had fallen for the ruse, which could only work to Teddy's favor.

"And yours?"

He scooped up a spoonful of cereal, glancing at Jordan before taking the bite. "Disappointing and frustrating." And a multitude of other emotions he didn't care to verbally analyze.

Jordan digested that, appearing sympathetic. "Care to talk about it?"

Austin wasn't one to spill his guts about personal issues, but Jordan had always been a good listener, reflective without judging, and Austin needed that quiet male camaraderie and support right now. "The night itself was great. In fact, I can't remember the last time I had such a good time with a woman. Teddy is smart, sexy, amusing...and entirely too determined," he added on a note of annoyance.

Jordan lifted an eyebrow. "Usually that's a good thing."

Austin pushed his half-eaten bowl of Cap'n Crunch aside. "She's determined to the point of seeing nothing beyond her promotion."

"Can't begrudge a person for wanting to be successful."

Austin didn't miss the bitter note to his brother's voice that had nothing to do with Teddy.

"I don't begrudge Teddy for wanting that promotion, but what about being successful *and* making time for a relationship?"

Jordan picked up his glass of orange juice. "Depends on the person's priorities."

Austin snorted. Teddy had made it patently clear where her priorities lay—in the hands of Sharper Image. "I guess I went with her to this party expecting something...different. Like maybe another date, where we could get to know one another without that ridiculous charade between us." Shaking his head, he scrubbed a hand over the light stubble covering his jaw. "Man, it's been a long time since I've felt that way about a woman."

Jordan chuckled, the sound entirely too gleeful. "She certainly has you tied up in knots."

Austin scowled, but knew he'd be a hypocrite if he denied what was so obviously the truth. Teddy did have a hold on him, one he couldn't shake. She made him think about things he'd decided were beyond his reach until his landscaping business was financially stable. She made him think about what it would be like to come home to her smiles in the evening and her soft, feminine scent filling this old Victorian house. And then there was the luxury of making love to her every night, and waking up beside her for the next fifty years.

Commitment. Security. And the comfort of having a family. After years of playing the field, the notion appealed to him. More and more with each passing year.

Folding his hands over his bare belly, Austin leaned back in his chair, rocking on the solid hind legs. "Jordan, you ever think about settling down?"

Stacking his fork and knife on his plate, Jordan shrugged noncommittally. "I thought I was close once, but it didn't work out, which is just as well because look at where I am now. If I had a family to support, I never would have been able to quit and walk out on those dishonest bastards."

Austin nodded in understanding.

"Now, I'm an unemployed architect, living with my bachelor brother, and I have no idea what the future holds."

"You could always take over Fantasy for Hire," Austin offered with a devilish grin.

Jordan visibly shuddered. "I'm nobody's fantasy, and I prefer to conduct business with my clothes *on*, thank you very much."

"You don't give yourself near enough credit. I'm sure there are women out there who fantasize about straitlaced architects." Austin ignored the dirty look Jordan cast his way. "I'd sell you the business real cheap."

"What, you thinking of giving up being the object of every woman's fantasy?" Humor threaded through Jordan's voice.

"I've been considering selling the business for a while now," Austin admitted. "Not only is Fantasy for Hire becoming too much for me to handle along with all the business coming in for McBride Landscaping, I'm tired of all the pretense."

"Feeling a little taken advantage of, hmm?"

He hadn't, not until he'd met Teddy. For this particular reason, he'd always been careful to draw the line between his job as a fantasy for hire and the customer he performed for, but that's where he'd failed with Teddy Spencer. He'd brazenly stepped over that line because of an intense, mind-boggling attraction, and he'd gotten burned for his efforts.

Teddy would rather cling to the fantasy than grasp the reality of what was between them.

"I want a normal life," Austin said, hearing the frustration in his own voice. "And when I meet a woman, I want to be sure that she's interested in me because of who I am, and not what particular fantasy of hers I might fulfill."

Jordan stood and carried his dishes to the sink, rinsing them. "Sounds like you've got some decisions to make."

"Yeah." He'd already come to the conclusion to put Fantasy for Hire on the market, and after the holidays he'd see if he could find an interested buyer for the business. Then, he'd see what he could do about finding a woman who wanted the *real* Austin McBride.

THE CORDLESS PHONE in Teddy's lap rang, and she tossed aside the woman's magazine she'd been thumbing through and clicked the connect button before the sound completed its cycle.

"Hello?" she answered.

"You are a *very* bad girl, Teddy Spencer."

Teddy immediately recognized her sister-in-law's low, throaty voice. Relief mingled with the awful anxiety that had been her constant companion all day long, easing the knot in her chest by a few degrees. Normally, Sundays were her day to relax and catch up on personal errands and chores. Today, she'd been too intent on talking to Susan to move more than an arm's stretch away from the phone. She hadn't even taken a shower yet because she'd feared missing the call. The only thing she'd allowed for her vigil was a quick change into leggings and an oversize sweatshirt, a scrubbed face, brushed teeth and a ponytail.

Not wanting to appear too anxious, she strove for a casual air. "It's the bad girls that have all the fun."

Susan laughed. "You certainly seem to be having your share," she said, her tone sly. "When were you going to tell the family about Austin? Or were you going to keep this guy all to yourself?"

The latter, but Susan's phone call last night had nixed that plan. Not quite ready to answer that question until she had a chance to feel Susan out, she said, "It's after five. Where have you been? I've been trying to get hold of you all day."

"No kidding." Susan snickered. "Thirteen messages on the answering machine is a bit excessive, don't you think?"

"No." Teddy straightened indignantly. "Not when I needed to speak with you about eight hours ago."

"Brent, the kids and I were out of the house early this morning," Susan said breezily. "We went to brunch with your brother Russ and his family. I would have invited you to come along, but thought you'd have better things to do this morning."

The insinuation in Susan's tone caused Teddy's face to warm and a horrifying thought to invade her mind...the very real possibility that Susan had shared that assumption with her brother Brent. "Susan—"

"Then Brent and Russ took the kids to see that new animated Christmas feature playing at the movies, and me and Natalie went shopping with your mother for Christmas presents for the kids. Santa went broke this year, and what I didn't get on the kids' Christmas list, Grandma insisted on buying."

Teddy shot up off the sofa, her heart slamming against her ribs. Oh, this didn't sound good at all! "You went shopping with my mother?" The question came out as a croak.

"She was on her best behavior," Susan assured her. "I swear, there's something about the holidays that brings out the very best in her. And when I told her about your new guy, she actually beamed."

Teddy squeezed her eyes shut, imagining her mother's pretty face, alight with happiness at the thought that her only daughter was finally coming to her senses and settling down. "No," she moaned.

"Yeah, she actually beamed," Susan reiterated, misinterpreting Teddy's denial. "She looked radiant."

Teddy shook her head, then realized that Susan couldn't see the silent gesture. She didn't know whether to laugh deliriously, or scream at the dreadful turn of events.

All day, her active imagination had come up with various scenarios of how her sister-in-law might have handled last night's conversation with Austin. She'd expected Susan to mention Austin to Brent, of course, and knew she could have quashed any rumors between the two before they'd circulated through the family. But this...this was her worst nightmare!

"Austin McBride is just a *friend*," she blurted desperately.

"Oh, sure he's just a friend, Teddy," Susan said, clearly expressing her disbelief. "The tiger is out of the bag, honey, and I have to say, he was an incredibly charming, sexy-sounding tiger. The whole family is dying to meet him—"

"The whole family?" she wailed, feeling pushed to the edge of hysteria.

"Of course the whole family. Since he agreed to come for Christmas Eve, I didn't see any reason to keep this exciting news all to myself."

"He *agreed*?" Teddy wheezed, collapsing back onto the sofa. Why hadn't Austin informed her of that minuscule fact? She replayed her conversation with Austin in her mind, and remembered telling him she'd take care of the discussion he'd had with Susan.

"Well, I admit to a teensy-tiny bit of coercion on my part," Susan added impishly.

Teddy rolled her eyes. "You don't know the meaning of subtle."

Susan laughed, as if Teddy had issued her a compliment. When Teddy didn't join in on the humor, Susan attempted to smooth things over. "Honey, I don't know why you're so upset. This is a good thing, really. Your mother is thrilled that you're dating again, especially since this is the first guy we've heard about since Bart."

Just the mention of the fiasco with Bartholomew Winston gave Teddy a migraine.

"And even if Austin *is* just a friend, there is a bright side to all this," Susan offered.

All Teddy saw was doom and gloom in her future. "Which is?"

"Well, I know how particular your parents can be when it comes to who their children date, but I'm thinking that if they see that you're at least making an effort to find a potential husband—not that you are," Susan quickly amended, knowing what a hot button that was for Teddy. "But if your parents believe that, then maybe your mother will leave you alone and quit obsessing about finding you a suitable man."

Teddy rested her head against the back of the sofa and stared up at the ceiling, her instincts rebelling against Susan's preposterous plan. Austin was hardly what her parents would consider "suitable". Yet he'd managed to fool everyone at Sharper Image, her conscience reminded her.

As she mulled over the suggestion, she began to see the merit behind the idea. Introducing Austin to her family didn't mean she had to marry him, for goodness' sake, but showing up with a date would at least pacify her mother into believing her daughter was finally circulating, instead of devoting so much time to "that silly little job" of hers.

Oh, yeah, her mother would be tickled pink. But this grand scheme required seeing Austin again, and that was the tricky part. Not only did the man set off disturbing sensual cravings and make her yearn for things she had no room in her life for, but she was pretty certain she'd chafed that male pride of his with her well-rehearsed speech last night. Which meant she'd be swallowing a large dose of her own pride if she asked this favor of him.

"So, is Austin as scrumptious as he sounds?" Susan asked, her excitement traveling over the phone lines.

Taking a deep breath, she forced a cheerful note to her voice. "You'll have to wait, and see for yourself."

7

TEDDY'S HEAD was killing her. Nearly twenty-four hours after hanging up the phone with Susan, what had started as a slow throbbing in her temples had escalated into full-blown pounding in her skull. Dread was the culprit for her headache. She'd yet to call Austin, and considering Christmas Eve was only a few days away, she knew she couldn't stall the inevitable another day, or even another hour.

Desperate for relief, and wanting her mind calm and focused before she spoke with Austin, she removed her purse from the bottom drawer in her desk and dug for the small bottle of aspirin she carried with her. A loose piece of paper crinkled, and she withdrew the yellow slip, recognizing it as the receipt Austin had given her for the money she'd paid him to escort her to the Christmas party. Except he hadn't accepted her payment, and had instead donated the money to a needy organization. There was nothing to indicate his generous donation on the receipt, but she didn't doubt for a second the sincerity of his claim. Austin was genuine, through and through, and she was about to take advantage of that generosity. Again.

Not wanting her thoughts to travel that road for fear she'd talk herself out of calling him, she tucked the receipt in her desk drawer, right beneath his Fantasy for Hire business card, and continued her search. Finding the plastic bottle, she twisted open the top and shook three tablets into her palm.

Needing water, she headed out of her office, down the

plush halls of Sharper Image, to the small, unoccupied kitch-enette at the end. Plucking a small paper cup from the dis-penser next to the watercooler, she filled it, tossed the pills into her mouth and washed them down in one huge gulp. She closed her eyes, and forced herself to relax, hoping her headache would ebb soon.

Something brushed across her skirt-clad bottom, jolting her back to awareness. Startled, she glanced around and found Louden standing two feet away from her, his pale blue eyes giving nothing away. The caress had been so sub-tle, she would have thought she'd imagined it if she'd been by herself. She didn't trust Louden, but neither could she prove anything had just happened.

Uneasiness slithered through her. Not wanting to be alone with him, she tossed her paper cup into the trash and turned to leave the kitchenette. He grabbed her arm before she could escape, gently, but firm enough that she couldn't dis-miss the gesture.

She glanced sharply at him, and he slowly released his hold, though he remained in her direct path. "I haven't had the chance to ask if you enjoyed the party Saturday night."

He hadn't had the opportunity because she'd deliberately avoided him all day. She'd decided steering clear of Louden as much as possible was the smartest course of action until after next week, when the promotion was either assigned to her, or Fred Williams.

She straightened, meeting his gaze head-on. "The Christ-mas party was great. Austin and I had a wonderful time."

"Ah, yes, Austin," he murmured reflectively. "What a sur-prise it was to finally meet your boyfriend. You two certainly seemed convincing."

Teddy managed a bland smile. "I'm not sure I know what you mean."

"Only that for a man who seemed so attentive during the party, he hasn't shown much devotion otherwise." A smile curved his thin mouth, but didn't reach his eyes. "No flowers on your birthday, no phone calls at work, no lunch dates..."

Teddy shrugged. "He's a busy man."

"I'm sure." He let that insinuation dangle between them as he withdrew a paper cup and filled it with cold water from the cooler. "Care to have a drink with me this evening to discuss the senior graphic design opening?"

In her opinion, there was nothing left to discuss. She qualified for the job in every way that mattered. "No, thank you. I already have other plans." Not caring for the slant of their conversation, she stepped around Louden and headed for the hallway.

"For a woman who wants the position, you're not showing much dedication to Sharper Image."

Teddy immediately stopped, her blood beginning a slow simmer in her veins. Turning, she pinned Louden with a direct look. "My dedication shows in the quality of my work, the deadlines I've never missed and the long hours I put in when necessary."

He sighed, shaking his head regretfully. "But you're not very accommodating when the situation requires it." He took a drink of water, as if he hadn't just issued a double-edged comment.

She forced a calm she was far from feeling. "I don't think Austin would appreciate me meeting with you after hours."

He crushed the paper cup in his hand, as if to prove how easily he could demolish her dreams. "It's just a drink between colleagues, Teddy. I would think if your boyfriend knew how important this promotion was to you, he'd understand."

Teddy's stomach pitched. After all she'd gone through to establish Austin as her boyfriend, it appeared Louden didn't care that she was committed to someone else.

Crossing her arms over her chest, she smiled sweetly at her boss. "Why don't you see if Fred Williams is able to have

a drink with you this evening, and discuss the promotion?
Maybe he'll be more accommodating." She turned to leave,
but not before she caught a glimpse of Louden's complexion
turning an unflattering shade of red.

Feeling wonderfully liberated, she walked back to her office with a light step, shut the door and sat behind her desk.
Clinging to that boost of confidence, she picked up the
phone, dialed the number for Fantasy for Hire off the business card in her top drawer—the only number she had for
Austin—and mentally rehearsed her request while the line
rang.

The business recorder clicked on, and as much as she
hated leaving a message for Austin when she'd rather talk to
him in person, she had no choice. "Hi, Austin, this is Teddy.
I'd really like to talk to you—"

The line picked up, interrupting her one-sided conversation. "Hello?"

The voice, though deep and male, wasn't Austin's. Another Fantasy for Hire employee, possibly? "I'm calling for
Austin. Is he there?"

"No, he's not, but I can take a message for him."

The voice sounded a bit too eager. "All right," she said,
deciding she had no choice. "This is Teddy Spencer. He has
my home and work numbers. Tell him I'd really like to talk
to him, in person preferably."

"Got it." The friendly voice hesitated a moment, then
added, "You know, you're welcome to come by the house
and talk to Austin. He should be home in about half an
hour."

"The house?" Confusion wove through her. "Isn't this
Austin's business?"

"One and the same," he confirmed. "He runs Fantasy for
Hire out of the house."

"Oh." She imagined a dozen males in Austin's house,
dressed in various sexy costumes as they consulted their

schedules for fantasy appointments. Doubt filled her—maybe going to Austin's house wasn't such a great idea. "Uh, I don't think I should infringe on Austin's business time—"

"You wouldn't be," he assured her. "This is Austin's brother, Jordan," the male voice went on to explain. "He's told me about you, Teddy. I'm sure he wouldn't mind if you stopped by to see him."

She had to trust that Jordan knew Austin well enough to make such a statement. "Okay." She jotted down the address Jordan gave her. "I'll be there in an hour."

"Great," he said effusively. "I can't wait to meet you."

Teddy hung up the phone, hoping Austin shared his brother's enthusiasm about her surprise visit.

"YOU DID *WHAT*?" Austin glared at his meddlesome brother.

Jordan held his hands up in a supplicating gesture. "Hey, she said she needed to talk to you in person. It sounded important, and I'm not one to turn down a woman in distress."

"Distress?" Austin laughed dryly at Jordan's description. "Teddy can take care of herself just fine. Whatever she needed to talk to me about could have been done over the phone." He would have preferred that, actually. The past two days, he hadn't been able to think about anything but her. One date, if he could even term escorting her to her Christmas party as such, and she had his hormones and emotions twisted into something he refused to examine. Seeing her in person again, being close enough to touch her, was going to kill him.

And what in the world could be so important that she had to talk to him in person?

"Regardless, she'll be here any minute," Jordan said, then frowned at Austin. "And you look like you've been digging ditches all day."

"Pretty damn close." He'd been shorthanded today on the

landscaping project under development for a newly built condominium complex and had spent the afternoon helping his guys install an elaborate sprinkler system, along with planting trees, shrubs and ground cover. Digging ditches wasn't beneath him, not in his chosen profession.

Jordan waved an impatient hand toward the upper facilities. "I suggest you go and take a shower before she gets here."

Austin glanced down at himself, a slow grin pulling up the corners of his mouth. He'd taken off his dirt-encrusted work boots at the back door leading into the kitchen, but the rest of his attire was just as filthy. A combination of soil and sweat coated his skin and adhered to his T-shirt and jeans. Dust layered his thick hair. Hell, he could even taste the day's grime in his mouth. He was half tempted to greet Teddy just as he was, to give her a good look at what her investment broker looked like at the end of a workday.

"Well?" Jordan prompted, wrinkling his nose at him. "Time's a ticking, and the longer you stand here, the more Glade freshener I'm going to have to use to cover up that outdoorsy scent of yours."

Austin spouted an obscene gesture that made Jordan's mouth twitch with amusement. "Since you invited her over, you can entertain her until I'm cleaned up," Austin said, none too happy about the situation.

"Hey, I thought I was doing you a favor," Jordan called after him as he climbed the stairs to his room.

"Yeah, well, next time, *don't*," Austin said over his shoulder.

He heard Jordan mutter something about what an ungrateful brother he was, and took it all in stride. Heading into the bathroom, he peeled his dirty shirt over his head, tossed it into the hamper, then removed his jeans. By the time he exited the shower fifteen minutes later and pulled on a pair of cutoff shorts and a clean T-shirt, he could hear

Teddy's voice drifting from downstairs. He headed in that direction, following the sounds to the living room, where Jordan and Teddy were standing near the potted Douglas fir he'd brought home a week ago. He'd retrieved the small box of Christmas ornaments from the attic last night and placed it next to the tree, but hadn't had the chance to decorate it yet.

Not quite ready to make his presence known, Austin leaned against the door frame and crossed his arms over his chest, watching the two of them interact.

Jordan scratched his chin, a disapproving expression on his face. "I tried telling Austin that the tree was a bit on the piteous side, but he seems to think a string of garland will spruce it up."

Tucking her silky blond hair behind her ear, Teddy tilted her head, a soft smile on her face as she scrutinized the tree. "Oh, I don't know. I think the tree has potential. Garland might overpower the branches, but maybe we could find something in this box to liven it up without weighing it down." She glanced at Jordan hesitantly. "Would you mind if I gave it a shot while we're waiting for Austin?"

A too-cheerful smile curved Jordan's mouth. "By all means, help yourself."

Traitor, Austin thought with a dark scowl. He opened his mouth to announce his presence, then snapped it shut when Teddy bent over to rummage through the box of decorative items, which pulled her skirt taut over her bottom and lifted the hem a few inches. Man, oh, man, the woman had a fine backside, not to mention a pair of long, slender legs that inspired erotic thoughts. Images flitted through his mind, of coming up behind her and skimming his hands over her slim hips and pressing his hard body to hers...of her widening her stance as he shimmed up her skirt, caressing her firm thighs...

She straightened abruptly, flashing a spool of red ribbon Jordan's way. "What do you think about this velvet ribbon?"

Austin liked the idea of velvet ribbon, a whole lot... especially if those possibilities included mutual, pleasurable bondage and erotic explorations...

"I could make some small bows to tie around the branches," she suggested, her face radiant and her eyes sparkling with excitement. "And here's a piece of green velvet we can use around the base."

Jordan withdrew a pair of scissors from the Queen Anne desk next to him and handed the shears to Teddy. "Perfect."

Yeah, she was perfect, Austin thought. Beautiful, smart, a fabulous kisser, fun to be with...and she didn't want anything to do with him, he sternly reminded himself.

Teddy snipped a section of red ribbon and twisted it into a pretty bow. "It's been years since I've decorated a tree," she said, a touch of melancholy in her voice.

Jordan cast her a sideways glance as he took over the job of cutting sections of ribbon for her to tie. "Your parents don't get a tree at Christmas?" He sounded as curious as Austin was.

"Oh, they do, usually a twelve-foot blue spruce. But my mother hires a professional to decorate the tree so the trim and ornaments match with the house and look evenly distributed on the branches." She added another bow, swaddled the green velvet around the base to cover the plastic pot, then stepped back to admire her handiwork. "When I was a child, my mother used to let me hang a few of the decorations just to appease me, but by the next day my ornaments were either gone, or rearranged on the tree."

"That must have been tough," Jordan commented insightfully.

Austin didn't want to care about Teddy and her *underprivileged* youth, yet something near the vicinity of his heart tugged for the little girl Teddy had been, and how she'd been denied one of Christmas's favorite rituals enjoyed by most kids. He could easily picture her as a mischievous little girl, full of energy and curiosity.

Teddy shrugged, as if having come to terms with her mother's peculiarities long ago. "Now that I live alone, buying a tree and decorating it seems like so much work, especially when I don't have anyone to share it with."

For as much as she declared the importance of embracing her freedom, Austin heard the note of loneliness in her voice, and wondered how much of her need for independence was pure rebellion. Ninety percent of it, he'd bet.

Finished with the last of the bows, she rummaged through the box and withdrew an old, fond memory of Austin's. A dazzling smile lit her face. "This papier-mâché star is great!"

A wry smile curved Jordan's mouth. "Austin made that for our mother for Christmas when he was in the seventh grade. She loved it and used it every year until she died."

Teddy touched the handmade ornament reverently. There was nothing special or fancy about the star—it was just a hodgepodge of paper, glitter and yarn a twelve year old boy had glued together—but Austin imagined Teddy silently wished her own mother would have been so accepting of a gift handcrafted with youthful love and enthusiasm.

She glanced back at Jordan. "It's the perfect decoration to top the tree, wouldn't you agree?"

Her softly spoken question asked Jordan's permission to adorn the Douglas fir with Austin's star. He nodded. "Yeah, I do."

Austin steeled himself against the rush of feeling that stirred to life within him. This scene was too cozy, a false illusion when he knew Teddy would never allow those emotional needs he'd glimpsed in the past few minutes to interfere with her personal goals.

That sobering thought prompted him to push off the doorjamb and fully enter the room, startling both Jordan and

Teddy. His brother looked at him questioningly, while an anxious look flitted across Teddy's expression. She wiped her palms down the sides of her skirt, making him wonder why she'd sought him out again when she'd made it abundantly clear she didn't have time in her life for a relationship. Or for him.

Another business proposition, he guessed. The thought rubbed him raw, but he couldn't help being curious. Neither could he help wanting her as badly as he did.

Man, she did have him tied up in knots.

He closed the distance between them, catching the awareness glittering in her gaze, the flutter of her pulse at the base of her throat and the slight quiver of her breasts beneath the dark green, silk blouse she wore. The satisfaction he experienced was heady.

"I see you've met my brother," he drawled, smiling pleasantly.

"I, uh, yes," she stammered, a nervous smile on her lips. "We were just trying to make your tree a bit more presentable for Santa."

His gaze flickered to the ugly duckling of a tree she'd transformed into a swan, then back to her. "As much as I'm sure Santa will appreciate your efforts, I'm certain you didn't drop by to make sure I had a well-decorated tree for the holidays."

Jordan frowned at his brother's cool tone. But in Austin's mind, even though their mother had taught them to be gentlemen, there was the matter of his ego being bruised.

"No, I didn't," she admitted, that chin of hers lifting a notch. "I'd like to talk to you. Privately, if that's okay."

He stared into her unwavering brown eyes, tempted beyond all reason. For all of three seconds he considered telling her no, that whatever was on her mind could be said in front of Jordan, but he wasn't that much of a cad. Besides, he really didn't care to share this conversation with his brother.

"Private it is," he said. "Why don't we step into my office."

"Behave yourself," Jordan muttered beneath his breath.

Austin glared at his brother's protective gesture toward Teddy before heading toward the back room. Geez, whose side was Jordan on, anyway?

Teddy watched Austin go, suddenly doubting the wisdom of her visit. Austin was hardly welcoming, nor did he seem inclined to accommodate yet another request of hers.

A gentle hand nudged her. "Go on," Jordan murmured from beside her. "He's all bark and no bite."

Encouraged by Jordan's support, she smiled her thanks and followed the sexy, moody man she couldn't get out of her mind through a door that connected to a kitchen, where he stopped to grab a can of root beer from the refrigerator. Popping the top, he offered her a drink of her own that she declined, and they continued, to another room transformed into a makeshift office. He closed the door behind her, and her heart leaped in response to just how alone they were.

There were no chairs other than the one behind the scarred desk dominating the room, so she advanced no farther. The phone rang at that moment, and Austin rounded the desk, propped his jean-clad hip on the surface and reached for the receiver.

"Fantasy for Hire," he greeted the caller.

Teddy tried not to let that deep, rich voice of his affect her, but her attempts were futile. The warm male tones stroked her senses and settled in the pit of her stomach like a potent shot of liquor.

"Hi, Don," Austin said after a moment, and turned to flip through the schedule open on the desk. His index finger scanned down a page, then stopped. "I've got you lined up for two fantasies tonight. A fireman at seven-thirty, and Zorro at ten."

Teddy listened to the conversation with some amusement

as she glanced around the cluttered office, trying not to think about Austin performing his share of fantasies for countless women. In her attempt to keep her mind occupied, her gaze was inevitably drawn to his wide, muscled shoulders stretching the cotton of his T-shirt, then moved to his profile, and eventually stopped on those incredible lips of his.

He grinned at something the caller said. "Hey, you're the one who thought up the Zorro costume, and it's become a favorite. Just be careful with that sword of yours." Austin chuckled at the other man's response, which Teddy didn't doubt was a bawdy one.

Excusing himself from the conversation for a moment, Austin covered the mouthpiece with his hand, his gaze on her. "C'mere and sit down, Teddy." With his bare foot, he pushed the rolling high-backed chair out a few inches from where he sat. "I'll be done in a minute."

To refuse would make her look uptight, so she sat down and waited while Austin gave his employee directions to each performance. He hung up the phone, then turned those sexy, intense green eyes on her.

"So, what can I do for you, Ms. Spencer?" Picking up his root beer, he took a long swallow while he waited for her to answer.

She crossed one leg over the other, taking a second to gather her courage. "I need to ask a favor."

The faintest hint of a smile tipped his mouth. "Another fantasy?"

Seeing the spark of insolence in his eyes, she knew he wasn't going to make this conversation easy on her, not that she blamed him after the way they'd parted Saturday night. There was no way to sugarcoat her request, so she just came out with it. "No, I was hoping you would come with me to my parents' house Christmas Eve."

Surprise crossed his gorgeous features. "Now, why would I want to do that?"

Yes, *why?* her conscience taunted. "Because you promised my sister-in-law that you would, and she told the rest of the family you'd be there."

He finished his root beer, appearing unconcerned. "Your sister-in-law made assumptions, and you were supposed to clear them up."

Frustration nipped at her. "I did." At least she'd tried to, not that it had worked.

"Another charade?" he guessed, his mouth thinning in disdain.

Her entire life was beginning to feel like one big scheme—at work, with her family. Everything was a carefully orchestrated plan...except for her feelings for Austin, which were too real, and becoming more complicated than she'd ever expected. "No, not another charade," she told him. "I explained that you were just a friend."

He tensed, the muscles across his chest flexing with the movement. "How convenient."

She closed her eyes, hating his contempt, but taking full responsibility for his resentment. Lifting her lashes, she met his dark, penetrating gaze, inwardly admitting defeat. "You know what, I think coming here was a big mistake."

She stood to leave, but he was faster, moving like a lithe panther. Propping his bare feet on either side of her thighs, he reeled the chair in closer to him with the strength of his legs, jarring her back into her seat. He leaned forward, looming over her. His strong, powerful thighs were close enough to touch...and so was that solid chest of his. Trapped between the chair and two hundred pounds of pure male essence and heat, her heart fluttered uncontrollably...with shameless excitement, and apprehension.

"What do you *really* want from me this time, Teddy?" he asked, his tone low and rough. "I gave you a cowboy. I gave you a lover. What fantasy do you expect me to be now?"

The frustrated undertone to his voice perplexed her, as did

this issue he had with being a fantasy for her. "I don't want you to be any fantasy. I want you to be...a friend. I could really use a friend right now." Between the pressures of her family, and Louden's strong-arm tactics, she desperately needed someone in her corner.

Something in his expression softened, then was quickly replaced with ruthless intent. "That poses a little problem, honey, because when I look at you, friendship isn't what comes to mind."

Yeah, Teddy, why would he want to be your friend after the way you treated him? To her consternation, her throat tightened and a suspicious moisture burned the backs of her eyes. "I know you probably hate me for how I ended things Saturday night—"

"Hate you?" Harsh, incredulous laughter erupted from him. "No, I don't hate you, Teddy. I *want* you." He stared at her face, and slowly lifted his hand, tracing a finger along her jaw. "I haven't slept the past few nights because every time I close my eyes I think of you and remember the heat and softness of your mouth..." He stroked his thumb along her full bottom lip, dipping just inside to dampen the pad of his finger. "The silky texture of your skin..." Those sensual fingers skimmed down her throat in a languid caress that made her breathing raspy, and caused her chest to rise and fall rapidly. "The warm taste of your breasts..." He brushed his knuckles over the slope of those swelling mounds, teasing her nipples into hard, achy points.

And just like that, her body hummed with arousal and an excruciating need.

He lifted his slumberous gaze from her breasts. One look into those striking green eyes filled with steely determination and she knew he wasn't done tormenting her.

A wicked smile lifted his lips. "And if that isn't enough to drive me crazy, I imagine what it would feel like to be inside you, as deep as I can get, and hear my name on your lips when you come..."

A surge of liquid warmth pooled in her belly, and lower. Her mind spun dizzily. "Austin..." she moaned raggedly.

"Yeah, just like that, Teddy." His voice vibrated with husky gratification, and he moved back slightly. His eyes, however, had no qualms about seducing her. "I'm not even inside you, not even touching you as intimately as I'd like to, but just thinking about having your legs wrapped around my hips and making love to you makes me hard enough to go off like an untried teenager."

She had a clear view of just how hard and impressive that part of his anatomy was beneath the faded denim of his shorts. Swallowing the thickness gathering in her throat, she pressed her knees together in a valiant attempt to ease the throbbing need he'd cleverly ignited. The attempt was useless.

Her gaze traveled upward, to his face. "So, you really don't hate me?" For some reason, having him confirm that was important to her.

He shook his head, his gaze honest. "No, I don't hate you, Teddy. I think you're nervous about what you feel for me and how fast our attraction has grown...and where it might lead."

She bit the inside of her cheek, unwilling to admit how accurate he was. She'd never planned for this, for him, and she feared she'd never be able to balance a career, and relationship—and that ultimately, she'd have to choose between the two.

"Then will you come with me to my parents' on Christmas Eve?" This time, she wasn't talking about a business arrangement. She wanted him to accompany her, and be a part of that special, magical evening before Christmas—and hopefully, his presence would banish the loneliness that always threatened to overwhelm her when she left her parents and realized that she was the only one in the family who didn't have anyone to share the holidays with.

Pure Christmas melancholy, she knew, but the desolate feeling never failed to creep up on her and hang on through the first of the year. Maybe this year would be different.

"If I say yes, I don't want any pretenses between us this time," Austin said, clasping his hands loosely between his knees so that he was no longer touching her. "Just you, and me, and whatever happens from there. And if all this leads to just friendship, then I'll accept that."

She found his terms more than fair. "All right."

A devastatingly charming grin transformed his features. "You brave enough to put your promise where your mouth is?"

She swallowed hard, knowing she was playing with fire...but she found Austin's brand of virile heat impossible to resist. The dare in his eyes spurred the recklessness she tried to keep buried.

Dampening her bottom lip with her tongue, she reached out, curled her fingers into the material of his shirt and pulled him down for a kiss the same time she sat up and met him halfway. Her lips crushed his, parted with immediate warmth, skipping all preliminary foreplay and going straight to the heart of the matter. The kiss was a hot, lusty, tongue-tangling mission to drive him as wild as he made her.

But something changed during the course of her provocative goal—an internal realization that overrode the pleasure of his generous mouth surrendering to her whims. She'd missed him. Two days apart, and she longed to see that wicked glint in his eyes, ached to experience the special way he made her feel, and especially craved the effortless way he made her body, her soul, come alive.

It was a frightening, overwhelming sensation.

With a low growl that rumbled in his chest, he grasped her hips in his hands, pulling her up and out of the chair and between his thighs. His large palms smoothed over her bottom, anchoring her intimately close. Her belly encountered the stiff ridge of his erection, and her heart slammed against her ribs. She moaned into his mouth as a very urgent, naughty thought crossed her mind, of pressing him down on his desk, hiking up her skirt and finishing what he'd started with his erotic monologue a few minutes ago.

It was Austin who ended the embrace, slowly pulling back and letting his lips slide from her mouth, to her jaw. "Oh, yeah, Ms. Spencer," he growled into the curve of her neck, where he nuzzled and pressed damp, open-mouth kisses on her skin. "That's a fantastic start to making good on your promise."

A delicious shiver rippled down her spine and she stepped back, until he had no choice but to let her go. Meeting his fiery emerald gaze, and witnessing his cocksure grin, her heart gave a tiny flip-flop of realization. It was useless to deny that what had transpired between them was anything less than powerful, and nothing even remotely close to resembling friendship.

And that meant trouble for her. Big trouble.

8

HE'D PLAYED DIRTY. Austin had acknowledged that fact minutes after Teddy left his house Monday evening, but three days later, he still didn't regret his unabashed behavior in prodding her to admit there was something between them. Her admission hadn't been verbal, but that mind-blowing kiss she'd initiated spoke volumes.

At first, he'd been annoyed that she'd had the nerve to ask him for yet another favor, but during the course of their conversation, he'd seen glimpses of contradicting emotions, of her wanting him as much as he wanted her, and a latent fear that kept her from completely opening herself to him. It had been that honest vulnerability that had softened him. Though he'd accepted her invitation for Christmas Eve, he'd been the one to establish the rules. No pretenses. So far, she'd adhered to his personal request, accepting and openly responding to the intimate kiss he'd greeted her with when he'd arrived at her condo to pick her up.

The woman was an inherently sensual creature, and despite her reservations, she certainly indulged wholeheartedly in kissing him, and took pleasure in the way he touched her. The low-cut, clingy red knit dress she'd worn in celebration of Christmas had tempted his hands to skim those ultra-feminine curves of hers—from the sleek line of her spine, over her bottom, and up and around to her hips, her waist, to just below the gentle slope of her breasts where his thumbs brushed along those full, soft mounds.

She'd moaned in acquiescence and arched toward him for

a deeper, more provocative contact, but he'd resisted the invitation. Satisfying the hunger he'd tasted in her kiss would take more than the few minutes they had before leaving for her parents'. The woman was in need of personal attention, emotionally and physically, and he planned to give her as much as she could handle, and then some, until she came to the realization that what was between them was worth pursuing.

Satisfied with his plan, Austin glanced over at Teddy sitting in the passenger seat of the Mustang as they drove to her parents' house in Pacific Heights. She was rummaging through her purse for something, and he switched on the overhead reading light for her. She smiled her thanks and withdrew a tube of lipstick.

"So, how are things with Louden?" he asked, curious if his presence at the company Christmas party had made any difference in her boss's attitude.

Flipping down the lighted mirror in front of her, she uncapped the tube and covered her kiss-swollen lips with a slash of pink-cinnamon color. "Just fine," she said too brightly.

He frowned as he made a left-hand turn onto the street Teddy had indicated. "Is he leaving you alone?"

She fluffed her hair that he'd unintentionally mussed during their kiss. She had the silkiest hair, and he loved running his fingers though the warm strands. She didn't seem to mind his fascination with her hair, either.

"I'm beginning to realize that Louden has the morals of an alley cat," she said, her tone tempered with disgust. "Which means he'll continue to prey until a bigger cat comes along and knocks him down a peg or two."

A flare of possessiveness gripped him, and his hands tightened on the steering wheel. "How about I pay Louden a personal visit and let him know just how close he is to being neutered?"

She laughed, but the sound was strained. "Austin, I can handle Louden. By the end of the next week, one way or another, this will all be over with. I'll either get the promotion, or I won't."

She didn't sound very positive, and that bothered him. "And if you don't?"

"Then I update my résumé and start over," she said in quiet resignation, putting the lighted mirror back in its place. "And I can't begin to tell you how much I dread doing that. It means proving myself all over again."

He heard the frustration in her voice, and knew she was referring to more than just establishing herself with another employer, but with her family, too. Strangely enough, he understood her resentment, and respected her determination to overcome it.

Reaching across the console, he gently laid his hand on her knee, offering silent support. "Getting that promotion is really important to you, isn't it?"

"Yeah, it is, for so many reasons," she admitted, then drew a deep breath as if to dismiss the entire subject. "Turn right here, then make another right on Vallejo. My parents' house is on the left-hand side."

He followed Teddy's directions, impressed with the ritzy area of San Francisco and multimillion-dollar homes overlooking the Bay, even though he'd expected as much. Trying not to allow old insecurities to assail him, he made the final turn onto Vallejo Street, determined to make the best impression on Teddy's family that he could, and hoped they accepted him for who he was. Nothing more. Nothing less.

"Which house?" he asked, glancing at Teddy. He frowned when he saw her struggling with the ruby and diamond band she wore on her ring finger.

"Stop the car for a minute," she said, her tone exasperated.

He slowed the Mustang to a halt as close to the side of the

narrow road as he could, put the vehicle in park, and turned to face her. "What are you doing?"

She tugged and twisted on the band, her face contorted with frustration. "I'm trying to take off my ring."

"Why?"

She exhaled loudly and continued her determined attempt to remove the ring, which refused to slip over her first knuckle. "Because my parents gave me this band when I graduated from high school, and they've never seen it on my left hand."

He couldn't help the grin spreading across his face. "Ah, so the illusion of being 'taken' is for every one else's benefit, but not your family's."

"Yeah, something like that," she muttered vaguely.

He continued to watch her struggle, amused with her thinking. "Don't you think you're making the issue more complicated than it needs to be?"

"No." Her succinct answer segued into a wince of pain, then a very unladylike curse when the gold cut into her flesh. "I must be retaining water," she said hopelessly.

Taking pity on her, he reached for her left hand. "Here, let me help."

"What?" she asked incredulously as he examined her finger. "You've got a pair of clippers in your glove box to cut the ring off my finger?"

He chuckled at her sarcasm. "Nope. Don't need any."

She snorted in disbelief. "Well, that ring isn't going to come off any other way..."

Her sassy comment rolled into a surprised gasp as he lifted her palm and used his tongue to dampen the skin where the ring encircled the digit, then closed his mouth over her finger to moisten the entire length. He suckled gently, swirling his tongue up and down her finger, thoroughly wetting her sensitized skin. Her eyes widened, her hand went limp in his, and an arousing groan slipped past her parted lips.

Once he was confident that her skin was slick enough, he dragged her finger from his mouth and gave the ring a twist and a gentle tug. The band slipped to her knuckle, and tightened around the bone. She let out a discouraged sigh, but he wasn't about to admit defeat, and slipped her finger into his mouth again, using his teeth and tongue to work the ring over her knuckle.

This time, he succeeded. Removing the band from his mouth, he turned her hand over and dropped the ring onto her palm.

"Thank you," she said breathlessly.

"Anytime." He grinned wickedly. "Do you need help putting it on your other finger?"

She quickly shook her head, but not before he saw the spark of desire that colored her brown eyes. "I think I can manage on my own." She did the deed herself, without any problems.

Putting the car into drive, he eased back into the street. "If you insist on wearing a ring on your left-hand finger, you need to think about getting yourself one that fits." He extended the comment mildly, but a fleeting, possessive thought crossed his mind as he turned into the Spencers' driveway. He wanted to be the one to put a ring there.

"So, Austin, how did you and my daughter meet?" The elder Evan Spencer the third asked as he handed Austin the double shot of Bailey's he'd poured for him.

Austin glanced around the expensively furnished parlor, complete with a professionally decorated twelve-foot blue spruce, and noted that all eyes were on him—from Teddy's parents, to each one of her three brothers and their respective wives, to Teddy herself. The eight nieces and nephews he'd met in a blur upon arriving were now in an adjoining playroom, watching videos, playing on the pinball and arcade games, and from the sounds of their laughter, having a good time with all the high-tech toys Grandma and Grandpa had purchased for their enjoyment.

"Yes, *how* did you meet?" Teddy's mother, Gloria, insisted on knowing. She tilted her blond head questioningly, appearing very much the well-bred hostess.

Teddy stood a few feet away, next to her mother, her luminous gaze pleading with him to be gentle with his answer.

No pretenses, he'd told her, yet he found he didn't want to embarrass Teddy, either. He'd only known the Spencers for less than half an hour, yet he got the distinct impression that Teddy's parents would find the truth distasteful and him unsuitable for their only daughter. The last thing he wanted was two strikes against him before he had a chance to convince Teddy how good they could be together.

He grinned at everyone, then settled his gaze on Teddy, giving her a private smile. "We met on her birthday, at the Frisco Bay."

Gratitude colored Teddy's eyes, but her relief was short-lived.

Gloria gasped, her hand fluttering to the pearl necklace layering the front of her cream silk blouse as she stared at her daughter in mortification. "You were picked up in a bar?"

Susan and Natalie, two of Teddy's sisters-in-law who were sitting next to each other on the sofa, smothered amused laughter. The sympathetic look they sent Austin's way led him to believe that their mother-in-law's theatrical display was a normal occurrence.

"No, Mother," Teddy said patiently. "I was with Brenda and Laura, having a drink for my birthday, and Austin didn't 'pick me up.' He was very much a gentleman, and we hit it off well."

"So well that she took him to her Christmas party," Susan

announced, just in case that tidbit of information hadn't made the rounds.

"Wow, must be serious, Theodora," Teddy's oldest brother, Evan, Jr., commented, winking at his little sister. "It's been so long since you've dated, we were beginning to worry that you were thinking about joining a convent."

Teddy glared at her brother. "You live to torment me, Evan."

"You're wrong, Evan," her other brother, Russ, added. "She'd rather be a CEO than a nun."

That earned a harrumph from her father. "I just don't understand you and your silly whims, Teddy," Evan, Sr., said sternly, swirling his martini. "We raised you to be a respectable young woman—"

"I'm an *independent* woman," Teddy interrupted her father's tirade.

"No argument there," Brent agreed with a grin. "Independent, stubborn and full of sass." Brent saluted Austin with his own drink of Jack Daniel's and soda. "If you can handle the independent gal, you can have her."

"No man worth his salt is going to allow his wife to work," the senior Evans said gruffly. Susan rolled her eyes as if to state she'd heard this lecture before, and the other two merely shook their heads.

"Isn't that right, Austin?" Evan, Sr., asked, looking for approval.

The cable-knit sweater Austin had worn suddenly felt heavy, hot and suffocating. Teddy's three sisters-in-law leaned forward in their seats, looking on in avid interest. Her brothers were obviously finding a lot of humor in the situation, and Teddy's mother was standing by her man and his old-fashioned ways. Even Teddy's expression showed she was curious about his answer.

This one he had to ride out on his own, and since there was only one person he wanted to please, he spoke the truth.

"Well, sir, I'm all for a woman working and having a career, if that's what she really wants."

The three sisters-in-law grinned at one another, as if Austin's statement had marked a major milestone in the Spencer household. Something in Teddy's gaze softened perceptibly, and Austin grasped and held on to the emotion, tucking it away for later.

"And who'll stay home and raise the kids?" Evan, Sr., argued.

"Dad, this is a moot point," Teddy interrupted before Austin could reply, her cheeks flushed a faint shade of pink. "I have no intention of getting married anytime soon, let alone having kids."

Her father shook a finger at her. "You're too stubborn for your own good, Theodora."

Russ stepped up to his father and slapped him good-naturedly on the back. "Dad, I think she's got you beat on this one."

"She already passed up one great catch," Gloria interjected. "How many others will she go through before she runs out of suitable men to marry?"

Evan, Sr., glanced at his only daughter, frowning. "I don't know many men who'll wait around while a woman chases after a fanciful hobby that keeps her too occupied to be a proper wife."

The hurt in Teddy's eyes was unmistakable, as was the resignation that her parents would never understand her choices.

The maid announced dinner, dispelling the awkward moment, and the family moved to the formal dining room. Austin remained behind with Teddy for a few extra seconds while she regained her composure.

"It's like this every time," Teddy said wearily.

Not knowing what to say to that, Austin touched his hand to the small of her back in a supportive gesture as they entered the adjoining room. Her parents didn't understand what drove Teddy, but he certainly did. The woman was strong and independent, but what no one realized was just how much her struggle to establish her own individuality was costing her emotionally.

Beneath a glittering chandelier, a long cherry-wood table was draped with cream linen and set with fine china, gleaming silver and elegant crystal. The adults sat at the formal table, while the kids were served at the picnic-style table in the game room established just for them.

The meal was an enjoyable feast of rack of lamb, sweet potatoes, fresh green beans and warm, crusty bread. Dinner conversation centered around Teddy's brother's professions of surgeon, lawyer and optometrist, and the various charities her mother and sisters-in-law had donated their time to during the holidays. All in all, Austin found the discussions entertaining, shared his opinion when asked, and enjoyed the humor and anecdotes thrown in by Teddy's brothers and sisters-in-law. It had been a long time since he'd been in a family setting, and it reminded him just how lonely his own life was when Jordan wasn't around.

They made it all the way to coffee and a rich, decadent dessert of chocolate truffle cheesecake without incident, when Evan, Sr., leaned back in his chair at the head of the table and addressed Austin specifically.

"So, Austin, what are your intentions toward Teddy?" The question was asked congenially enough, but Austin didn't doubt the seriousness behind the query.

Teddy stiffened beside him. "Dad!" she whispered harshly, obviously mortified.

Gloria, who sat on the other side of Teddy, patted her daughter's hand consolingly. "Now, Theodora, your father is just looking out for your welfare."

Austin smothered a grin as he watched that chin of Teddy's lift mutinously and fire enter her eyes. "I'm a big girl, Mother, and more than capable of taking care of myself."

"Well?" the senior Evans prompted, ignoring Teddy's statement.

Austin did a quick survey of the other residents at the table, none of whom looked ready to jump to his defense. "Intentions?" He mulled over the word while taking a drink of his coffee. "Well, I hadn't really thought of Teddy in those terms. I care for your daughter very much. I guess we'll have to see where it leads."

Evan, Sr., nodded and rubbed his chin thoughtfully. "Can you support her appropriately?"

Teddy nearly choked on the bite of cheesecake she'd been swallowing. Once her coughing fit was under control, she cast a beseeching glance her father's way. *"Dad,"* she said between gritted teeth, the word sounding suspiciously like a warning.

"Now, Theodora," her mother chastised. "These are perfectly legitimate questions for your father to ask of any young man who expresses an interest in you."

"Or a *woman* who might express an interest in one of your brothers," Susan added oh-so-helpfully, letting Austin know that no one was safe from the elder Spencers' interrogation.

"I'm not rich by any stretch of the imagination," Austin admitted, pushing aside his half-eaten dessert. "But the house I live in is paid for, and I make a decent living, certainly enough to support a family."

An inquisitive look entered Evan, Sr.'s, gaze. "I don't believe you've said what you do for a living."

"He's an investment broker," Teddy announced eagerly, the same moment that Austin said, "I own my own landscaping business."

It didn't take a rocket scientist to guess that Teddy had feared he'd reveal his Fantasy for Hire gig.

Dead silence followed, and everybody seemed to go perfectly still as eight pair of eyes scrutinized him like an insect under a microscope. Even Teddy seemed to stop breathing, and he couldn't help wondering if she'd approve of what he *really* did for a living—digging ditches.

"You're a busy man, Mr. McBride," Brent said with some degree of amusement, breaking up the stagnant silence that had settled in the dining room.

"Certainly very enterprising," Evan, Sr., agreed, sounding begrudgingly impressed.

"Actually, I'm no longer an investment broker," he said, certain he saw Teddy's shoulders slump at that announcement. "I'm concentrating on the landscaping business."

"Oh," Gloria said, and the sound wasn't a complimentary one.

Austin knew if he intended to see Teddy again, he wanted the truth out on the table now. "I know landscaping doesn't sound as glamorous as an investment broker. It's a lot of hard work, and some days long hours, but overall I find it very satisfying."

Evan, Sr., glanced from Teddy, then back to the man she'd brought to meet their family. Austin was certain he wasn't what the elder Spencer and his wife had in mind for their daughter, but Austin was exactly what he said he was. What they saw was what they got.

"And your parents," Evan, Sr., went on, as if striving to find some redeeming quality. "What do they do?"

"Both of my parents are dead." Knowing he had nothing left to lose, he added, "It's just me and my brother, Jordan, who is currently an unemployed architect."

Dismay filled Gloria's eyes as she looked at Teddy, as if she couldn't believe her daughter had settled for less than one of the prominent businessmen in their league.

Teddy's five-year-old niece, Katie, came out of the playroom at that moment, anticipation wreathing her pretty face.

"Grandma, we all ate our dinner. When do we get to open our presents?"

An adoring smile softened Gloria's features as she looked at her granddaughter, and Austin had the thought that this woman was a marshmallow beneath her haughty exterior. "I suppose now would be a good time, since you all have to get to bed soon so Santa can come visit. Why don't you get everyone to wash up and meet us in the parlor?"

Katie raced from the room, her little-girl voice announcing to her cousins, "We get to open our presents!"

The adults laughed at the responding squeals of delight and "yipees" that drifted from the playroom, and they all moved back into the parlor. Austin made himself comfortable on the sofa while Teddy helped pass out the gaily wrapped Christmas presents under the tree, obviously having fun with the task. For as much as she'd claimed that kids weren't her forte, Austin couldn't help noticing how much she enjoyed playing the role of aunt, and how loving she was with each child. A smile played at the corner of his mouth as he watched Teddy divide her attention between helping Drew, her three-year-old nephew, put together a chunky wooden puzzle, and her six-year-old niece, Molly, diaper her new "Baby-wets-a-lot." Her maternal instincts weren't as suppressed as she might want to believe.

Susan settled herself next to Austin, and he smiled amicably at her. There was mischief in the other woman's gaze, and a glint of determination. Leaning close, taking advantage of Gloria and Evan, Sr.'s, distraction, she said in a low voice, "Don't sweat the small stuff, Austin. The Spencers are a different breed. Everyone goes through the initial interrogation process. What ultimately matters is how Teddy feels about you."

Austin appreciated Susan's encouragement, but after that enlightening dinner conversation, he wasn't so sure fitting into Teddy's life would be as easy as surviving the Spencer's third-degree. Not only did he feel as though he'd never measure up, he honestly had no idea where he stood with Teddy—if what he did for a living mattered to her, or how she truly felt about him—beyond their "agreements."

Maybe it was time he found out.

9

TEDDY LEANED her head against the passenger seat's head-rest and released a long pent-up breath—in relief, exhaustion and a good part frustration. Beside her, Austin was quiet as he pulled out of her parents' driveway, the moonlight reflected through the windshield illuminating his pensive features.

"That was a disaster," she said, shaking her head in disappointment.

"Not the entire evening," he graciously conceded with a smile that wasn't quite as sexy and breathtaking as usual. "I enjoyed watching the kids open their presents, and talking to your brothers and their wives."

Her siblings seemed to like him, too, which pleased her. However, Teddy didn't miss the fact that he had no compliments for her parents—not that they'd deserved any accolades after the way they'd grilled him. "I never would have thought my parents would behave so atrociously," she said, her tone contrite.

He brought the car to a halt at a stop sign and glanced over at her, his gaze expressing an odd combination of understanding and regret. Reaching across the console, he gently brushed his fingers along her cheek. "I suppose they're just concerned about who their little girl is getting involved with."

Her skin tingled where he touched her, eliciting a sensual warmth that spread through her entire body. "As if they have any say in the matter," she said, forcing an indignant note over the quiver of awareness infusing her voice. "If my parents had their choice, they'd have me married off to some stuffy blue blood, being a *proper* wife."

"I can't imagine it," he murmured, a sly smile curving his mouth.

She exaggerated a shudder, adding to the humor of the situation. "Neither can I."

They both laughed, his low, husky chuckles mingling with her lighter ones, the sound pleasant and very intimate in the close confines of the car. The lighthearted moment released some of the tension she'd sensed in him a half hour after arriving at her parents'. The evening had only gotten worse, and certainly more complicated than she'd expected.

Austin drove on, maneuvering the car through the streets of Pacific Heights. He wasn't taking the normal way back to her condo, but she didn't mind if he wanted to take a longer route, which would give her more time with him. It was Christmas Eve, and for the first time since she could remember, she dreaded being alone.

"Austin..." She fiddled with the strap of her purse. "I'm really sorry for my parents' behavior tonight, and that you had to lie about owning your own landscaping business. I'll be the first to admit that my parents can be judgmental, but they'll come around."

He glanced her way. "You planning on bringing me to another family get-together?"

Her heart thumped in her chest, and a flood of emotions shook her to her soul. There was no denying she enjoyed everything about Austin, from his humor and honesty, to the feminine way he made her feel. But he made her yearn for things that conflicted with everything she'd worked so hard to attain, and the strength of those feelings frightened her.

She gave a noncommittal shrug, which was the best she could offer him. "You never know."

He stared at her for a long, intense moment, then switched

his gaze back to the road. "Does it matter to you what I do for a living?" he asked quietly.

She glanced out her window to the darkness beyond, giving his question serious consideration. If she was honest with herself, she had to admit that on some level Austin owning Fantasy for Hire bothered her, because she disliked the thought that other women fantasized about him and lusted over that gorgeous body while he performed a sexy striptease for them. She was beginning to think of Austin as *her* fantasy, and she didn't want to share. Jealousy was a foreign emotion to her, one she'd never experienced in a relationship with a man, but she quickly realized she wasn't immune to the green-eyed monster.

So how did she answer his question without sounding like a possessive shrew? "I'd be lying if I said it didn't matter to me what you did for a living. But I suppose I can learn to get used to you stripping for other women."

"And what if I really did own my own landscaping business?" he asked, his voice slightly anxious. "Would that line of work make a difference to you?"

She studied his face, seeing the taut line of his jaw, the tense set of his shoulders beneath his cable-knit sweater, and the truth finally dawned on her. "You really are in that line of work, aren't you? Along with Fantasy for Hire."

He nodded, and turned onto another darkened street that climbed upward and overlooked Pacific Heights. "Yep. McBride Commercial Landscaping is a real, solid business. I'm not rich, but I'm successful enough to support myself, and I love my job."

She tilted her head, fascinated with this facet of Austin's life. "And Fantasy for Hire?"

"It's been a lucrative business, and it helped to support me when I needed the money, but I've definitely outgrown it. I'm going to sell the business so I can devote my time to McBride Landscaping."

The car rolled to a stop. Austin cut the engine and turned to look at her with searching eyes, as if gauging her reaction to his newest revelation. It struck her then, that as confident as Austin appeared, he harbored a few insecurities of his own.

"Why does what I think matter so much to you?" she whispered, breaking through the quiet that had settled in the car.

"Because this is who I am, Teddy," he said, his warm gaze falling from her eyes, to her mouth, then back up again. "What you see is what you get, and I want to be sure you're okay with that."

Liquid heat pooled in her belly. "Yeah, I am."

"I'm not some blue blood with a fancy investment-broker image, Teddy—"

She pressed her fingers to his lips to stop his words, and the jolt of electrical heat that passed between them made her shiver. "That's probably why I'm so attracted to you."

Gently, he grasped her wrist, lowering her hand so her palm pressed against his chest, so she could feel the steady beating of his heart. "And your parents?"

She understood the reassurances he was searching for. Her mother and father hadn't issued full approval of Austin, and he wanted to make sure it made no difference to her. "Do you honestly think it matters to me what my parents think?"

His eyes burned into hers, hot and filled with an honest, primitive need that tapped into every responding nerve in her body. "I just want to be sure before we go any further."

Knowing where the next step in their relationship would lead, an equal measure of excitement and apprehension swirled within her. "I'm...sure."

The lazy, sexy grin that settled on his mouth was sheer male, and the dark look in his green eyes was very, very pleased.

Needing a moment to absorb what she'd just agreed to, she glanced around at their surroundings. Wherever he'd parked was pitch-black and deserted. They were alone, except for the breathless view of the bay below them and the star-studded sky above. A renewed rush of warmth seeped into her midsection.

"Where are we?" she asked, peering out the window.

His long fingers trailed along her shoulder and toyed with her silky hair. "It's a secluded place that not many people know about."

She cast him a teasing look. "And how do you know about it?"

He grinned, a wicked light brightening his gaze. "When I was in high school, I'd bring girls up here to make out with them." He looked off in the distance, amusement in his expression. "One time, when I was sixteen and had just gotten my driver's license, I brought a girl up here on a Saturday night. Not fifteen minutes later, another car pulled up, and it was Jordan and his date." Austin chuckled, shaking his head. "He didn't so much as get the chance to kiss his girl, because he was so furious at finding me up here, making out with my date."

Teddy laughed at the fond memory he shared, reminded too much of how her own brothers had been with the guys she'd dated. Protective and ruthless. "It must be an older-brother thing."

His thumb rubbed along her sensitive earlobe, then found the spot that made her shiver with pleasure. "You got caught necking, too?"

"No, never. I missed out on that particular fun." She sighed with a small measure of regret, because she'd been too busy with debutante balls and country-club dances. And though she'd been rebellious enough to go along with the suggestion, no boy had issued the invitation. "I just meant that my brothers were overly protective of me, too. Who I went out with, where my dates took me, and all that stuff. Not that they had anything to worry about. The boys I was allowed to date came from prestigious families that were friends of my parents, and they wouldn't have dared touched me the wrong way. I was deemed a 'good girl,' and my brothers made sure I kept that reputation."

"Well, you're all grown up, your brothers aren't anywhere around, and I'm not one of those saps who come from a highfalutin family." He leaned close, and her senses spun at the hot, hungry look in his eyes. "Wanna neck?"

Being a bad girl suddenly held enormous appeal. Feeling reckless, she met him halfway to the console. "Yeah, I think I do."

The hand caressing her throat moved up and slid into her hair, threading through the warm strands. The last thing she saw was the sinful grin curving his mouth, then his lips covered hers and he was kissing her—long, deeply intimate kisses that brought her to a fever pitch of need in no time flat. Her body swelled with arousal, her breasts grew heavy, and an achy emptiness settled in the pit of her belly.

They made out like two lust-filled teenagers, both attempting to find a comfortable position that would allow them more freedom to use their hands without putting a crick in their necks. Austin managed to cup her breast in his hand, and when she shifted to move closer, his arm twisted awkwardly and fell away. She touched his thigh, but the other hand supporting her slipped off the console and she nearly bit his lip as the impact jarred her entire body.

A giggle escaped her. "This is crazy."

He nuzzled her neck, his breath hot and damp against her skin. "But fun and kinda sexy, don't you think?"

Delicious and thrilling, she agreed, if only her back didn't ache from her awkward position. "I can't get close enough," she complained.

"Yeah, you can." Moving back to his side of the car, he slid the leather seat back, making more room between him and the steering wheel. "C'mere, Teddy," he murmured huskily, his eyes ablaze with a sweet, sexual promise that dared her to be just as bold. "I want you to sit on my lap so I can touch you the way I've been wanting to since the night of the Christmas party."

His words made her shiver, made her melt, made her eager for what they both wanted. Judging the distance between them and deeming it as too far, she climbed over the console with his help, but not without whacking her leg on the steering wheel, losing a shoe on the trek and elbowing him in the ribs. They laughed at their bumbling, but all amusement ceased once she was straddling his thighs...their embrace so snug and intimate there was no mistaking how much he wanted her.

He skimmed her hips with his hands and smiled a roguish grin that told her he'd had way too much experience as a young teen at this sort of thing. "Close enough for you?"

"Yeah." Her fingers found their way beneath the hem of his sweater. His flat abdomen clenched as she stroked his belly, luxuriating in his vibrant, muscular body. "Can I take off your sweater?"

"Honey, you can do anything to me that you'd like to," he urged. "Be as bad as you want to be. I won't tell a soul."

Licking her dry lips, and enjoying the thrill of being naughty, she lifted the cable-knit over his head and spent a minute exploring his magnificent chest and the hot, tight feel of his skin all the way down to the waistband of his slacks. His hips rolled enthusiastically beneath her, but instead of giving him the attention he sought, she touched her knees, which bracketed his hips. Slowly, she skimmed her palms upward, dragging the hem of her knit dress up her thighs, tempting him with the lacy band holding up her silk stockings and a glimpse of smooth, pale skin.

His breathing deepened as he watched her brazen, shame-

less display on his lap, and she gently tipped his chin up
with a finger so his eyes met hers. Not quite done seducing
him, she grasped one of the hands cinching her waist and
flattened his palm at the base of her throat, then guided his
hot, callused fingers inside the low-cut collar of her dress.

Stopping just above where the upper slope of her breast
swelled from her bra, she whispered invitingly in the shadowed interior of the vehicle, "Touch me the way you've been
wanting to since the Christmas party."

With a low-throated growl, he slipped the shoulders of her
dress down, until the stretchy material tightened around her
arms, and the front bunched around her waist. He didn't
bother with the back clasp to her sheer, lacy bra, and instead
lowered the cups so that her breasts sprang free from the
binding—firm, full and eager for attention. His hands
shaped her, his thumbs rasped across her sensitive nipples,
and then he dipped his head and took one puckered tip into
his hot, wet mouth.

Moaning in pure, unadulterated pleasure, Teddy let her
head drop back, arched her spine and clenched her fingers in
his thick, soft hair. He teased the crest with his teeth, then
soothed the gentle bites with the damp swirl of his tongue
until her breasts grew swollen and heavy.

Her flesh thrummed. Her blood pounded. A sultry heat
swirled within the car, making her skin slick, and his just as
damp. Idly, she noticed that the windows were completely
fogged, cocooning them in their own private world. The
arousing, male scent of him filled every panting breath she
gulped, and suddenly she wasn't near close enough for what
she needed. Gripping his bare shoulders, she rocked into
him, so that the hard ridge beneath the fly of his pants
pressed against the apex of her thighs, rubbing enticingly.
She gasped at the erotic friction of wet silk against pulsing,
aroused flesh. He groaned and grew impossibly thicker.

A ragged sob caught in her throat, and she grappled frantically with the thin leather belt at his waist, wanting to touch him, stroke him, feel him inside her where she needed him the most.

He caught her wrists, laughing harshly, stopping her before she attained her goal. She gazed down at him in confusion, finding nothing humorous about the situation.

His smoky gaze flickered over her, taking in her wanton display on his lap—the way the front of her dress was pulled low to reveal the pale curves of her breasts, and the hem that flashed a tempting expanse of thigh and held the promise of something far more alluring. She trembled, as if he'd physically stroked her in all those inflamed places.

Visibly drawing in a steady breath, he brought his gaze back to hers. "Teddy, honey, I want you so badly I can't think straight. But I don't have any protection with me, and I won't risk you that way."

She closed her eyes, ignoring the deep, internal throb demanding release, but her attempts failed. "You're experienced at this sort of thing," she said, frowning playfully at him. "Didn't you come prepared?"

A rakish grin slashed across his features at her complaint. "Not to make love to you. When we do, I want a nice, soft bed beneath us, and hours to enjoy us being together, not a quickie in my car."

She rolled her eyes in mock disgust. "What a time to be chivalrous."

A deep chuckle rumbled in his chest. Letting go of her hands, he nuzzled her neck, skimming his lips up to her ear. "You'll thank me later, but right now, let me take the edge off for you."

She opened her mouth to tell him no, that she didn't want to experience that sexual release without him, but those clever hands of his were already rasping along her stockings and disappearing beneath the hem of her dress. He stroked the soft, sensitive flesh of her inner thighs, and the only sound that emerged from between her lips was a low, needy groan.

Her hips shifted, tilting toward him instinctively. His fingers leisurely traced the elastic band of her panties along the crease of her leg, brushed erotically over the strip of silk covering her feminine secrets, then finally slipped beneath that barrier to glide his thumb over that slick, aching bud of flesh.

A shock wave of pleasure rolled through her. She bit her bottom lip to keep from crying out and squeezed her eyes shut to maintain some control. He made her wild. He made her shameless. Her body never felt so vibrantly alive, and the foreign sensation was as thrilling as it was startling.

"Look at me, Teddy." Austin's voice was dark and coaxing, gentle and reassuring.

She tried. Oh, Lord, she tried—barely managing to lift her lashes and meet his dark, hungry gaze. He sat back in his seat, watching her, his muscular body tense, his breathing just as erratic as hers as his fingers continued to ply a delicious, forbidden kind of magic.

She quivered from head to toe, and pressed her hands against his chest for support. Uncertainties assailed her. "Austin..."

"Shh..." Somehow, someway, he understood her fears of letting go. "I want to watch you, just like this." He stroked her slowly, rhythmically, building the exquisite pressure. "You're incredibly beautiful, Teddy, and very sexy...come for me."

His words, his touch, the reverent way he looked at her, pushed her to the edge, then over that precipice. While he watched, she came undone for him, letting the climax roll over her in waves of intense pleasure that seemed to go on and on. A long, low moan ripped from her, and he groaned right along with her, the provocative sound setting off additional surges of sensation that extended the deep, internal shudders rippling through her body.

Satiated, she collapsed against his chest, burying her face in the crook of his neck as she struggled to breathe normally. The interior of the car was warm and humid from the heat they'd generated, and her breasts slid against his damp chest, arousing her all over again.

Austin adjusted the top of her dress, covering her, then smoothed his hands down her spine in a languid caress. "You're incredible, Teddy."

Smiling drowsily, she lifted her head and brushed her fingers across his lips, reveling in the contentment she felt with this man. "I think you deserve all the credit for what just happened."

His grin was pure male satisfaction, and she discovered that she didn't want this night to end. Not this soon.

"Austin, I know it's Christmas Eve, and you probably spend Christmas morning with Jordan, but I don't want to be alone tonight." She swallowed hard. The admission cost her emotionally, but her need for him went beyond anything she'd ever experienced. "If you have a few spare condoms we can use, I have a nice, soft bed at home we can make good use of." Her tone was light and teasing, but her insides tied up in knots at the thought that he might refuse her.

He smoothed her disheveled hair from her face. The undeniable need reflecting in his eyes eased her fears of rejection. The rakish grin tipping the corners of his mouth made her heart swell with powerful emotions. "The condoms are at home."

She worried her bottom lip between her teeth, briefly considering her brazen request. "Maybe you could drop me off at my place, then go and get them, and a spare change of clothes?"

He stared at her, searching her expression—for what, she couldn't be certain. "Are you sure about this, Teddy?"

For a moment, her heart faltered. Trapped by the hunger glittering in his eyes, her breath fluttered in her throat. He wasn't asking for a lifetime commitment, she told herself, just the certainty that she was ready for a more intimate relationship. Adults indulged in mutual pleasure all the time, and she desperately craved that sensual connection with him.

"Yeah, I'm sure," she whispered. Framing his face between her hands, she lowered her parted lips to his to prove just how certain she was about becoming his lover.

A rapid tapping against Austin's window startled Teddy, and it took a few heartbeats and Austin's comical expression for her to realize that someone had caught them making out. Horrified at the prospect, but grateful for the fogged windows which offered a modicum of privacy, she scrambled back to her side of the car. Her dress caught on the gearshift, and the vehicle rocked with her swift movement over the console. Finding Austin's sweater on the floorboard, she tossed it at him.

"Put that on!" she ordered frantically.

"Kinda late for modesty, don't you think?" he drawled, tugging the sweater over his head and adjusting it over his torso.

She glared at him, tamping down the bubble of laughter working its way up. The situation was hilarious, if not a bit humiliating, but she wasn't going to give him the satisfaction of humoring him.

"Hey, kids, roll down the window," a gruff voice commanded. "It's past curfew, and I don't think your parents would appreciate being called down to the police station on Christmas Eve."

Austin did as he was instructed, rolling his window halfway down while Teddy gave the hem of her dress a fierce tug, stretching the material to her knees. "Good evening, sir," he said respectfully to the uniformed officer standing outside the Mustang.

The cop crouched down, and a beam of light searched the

interior of the car, bouncing from Austin to Teddy. Her cheeks flamed with embarrassment.

The officer grinned, clearly expecting teenagers, not two grown adults. "Considering you're both consenting adults, I'm guessing your parents wouldn't give a damn if you spent the night in the slammer."

"Uh, no, sir," Austin replied politely.

The cop snapped off his light. "I'll give you five minutes for the windows to clear, then I suggest you take this to a private place," he said, amusement obvious in his voice.

Austin nodded his gratitude. "We'll do that, sir."

The officer headed back to his squad car, and Austin turned and grinned impishly at her. "Well, you've just experienced the full effect of making out on a dark, secluded road." He turned the ignition and put the window defroster on full blast. "That was probably just as embarrassing as getting caught by one of your brothers."

Teddy groaned and slumped against her seat. "Thank you for the unique experience."

Austin winked at her. "It was my pleasure."

AUSTIN STUFFED a clean change of clothes into his duffel bag, then crossed the wooden floor of his room to the bathroom, the spurs he'd attached to his cowboy boots jangling with each impatient step. Grabbing his toothbrush and a few other necessities, he returned to the bed, tossed the toiletries into the duffel, then went to retrieve the most important item for his sleep-over at Teddy's.

Just as he withdrew the unopened box of condoms he'd had stashed in his nightstand for the past six months, he heard a brisk knock on the open bedroom door. Like a kid being caught with something forbidden, the tips of his ears warmed, and he discreetly buried the box in his bag. His reaction was insane, considering he was a grown man, but there was something about Teddy that made what was going to happen tonight special. He didn't want to spoil his own mood, or tarnish Teddy's reputation, by enduring Jordan's ribbing.

However, explaining the costume he was wearing was something he hadn't considered.

Reluctantly, he turned to face Jordan, who was leaning against the doorjamb, his hands buried in the pockets of his robe.

A grin twitched the corners of Jordan's mouth as he took in Austin's cowboy attire, complete with Stetson, chaps and shiny silver spurs he'd bought to complete the Fantasy for Hire ensemble.

Jordan moved into the bedroom, curiosity brimming in his eyes. "I was expecting to hear Santa tonight, but the jangling noise I heard didn't sound like Christmas bells, so I thought I'd better investigate."

Austin zipped up the duffel, anxious to be on his way. "I'm sorry if I woke you up."

"Where in the world are you going dressed like that on Christmas Eve?" Jordan's amusement faded into a frown of disapproval. "Don't tell me that you've got a gig tonight."

Austin was beginning to feel like tonight's "gig" would be the performance of his life. Slinging the duffel over his shoulder, he grinned at his brother. "Don't wait up for me, pardner," he drawled humorously, tipping his Stetson at Jordan. "I've got one last fantasy to fulfill, and I have a feeling it's going to take all night long."

A slow grin spread across Jordan's face as understanding dawned.

Before Jordan could comment, Austin headed out the door and down the stairs. The metallic sound of the spurs' rowels chinking against wood rang throughout the house.

Jordan stood at the top of the stairs, and called after Austin, "Be careful that you don't hurt Teddy with those spurs!"

Austin chuckled. It was obvious that his brother adored Teddy as much as he did. Now it was just a matter of convincing Teddy how much she belonged in his life.

10

AUSTIN DIDN'T KNOW what to expect when he returned to Teddy's condo, but it certainly wasn't the sultry vixen who greeted him. Just like him, Teddy had changed, but her attire was far more enticing, and certainly more revealing. Soft chiffon and sheer lace in a deep shade of purple shaped her full breasts and draped along her curves to midthigh, accentuating everything womanly about her. Her hair was tousled around her head, her eyes shone bright with anticipation, and she smelled delicious, like citrus and something infinitely soft and feminine.

"Very nice," he murmured appreciatively, forgetting all about the role he'd wanted to play for her.

She shifted anxiously on her feet, and the hem of the nightie flirted along her thighs. "I got the nightgown for my birthday, and I thought I'd put it to good use," she explained, a faint blush touching her cheeks.

He didn't bother to point out that she wouldn't be wearing it for long.

He waited for her to invite him in, but she didn't seem in any hurry to do so. Her gaze leisurely traveled the length of him, and he could have sworn he heard her breath catch when she reached the spurs attached to his boots. There was no mistaking the excitement wreathing her expression when she glanced back at his face.

"Hello, cowboy," she said in a husky, come-hither voice.

He touched the brim of his hat politely, ignoring the swift

current of heat rushing through his veins so he could play along with the fantasy he wanted to create for her. "Ma'am."

Her small, pink tongue licked her bottom lip, and she leaned against the wall in the entryway, looking entirely too tempting. Blinking innocently, she asked, "So, cowboy, what brings you to my neck of the woods?"

Austin quickly realized that the woman he'd planned to seduce was turning the tables on him. Not that he minded having a willing counterpart, but if she wasn't careful, her provocative act was going to send him over the edge sooner than he'd anticipated. "I'm looking for a place to bunk down for the night," he drawled, struggling to maintain his composure when all he wanted to do was take this woman up against the wall, finesse be damned. "And I was hoping you could accommodate a lonesome cowboy."

Batting her lashes demurely at him, she skimmed her fingers over the swell of her breasts. Austin's mouth went dry as her nipples tightened.

A seductive smile added to her beguiling act. "Well, you're more than welcome to sleep in the stable with your horse."

He chuckled at her unexpected reply. "In that case, I guess I'm going to have to confess that I'm actually an outlaw seeking refuge, and I'll be taking you hostage." Making good on his threat, he moved into the entryway, closed the door behind him, and forced her up against the wall with the muscular heat of his body.

Her luminous brown eyes widened in mock fear and genuine excitement as she entwined her arms around his neck. "Dare I hope you'll be ravishing me?"

Dropping his duffel bag, he plowed his fingers into her hair so he could lift her mouth to his—not that she was resisting much. "Didn't your parents ever warn you just how dangerous an outlaw could be?" he growled.

"Oh, yeah, they've tried, but I can't help my attraction to a man in chaps and spurs," she admitted, her voice dropping to a honeyed purr. She lifted her hips, encountering the thick length of his erection framed between the crotch of his chaps. "Especially an outlaw who has a weapon as impressive as yours. I hope you aren't afraid to use it."

A guttural groan ripped from his chest. He'd been hard for the past ten minutes, ever since she'd opened the door, but her teasing, arousing monologue increased the pressure in his groin to near pain. "Damn, but you're feisty."

She flashed him a sassy grin. "Shut up and kiss me, cowboy."

Not one to refuse such a tempting offer, he gave her exactly what she demanded—a hot, deep French kiss that quickly had them both wild for so much more. He lifted his mouth from hers long enough to pick up his duffel, then he swung her into his arms, swallowing her squeal of alarm as his lips closed over hers once again for another tongue-tangling kiss. Maneuvering her through the condo to the bedroom took effort, especially since she now had his face between her hands and was kissing him senseless. With every jangling step he took, her breathing deepened, and her urgency seemed to mount, matching the frenzied beat of his heart.

He found the bedroom minutes later, but not before taking a quick tour of her office, where Teddy breathlessly informed him they were in the wrong room—unless he wanted to use her desk. Tempted, but determined to make love to her properly this first time, he continued, stopping briefly in the hallway to readjust his hold on the woman in his arms while she placed damp, openmouthed kisses on his neck that made him weak in the knees. He bumped his hip against the dresser, muttered an oath that made her giggle, and blindly searched for her bed in the dark. Finally, his knees connected with something soft and wide, and he unceremoniously dropped her onto the mattress. She yelped in surprise, and he heard the springs creak as she bounced.

Setting the duffel close by, he switched on the lamp on the nightstand, illuminating the room, and Teddy, in a soft glow of light. She was sprawled on top of the floral comforter covering the bed, her blond hair a cloud of silk around her head, her eyes alight with awareness, and that scrap of nothing nightie up around her hips. He was certain the diaphanous panties barely covering her mound were designed to drive a man to primitive measures. He was nearly there.

Tipping the Stetson back on his head, he eyed those long, slender limbs of hers with unabashed male appreciation. "I think this is the part where I ravish you," he said wickedly.

A pretty shade of pink flushed her skin, and she tilted her head speculatively as her gaze once again took in his attire. "Why are you dressed up like this?" she asked, her voice as soft as the moonlight filtering in through the bedroom window.

"This last fantasy is for you, Teddy," he said, and knew by the slight catch to her breathing that she understood the significance of this final performance as *her* cowboy.

She stared at him in anticipation as he lifted a small recorder from his bag, put it on the nightstand, and hit play. Seconds later, the same upbeat, rockabilly tune he'd danced to for her birthday filled the silence of the night, the pulsing sound as provocative as the look darkening her eyes.

Spotting the Stetson he'd given her that same night, he retrieved it from the dresser, and settled it on her head, grinning at the luscious picture she made. "Merry Christmas, honey."

He straightened, intending to get the show on the road and give this woman a fantasy she'd never forget—and an incredible night that would hopefully change the course of their relationship. Rocking and rolling his hips to the rhythm of the country beat, he reached for the top snap on his western shirt to rip it open.

"Wait!" she blurted, holding up a hand to stop him.

He immediately ceased all movement, paralyzed with the unsettling possibility that she might be having second thoughts about them, about this.

Sitting up on her knees in front of him, she chewed on her lower lip uncertainly. "Would you be terribly disappointed if I undressed you, instead of you stripping for me?" Her voice quivered with an endearing hesitancy, then her chin lifted with that sassiness he was coming to adore. "I mean, after all, this is *my* fantasy."

He chuckled, unable to help himself. God, he loved how sexy and bold she was, and knew life with her would always be invigorating. "There's nothing that would please me more," he told her, a small part of his mind wondering how he'd be able to withstand such torment. "Where would you like to start?"

She crooked her finger at him. "Come a little closer."

The rowels on his boots chinked seductively as he did as she requested. Now it was her hips that swayed to the music, her hands that lifted to his chest. Gripping the material in her fists on either side of the pearl buttons, she ripped open his shirt.

A groan of pure pleasure rumbled in her throat as she smoothed her palms over the heat of his skin and explored to her heart's content, pushing him to the brink of madness. Following the light sprinkling of hair on his chest downward, she splayed a hand low on his taut belly and nudged him back a foot and stood.

With an intoxicating, feminine confidence that made him burn, she slid the tips of her fingers upward, flicking over his flattened nipples on her journey up to his shoulders, where she slowly dragged the shirt down his arms. And during this gradual striptease, when she had his hands tangled in cotton, she moved close and brushed her body against his to the beat of the music—her breasts, her belly, her thighs, all inflaming his senses.

His nostrils flared, and as soon as she tugged his shirt off and tossed it somewhere behind him, he caught her around the waist with one arm, slid a thigh between hers, and brought her flush to his hard length, trapping her arms between them.

She wasn't intimidated by his domination, or the fierce arousal pressing against her belly. "Hold your horses, cowboy," she whispered against his mouth, her gaze hot and eager for what was to come—albeit in her own sweet time. "This is my fantasy, and I'm not done yet."

Austin groaned, certain he'd never be able to hold out.

With her arms locked between them, her hand found the bulge tightening the front of his jeans. Shamelessly, she cupped the fullness in her palm, stroked him to the beat of the music as her own hips gyrated provocatively against his. Austin gritted his teeth as a shudder ripped through him. Heeding that fierce warning, he let her go the same moment her fingers hooked around the sides of his chaps and she gave a hard yank. Velcro tore apart, and with a triumphant grin, she flung the soft leather aside.

And from there, with each article of clothing she playfully removed from his body and tossed haphazardly in the room, from his cowboy boots with those spurs he'd worn just for her, to his jeans and briefs and then finally his Stetson, she totally captivated Austin, bringing warmth and laughter to a place deep within him that had been cold and lonely for too long. She was wicked, amusing, damn sexy, and everything he wanted in a woman.

Teddy stared breathlessly at the gorgeous, naked man standing in the middle of her bedroom—*her fantasy.* Austin was, in a word, *magnificent.* He was solidly aroused, all aggressive male, and she thrilled at the notion that she'd brought him to this.

Not quite ready to relinquish the heady rush of feminine power coursing through her veins, she circled him, languidly caressing the firm slope of his back, his tight buttocks, and planting teasing, biting kisses along his throat and chest. Closing her eyes, she slid lower, until the very male essence of him brushed her lips—and heard a rough, strangled sound catch in his throat that was half pain, half pleasure.

Reckless excitement curled through her, settling in the pit of her belly, spreading outward. Eager to taste him in a way she'd never experienced before, she closed her mouth intimately over him, indulging in the smooth, velvety texture of his skin, the virile heat of him sliding along her tongue...

His entire body instinctively bucked toward her, and he sucked in a swift, shocked breath. His hands lifted, knocking the Stetson on her head to the floor. His long fingers tangled in her hair, at first guiding her untutored, but very erotic offering, then in a frantic attempt to pull her away.

Swearing viciously, he dragged her back up again. She caught a quick glimpse of the hot need glowing in the depths of his gaze before he fluidly, effortlessly, turned her, banded his strong arms around her waist, and tucked her backside against the front of his body.

She gasped, her heart slamming against her ribs. It was like being surrounded by fire...so much heat, raw and intense. Flames licked along her back, her thighs, and that out-of-control wildfire even found its way to the tips of her breasts, and her belly, where he'd splayed one of his hands to keep her bottom nestled close to his groin. The dresser mirror in front of them gave her a perfect view of their intimate position, enabling her to see the flush on her skin, the exhilaration in her eyes. The alluring sight aroused her, made her pulse flutter anxiously for what was to come.

He buried his face against the side of her neck, and she

shivered as his harsh breathing branded her skin. Gradually, his mouth charted a warm, damp path to her ear. "I feel at a distinct disadvantage here, darlin'," he drawled in a low voice that rumbled along her nerve endings. "I'm buck naked, and you've got way too many clothes on."

She wanted to laugh at his attempt at levity, but all she could think of was his hands sliding on her skin, his body easing into hers, and the wild ride he'd give her. "Then take them off," she dared impudently.

A warm chuckle reverberated against her neck. "Yes, ma'am." Sliding his hands beneath the hem of her gown, he slowly drew the soft material up and over her head, and tossed it somewhere in the room, leaving her clad in just her panties. She felt no embarrassment, only an acute desire for him to touch her as intimately as she'd touched him.

Somehow, he knew. As his gaze met hers in the mirror, he lifted his hands and cupped her swollen breasts in his palms, rasped his thumbs across her nipples until they were stiff and aching. Biting back a soft moan, she pressed her hands to the sides of his thighs, rolled her head back onto his shoulder, and arched her body more fully into his hands. He nuzzled her neck, stroked his fingers down her trembling belly and teased her through the damp, silky material of her panties until a whimper escaped her and her knees threatened to buckle.

Turning in his arms, she sought his mouth with hers, and he didn't hesitate to give her the kind of kiss she craved. No more teasing. No more gentle humor. Just intense passion and sizzling desire. She wanted it all, and she wanted it with him.

While his mouth consumed hers, and his tongue delved deep, he moved with her toward the bed. The back of her knees hit the edge, and he urged her down upon the mattress, pushing aside the Stetson that had landed there earlier so she could lie down, though he didn't join her. Instead, he dragged her panties over her slim hips and down her long limbs. Then he leisurely kissed his way up first one leg, then the other, stopping to explore every erogenous zone with his lips and tongue and the soft strum of his fingers.

The seductive journey took him all the way up to her quivering thighs, where he nipped the sensitive flesh with his teeth, then soothed the bites with long, slow laps of his tongue. He moved on to her belly, swirled his tongue in her navel, then closed his mouth over her breast and suckled the tender flesh until her entire body throbbed for that mystical release...

"Austin, please," she begged.

He lifted his head, a wholly wicked grin slashing across his features. "But I'm not done ravishing you, darlin'. Any cowboy worth his chaps isn't gonna leave his lady so worked up."

Just when she thought she couldn't stand any more of the dizzying sensations, he slipped down on the bed, used his palms to nudge her thighs apart, and claimed her in the most intimate kind of caress of all. His fingers filled her, sliding deeply. The heat of his mouth engulfed her. And the silky, rhythmic glide of his tongue sent her soaring straight into the realms of bliss.

Her release was swift and powerful, her cries lusty and unabashed. Her fingers twisted in the covers in an attempt to keep her grounded, but she flew apart anyway, reveling in the luxurious climax that seemed to go on and on. And when she finally tumbled back to earth, panting for breath, her body limp, she opened her eyes to find Austin standing by the side of the bed, sheathing himself in a condom.

"Wow," she whispered, awed by her body's ability to melt and surrender at Austin's whim—first in his car earlier, and now. "Twice in one night. Incredible."

Finished with the necessary protection, he knelt between her spread knees, then moved over her, settling himself be-

tween her still-quivering thighs. Bracing his forearms on either side of her head so they were face-to-face, he allowed a
devilish grin to claim his lips. "Darlin', we're going for a
third."

Her pulse quickened, and leaped again when his thick sex
slid against her damp cleft, the velvety tip of his erection
finding the entrance to her body. She was primed and ready,
but he didn't penetrate more than a teasing inch. "I
couldn't..."

"Oh, yeah, you can." His fingers wove through her hair,
cradling her head in his big hands as he eased his chest
against her breasts, crushing her with the delicious weight
and heat of his body. His dark green eyes glittered with hunger, and powerful emotion that seemed to touch her soul.
"And this time, I want to hear my name on your lips when
you come..."

And with that demand, he filled her with one smooth,
hard thrust. She gasped as her body stretched to accommodate him. He let out a low, animal groan as her sleek, inner
muscles clenched him tight. Instinctively, she wrapped her
legs around his hips and arched into him. He growled in response to her seductive move and surged against her, sliding
deeper still.

She saw his restraint in the tight clenching of his jaw, felt it
in the taut line of his body. Sliding her hands down his muscled back and over his firm buttocks, she urged him to take
what he wanted and give in to those primal desires. "This
ride is all yours, cowboy," she murmured in a husky whisper.

He shook his head, humor dancing in those smoky eyes of
his. "Ladies first," he said, male arrogance tinging his deep
voice. "I insist."

She laughed lightly, but the playful sound ebbed into a
moan when he bent his head and captured her lips with his,
kissing her in the same erotic manner he made love to her.

He had a point to prove, and set out to demonstrate the wonders of a female body, and just how well he knew hers.

He continued to kiss her, ruthlessly maintaining a steady rhythm designed to push her closer to that sublime ecstasy. Her heart raced, and incredibly, with each slow, measured stroke, each primal lunge, she felt the gradual building of yet another climax. Intense pleasure coiled inside her, urging her to move with him, toward the promise of something lush and wild and spectacular.

She was close...so, so close.

He lifted his head, sliding his mouth from hers to watch her expression. His gaze locked with hers, demanding and fiery. There was no way she could hide anything from him, he wouldn't allow it. He coaxed not only her physical surrender, but an emotional one, too...and she found the feelings swirling within her thrilling, arousing and terrifying, because she'd never given a man what Austin silently asked for...her complete acquiescence, heart, body and soul.

"Let it go, baby," he rasped, as if he understood her fears. "I'll catch you when you fall."

Helpless to deny him, she closed her mind to everything, ceasing to exist past the feel of him moving in her, over her...and then it happened, a blinding rush of sensation that stole her breath and spilled through her like liquid fire.

The orgasm was so intense, she grasped his shoulders for fear of flying apart. And just as she reached the peak and her body convulsed with the exquisite, sensual gratification, she gave him what he'd ultimately wanted.

"*Austin...*" she moaned huskily, raggedly.

A satisfied light glimmered in his eyes. "Yeah, just like that..."

In a series of hard, swift strokes he thrust into her, and as she watched him toss back his head and give himself over to his own violent climax, she realized she'd gone and done something utterly foolish.... Something that would only lead to a wealth of heartache for her, false expectations from her parents, and a string of disappointments for the man who'd possessed her body so thoroughly.

She'd fallen hard and deep for Austin McBride.

STANDING BY the side of the bed, Austin stared down at the woman sprawled on her stomach amidst the tangle of sheets and blankets, unable to help the lazy smile tipping his mouth, or the warm inner glow chasing away the chill still clinging to his skin from his predawn quest through the misty, rainy morning to find Teddy a special Christmas surprise. No easy feat, considering every tree lot he'd driven to had sold out the night before.

Finally, his persistence had paid off. He'd found a lone, solitary tree in an abandoned lot, a scrawny five-foot Douglas fir with a broken limb and a crooked trunk that wobbled haphazardly on the wooden base it had been nailed to. Knowing how effortlessly Teddy could transform such imperfection, he'd claimed the tree. While he was trying to secure the five-foot shrub to the top of the Mustang, it had started to rain, a cold drizzle that gradually soaked through his shirt and jeans.

The slight discomfort would be worth seeing Teddy's face light up with joy when she saw her surprise. Her very own Christmas tree, to decorate as she pleased, and to share with him. This year, she wouldn't be alone on Christmas morning. This year, he'd give her every reason to celebrate.

He had nothing to wrap and put beneath the tree for her. The thought had crossed his mind on the drive back to her place, but he'd decided that he wanted to give Teddy something more personal than a tangible gift, something precious and priceless, something all the money in the world couldn't buy. Something she was in dire need of, even if she didn't realize it yet.

His love.

Yeah, he loved her. The emotion had snuck up on him when he'd least expected it, stealing into his heart and making him realize he needed this feisty, stubborn, too-independent woman in his life. He wanted a wife to come home to at night and share his life with, and he wanted children to bring love and laughter to a home that hadn't experienced much merriment since his parents had died. He imagined all those things, and more...and in every mental picture that projected in his mind, Teddy played a central part in his future.

His feelings for her were crazy, nothing he'd ever prepared himself for, yet there was no denying what he felt for her exceeded anything he'd ever experienced. And despite their different backgrounds and her parents' uncertainties about him, the only person's opinion that mattered to him was Teddy's.

He knew that needing someone didn't come easily to Teddy, but he harbored enough confidence to believe her feelings for him were just as strong as his were for her, which, at the very least, gave them a solid foundation to build on. He'd seen the emotion in her eyes when he'd made love to her last night, the uninhibited way she'd responded to him told a tale of its own. But he'd also sensed her uncertainty after that first joining, felt the barest hint of reservation. And he wasn't going to give her time to come up with any regrets.

Luckily for him, she was easily distracted. He'd kept her mouth and hands and mind as busy as his own. He'd fanned the flames of desire all over again, taking her in possessive, erotic ways that had at first shocked Teddy, then incited her to new, feverish heights. They'd made good use of the box of condoms he'd brought, and in the dark hours of the night he hoped he'd managed to strip away a few layers of that frustrating reserve.

She let out a soft, slumberous sigh and shifted on the mattress, stretching out more fully on her belly and sprawling those gorgeous legs of hers across most of the bed. He couldn't help but grin. If he'd still been lying beside her, she would have kicked him right off the edge. The woman was a bed-hog.

The covers wrapped loosely around her slender hips and tangled around her shapely legs, leaving the smooth slope of her back bare to his gaze, and hinting at the soft, warm nakedness beneath the sheet. Her arms were folded around a pillow, her face buried in the softness, and the slight curve to her body afforded him a glimpse of one full, pale breast.

Not so surprisingly, sexual heat surged through his body, settling into an insistent throb in his groin. Amazingly, he grew full and heavy beneath his cold, wet briefs and the denim molding to his hips and thighs. Welcoming the rush of warmth and anticipating the greater heat of Teddy's body, he stripped his damp T-shirt over his head and dropped it to the floor. He toed off his shoes, tugged off his soaked socks, and struggled to push the wet denim over his hips and down his legs. Completely naked, and fully aroused, he slipped beneath the covers and moved toward Teddy.

The moment his chilled flesh touched hers she gasped and came awake, her head lifting from the pillow. She looked disoriented, her tousled hair falling over her face, her eyes hazy. Before she could turn around or scramble away, he aligned his body over hers from behind, pressed her back down on the mattress, and pulled the blankets up around them.

"Austin?" she said, her voice husky and a little bewildered.

He dragged his open mouth along her jaw, nuzzled the warm, fragrant hollow of neck, tasting her skin with his lips and the touch of his tongue. "'Morning," he murmured, his rumbly voice low and intimate in the shadowed gray before dawn. The soft, rhythmic pitter-patter of rain against the window added to the lazy, sensual morning.

She released a drowsy, complacent "Mmm" as he caressed along the indentation of her waist with his hands, then shivered when he slipped his palms along her ribs and finally tucked his chilled hands between her breasts and the mattress to warm them.

She sucked in a swift breath as her nipples beaded against his icy palms. "You're freezing," she complained as another shudder ran though her, though she made no move to push him off her.

Nudging her thighs apart, he settled between that warm, welcoming harbor. "I won't be for long," he whispered, gently rubbing his stubbled cheek along her smooth shoulder. His damp hair brushed her skin, and he felt her shiver again.

"And you're wet," she said, her voice filled with confusion.

"I think that's my line." He rolled his hips forward, gliding his hot, male flesh along her slick, feminine cleft, proving his point.

She laughed huskily, and wriggled her bottom beneath him, impatiently seeking the deeper contact he planned to give her in his own sweet time. She drew a deep breath, and released it slowly. "You smell like rain, and pine."

"Imagine that." Smiling at the puzzled note to her voice, he eased a hand away from her breast, slid his flattened palm down her belly, and threaded his way through silky, damp curls to a greater fire, a more desperate need. Sultry desire drenched his fingertips the moment he touched her.

She whimpered beneath him, and he groaned, the heaviness and hunger inside him intensifying. "Ah, you feel so damn good, Teddy," he breathed. Sinking deeper into her lush heat, he plied that tiny nub of flesh, giving her nothing but pleasure. Her breathing quickened, and he had the fleeting thought that he might be crushing her with his weight. "Am I too heavy for you?" he murmured against her ear.

"Nnnnooo," she moaned, her legs parting wider for his touch, while her fingers gripped the pillow. She turned her head to glance back at him, but got caught up in the tremors shimmering through her body. He watched her eyes roll back in ecstasy, her lips part, and a long, keening cry rip from her throat as she gave herself over to the erotic sensations.

Satisfaction swelled in his chest, and he continued to stroke her, slowly, exquisitely, reverently, until the last bit of rapture ebbed—reveling in the fact that this time, she didn't even try to temper the emotional climax.

Her unconditional response turned him on, humbled him, even. Wanting to give the same in return, he dragged his palms from beneath her, found her hands, and laced their fingers together at the side of her head. "Lift your hips for me, Teddy," he rasped near her ear, desperate to be inside her.

She accommodated his request without hesitation, and he slid into her with a sleek, heavy glide, surrounding her with flesh that was no longer chilled, but now burned with the wild need to possess her in the most elemental way possible.

Mutual groans coalesced, and his hips began pumping harder, faster. Her fingers tightened around his, and she whispered his name, over and over, a sweet, drugging litany that dragged him deeper into the flames.

The sensations crashing over him stole his breath. The powerful emotions he felt for this woman touched his heart, overwhelming him, sending him careening straight over the edge of control. Burying deep, he arched against her and rode with the most excruciating pleasure he'd ever known.

11

SIGHING CONTENTEDLY, Teddy draped her leg over Austin's and rested her head in the crook of his shoulder, unable to think of a nicer way to wake up in the morning—making love to an exceptionally sexual, virile man who was as generous with her pleasure as he was greedy about taking his own satisfaction. The delicious, satiated glow spreading through her was something she could get to.

Sex had never been a necessity for her, certainly not something she'd given much importance to in her pursuit to establish her career, but she quickly realized it was a matter of making love to the right man. She couldn't get enough of Austin, the excitement of his kisses, the thrill of his touch, and even the sexy way he looked at her that could make her smolder and burn until he extinguished those internal flames of desire.

Their sexual compatibility and sizzling attraction was a win-win situation, and though her startling realization last night had scared her on an emotional level, she'd put her feelings for Austin into perspective during the night and decided to handle the situation like any other independent woman would. She'd have an affair with Austin. A simple, undemanding relationship that wouldn't interfere with the goals she'd worked so hard to achieve, or threaten the unrestricted life-style she'd finally established for herself. A no-strings tryst that wouldn't give Austin any false illusions about a forever kind of future together. No promises. No long-term commitment.

Satisfied with her plan, she lifted her head to look at Austin, furrowing her fingers in the soft, curly hair on his chest. His eyes were closed, and he looked exhausted, completely wiped out. And totally gorgeous with dark morning stubble lining his lean jaw. She thought about that roughness against her neck and shoulders during their last erotic interlude, and her skin tingled with renewed awareness. Slowly, she skimmed her palm down to his belly, slipped her hand beneath the sheet draped over his hips, and curled her warm fingers over his semierect shaft.

He groaned, and grabbing her wrist, he pulled her hand back up so it rested over the steady beating of his heart. "Have mercy, woman. I need a little time to recuperate," he muttered, eyes still closed.

She laughed softly, and took pity on his poor, abused body. "Okay, I'll give you ten minutes, and if you're still being uncooperative, I'll just have to climb on top and straddle you while you're sleeping."

The corner of his mouth twitched. "You're a shameless hussy."

"It's all your fault," she said, reaching up to run her fingers through Austin's still-damp hair, which brought to mind how cold and wet he'd been when he'd slipped into bed with her just a little while ago. "So tell me, why were you all wet?"

"As you can see, it's raining outside," he said, his voice a deep, rumbling murmur.

She glanced toward the window, watching rivulets of water run down the pane. The soft sound of rain outside soothed her. "Hmm, so it is." But that didn't really answer her question, so she rephrased it. "What were you doing out *in* the rain?"

The eye closest to her opened halfway, enough for her to glimpse feigned exasperation. "You're not going to let me sleep, are you?"

"Nope." Smiling at his poor attempt to appear annoyed, she stacked her hands on his chest and rested her chin on top. "What were you doing out in the rain?" she repeated.

Both eyes opened, brilliant green and full of mischief now. "Getting your Christmas present."

Her heart flip-flopped in her chest at that surprising announcement. It *was* Christmas morning, and the last thing she expected was a gift from Austin, especially when she hadn't gotten him anything in return. "You didn't have to do that."

"I wanted to." He brushed a strand of hair off her cheek, his touch infinitely tender, the look in his eyes just as adoring.

The swell of emotion she experienced for this man at that moment terrified her, and she quickly suppressed it. "What store would be open on Christmas, at six in the morning?"

He lifted a dark eyebrow. "Well, Ms. Skeptical, why don't we just go find out?"

Like a giddy kid on Christmas morning, Teddy sprang from the bed and grabbed the long, cotton robe hanging on the hook behind the bathroom door. Slipping into it, she came back to the bedroom and found Austin sitting on the side of the bed, still naked, and frowning at the garments on the floor.

He glanced up at her. "My clothes are all wet, except for my costume, and I'm afraid those chaps might be a little drafty."

She laughed, though the thought of all that gorgeous masculinity framed in nothing but leather chaps made her pulse quicken. "But oh so sexy," she said breathlessly.

"I'd be happy to oblige that fantasy later, darlin'," he drawled huskily. "But right now, I'd prefer to keep the important parts warm."

She tightened the sash on her robe, and extended an offer

before she lost the nerve. "Maybe you ought to leave a few extra changes of clothes here."

His gaze held hers for an immeasurable moment, dark and searching. "Maybe," he said, his tone completely noncommittal.

Not wanting to delve any deeper into that subject at the moment, she rummaged through her dresser drawers, withdrawing a pair of light pink drawstring sweat shorts she wore around the house. Turning, she held them out to Austin. "This should work, for now. I know they look small, but they stretch, and they're comfortable."

His expression turned doubtful, but without any other options available, he went ahead and stepped into the snug shorts. Sure enough, the fabric stretched to accommodate his muscular form. The soft pink cotton molded to everything male about him, from his lean hips and tight buttocks, to the masculine bulge between his hard thighs.

"Wow, the color pink really suits you," she teased.

He propped his hands on his hips and glared. "I'm sure your parents would be thrilled to find out I wear women's clothing."

She smothered a giggle. "My lips are sealed." Grabbing his hand, she tugged him toward the bedroom door. "So, where's this surprise?"

"In the living room."

She headed in that direction, but before they reached the end of the short hallway, he stopped her, turning her to face him. Uncertainty flickered in the depth of his eyes, touching a chord deep within her.

"It's really not much, but it's something I hope might become a tradition."

His words puzzled her, but she didn't have much time to ponder them. He asked her to close her eyes, and once she did, he rested his hands lightly on her shoulders and guided her into the living room. The scent of pine added to her bewilderment.

"Merry Christmas, sweetheart," he said from behind her, his words warm and heartfelt.

Teddy opened her eyes, and gasped at the sight of the Christmas tree sitting in the corner of the room, crooked and fractured in places, but its spirit not broken. The tree was nothing grand, a misfit among Douglas firs, but the sentiment behind Austin's gesture transcended grandeur. The lengths he'd gone through to offer her this special gift exceeded anything anyone had ever done for her.

"It's all yours, to decorate as you please," he said, pressing a soft kiss against her hair. "And you're not alone this year. You can share it with me."

Realizing he must have overheard the conversation she'd had with Jordan about her childhood, her throat tightened and tears burned the back of her eyes.

It's really not much, but it's something I hope might become a tradition.

Now his words made sense, the meaning behind his remark teeming with assumptions...and complications. "Tradition" implied something lasting, tied up with commitment, and the future. A custom passed on from year, to year, and shared with loved ones.

Oh, Lord. While she wanted to maintain a casual relationship with Austin, he'd sailed headlong into forbidden territory, making subtle insinuations she wasn't near ready to face.

Feeling suffocated, and unable to think straight, she pasted on a smile, and turned to face him. "This is great," she said way too brightly. "Let's decorate it. I'll make some popcorn and we can string it and put it on the tree."

She started toward the kitchen, but he caught her arm, stopping her. His gaze flickered over her face, and she desperately tried not to let her fear show.

"This isn't everything, Teddy." His tone was so gentle, she wanted to weep.

"It's certainly enough," she said, the double meaning escaping on choked laughter.

He hesitated, his own expression momentarily uncertain. Then his gaze cleared, and his fingers slid from her upper arm down to her hand, which he held loosely in his palm. "I love you, Teddy."

Her stomach sank, and she visibly flinched at the words, so sweet, so powerful...so smothering. She shook her head in denial. "No, please, don't."

"Don't love you?" he asked, surprise etching his features. "It's too late, because I'm already too far gone. Don't say the words? I have to, because I want you to know how serious I am about you. About us."

She pulled her hand from his. "This is too much, too fast..."

The beginnings of a frown appeared on his face, exposing a niggling of concern. "I know you told me that you don't have time for a relationship right now, but I'd think after the past week, hell, after last night, you'd make time. What we have together is more than just an itch we both need to scratch."

Her face flushed, yet she couldn't shake the feeling of being smothered. Of becoming just as accommodating as her sisters-in-law, and her mother. "Why can't we just have an affair, and enjoy our time together for as long as it lasts?"

He jammed his hands on his hips, his eyes darkening to a fierce shade of green. "So, you want to use me for sex?"

His harsh voice sent a trickle of uneasiness skidding down her spine. She'd obviously provoked him, but admitting the truth was far better than leading him astray with false promises. "I enjoy being with you, Austin, but I've got a job to think about, and a committed relationship would demand more time than I have to give right now." Her words sounded selfish to her own ears but, dammit, she cherished her independence, the freedom to come and go as she pleased, without answering to anyone.

Her mental assurance lacked a certain conviction she refused to analyze.

Irritation tightened his jaw. "I've got my own business to run, and I'm not demanding anything more from you than you're willing to give. I was hoping we could meet somewhere in the middle."

She rubbed her forehead wearily, knowing from experience that it rarely worked out so compatibly. Relationships turned demanding in time, and eventually destructive. She shook her head, feeling torn and confused, but ultimately holding on to the belief that balancing a career and relationship wasn't for her. "I...can't," she whispered achingly.

"Why not?" he persisted.

His direct question stirred up many answers, and a whole lot of resentments she'd kept tucked away for so many years. Turning away, she moved deeper into the living room, away from the vibrant heat of Austin's body, and attempted to explain her reasons the best she could. "It's taken me years to finally become my own person, to finally break free of my family's influence. Ever since I was a little girl, my parents have had certain expectations of me. As a teenager, I was groomed to be a 'lady,' went to every country-club dance there was and dated 'respectable' boys. And when I graduated from high school, my mother set me up with an endless string of potential husband prospects. Every guy I went out with came from an affluent family, and usually after the second or third date my mother was hinting at a wedding. That's when I broke things off with the guy I was dating, before my mother had the chance to throw an engagement party."

Standing by the Christmas tree, she reached out and tentatively touched one of the limbs, trying not to let the sentiment behind Austin's gift get the best of her. She'd never known a man so sweet, so selfless, yet her misgivings wouldn't allow her to accept what he so generously offered.

Swallowing the huge knot forming in her throat, she continued. "All I wanted was to go to college and pursue a career in graphic design, which I loved. All I got from my parents was nothing but grief, because I was too focused on a career when there was no need for me to work. They disapproved of my choices, and ever since the age of eighteen, I've been nothing but a disappointment to them." She glanced over her shoulder at Austin, meeting his gaze and praying he wouldn't hate her too badly once this was over. "You saw what I went through last night."

Something in his eyes softened, and he stepped toward her. "Teddy—"

She held up a hand to ward him off, wanting him to know everything. One touch from him, and she'd lose all train of thought. "Then there was Bartholomew Winston, who was, of course, handpicked by my father and came with my mother's full approval. He was a banker like his father and grandfather before him, came from old money, and was wealthy enough to impress my parents. After a few months of dating Bart, I finally gave in to the pressure. I had a ring on my finger, a wedding date set, and china patterns all picked out."

"Did you love him?" Austin asked, that question seemingly important to him.

"No, I didn't love him," she admitted, a sad smile touching her mouth. "I cared for him, and I thought that was enough, because he was the first guy who understood and accepted my goals." She'd learn later that his approval was all an illusion, a way to temporarily appease her. "For the first time in longer than I could remember, my mother and I had a decent relationship. She was in her glory making wedding plans, and I tried to convince myself that I could be happy." She couldn't contain the self-deprecating laugh that bubbled out of her. "About three months before the wedding, my parents sat Bart and I down and told me that now that I was getting married to a very prominent man, I should give up this foolishness of having a career. Certainly I couldn't be a proper wife if I was busy working outside the mansion," she added sarcastically.

He stood there, too far away, arms crossed over his wide chest, watching her with unfathomable eyes, listening, waiting. He appeared so patient, so understanding, yet there was something in his stance that promised something a bit more charged.

She drew a deep breath, and tightened the sash on her robe, not to keep the lapels together, but in an attempt to keep herself from falling apart. "Bart agreed with my parents, when I thought all along he understood how important being a graphic designer was to me. But he changed his tune, insisting that he wouldn't have a wife who worked when there was no need for her to do so. And so I insisted that he take his ring back and find a more submissive female who wanted to be his keeper."

Dragging a hand through her disheveled hair, she inwardly winced as she remembered the fiasco that erupted in her father's study after her very indelicate declaration. "My parents totally freaked out, but I'd never felt so liberated as I did in that moment. And from then on, I vowed that I'd depend on no one but myself. I moved out of the house, much to my parents' dismay, and I've been supporting myself ever since. I've totally disgraced them, but the move bolstered my confidence." She watched Austin slowly move closer, and her chin rose in a stubborn show of bravado. Unfortunately, her insecurities couldn't be so easily masked. "I like my independence. I've struggled for it. I've earned it, and I don't want to give it up."

Very gently, he used his thumb and forefinger and lowered her chin back down, as if silently telling her she had no reason to be defensive with him. "Who said anything about giving it up?" Before she could issue a response, he continued. "What makes you think you can't have a relationship *and* a career? What makes you think I'd ever try and stifle you like your parents have tried to do?"

His barrage of questions made her head spin. His nearness made her long to put her arms around his neck, cling to his strength, and forget about every one of her doubts. "Because that's what ultimately happens! I've been through it personally, and I've seen my brothers do it to each of their wives—"

He scoffed, a harsh sound that cut through her protests. "Oh, you'd be surprised, Teddy. If I learned anything last night, it's that your sisters-in-law are hardly the submissive types. They let your brothers think they have the upper hand and put on a good show for your mother and father, but every one of them is an independent, self-sufficient woman who seems to have found an equal balance with her husband."

His insightful view astounded her, and left her speechless.

He took advantage of her wide-eyed stare. "You have nothing to prove to me, Teddy," he said. "Nothing at all. I love you just the way you are, stubborn, independent and determined to grasp that promotion you want so badly. And I'd never do anything to change the person you are, or interfere with what's important to you."

She heard his words, and really wanted to believe them, but couldn't stem the rise of panic that flooded her...a deep-rooted fear that his understanding would wane in time.

She thought into the future, to where a committed relationship with Austin would lead, and her doubts were confirmed. "But you want a wife, and babies."

"Yeah, I do," he admitted. "Eventually."

"I don't want that," she said, issuing the denial out of self-preservation.

"Don't you?" His deep voice was calm and soothing, but his eyes pierced her with a perception that shook her to the depths of her soul.

She paced away from him, the intensity of her feelings for Austin deluging her with more unsettling thoughts. Her deep longing for him seemed to eclipse her lifelong need for independence and made her wonder what her life would be like if she eventually married Austin and gave him the babies he wanted.

And that's where everything became a jumbled, conflicting mess in her mind. She'd been taught that women were supposed to be complacent, dutiful wives, and when babies came along, women stayed at home, falling into a maternal role that didn't include the career Teddy had spent years working toward.

Dread balled in her stomach, overriding sense or reason. "No, I don't want that," she forced herself to say, and tried her best to believe those words. Sinking into the cushions of the couch, she beseeched Austin with her gaze. "All this has taken me by surprise. I wasn't expecting to fall for you. And I don't think I can be what you ultimately need in your life." The statement came out as a tight, aching whisper.

His mouth stretched into a grim line. "You're not even willing to try."

"I'm willing to give you what I can." She hated the uncertain quiver in her voice. Hated even more the fear that ruled her emotions.

"A no-strings affair," he said, his tone flat.

Right now, it was all she could offer him. "Yes."

"No way. It's not enough." His expression turned angry. "I've been used like that before, and I won't be anyone's part-time plaything again."

Hearing the heated condemnation in his voice, and suspecting he, too, had been played for a fool in the past, she regarded him cautiously. "What are you talking about?"

"The last relationship I was in, if you could even call it that, was with a woman who was out for a good time, and I was it. Her name was Diane, and she was a Fantasy for Hire customer. Just like you, she was looking for a personal fantasy."

Teddy's heart sank as she realized the correlation between her own behavior and this other woman's. Beyond Austin's anger, she also heard the hurt in his deep voice, and realized that this other woman had trampled on his emotions and had given him a few insecurities of his own.

"She used me, Teddy, and when the affair came down to something more serious for me, she blew me off." Tension bunched the muscles across his chest and in his arms as he stood on the other side of the coffee table. "Bottom line, I wasn't good enough for her, and the life she led. Not on a permanent basis anyway."

She winced at the lash of his words, and the bitterness seeping into his tone. "I'm sorry," she said, her voice tight and aching.

"Yeah, me too." His cold gaze held hers relentlessly. "So no, I don't do convenient affairs, Teddy. I need some kind of commitment when I'm serious about a woman. No matter how old-fashioned it may seem, when I fall in love, I'm an all-or-nothing kind of guy. And I expect the same from the woman I'm involved with."

Her throat closed up, making speech impossible. His rare declaration of fidelity and devotion was what women dreamed of, and Teddy's heart swelled with so many regrets, so many fears...and the overwhelming need to believe him, and accept his precious offering. The upheaval of emotions swamped her, pulling her in two different directions.

Letting out a low sigh of defeat, he headed for the hallway that led to her bedroom—to gather up his things, she suspected—then stopped before disappearing. "And just for the record, Teddy, I've never told another woman that I was in love with her. You're the first, and I didn't make the declaration lightly."

She closed her eyes, listening to the rustling sounds drifting from down the hall, and tried to convince herself that it was best that things ended now, instead of when the relationship became more complicated. More demanding.

Her heart twisted unmercifully, rejecting the convenient excuse she desperately tried to cling to. Emotionally, she was already over her head—and the realization was alarming.

He returned to the living room minutes later, changed into his damp clothes, duffel bag in hand. "You're still hanging on to the fantasy, Teddy," he said, his gaze uncompromising as it held hers. "I'm offering you the real thing, and I won't accept anything less from you, either."

And then he was gone. As the silence and solitude she'd always cherished surrounded her, hot tears scalded her eyes. Seconds ticked into minutes, which turned into hours as she sat on the couch and stared at the Christmas tree Austin had bought for her, to share with her. Yet she'd pushed him out of her life, so determined to preserve her independence...so afraid to trust him with her heart.

"ARE YOU SURE I can't convince you to join Brenda and me for a drink at the Frisco Bay?" Laura asked, her concerned voice attempting to cajole Teddy into accepting the invitation.

"I'm sure." Teddy appreciated her friend's attempt to cheer her up, but there were too many memories of Austin at the Frisco Bay, and she just wasn't up to making polite conversation when her heart ached like nothing she'd ever experienced before.

It had been a week and a half since Christmas morning, when Austin had walked out of her life. She hadn't heard from him, not that she'd expected to after the angry way they'd parted. She'd spent the holiday weekend by herself, alone and lonely and wallowing in misery. The tree in her living room had remained undecorated, yet she couldn't bring herself to remove it from the condo, either.

She'd refused the New Year's Eve parties Laura and Brenda had invited her to, feeling as though she had little to celebrate. Her parents had invited her and Austin over for New Year's Day brunch at the house, hoping to "get to know Austin better," since it seemed the two of them were serious about each other. Teddy declined that gracious offer with a convenient fib that she had other plans. She didn't have the heart to tell her mother that Austin was no longer a part of her life.

And after she'd hung up the phone, Teddy recognized the irony of her parents accepting Austin, even if it was on a tentative level, when she'd been the one to judge him so harshly.

Pushing that awful thought aside, she reached for a file on her desk and resumed her conversation with Laura. "I've got a proposal to finish up here at work," she said, pulling out the first draft copy of a resort brochure. "So I'll be here late tonight. You and Brenda go and have a good time."

"All right," Laura reluctantly agreed. "Hey, isn't tomorrow the day you find out if you get the senior graphic design promotion?"

Teddy found she couldn't even summon a small bout of enthusiasm over what once had been her sole ambition. "Yeah. There's a board meeting first thing in the morning. I should know by noon."

"Well, good luck, and keep me and Brenda posted."

Teddy managed a small smile, grateful for her friends' support. "Thanks, I will."

Hanging up the phone, she continued working on the brochure, making notes for narrative, and jotting down ideas for what she thought would make for an attractive, trifold advertisement. She welcomed the diversion—it kept thoughts of Austin at bay.

It was a little after 6:00 p.m., and outside her office she could hear other employees leaving for the evening. The building grew quiet, except for the occasional hum of the copier being used by an ambitious employee working late like herself, or the ring of the outer telephone that someone else picked up. Another hour, she decided, and she'd pack up her work and head home, though the thought of entering her condo made her dread the lonely, solitary night ahead. It no longer seemed to matter that she'd once cherished the privacy and freedom that came with being an unattached woman.

"Trying to make a last-minute impression on me?"

Louden's sly voice slithered down Teddy's spine, and she glanced up to find her boss standing in the doorway to her office. "No, I'm trying to do my job and meet my current deadline. I'm sure you've made up your mind by now who will get the promotion."

Very casually, he entered the room, closing the door behind him. Her heart gave a distinct thump in her chest, and uneasiness congealed in her belly.

His pale gaze flickered over her silk blouse, then rose to her eyes again as he moved closer to her desk. "I submit my final choice tomorrow morning, *before* the board meeting begins. It's still not too late for me to put you at the top of the list." His insinuation rang clear—as of this moment, she wasn't his top candidate for the position. "How about dinner tonight?"

Feeling very uncomfortable being alone with Louden in her office, she stood and reached for her briefcase, deciding it was time to pack up and leave. "I don't think so. Austin is expecting me home shortly."

"Cut the pretense, Teddy," he said in a light, mocking tone that was at odds with the ominous glint in his eyes.

Her pulse leaped in apprehension. Trying to keep calm, she gathered important files and stacked them in her brief-case. "I have no idea what you're talking about."

Bracing his hands on the desk across from her, he leaned in close. "He's a stripper," he said, his gaze sparkling with the trump card he'd just played.

A cold chill tingled along the surface of her skin, and her belly tightened with tension. She let none of her anxiety show. "Excuse me?" she asked, infusing her voice with a credible amount of bewilderment.

A slow, insidious smile curved his thin lips as he straight-ened. "Austin McBride is a stripper, a fantasy for hire, or in your case, an escort for hire who received a higher price than I'd ever demand for services rendered."

He knew too much, and she had no idea how Louden had discovered the truth about Austin. She watched him circle her desk, like a predatory animal closing in for the final vic-tory, and snapped the locks closed on her briefcase.

"Aren't you the least bit curious how I know about Aus-tin?" he asked. "Janet mentioned to me that she thought your boyfriend looked familiar at the Christmas party, and then it dawned on her where she'd seen him before...dressed as a cop, one who stripped for a living. Needless to say, I found that extremely interesting, and while you were at lunch today I found a business card and a receipt for a thou-sand dollars for 'services rendered' in your desk drawer."

White-hot fury filled her, and she turned to face Louden—who stood way too close for her comfort. "You went through my things?"

He shrugged, as if invading her privacy didn't violate a se-rious code of ethics.

Months of enduring Louden's tactics finally got the best of her. Fists clenching at her sides, she met his gaze challeng-ingly, and let her temper boil over. "You had no right!"

He merely smiled, looking pleased with himself. "It

proved what I already suspected. Austin is a fraud, so now that the truth is out in the open, there's no longer a reason for you to play coy and pretend that you're unavailable." He slid his fingers down her bare arm. "Now, about your promotion..."

She jerked away from him, gaping incredulously at his nerve. She was tired of battling this man for something she knew she deserved, and she refused to compromise her morals to get it.

And in that moment, she came to a startling realization. This promotion was important to her, yes, but not as much as it once had been. She'd thought she needed to prove to her family that she was self-sufficient, determined and confident, and had put too much emphasis on the senior graphic design position being the direct link to her happiness. Her priorities shifted, and the one topping the list was ultimately pleasing herself—and that meant standing up to this man who believed he wielded so much control over her.

"You know what, Louden? You can take the promotion and shove it," she said matter-of-factly, feeling more unencumbered than she had in years. "And I'm sure the board of directors will find it interesting tomorrow morning to find out exactly how you choose your candidates."

An incensed shade of red traveled up his neck and suffused his face. "It's your word against mine," he said, his tone low and dark with menace.

Grabbing her purse and briefcase, she met his gaze evenly, telling him without words that she wasn't intimidated by him. "I'm willing to take that chance. The last thing I knew, sexual harassment was against the law."

With that parting remark, she started around the opposite side of the desk, her eye on the closed door and her thoughts on quickly escaping this man's hostility. She'd only managed two steps when strong fingers manacled her wrist in a painful grip.

She glared back at Louden, refusing to cower. "Let me go."

A malicious sneer curved his lips. "If you're going to file a complaint, we might as well legitimize it."

And with that, he jerked her around and shoved her against the wall, hard enough that she smacked her head, causing her to lose her grasp on her briefcase and purse, and momentarily paralyzing her entire body. A picture crashed to the floor from the jarring impact, the sound of shattering glass sharp in Teddy's mind.

Stunned and dazed, and trying desperately to gulp air into her lungs, she felt his hands grope at her blouse, then viciously rip it open. Her lips parted to scream, but he clamped a hand over her mouth, nearly smothering her. Refusing to be a victim, she struggled against him as his other hand tugged at the hem of her skirt, then his hand touched her thigh. Swallowing the bile rising in her throat, she shoved against his shoulders, adrenaline lending her a strength she never knew she possessed.

"Oh my God!"

Teddy heard her co-worker's exclamation from somewhere in the office, and it was enough to alarm Louden. He didn't let her go, but instead looked over his shoulder at the intruder. Taking advantage of the distraction, Teddy brought her knee up against his groin, hard. Louden's hands fell away from her to grab himself, and he gaped at her in wide-eyed astonishment. His shock turned to outrage, and though he was in obvious pain, he growled low in his throat and made a last attempt to lunge at her. Her hand shot out to protect herself, and the base of her hand slammed into his nose.

She heard something crack, watched as Louden fell to his knees, clutching both his groin and now-bloody nose. An anguished moan ripped from his chest, and Teddy didn't spare another second to put some distance between them.

On shaking, trembling legs, Teddy managed to round her desk and reach Anna, one of the secretaries in the firm. The woman appeared as shocked as Teddy felt.

"Are you all right?" Anna asked just as two other employees entered her office, obviously having heard the commotion.

"I'm...fine," she assured them all, and with less than steady hands pulled the ends of her blouse back together over her chest. "Someone, call the police, please. I want this man arrested for sexual assault."

12

IT WAS A COLD, cloudy, overcast Saturday afternoon, and neither McBride brother was home, much to Teddy's disappointment. She hadn't called beforehand, afraid that Austin might refuse to see her, and she didn't want to discuss this private matter over the phone.

Sitting on the porch steps leading to the charming old Victorian house that Austin shared with his brother, she waited for over an hour for him to come home, knowing she'd sit there forever if that's how long it took to convince Austin that he was the single-most important thing in her life.

Him, and his love and belief in her.

Coming to that conclusion had been a soul-searching event, but her realization had put so many things into perspective for her. After Louden's attack, she'd spent a few days prioritizing her life, putting her own happiness first on that list, her love for Austin second, and her career third. She no longer felt the need to validate her self-worth to her family, or anyone else, by climbing the corporate ladder. No longer believed that sole independence was the means to ultimate happiness and emotional gratification. She'd put way too much stock in her ambitious goals, when the key to her contentment lay in her heart.

And Austin was in her heart and certainly a part of her soul. She hadn't expected to fall in love with him, never believed a man could make her feel so whole, so emotionally complete. She'd never imagined that the thought of living without him would make her heart ache so unbearably.

Sighing to chase away the nerves fluttering in her stomach, she closed her eyes and leaned back against the stair railing, silently praying that her revelation hadn't come too late.

Fifteen minutes later, his black Mustang turned the corner and drove up the street. Austin glanced out the driver's window, saw her sitting in front of the house, and parked his car in the driveway. Neither brother exited the vehicle, and she could see Austin talking to Jordan, or rather, arguing, if the irritable look on Austin's face was anything to go by.

Finally, Jordan got out of the Mustang, a wide, welcoming smile spreading across his handsome face. "Hi, Teddy," he said, waving her way as he headed toward the front porch. "It's great to see you again."

Austin followed behind at a slower pace, unsmiling, his expression not at all as inviting as Jordan's. Despite his cranky disposition, one that she was no doubt responsible for, he looked absolutely gorgeous in his well-worn jeans and leather jacket, his dark hair tousled so enticingly around his head.

Heart pounding with apprehension, Teddy stood and forced herself to return Jordan's smile. "It's nice to see you again, too, Jordan."

He sauntered casually up the porch stairs, and hooked a finger over his shoulder to indicate Austin. "I'm seriously hoping that you're here to give my brother a much-needed attitude adjustment."

Austin scowled from behind Jordan, but the temperamental gesture was lost on the elder sibling who had way too much mischief glinting in his eyes. "I thought if I sprung for pizza and beer that it might improve his mood, but the man isn't easily swayed by our favorite pastime."

"Jordan," Austin said, his voice vibrating with a low warning.

"Well, it's true," Jordan said as Austin slowly, reluctantly, climbed the stairs to join Jordan and Teddy. "You've been acting like the Grinch since Christmas morning."

Austin's dark green gaze flickered to Teddy, the depths of which were filled with a misery she was all too familiar with. "Maybe that's because someone stole *my* Christmas."

Teddy's heart sank to her knees. What if Austin had decided that he no longer wanted a relationship with her? What if she'd hurt him so badly he no longer trusted her with his love? And what if she'd destroyed the one thing she needed the most from him—the way he believed in her, his unconditional acceptance of who and what she was. She had to make him realize that what she was offering this time wasn't a convenient fling, or a part-time fantasy. It was *the real thing*.

Jordan leaned close, but didn't bother lowering his voice when he spoke. "If my brother is stupid enough to let his pride get in the way of the best thing that's ever happened to him, I'm always available." He gave her a teasing wink, one she suspected was designed to rile his brother.

Jordan's scheme worked. Austin visibly bristled and a possessive light sparked in his eyes. "Get lost, Jordan," he growled fiercely.

A huge, unrepentant grin lifted the corners of Jordan's mouth. "Hey, consider me gone."

Austin stared after his brother with a frown, waiting until Jordan had unlocked the front door and stepped inside the house, leaving them well and truly alone. His unfathomable gaze traveled back to her, though he said nothing, letting the awkward silence stretch between them.

Since he didn't seem inclined to start any conversation, she shifted anxiously on her feet and attempted a truce. "Hi," she said, hating the quiver in her voice.

He didn't offer a polite greeting in return, but cut right to the chase. "What are you doing here, Teddy?"

"Pleasing myself," she said, the truthful declaration slipping from her prematurely.

His eyebrows rose, making her realize how selfish that had sounded, when she'd meant it to be a liberating statement—that she'd finally realized what was important to her.

"Excuse me?" he asked.

Deciding that starting from the beginning would be the most logical approach, she drew a calming breath and said more steadily, "I'm here because I wanted to talk to you."

He leaned against the opposite railing, folded his arms over his chest and crossed his legs at his ankles. He offered no verbal encouragement; his seemingly casual pose the only indication that he was willing to listen to her.

"I, um, got the promotion," she said, thinking they could start on neutral territory and work their way to more personal issues—if he softened up along the way.

"I'm happy for you. I had no doubt you'd get it."

He sounded genuine, and beyond the reservation in his gaze she caught a glimpse of warmth and sincerity. Knowing that he still cared gave her hope for what lay ahead.

As much as she wanted to close the distance between them, she stayed where she was and forged on, knowing she had to tell him everything, even as unpleasant as some of the recollections were. "Louden was arrested for assault, and I was the one to press charges."

His entire body tensed at that announcement, his expression turning fierce and intense. "What happened?"

She explained the confrontation with Louden in full detail, how he'd assaulted her, how Anna had witnessed the attack, and the fact that Louden spent the night in jail and was fired from Sharper Image. And during her spiel, she watched Austin's body language shift, watched how protective and outraged he became on her behalf. Surprisingly, she found his possessive behavior endearing and chivalrous, not at all smothering.

"Since that incident, three other women in the company have stepped forward with claims of sexual harassment against Louden."

"Good," he said gruffly. "Hopefully, Louden will get his comeuppance."

"Yeah," she agreed. "It looks like he will."

Austin scrubbed a hand along his jaw and released a heavy breath. "So, it sounds like you've got everything you want."

No bitterness coated his words, no resentment, just a resignation that Teddy refused to accept. "Not quite everything," she said quietly, curling her fingers around the top of the railing on either side of her hips. "I want *you*."

His smile was a little sad. "With that promotion, I doubt you'll have time for me in your life."

She'd given him every reason to express that skepticism, to be leery of her claim. And then she realized that there was one thing left for her to prove after all...her love for Austin.

"You know, the incident with Louden was a real eye-opener," she said, capturing his attention once again.

He frowned at her, though he appeared curious over her statement. "How so?"

"Because it took what happened with Louden to make me realize exactly where my priorities lay." Her fingers gripped the railing tighter, keeping her grounded and focused. "I allowed my narrow-minded goals, and the need for this promotion, to totally consume my life."

His gaze sharpened, turned cautious. "And it no longer matters to you?"

"Oh, it matters," she admitted, knowing she owed him honesty. "But it's not the most important thing in my life anymore. You see, I now have the career I always wanted, but I have no one to share it with." Swallowing the huge knot forming in her chest, she risked everything she had. "And I'm in love with this man who is incredibly generous and understanding and would never do anything to stifle me, but I was too afraid to trust him."

"And he was afraid that he wasn't good enough for you," he replied, his voice a tad rusty.

"What?" she whispered.

"Yeah, it's true." He met her gaze directly, revealing insecurities of his own. "We're so different, you and I. How we were raised, and what we come from. I'm not a blue blood, just a down-to-earth man who doesn't wear a suit unless I absolutely have to. I have no interest in politics, or money, or being an investor, and I own a landscaping business. Most often than not, I come home at night filthy. After meeting your parents, and getting a good idea of what they expect for you, I don't think I would fit in."

She laughed, not because she found his concerns amusing, but because none of those things mattered to her. And judging by the few conversations she'd had with her mother the past two weeks, her parents had warmed to him, too.

"Oh, Austin," she said with a bright smile, one as warm and glowing as their future together. "First of all, I don't give a damn what my parents, or anyone else, thinks about you. *I* love you, just the way you are. But I don't think you have to worry about impressing my mother and father. I get the feeling that they like you. My mother has asked me twice now when I plan to bring you over for dinner again."

"You love me?" he asked, his voice ragged, his gaze filled with pleasure and excitement, and just a hint of disbelief.

"Yeah, I do." Finally closing the distance between them, she wrapped her arms around his neck and pressed her body to his, craving his heat. "And just for the record, Austin, I've never told another man that I loved him," she said, repeating the same words he'd told her Christmas morning. Her feelings for Bart had never extended beyond caring. "You're the first, and I don't make the declaration lightly."

A full-fledged, sexy grin claimed his mouth, and his hands

found their way inside her lambskin coat, sliding around to stroke over her jean-clad bottom. "Damn, but you're bossy."

"Yeah, I am, so you'd better get used to it," she said with an impudent smile. Twining her fingers through his thick, soft hair, she brazenly pulled his mouth down to meet hers. "Now shut up and kiss me, because I've missed you so much."

His reply was a deep, thrilling groan that vibrated against her lips. Their time apart dissolved beneath the onslaught of a hot, needy, tongue-tangling kiss. They made magic. They affirmed their love. They both moaned in frustration when the melding of their lips was no longer enough to quench the burning, out-of-control desire that had ignited between them.

"Too many clothes," she complained breathlessly as she stole another deep kiss to assuage her hunger for the taste of him, then slipped her cool hands inside his jacket and beneath his shirt so she could touch his heated flesh. She lost all sense of time and place—she could only think of this man and how he made her feel.

Her entire body tingled, causing her thoughts to shift to more urgent matters. Breaking their kiss, she said huskily, "I want you naked."

His low rumbling laughter tickled her skin as his mouth found the soft hollow under her ear. He nuzzled the sensitive flesh, and she shivered. "I don't think the neighbors would appreciate the public display."

She bit her bottom lip, imagining that sensual mouth on her breasts. Knowing too well the delicious, exquisite sensation of her nipple being finessed by his tongue, she melted a little more. "Should we go back to my place?" she whispered.

He lifted his head, shaking it, his eyes feverish and impatient. "I can't wait that long."

The unmistakable erection pressing against her belly attested to his barely suppressed restraint. Excitement and awareness seized her. "Me neither."

They stared at each other for what seemed like an eternity to Teddy, both of them uncertain as to what to do about this awesome need they had for each other, and how to satisfy it. Then a reckless grin slashed across his features, and she sensed trouble was about to begin. He bent his knees, and in one fluid motion hefted her over his shoulder caveman-style.

A surprised shriek escaped her. By the time she'd dragged in a breath and could talk again, they were inside the house, and he was carrying her across the foyer toward a set of stairs that led to the second landing. Blood rushed to her head, making her dizzy. "Austin!" she said, choking back laughter, and managing to prop herself up by bracing her hands on his backside. "Put me down!"

He gave her thigh a loving, intimate squeeze. "In a minute."

Jordan rounded the corner from the living room into the foyer at that moment, a comical expression on his face when he saw the two of them. Teddy blushed to the roots of her hair.

Austin didn't stop his stride. "Don't mind us, Jordan," he said, then loped up the stairs, two at a time, giving Teddy a jarring ride. "We've got an itch that can't wait to be scratched."

A grin quirked Jordan's mouth, and he reached for the set of keys on the small table by the front door. "Gotcha. I'll take this as my cue to 'get lost' again, this time for a few hours."

"At least," Austin agreed wholeheartedly, shamelessly. Entering a room, he kicked the door shut behind them, then lowered her back to her feet.

Light-headed, she swayed slightly, and he grabbed her hand to steady her. As she gained her balance, Teddy glanced around, registering the warm, masculine tones of Austin's room, and the big four-poster antique bed dominating the middle. Her pulse quickened, and she brought her gaze back to Austin, who was looking at her very intently, their earlier play replaced by something serious and intimate.

"Will you marry me, Teddy?" he asked, his voice strong, and clear, and infinitely tender. "If you need time, I'll give it to you, but I need a commitment."

"You've got it," she assured him, smiling. "I don't need any more time to know that you're the perfect man for me. Yes, I'll marry you."

Relief touched his expression. Framing her face between his palms, he brought her mouth up to his for a kiss that started out gentle and sweet, but quickly escalated into a full-blown seduction. Eager again, she slipped her hands into his jacket and shoved the heavy material off his shoulders and down his arms, letting it fall to the floor. He groaned, and rid her of her coat, too, then lifted her sweater over her head and tossed it aside. Less than five seconds later her bra followed, and he filled his hands with the warm, resilient flesh, rubbed his thumbs over the beaded nipples until her breath caught in her throat.

"Do you mind living here?" he asked, raising his arms so she could peel his shirt off while he toed his loafers off his feet.

She couldn't imagine them living in her small condo when they had such a lovely place to call home. "I'd love to live in your house...and I'd love to have your babies."

That stalled him for a moment, just as he'd unsnapped her jeans and started to unzip them. His gaze jerked to hers, hopeful and searching. "What about your career?"

Giving him a provocative smile, she went to work on his belt buckle. "Weren't you the one who told me I could have it all?" Done with that first task, she took care easing his zipper over the full erection straining the fly of his jeans.

"Yeah, and I'm glad you believe it." He released a tight

hiss of breath when her hands slid into his briefs and she took all that hot, hard masculinity into her hands.

Grasping her wrists, he pulled them away from his body and walked her back toward the bed—until the mattress connected with her knees and she was forced to sit. Then he knelt before her and pulled off her leather boots and socks.

"You'll make a great mom," he said knowingly.

She believed that, too, especially when she had him by her side, supporting her, loving her. He hooked his fingers into the waistband of her jeans, and she lifted her hips so he could pull them off. Then he slowly removed her panties, trailing hot, damp kisses along her belly, her hip, her feminine mound, her quivering thighs…all the way down to her feet.

Dewy and restlessly inflamed, she struggled to keep her mind focused on important issues for just a few minutes longer. "How do you feel about eloping?"

The smoky gaze traveling leisurely, hungrily, up her long legs jumped immediately to her face. "Are you serious? You don't want a big wedding?"

She exaggerated a shudder. "No." She'd been that route before, and didn't need all that pomp and circumstance to pledge her eternal love to Austin.

He raised an eyebrow, and with a tantalizing, calculated roll of his hips that was all for her pleasure, he shimmied out of his own pants. A smile curved her mouth. She planned to extract many more private performances in the future.

"I thought all women wanted a big, fancy wedding," he said, curious and confused.

Anticipation and desire quickened her pulse as she took in his magnificent body. She wriggled back on the bed, until she lay in the center. "I'd strangle my mother before we made it to the ceremony," she said jokingly. "Besides, I want to marry you soon. I don't think I could wait months and months to live with you, and wake up to you every day…"

Grinning in obvious agreement, he moved up onto the

bed, and over her, settling his hips between her welcoming thighs, teasing her with the tip of his shaft. "Is three weeks enough time to make arrangements, and schedule yourself a nice, lengthy vacation?"

"That would be perfect," she murmured, wrapping her legs around his thighs to urge him closer, and drawing his head down so she could kiss him. "But I don't think I can wait another minute for you to make love to me."

"Yes, ma'am," he drawled with a sinful grin, and obliged her, taking her breath away in one smooth, silky thrust of his hips against hers. He touched her heart with his love, filled her soul with that unconditional faith of his, and in the process redefined the word *perfect*.

Epilogue

A MONTH LATER, Teddy and Austin eloped to Waikiki, Hawaii, where they were married by a minister on a bluff overlooking the crystal blue Pacific Ocean. The bride wore a simple cream silk dress complemented with a lei of orchids, and the groom sported dark brown slacks, a cream-colored shirt and an adoring smile as he exchanged wedding vows with the woman who'd stolen his heart.

Afterward, they ordered room service in their bridal suite and sat out on their lanai and fed each other lobster, buttered potatoes and slices of raspberry white-chocolate cheesecake. And when their appetite for food had been appeased, they'd moved to the bedroom and satisfied a more physical and emotional hunger, consummating their love in a ritual as old as time.

Two hours after becoming Mrs. Austin McBride, the only thing Teddy wore was the orchid lei, which Austin had insisted upon, a pink flush on her skin from Austin's loving and the huge rock of a diamond her husband had surprised her with during their wedding ceremony. The ring now replaced the ruby and diamond band she'd worn there for the past year.

Austin propped himself up on his elbow and stared down at his wife, amazed that one woman could make his life so incredibly rich. She looked beautiful, and entirely too pleased with herself. He knew the reason why.

"You do realize, don't you, that your parents are going to hit the roof when they get your 'wedding announcement' in the mail."

"Yeah." Amusement threaded her husky voice and sparkled in her eyes. She'd asked the minister's wife to take a Polaroid snapshot of the two of them after the ceremony, then on a piece of the hotel's stationery she'd written, "Teddy and Austin announce their wedding to one another," along with the date. She'd sealed both in an envelope, and sent it to her parents in San Francisco so they'd receive the news before Austin and Teddy arrived back home.

She rolled to her back and smiled up at him, looking tousled, and thoroughly satiated. Her breasts were tipped in fragrant orchids, and a few crushed petals clung to her still-damp skin. "I have to admit that it felt good to buck convention."

He laughed. Leave it to Teddy to indulge in one final act of rebellion with her parents. "You sure you're okay with this?"

"Absolutely," she assured him, touching her hand to his jaw. "I couldn't be happier, or more in love, and I don't need a huge ceremony or reception to validate how I feel about you." Then a small frown creased her forehead. "My parents will survive this little catastrophe, though I'm a little worried about Jordan."

"Jordan?" he questioned, wondering what his brother had to do with all that. "Why?"

Her hand absently caressed his chest, and the diamond on her finger caught the light, glittering like a brilliant star. "Well, I know you're trying to sell Fantasy for Hire, but he didn't seem too thrilled about handling the business while you're away."

"He'll be fine." Austin grinned with wry humor. "It's not as though he's got to worry about fulfilling anyone's fantasy. I only need him to book the dancers."

"I guess you're right, but wouldn't it be great if he found someone like we found each other?" The hopeful quality in Teddy's voice attested to the fondness she seemed to have for Austin's brother. "I mean, I'm sure he's some woman's ideal fantasy."

Austin thought about the possibility of Jordan shedding his conservative image to play some woman's fantasy, but knew his brother would never go for that kind of public performance. Jordan tolerated Fantasy for Hire, but he'd never personally advocate being hired out as someone's fondest desire.

He shook his head at Teddy. "Naw, it'll never happen."

Moving over Teddy, he fitted himself snugly between her thighs, his need for her already fierce and rampant. "Now, what do you say we forget about Jordan, and your parents, and enjoy our honeymoon. I want you, wife."

Smiling a sultry, seductive smile, she lifted the lei of orchids from around her neck and placed it over his head, letting the fragrant flowers fill the air between them. "Consider yourself laid, husband."

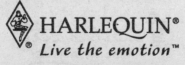

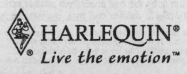